Washington Irving

Biographies and Miscellanies

Washington Irving

Biographies and Miscellanies

ISBN/EAN: 9783743309944

Manufactured in Europe, USA, Canada, Australia, Japa

Cover: Foto ©Andreas Hilbeck / pixelio.de

Manufactured and distributed by brebook publishing software
(www.brebook.com)

Washington Irving

Biographies and Miscellanies

BIOGRAPHIES

AND

MISCELLANIES

BY

WASHINGTON IRVING

EDITED BY HIS LITERARY EXECUTOR

PIERRE M. IRVING

NEW YORK

G. P. PUTNAM'S SONS

27 AND 29 WEST 23D STREET

CONTENTS.

LETTERS OF JONATHAN OLDSTYLE, Gent.

[The letters under the signature of Jonathan Oldstyle were written at the age of nineteen, when the author was a student at law in the office of Josiah Ogden Hoffman, and the city he was seeking to amuse by these juvenile productions contained scarce sixty-five thousand inhabitants. The series consisted of nine contributions to the " Morning Chronicle," a daily paper started by his brother, Dr. Peter Irving, his senior by eleven years, on the 1st of October, 1802. The introductory letter appeared in its columns on the 15th of the following month, and would seem to have been overlooked by the printer who collected and published the others in pamphlet form in 1824, without the author's knowledge. This opening letter is now reproduced after the lapse of sixty-four years, and is of interest, if in no other respect, as being the first essay in print of a writer afterwards so much admired for the graces of his style. The last four letters of the series are omitted in deference to the wishes of the author, who marked them as "not to be reprinted," when there was question of including the pamphlet of Oldstyle papers in a collective edition of his writings. Of the literary merit or demerit of these early productions I do not propose to speak. Of the local effect of the portion which touches on the drama, Dunlap, in his "History of the American Theatre," remarks : "Though always playful, the irritation caused was excessive." Meaning of course among the actors, for to the town they afforded great entertainment.

The theatre which was the place of performance at the date of these letters, and which offered almost the only intellectual recreation in New York, stood in front of the Park, nearly midway between Ann and Beekman Streets.—ED.]

LETTERS

JONATHAN OLDSTYLE, GENT.

LETTER I.

R. EDITOR,—If the observations of an odd old fellow are not wholly superfluous, I would thank you to shove them into a spare corner of your paper.

It is a matter of amusement to an uninterested spectator like myself, to observe the influence fashion has on the dress and deportment of its votaries, and how very quick they fly from one extreme to the other.

A few years since the rage was,—very high crowned hats with very narrow brims, tight neckcloth, tight coat, tight jacket, tight small-clothes, and shoes loaded with enormous silver buckles; the hair craped, plaited, queued, and powdered;—in short, an air of the greatest spruceness and tightness diffused over the whole person.

The ladies, with their tresses neatly turned up over an immense cushion; waist a yard long, braced up with stays into the smallest compass, and encircled by an enormous hoop; so that the fashionable belle resembled a walking bottle.

Thus dressed, the lady was seen, with the most be-witching languor, reclining on the arm of an extremely attentive beau, who, with a long cane, decorated with an enormous tassel, was carefully employed in removing every stone, stick, or straw that might impede the prog-ress of his tottering companion, whose high-heeled shoes just brought the points of her toes to the ground.

What an alteration has a few years produced! We now behold our gentlemen, with the most studious care-lessness and almost slovenliness of dress; large hat, large coat, large neckcloth, large pantaloons, large boots, and hair scratched into every careless direction, lounging along the streets in the most apparent listlessness and vacuity of thought; staring with an unmeaning counte-nance at every passenger, or leaning upon the arm of some kind fair one for support, with the other hand crammed into his breeches' pocket. Such is the picture of a modern beau,—in his dress stuffing himself up to the dimensions of a Hercules, in his manners affecting the helplessness of an invalid.

The belle who has to undergo the fatigue of dragging along this sluggish animal has chosen a character the very reverse,—emulating in her dress and actions all the airy lightness of a sylph, she trips along with the great-est vivacity. Her laughing eye, her countenance enlivened with affability and good-humor, inspire with kindred animation every beholder, except the torpid being by her side, who is either affecting the fashionable sang-froid, or is wrapt up in profound contemplation of himself.

Heavens! how changed are the manners since I was young! Then, how delightful to contemplate a ball-room,—such bowing, such scraping, such complimenting; nothing but copperplate speeches to be heard on both sides; no walking but in minuet measure; nothing more common than to see half a dozen gentlemen knock their heads together in striving who should first recover a lady's fan or snuff-box that had fallen.

But now, our youths no longer aim at the character of pretty gentlemen; their greatest ambition is to be called lazy dogs, careless fellows, &c., &c. Dressed up in the mammoth style, our buck saunters into the ball-room in a surtout, hat under arm, cane in hand; strolls round with the most vacant air; stops abruptly before such lady as he may choose to honor with his attention; entertains her with the common slang of the day, collected from the conversation of hostlers, footmen, portors, &c., until his string of smart sayings is run out, and then lounges off to entertain some other fair one with the same unintelligible jargon. Surely, Mr. Editor, puppy-ism must have arrived to a climax; it must turn; to carry it to a greater extent seems to me impossible.

JONATHAN OLDSTYLE.

NOVEMBER 15, 1802.

LETTER II.

IR,—Encouraged by the ready insertion you gave my former communication, I have taken the liberty to intrude on you a few more remarks.

Nothing is more intolerable to an old person than innovation on old habits. The customs that prevailed in our youth become dear to us as we advance in years; and we can no more bear to see them abolished than we can to behold the trees cut down under which we have sported in the happy days of infancy.

Even I myself, who have floated down the stream of life with the tide,—who have humored it in all its turnings, who have conformed in a great measure to all its fashions,—cannot but feel sensible of this prejudice. I often sigh when I draw a comparison between the present and the past; and though I cannot but be sensible that, in general, times are altered for the better, yet there is something, even in the imperfections of the manners which prevailed in my youthful days, that is inexpressibly endearing.

There is nothing that seems more strange and preposterous to me than the manner in which modern mar-

16

riages are conducted. The parties keep the matter as secret as if there was something disgraceful in the connection. The lady positively denies that anything of the kind is to happen; will laugh at her intended husband, and even lay bets against the event, the very day before it is to take place. They sneak into matrimony as quietly as possible, and seem to pride themselves on the cunning and ingenuity they have displayed in their manœuvres.

How different is this from the manners of former times! I recollect when my aunt Barbara was addressed by 'Squire Stylish; nothing was heard of during the whole courtship but consultations and negotiations between her friends and relatives; the matter was considered and reconsidered, and at length the time set for a final answer. Never, Mr. Editor, shall I forget the awful solemnity of the scene. The whole family of the Oldstyles assembled in awful conclave: my aunt Barbara dressed out as fine as hands could make her,—high cushion, enormous cap, long waist, prodigious hoop, ruffles that reached to the end of her fingers, and a gown of flame-colored brocade, figured with poppies, roses, and sunflowers. Never did she look so sublimely handsome. The 'Squire entered the room with a countenance suited to the solemnity of the occasion. He was arrayed in a full suit of scarlet velvet, his coat decorated with a profusion of large silk buttons, and the skirts stiffened with a yard or two of buckram; a long pig-tailed wig, well powdered, adorned his head; and stockings of deep blue

2

silk, rolled over the knees, graced his extremities; the flaps of his vest reached to his knee-buckles, and the ends of his cravat, tied with the most precise neatness, twisted through every button-hole. Thus accoutred, he gravely walked into the room, with his ivory-headed ebony cane in one hand, and gently swaying his three-cornered beaver with the other. The gallant and fashionable appearance of the 'Squire, the gracefulness and dignity of his deportment, occasioned a general smile of complacency through the room; my aunt Barbara modestly veiled her countenance with her fan, but I observed her contemplating her admirer with great satisfaction through the sticks.

The business was opened with the most formal solemnity, but was not long in agitation. The Oldstyles were moderate; their articles of capitulation few; the 'Squire was gallant, and acceded to them all. In short, the blushing Barbara was delivered up to his embraces with due ceremony. Then, Mr. Editor, then were the happy times: such oceans of arrack,—such mountains of plum-cake,—such feasting and congratulating,—such fiddling and dancing,—ah me! who can think of those days, and not sigh when he sees the degeneracy of the present: no eating of cake nor throwing of stockings,—not a single skin filled with wine on the joyful occasion,—nor a single pocket edified by it but the parson's.

It is with the greatest pain I see those customs dying away, which served to awaken the hospitality and friendship of my ancient comrades,—that strewed with flowers the path to the altar, and shed a ray of sunshine on the commencement of the matrimonial union.

The deportment of my aunt Barbara and her husband was as decorous after marriage as before; her conduct was always regulated by his,—her sentiments ever accorded with his opinions; she was always eager to tie on his neckcloth of a morning,—to tuck a napkin under his chin at meal-times,—to wrap him up warm of a winter's day, and to spruce him up as smart as possible of a Sunday. The 'Squire was the most attentive and polite husband in the world; would hand his wife in and out of church with the greatest ceremony,—drink her health at dinner with particular emphasis, and ask her advice on every subject,—though I must confess he invariably adopted his own;—nothing was heard from both sides but dears, sweet loves, doves, &c. The 'Squire could never stir out of a winter's day, without his wife calling after him from the window to button up his waistcoat carefully. Thus, all things went on smoothly; and my relations Stylish had the name—and, as far as I know, deserved it,—of being the most happy and loving couple in the world.

A modern married pair will, no doubt, laugh at all this; they are accustomed to treat one another with the utmost carelessness and neglect. No longer does the wife tuck the napkin under her husband's chin, nor the husband attend to heaping her plate with dainties;—no longer do I see those little amusing fooleries in company where the lady would pat her husband's cheek, and he chuck her under the chin; when dears, and sweets were as plenty as cookies on a New-year's day. The wife now considers herself as totally independent,—will advance her own opinions, without hesitation, though directly opposite to his,—will carry on accounts of her own, and will even have secrets of her own, with which she refuses to entrust him.

Who can read these facts, and not lament with me the degeneracy of the present times ;—what husband is there but will look back with regret to the happy days of female subjection.

JONATHAN OLDSTYLE.

NOVEMBER 20, 1802.

IR,—There is no place of public amusement of which I am so fond as the Theatre. To enjoy this with the greater relish, I go but seldom; and I find there is no play, however poor or ridiculous, from which I cannot derive some entertainment.

I was very much taken with a play-bill of last week, announcing, in large capitals, "The Battle of Hexham, or, Days of Old." Here, said I to myself, will be something grand—Days of Old,—my fancy fired at the words. I pictured to myself all the gallantry of chivalry. Here, thought I, will be a display of court manners and true politeness; the play will, no doubt, be garnished with tilts and tournaments; and as to those banditti, whose names make such a formidable appearance on the bills, they will be hung up, every mother's son, for the edification of the gallery.

With such impressions, I took my seat in the pit, and was so impatient that I could hardly attend to the music, though I found it very good.

The curtain rose,—out walked the Queen,* with great

---

* Mrs. Whitlock, a sister of Mrs. Siddons.—ED.

majesty; she answered my ideas: she was dressed well, she looked well, and she acted well. The Queen was followed by a pretty gentleman, who, from his winking and grinning, I took to be the court-fool; I soon found out my mistake. He was a courtier "high in trust," and either general, colonel, or something of martial dignity. They talked for some time, though I could not understand the drift of their discourse, so I amused myself with eating peanuts.

In one of the scenes I was diverted with the stupidity of a corporal, and his men, who sung a dull song, and talked a great deal about nothing; though I found, by their laughing, there was a great deal of fun in the corporal's remarks. What this scene had to do with the rest of the piece, I could not comprehend; I suspect it was a part of some other play, thrust in here by accident.

I was then introduced to a cavern, where there were several hard-looking fellows sitting around a table carousing. They told the audience they were banditti. They then sung a gallery song, of which I could understand nothing but two lines :—

> "The Welshman lik'd to have been chok'd by a mouse,
> But he pull'd him out by the tail."

Just as they had ended this elegant song, their banquet was disturbed by the melodious sound of a horn, and in marched a portly gentleman,* who, I found, was

* Hodgkinson, a versatile actor who filled all parts, from Falstaff to a Harlequin. — ED.

their captain. After this worthy gentleman had fumed his hour out, after he had slapped his breast and drawn his sword half a dozen times, the act ended.

In the course of the play, I learnt that there had been, or was, or would be, a battle; but how, or when, or where, I could not understand. The banditti once more made their appearance, and frightened the wife of the portly gentleman, who was dressed in man's clothes, and was seeking her husband. I could not enough admire the dignity of her deportment, the sweetness of her countenance, and the unaffected gracefulness of her action;* but who the captain really was, or why he ran away from his spouse, I could not understand. However, they seemed very glad to find one another again; and so at last the play ended, by the falling of the curtain.

I wish the manager would use a drop-scene at the close of the acts; we might then always ascertain the termination of the piece by the green curtain. On this occasion, I was indebted to the polite bows of the actors for this pleasing information. I cannot say that I was entirely satisfied with the play, but I promised myself ample entertainment in the afterpiece, which was called the "Tripolitan Prize." Now, thought I, we shall have some sport for our money; we will, no doubt, see a few of those Tripolitan scoundrels spitted like turkeys for

---

* Mrs. Johnson, a great favorite with the author and the public.

our amusement. Well, sir, the curtain rose—the trees waved in front of the stage, and the sea rolled in the rear; all things looked very pleasant and smiling. Presently I heard a bustling behind the scenes,—here, thought I, comes a band of fierce Tripolitans, with whiskers as long as my arm. No such thing; they were only a party of village masters and misses taking a walk for exercise,—and very pretty behaved young gentry they were, I assure you; but it was cruel in the manager to dress them in buckram, as it deprived them entirely of the use of their limbs. They arranged themselves very orderly on each side of the stage, and sung something, doubtless very affecting, for they all looked pitiful enough. By and by came up a most tremendous storm: the lightning flashed, the thunder roared, and the rain fell in torrents; however, our pretty rustics stood gaping quietly at one another, until they must have been wet to the skin. I was surprised at their torpidity, till I found they were each one afraid to move first, for fear of being laughed at for their awkwardness. How they got off I do not recollect; but I advise the manager, in a similar case, to furnish every one with a trap-door, through which to make his exit. Yet this would deprive the audience of much amusement; for nothing can be more laughable than to see a body of guards with their spears, or courtiers with their long robes, get across the stage at our theatre.

Scene passed after scene. In vain I strained my eyes

to catch a glimpse of a Mahometan phiz. I once heard a great bellowing behind the scenes, and expected to see a strapping Mussulman come bouncing in; but was miserably disappointed, on distinguishing his voice, to find out by his swearing that he was only a Christian. In he came,—an American navy officer,—worsted stockings, olive velvet small-clothes, scarlet vest, pea-jacket, and gold-laced hat—dressed quite in character. I soon found out, by his talk, that he was an American prize-master; that, returning through the Mediterranean with his Tripolitan prize, he was driven by a storm on the coast of England. The honest gentleman seemed, from his actions, to be rather intoxicated; which I could account for in no other way than his having drank a great deal of salt-water, as he swam ashore.

Several following scenes were taken up with hallooing and huzzaing, between the captain, his crew, and the gallery, with several amusing tricks of the captain and his son,—a very funny, mischievous little fellow. Then came the cream of the joke: the captain wanted to put to sea, and the young fellow, who had fallen desperately in love, to stay ashore. Here was a contest between love and honor; such piping of eyes, such blowing of noses, such slapping of pocket-holes! But Old Junk was inflexible,—What! an American tar desert his duty! (three cheers from the gallery), impossible! American tars forever!! True blue will never stain!! &c., &c. (a continual thundering among the gods). Here was a scene of distress;

here was bathos.   The author seemed as much puzzled
to know how to dispose of the young tar as Old Junk
was.   It would not do to leave an American seaman on
foreign ground, nor would it do to separate him from
his mistress.

Scene the last opened.   It seems that another Tripolitan cruiser had bore down on the prize, as she lay
about a mile off shore.   How a Barbary corsair had
got in this part of the world,—whether she had been
driven there by the same storm, or whether she was
cruising to pick up a few English first-rates, I could not
learn.   However, here she was.   Again were we conducted to the sea-shore, where we found all the village
gentry, in their buckram suits, ready assembled to be
entertained with the rare show of an American and
Tripolitan engaged yard-arm and yard-arm.   The battle was conducted with proper decency and decorum,
and the Tripolitan very politely gave in,—as it would
be indecent to conquer in the face of an American audience.

After the engagement the crew came ashore, joined
with the captain and gallery in a few more huzzas, and
the curtain fell.   How Old Junk, his son, and his son's
sweetheart, settled it, I could not discover.

I was somewhat puzzled to understand the meaning
and necessity of this engagement between the ships, till
an honest old countryman at my elbow said, he supposed
this was the Battle of Hexham, as he recollected no

fighting in the first piece. With this explanation I was perfectly satisfied.

My remarks upon the audience, I shall postpone to another opportunity.

JONATHAN OLDSTYLE.

DECEMBER 1, 1802.

IR,—My last communication mentioned my visit to the theatre; the remarks it contained were chiefly confined to the play and the actors. I shall now extend them to the audience, who, I assure you, furnish no inconsiderable part of the entertainment.

As I entered the house some time before the curtain rose, I had sufficient leisure to make some observations. I was much amused with the waggery and humor of the gallery, which, by the way, is kept in excellent order by the constables who are stationed there. The noise in this part of the house is somewhat similar to that which prevailed in Noah's ark; for we have an imitation of the whistles and yells of every kind of animal. This, in some measure, compensates for the want of music, as the gentlemen of our orchestra are very economic of their favors. Somehow or another, the anger of the gods seemed to be aroused all of a sudden, and they commenced a discharge of apples, nuts, and gingerbread, on the heads of the honest folks in the pit, who had no possibility of retreating from this new kind of thunderbolts. I can't say but I was a little irritated at being saluted, aside of my head,

28

with a rotten pippin; and was going to shake my cane at them, but was prevented by a decent-looking man behind me, who informed me that it was useless to threaten or expostulate. "They are only amusing themselves a little at our expense," said he; "sit down quietly and bend your back to it." My kind neighbor was interrupted by a hard green apple that hit him between the shoulders,— he made a wry face, but knowing it was all a joke, bore the blow like a philosopher. I soon saw the wisdom of this determination: a stray thunderbolt happened to light on the head of a little sharp-faced Frenchman, dressed in a white coat and small cocked hat, who sat two or three benches ahead of me, and seemed to be an irritable little animal. Monsieur was terribly exasperated; he jumped upon his seat, shook his fist at the gallery, and swore violently in bad English. This was all nuts to his merry persecutors; their attention was wholly turned on him, and he formed their target for the rest of the evening.

I found the ladies in the boxes, as usual, studious to please; their charms were set off to the greatest advantage; each box was a little battery in itself, and they all seemed eager to outdo each other in the havoc they spread around. An arch glance in one box was rivalled by a smile in another, that smile by a simper in a third, and in a fourth a most bewitching languish carried all before it.

I was surprised to see some persons reconnoitring the

company through spy-glasses ; and was in doubt whether these machines were used to remedy deficiencies of vision, or whether this was another of the eccentricities of fashion. Jack Stylish has since informed me that glasses were lately all the go ; "though hang it," says Jack, "it is quite out at present ; we used to mount our glasses in great snuff, but since so many tough jockeys have followed the lead, the bucks have all cut the custom." I give you, Mr. Editor, the account in my dashing cousin's own language. It is from a vocabulary I do not well understand.

I was considerably amused by the queries of the countryman mentioned in my last, who was now making his first visit to the theatre. He kept constantly applying to me for information, and I readily communicated, as far as my own ignorance would permit.

As this honest man was casting his eye round the house, his attention was suddenly arrested. "And, pray, who are these ?" said he, pointing to a cluster of young fellows. "These, I suppose, are the critics, of whom I have heard so much. They have, no doubt, got together to communicate their remarks, and compare notes ; these are the persons through whom the audience exercise their judgments, and by whom they are told when they are to applaud or to hiss." "Critics ! ha, ha ! my dear sir, they trouble themselves as little about the elements of criticism as they do about other departments of science and belles-lettres. These are the beaux of the present day, who meet here to lounge away an idle hour, and play off their little impertinencies for the entertainment of the public. They no more regard the merits of the play, nor of the actors, than my cane. They even strive to appear inattentive; and I have seen one of them perched on the front of the box with his back to the stage, sucking the head of his stick and staring vacantly at the audience, insensible to the most interesting specimens of scenic representation, though the tear of sensibility was trembling in every eye around him. I have heard that some have even gone so far in search of amusement as to propose a game of cards in the theatre, during the performance." The eyes of my neighbor sparkled at this information—his cane shook in his hand, the word "puppies" burst from his lips. "Nay," says I, "I don't give this for absolute fact; my cousin Jack was, I believe, quizzing me (as he terms it) when he gave me the information." "But you seem quite indignant," said I, to the decent-looking man in my rear. It was from him the exclamation came; the honest countryman was gazing in gaping wonder on some new attraction. "Believe me," said I, "if you had them daily before your eyes, you would get quite used to them." "Used to them," replied he; "how is it possible for people of sense to relish such conduct?" "Bless you, my friend, people of sense have nothing to do with it; they merely endure it in silence. These young gentlemen live in an indulgent age. When I was a young man, such tricks and follies were held in proper contempt." Here I went a little too far; for, upon better recollection, I must own that a lapse of years has produced but little alteration in this department of folly and impertinence. "But do the ladies admire these manners?" "Truly I am not as conversant in female circles as formerly; but I should think it a poor compliment to my fair country-women, to suppose them pleased with the stupid stare and cant phrases with which these votaries of fashion add affected to real ignorance."

Our conversation was here interrupted by the ringing of a bell. "Now for the play," said my companion. "No," said I, "it is only for the musicians." These worthy gentlemen then came crawling out of their holes, and began, with very solemn and important phizzes, strumming and tuning their instruments in the usual style of discordance, to the great entertainment of the audience. "What tune is that?" asked my neighbor, covering his ears. "This," said I, " is no tune; it is only a pleasing symphony, with which we are regaled, as a preparative." For my part, though I admire the effect of contrast, I think they might as well play it in their cavern under the stage. The bell rung a second time,— and then began the tune in reality; but I could not help observing that the countryman was more diverted with the queer grimaces and contortions of countenance ex-hibited by the musicians, than their melody. What I heard of the music I liked very well (though I was told by one of my neighbors that the same pieces have been played every night for these three years); but it was often overpowered by the gentry in the gallery, who vociferated loudly for "Moll in the Wad," "Tally-ho the Grinders," and several other airs more suited to their tastes.

I observed that every part of the house has its different department. The good folks of the gallery have all the trouble of ordering the music (their directions, however, are not more frequently followed than they deserve). The mode by which they issue their mandates is stamping, hissing, roaring, whistling; and, when the musicians are refractory, groaning in cadence. They also have the privilege of demanding a bow from John (by which name they designate every servant at the theatre who enters to move a table or snuff a candle); and of detecting those cunning dogs who peep from behind the curtain.

By the by, my honest friend was much puzzled about the curtain itself. He wanted to know why that carpet was hung up in the theatre? I assured him it was no carpet, but a very fine curtain. "And what, pray, may be the meaning of that gold head, with the nose cut off, that I see in front of it?" "The meaning,—why, really, I can't tell exactly,—though my cousin, Jack Stylish, says there is a great deal of meaning in it. But surely you like the design of the curtain?" "The design,—why, really, I can see no design about it, unless it is to be

3

brought down about our ears by the weight of those gold heads, and that heavy cornice with which it is garnished." I began now to be uneasy for the credit of our curtain, and was afraid he would perceive the mistake of the painter, in putting a harp in the middle of the curtain and calling it a mirror; but his attention was happily called away by the candle-grease from the chandelier, over the centre of the pit, dropping on his clothes. This he loudly complained of, and declared his coat was bran-new. "Pooh, my friend!" said I; "we must put up with a few trifling inconveniences when in the pursuit of pleasure." "True," said he; "but I think I pay pretty dear for it :—first, to give six shillings at the door, and then to have my head battered with rotten apples, and my coat spoiled by candle-grease; by and by I shall have my other clothes dirtied by sitting down, as I perceive everybody mounted on the benches. I wonder if they could not see as well if they were all to stand upon the floor?"

Here I could no longer defend our customs, for I could scarcely breathe while thus surrounded by a host of strapping fellows, standing with their dirty boots on the seats of the benches. The little Frenchman, who thus found a temporary shelter from the missive compliments of his gallery friends, was the only person benefited. At last the bell again rung, and the cry of "Down, down,—hats off," was the signal for the commencement of the play.

If, Mr. Editor, the garrulity of an old fellow is not tiresome, and you choose to give this view of a New-York Theatre a place in your paper, you may, perhaps, hear further from your friend,

JONATHAN OLDSTYLE.

DECEMBER 3, 1802.

IR,—I shall now conclude my remarks on the Theatre, which I am afraid you will think are spun out to an unreasonable length; for this I can give no other excuse than that it is the privilege of old folks to be tiresome, and so I shall proceed.

I had chosen a seat in the pit, as least subject to annoyance from a habit of talking loud that has lately crept into our theatres, and which particularly prevails in the boxes. In old times, people went to the theatre for the sake of the play and acting; but I now find that it begins to answer the purpose of a coffee-house, or fashionable lounge, where many indulge in loud conversation, without any regard to the pain it inflicts on their more attentive neighbors. As this conversation is generally of the most trifling kind, it seldom repays the latter for the inconvenience they suffer, of not hearing one half of the play. I found, however, that I had not much bettered my situation; but that every part of the house has its share of evils. Besides those I had already suffered, I was yet to undergo a new kind of torment. I had got in the neighborhood of a very obliging personage, who had

36

seen the play before, and was kindly anticipating every
scene, and informing those that were about him what
was to take place,—to prevent, I suppose, any disagreeable surprise to which they would otherwise have been
liable. Had there been anything of a plot to the play,
this might have been a serious inconvenience; but as the
piece was entirely innocent of everything of the kind, it
was not of so much importance. As I generally contrive
to extract amusement from everything that happens, I
now entertained myself with remarks on the self-impor-
tant air with which he delivered his information, and the
distressed and impatient looks of his unwilling auditors.
I also observed that he made several mistakes in the
course of his communications. "Now you'll see," said
he, "the queen in all her glory, surrounded with her
courtiers, fine as fiddles, and ranged on each side of the
stage like rows of pewter dishes." On the contrary, we
were presented with the portly gentleman and his ragged
regiment of banditti. Another time he promised us a
regale from the fool; but we were presented with a very
fine speech from the queen's grinning counsellor.

My country neighbor was exceedingly delighted with
the performance, though he did not half the time understand what was going forward. He sat staring, with open
mouth, at the portly gentleman,* as he strode across the
stage and in furious rage drew his sword on the white

* Hodgkinson.

lion. "By George, but that's a brave fellow," said he, when the act was over; "that's what you call first-rate acting, I suppose."

"Yes," said I, "it is what the critics of the present day admire, but it is not altogether what I like. You should have seen an actor of the old school do this part; he would have given it to some purpose; you would have had such ranting and roaring, and stamping and storming; to be sure, this honest man gives us a bounce now and then in the true old style, but in the main he seems to prefer walking on plain ground, to strutting on the stilts used by the tragic heroes of my day."

This is the chief of what passed between me and my companion during the play and entertainment, except an observation of his, "that it would be well if the manager was to drill his nobility and gentry now and then, to enable them to go through their evolutions with more grace and spirit." This put me in mind of something my cousin Jack said to the same purpose, though he went too far in his zeal for reformation. He declared, "he wished sincerely one of the critics of the day would take all the slab-shabs of the theatre (like cats in a bag), and twig the whole bunch." I can't say but I like Jack's idea well enough, though it is rather a severe one.

He might have remarked another fault that prevails among our performers (though I don't know whether it occurred this evening), of dressing for the same piece in the fashions of different ages and countries, so that while one actor is strutting about the stage in the cuirass and helmet of Alexander, another, dressed up in a gold-laced coat and bag wig, with a chapeau de bras under his arm, is taking snuff in the fashion of one or two centuries back, and perhaps a third figures in Suwarrow boots, in the true style of modern buckism.

"But what, pray, has become of the noble Marquis of Montague, and Earl of Warwick?" said the countryman, after the entertainment was concluded. "Their names make a great appearance on the bill, but I do not recollect having seen them in the course of the evening." "Very true,—I had quite forgot those worthy personages; but I suspect they have been behind the scenes, smoking a pipe with our other friends *incog.*, the Tripolitans. We must not be particular nowadays, my friend. When we are presented with a battle of Hexham without fighting, and a Tripolitan afterpiece without even a Mahometan whisker, we need not be surprised at having an invisible marquis or two thrown into the bargain. But what is your opinion of the house?" said I; "don't you think it a very substantial, solid-looking building, both inside and out? Observe what a fine effect the dark coloring of the wall has upon the white faces of the audience, which glare like the stars in a dark night. And then, what can be more pretty than the paintings in the front of the boxes,—those little masters and misses sucking their thumbs, and making mouths at the audience?"

"Very fine, upon my word. And what, pray, is the use of that chandelier, as you call it, that is hung up among the clouds, and has showered down its favors upon my coat?"

"Oh! that is to illumine the heavens, and set off to advantage the little periwig'd Cupids, tumbling head over heels, with which the painter has decorated the dome. You see we have no need of the chandelier below, as here the house is perfectly well illuminated; but I think it would have been a great saving of candle-light if the manager had ordered the painter, among his other pretty designs, to paint a moon up there, or if he was to hang up that sun with whose intense light our eyes were greatly annoyed in the beginning of the afterpiece."

"But don't you think, after all, there is rather a—sort of a—kind of a heavyishness about the house? Don't you think it has a little of an under-groundish appearance?"

To this I could make no answer. I must confess I have often thought myself the house had a dungeon-like look; so I proposed to him to make our exit, as the candles were putting out, and we should be left in the dark. Accordingly, groping our way through the dismal subterraneous passage that leads from the pit, and passing through the ragged bridewell-looking ante-chamber, we once more emerged into the purer air of the park, when bidding my honest countryman good-night, I repaired home, considerably pleased with the amusements of the evening.

Thus, Mr. Editor, have I given you an account of the chief incidents that occurred in my visit to the Theatre. I have shown you a few of its accommodations and its imperfections. Those who visit it more frequently may be able to give you a better statement.

I shall conclude with a few words of advice for the benefit of every department of it. I would recommend—

To the actors—less etiquette, less fustian, less buckram.

To the orchestra—new music, and more of it.

To the pit—patience, clean benches, and umbrellas.

To the boxes—less affectation, less noise, less coxcombs.

To the gallery—less grog, and better constables ;—and,

To the whole house, inside and out, a total reformation.

And so much for the Theatre.

JONATHAN OLDSTYLE.

DECEMBER 11, 1802.

BIOGRAPHICAL SKETCHES.

[The Naval Biographies which follow, were contributed to the "Ana-lectic Magazine," a monthly periodical, published in Philadelphia by the late Moses Thomas of that city, and edited by the author during the years 1813, 1814 ; the period of the war with Great Britain, in which the national character was so gallantly sustained on the ocean.

The "Memoir of Thomas Campbell," the Scottish poet, was originally prefixed to an American edition of his poems, in 1810, and was trans-ferred to the "Analectic Magazine" in March, 1815, revised and en-larged. To this copy, which is the one here introduced, is appended a letter from Mr. Irving respecting Campbell, written after the poet's death.

The notices of Allston and Talma were contributions, the first to "Duyckinck's Cyclopædia of American Literature," the last to the "Knickerbocker Gallery," the title of a collection of pieces from various hands, published in 1855.—ED.]

Biographical Sketches.

—•—

CAPTAIN JAMES LAWRENCE.

O speak feelingly, yet temperately, of the merits of those who have bravely fought and gloriously fallen in the service of their country, is one of the most difficult tasks of the biographer. Filled with admiration of their valor, and sorrow for their fate, we feel the impotency of our gratitude, in being able to reward such great sacrifices with nothing but empty applause. We are apt, therefore, to be hurried into a degree of eulogium, which, however sincere and acknowledged at the time, may be regarded as extravagant by the dispassionate eye of after-years.

We feel more particularly this difficulty in undertaking to give the memoirs of one whose excellent qualities and gallant deeds are still vivid in our recollection, and whose untimely end has excited, in an extraordinary degree, the sympathies of his countrymen. Indeed, the popular career of this youthful hero has been so transient, yet dazzling, as almost to prevent sober investigation. Scarce had we ceased to rejoice in his victory, before we were called on to deplore his loss. He passed before the public eye like a star, just beaming on it for a moment, and falling in the midst of his brightness.

Captain James Lawrence was born on the 1st of October, 1781, at Burlington, in the State of New Jersey. He was the youngest son of John Lawrence, Esq., an eminent counsellor at law of that place. Within a few weeks after his birth his mother died, and the charge of him devolved on his sisters, to whom he ever showed the warmest gratitude for the tender care they took of his infant years. He early evinced that excellence of heart by which he was characterized through life; he was a dutiful and affectionate child, mild in his disposition, and of the most gentle and engaging manners. He was scarce twelve years of age when he expressed a decided partiality for a seafaring life; but his father disapproving of it, and wishing him to prepare for the profession of the law, his strong sense of duty induced him to acquiesce. He went through the common branches of education, at a grammar-school, at Burlington, with much credit to himself and satisfaction to his tutors. The pecuniary misfortunes of his father prevented his receiving a finished education, and between the age of thirteen and fourteen he commenced the study of the law with his brother, the late John Lawrence, Esq., who then resided at Woodbury. He remained for two years in this situation, vainly striving to accommodate himself to pursuits wholly repugnant to his taste and inclinations. The dry studies of statutes and reporters, the technical rubbish, and dull routine of a lawyer's office, were little calculated to please an imagination teeming with the adventures, the wonders, and variety of the seas. At length, his father being dead, and his strong predilection for the roving life of a sailor being increased by every attempt to curb it, his brother yielded to his solicitations, and placed him under the care of Mr. Griscomb, at Burlington, to acquire the principles of navigation and naval tactics. He remained with him for three months, when, his intention of applying for a situation in the navy being generally known, several of the most distinguished gentlemen of the State interested themselves in his behalf, and wrote to the Navy Department. The succeeding mail brought him a midshipman's warrant; and between the age of sixteen and seventeen he entered the service of his country.

His first cruise was to the West Indies in the ship *Ganges*, commanded by Captain Thomas Tingey. In this and several subsequent cruises, no opportunity occurred to call forth particular services; but the attention and intelligence which he uniformly displayed in the discharge of his duties, the correctness of his deportment, and the suavity of his manners, gained him the approbation of his commanders, and rendered him a favorite with his associates and inferiors.

When the war was declared against Tripoli, he was promoted to a lieutenancy, and appointed to the command of the schooner *Enterprise.* While in this command he volunteered his services in the hazardous exploit of destroying the frigate *Philadelphia,* and accompanied Decatur as his first lieutenant. The brilliant success of that enterprise is well known ; and for the gallantry and skill displayed on the occasion, Decatur was made post-captain, while Lawrence, in common with the other officers and crew, were voted by Congress two months' extra pay, —a sordid and paltry reward, which he immediately declined.

The harbor of Tripoli appears to have been the school of our naval heroes. In tracing the histories of those who have lately distinguished themselves, we are always led to the coast of Barbary as the field of their first experience and young achievement. The concentration of our little navy at this point, soon after its formation, has had a happy effect upon its character and fortunes. The officers were most of them young in years, and young in arms, full of life and spirits, and enthusiasm. Such is the time to form generous impressions and strong attachments. It was there they grew together in habits of mutual confidence and friendship ; and to the noble emulation of so many young minds newly entering upon an adventurous profession, may be attributed that enterprising spirit and defiance of danger that has ever since distinguished our navy.

After continuing in the Mediterranean about three years and a half, Lawrence returned to the United States with Commodore Preble, and was again sent out on that station, as commander of Gun-boat No. 6, in which he remained for sixteen months. Since that time he has acted as first lieutenant of the *Constitution*, and as commander of the *Vixen*, *Wasp*, *Argus*, and *Hornet*. In 1808 he was married to a daughter of Mr. Montaudevert, a respectable merchant of New York, to whom he made one of the kindest and most affectionate of husbands.

At the commencement of the present war he sailed in the *Hornet* sloop-of-war, as part of the squadron that cruised under Commodore Rodgers. While absent on this cruise Lieutenant Morris was promoted to the rank of post-captain, for his bravery and skill as first lieutenant of the *Constitution* in her action with the *Guerriere*. This appointment, as it raised him two grades, and placed him over the heads of older officers, gave great offence to many of the navy, who could not brook that the regular rules of the service should be infringed. It was thought particularly unjust, as giving him rank above Lawrence, who had equally distinguished himself as first lieutenant of Decatur, in the destruction of the frigate *Philadelphia*, and who, at present, was but master and commander.

On returning from his cruise Captain Lawrence, after consulting with Commodores Rodgers and Bainbridge, and with other experienced gentlemen of the navy, addressed a memorial to the Senate and a letter to the

4

Secretary of the Navy, wherein, after the fullest acknowl-
edgments of the great merits and services of Captain
Morris, he remonstrated in the most temperate and respectful, but firm and manly language, on the impropriety
of his promotion, as being contrary to the rules of naval
precedence, and particularly hard as it respected himself.
At the same time he frankly mentioned that he should
be compelled, however reluctant, to leave the service, if
thus improperly outranked.

The reply of the Secretary was singularly brief; barely
observing, that if he thought proper to leave the service
without a cause, there would still remain heroes and
patriots to support the honor of the flag. There was a
laconic severity in this reply calculated to cut a man of
feeling to the heart, and which ought not to have been
provoked by the fair and candid remonstrance of Lawrence.

Where men are fighting for honor rather than profit,
the utmost delicacy should be observed towards their
high-toned feelings. Those complaints which spring
from wounded pride, and the jealousy of station, should
never be regarded lightly. The best soldiers are ever
most tenacious of their rank; for it cannot be expected
that he who hazards everything for distinction, will be
careless of it after it is attained. Fortunately, Lawrence
had again departed on a cruise before this letter arrived,
which otherwise might have driven from the service one
of our most meritorious officers.

This second cruise was in company with Commodore Bainbridge, who commanded the *Constitution*. While cruising off the Brazils they fell in with the *Bonne Citoyenne*, a British ship-of-war, having on board a large amount of specie, and chased her into St. Salvador. Notwithstanding that she was a larger vessel, and of a greater force in guns and men than the *Hornet*, yet Captain Lawrence sent a challenge to her commander, Captain Green, pledging his honor that neither the *Constitution* nor any other American vessel should interfere. Commodore Bainbridge made a similar pledge on his own part; but the British commander declined the combat, alleging that though perfectly satisfied that the event of such a rencounter would be favorable to his ship, "yet he was equally convinced that Commodore Bainbridge could not swerve so much from the paramount duty he owed his country as to become an inactive spectator, and see a ship belonging to the very squadron under his orders fall into the hands of the enemy."

To make him easy on this point, Commodore Bainbridge left the *Hornet* four days together off the harbor in which the *Bonne Citoyenne* laid, and from which she could discover that he was not within forty miles of it. He afterwards went into the harbor and remained there three days, where he might at any time have been detained twenty-four hours, at the request of Captain Green, if disposed to combat the *Hornet*. At length the

Constitution went off altogether, leaving Lawrence to blockade the *Bonne Citoyenne*, which he did for nearly a month, Captain Green not thinking proper to risk an encounter. It is possible that having an important public trust in charge, and sailing under particular orders, he did not think himself authorized to depart from the purpose of his voyage, and risk his vessel in a contest for mere individual reputation. But if such were his reasons, he should have stated them when he refused to accept the challenge.

On the 24th of January Captain Lawrence was obliged to shift his cruising-ground, by the arrival of the *Montagu*, 74, which had sailed from Rio Janeiro for the express purpose of relieving the *Bonne Citoyenne* and a British packet of 12 guns, which likewise lay at St. Salvador. At length, on the morning of the 24th February, when cruising off Demarara, the *Hornet* fell in with the British brig *Peacock*, Captain Peake, a vessel of about equal force. The contest commenced within half-pistol shot, and so tremendous was the fire of the Americans, that in less than fifteen minutes the enemy surrendered, and made signal of distress, being in a sinking condition. Her mainmast shortly went by the board, and she was left such an absolute wreck, that, notwithstanding every exertion was made to keep her afloat until the prisoners could be removed, she sunk with thirteen of her crew, and three brave American tars, who thus nobly perished in relieving a conquered foe. The slaughter on board of the *Peacock* was very severe; among the slain was found the body of her commander, Captain Peake. He was twice wounded in the course of the action; the last wound proved fatal. His body was wrapped in the flag of his vessel, and laid in the cabin to sink with her,—a shroud and sepulchre worthy so brave a sailor.

During the battle the British brig *L'Espeigle*, mounting 15 two-and-thirty-pound carronades and two long nines, lay at anchor, about six miles inshore. Being apprehensive that she would beat out to the assistance of her consort the utmost exertions were made to put the *Hornet* in a situation for action, and in about three hours she was in complete preparation, but the enemy did not think proper to make an attack.

The conduct of Lawrence towards his prisoners was such as, we are proud to say, has uniformly characterized the officers of our navy. They have ever displayed the liberality and scrupulous delicacy of generous minds towards those whom the fortune of war has thrown in their power; and thus have won by their magnanimity those whom they have conquered by their valor. The officers of the *Peacock* were so affected by the treatment they received from Captain Lawrence, that on their arrival at New York they made a grateful acknowledgment in the public papers. To use their own expressive phrase, "they ceased to consider themselves prisoners." Nor must we omit to mention a circumstance highly to the honor of the brave tars of the *Hornet.* Finding that the crew of the *Peacock* had lost all their clothing by the sudden sinking of the vessel, they made a subscription, and from their own wardrobes supplied each man with two shirts, and a blue jacket and trowsers. Such may rough sailors be made, when they have before them the example of high-minded men. They are beings of but little reflection, open to the impulse and excitement of the moment; and it depends in a great measure upon their officers, whether, under a Lawrence, they shall ennoble themselves by generous actions, or, under a Cockburn, be hurried away into scenes of unpremeditated atrocity.

On returning to this country Captain Lawrence was received with great distinction and applause, and various public bodies conferred on him peculiar tokens of approbation. While absent the rank of post-captain had been conferred on him, and shortly after his return he received a letter from the Secretary of the Navy, offering him the command of the frigate *Constitution*, provided neither Captains Porter nor Evans applied for it, they being older officers. Captain Lawrence respectfully declined this conditional appointment, for satisfactory reasons which he stated to the Secretary. He then received an unconditional appointment to that frigate, and directions to superintend the Navy Yard at New York in the absence of Captain Ludlow. The next day, to his great surprise and chagrin, he received counter-orders, with instructions to take command of the frigate *Chesapeake*, then lying at

Boston, nearly ready for sea. This appointment was particularly disagreeable to him. He was prejudiced against the *Chesapeake*, both from her being considered the worst ship in our navy, and from having been in a manner disgraced in the affair with the *Leopard*. This last circumstance had acquired her the character of an unlucky ship,—the worst of stigmas among sailors, who are devout believers in good and bad luck; and so detrimental was it to this vessel, that it has been found difficult to recruit crews for her.

The extreme repugnance that Captain Lawrence felt to this appointment induced him to write to the Secretary of the Navy, requesting to be continued in the command of the *Hornet*. Besides, it was his wish to remain some short time in port, and enjoy a little repose in the bosom of his family: particularly as his wife was in that delicate situation that most calls forth the tenderness and solicitude of an affectionate husband. But though he wrote four letters successively to the Secretary, he never received an answer, and was obliged reluctantly to acquiesce.

While laying in Boston Roads, nearly ready for sea, the British frigate *Shannon* appeared off the harbor, and made signals expressive of a challenge. The brave Lawrence immediately determined on accepting it, though conscious at the time of the great disparity between the two ships. The *Shannon* was a prime vessel, equipped in an extraordinary manner, for the express purpose of combating advantageously one of our largest frigates. She had an unusually numerous crew of picked men, thoroughly disciplined and well-officered. She was commanded by Captain Broke, one of the bravest and ablest officers in the service, who fought merely for reputation.

On the other hand, the *Chesapeake* was an indifferent ship; with a crew, a great part of whom were newly recruited, and not brought into proper discipline. They were strangers to their commander, who had not had time to produce that perfect subordination, yet strong personal attachment, which he had the talent of creating wherever he commanded. His first lieutenant was sick on shore; the other officers, though meritorious, were young men; two of them were mere acting lieutenants; most of them recently appointed to the ship, and unacquainted with the men. Those who are in the least informed in nautical affairs, must perceive the greatness of these disadvantages.

The most earnest endeavors were used, by Commodore Bainbridge and other gentlemen of nice honor and sound experience, to dissuade Captain Lawrence from what was considered a rash and unnecessary exposure. He felt and acknowledged the force of their reasons, but persisted in his determination. He was peculiarly situated; he had formerly challenged the *Bonne Citoyenne*, and should he decline a similar challenge, it might subject him to sneers and misrepresentations. Among the other unfortunate circumstances that attended this ill-starred battle, was the delay of a written challenge from Captain Broke, which did not arrive until after Captain Lawrence had sailed. It is stated to have been couched in the most frank and courteous language; minutely detailing the force of his ship; and offering, if the *Chesapeake* should not be completely prepared, to cruise off and on until such time as she made a specified signal of being ready for the conflict. It is to be deeply regretted that Captain Lawrence did not receive this gallant challenge, as it would have given him time to put his ship in proper order, and spared him the necessity of hurrying out, in his unprepared condition, to so formal and momentous an encounter.

After getting the ship under way, he called the crew together, and having ordered the white flag to be hoisted, bearing the motto, "Free trade and sailors' rights," he, according to custom, made them a short harangue. While he was speaking several murmurs were heard, and strong symptoms of dissatisfaction appeared in the manners and countenances of the crew. After he had finished, a scoundrel Portuguese, who was boatswain's mate, and acted as spokesman to the murmurers, replied to Captain Lawrence in an insolent manner, complaining, among other things, that they had not been paid their prize-money, which had been due for some time past.

The critical nature of the moment, and his ignorance of the dispositions and characters of his crew, would not allow Captain Lawrence to notice such dastardly and mutinous conduct in the manner it deserved. He dared not thwart the humors of men, over whose affections he had not had time to acquire any influence, and therefore ordered the purser to take them below and give them checks for their prize-money, which was accordingly done.

We dwell on these particulars to show the disastrous and disheartening circumstances under which Captain Lawrence went forth to this battle,—circumstances which shook even his calm and manly breast, and filled him with a despondency unusual to his nature. Justice to the memory of this invaluable officer requires that the disadvantages under which he fought should be made public.*

It was on the morning of the 1st of June that the *Chesapeake* put to sea. The *Shannon*, on seeing her come out, bore away, and the other followed. At 4 P. M. the *Chesapeake* haled up and fired a gun ; the *Shannon* then hove to. The vessels manœuvred in awful silence, until within pistol-shot, when the *Shannon* opened her fire, and both vessels almost at the same moment poured forth tremendous broadsides. The execution in both ships was terrible, but the fire of the *Shannon* was peculiarly fatal, not only making great slaughter among the men, but cutting down some of the most valuable officers.

* The particulars of this action are chiefly given from a conversation with one of the officers of the *Chesapeake;* and we believe may be relied on as authentic.

The very first shot killed Mr. White, sailing-master of the *Chesapeake*, an excellent officer, whose loss at such a moment was disastrous in the extreme. The fourth lieutenant, Mr. Ballard, received also a mortal wound in this broadside, and at the same moment Captain Lawrence was shot through the leg with a musket-ball; he however supported himself on the companion-way, and continued to give his orders with his usual coolness. About three broadsides were exchanged, which, from the closeness of the ships, were dreadfully destructive. The *Chesapeake* had three men shot from her helm successively, each taking it as the other fell; this of course produced irregularity in the steering, and the consequence was that her anchor caught in one of the *Shannon's* after-ports. She was thus in a position where her guns could not be brought to bear upon the enemy, while the latter was enabled to fire raking shots from her foremost guns, which swept the upper decks of the *Chesapeake*, killing or wounding the greater portion of the men. A hand-grenade was thrown on the quarter-deck, which set fire to some musket-cartridges, but did no other damage.

In this state of carnage and exposure about twenty of the *Shannon's* men, seeing a favorable opportunity for boarding, without waiting for orders, jumped on the deck of the *Chesapeake*. Captain Lawrence had scarce time to call his boarders, when he received a second and mortal wound from a musket-ball, which lodged in his intestines. Lieutenant Cox, who commanded the second division, rushed up at the call for the boarders, but came just in time to receive his falling commander. He was in the act of carrying him below, when Captain Broke, accompanied by his first lieutenant, and followed by his regular boarders, sprang on board the *Chesapeake.* The brave Lawrence saw the overwhelming danger; his last words, as he was borne bleeding from the deck, were, "Don't surrender the ship!"

Samuel Livermore, Esq., of Boston, who from personal attachment to Captain Lawrence had accompanied him in this cruise as chaplain, attempted to revenge his fall. He shot at Captain Broke, but missed him; the latter made a cut at his head, which Livermore warded off, but in so doing received a severe wound in the arm. The only officer that now remained on the upper deck was Lieutenant Ludlow, who was so entirely weakened and disabled by repeated wounds, received early in the action, as to be incapable of personal resistance. Owing to the comparatively small number of men, therefore, that survived on the upper deck, having no officer to head them, the British succeeded in securing complete possession, before those from below could get up. Lieutenant Budd, who had commanded the first division below, being informed of the danger, hastened up with some men, but was overpowered by superior numbers and cut down immediately. Great embarrassment took place, in consequence of the officers being unacquainted with the crew. In one instance in particular, Lieutenant

Cox, on mounting the deck, joined a party of the enemy through mistake, and was made sensible of his error by their cutting at him with their sabres.

While this scene of havoc and confusion was going on above, Captain Lawrence, who was lying in the ward-room in excruciating pain, hearing the firing cease, forgot the anguish of his wounds; having no officer near him, he ordered the surgeon to hasten on deck and tell the officers to fight on to the last, and never to strike the colors; adding, "They shall wave while I live." The fate of the battle, however, was decided. Finding all further resistance vain, and a mere waste of life, Lieutenant Ludlow gave up the ship; after which he received a sabre wound in the head from one of the *Shannon's* crew, which fractured his skull and ultimately proved mortal. He was one of the most promising officers of his age in the service, highly esteemed for his professional talents, and beloved for the generous qualities that adorned his private character.

Thus terminated one of the most remarkable combats on naval record. From the peculiar accidents that attended it, the battle was short, desperate, and bloody. So long as the cannonading continued, the *Chesapeake* is said to have clearly had the advantage; and had the ships not ran foul, it is probable she would have captured the *Shannon.* Though considerably damaged in her upper works, and pierced with some shot-holes in her hull, yet she had sustained no injury to affect her safety; whereas the *Shannon* had received several shots between wind and water, and, consequently, could not have sustained the action long. The havoc on both sides was dreadful; but to the singular circumstance of having every officer on the upper deck either killed or wounded, early in the action, may chiefly be attributed the loss of the *Chesapeake.*

There have been various vague complaints circulated of the excesses of the victors, and of their treatment of our crew after the surrender. These have been, as usual, dwelt on and magnified, and made subjects of national aspersion. Nothing can be more illiberal than this. Where the scene of conflict is tumultuous and sanguinary, and the struggle desperate, as in the boarding of a ship, excesses will take place among the men which it is impossible to prevent. They are the inevitable incidents of war, and should never be held up to provoke national abhorrence or retaliation. Indeed, they are so liable to be misrepresented by partial and distorted accounts, that very little faith is ever to be placed in them. Such, for instance, is the report, that the enemy discharged several muskets into the cockpit after the ship had been given up. This, in fact, was provoked by the wanton act of a boy below, who shot down the sentinel stationed at the gangway, and thus produced a momentary exasperation, and an alarm that our men were rising. It should be recollected, likewise, that our flag was not struck, but was hauled down by the enemy; consequently, the surrender of the ship was not immediately known throughout, and the struggle continued in various places, before the proper orders could be communicated. It is wearisome and disgusting to observe the war of slander kept up by the little minds of both countries, wherein every paltry misdeed of a paltry individual is insidiously trumpeted forth as a stigma on the respective nation. By these means are engendered lasting roots of bitterness, that give an implacable spirit to the actual hostility of the times, and will remain after the present strife shall have passed away. As the nations must inevitably, and at no very distant period, come once more together in the relations of amity and commerce, it is to be wished that as little private animosity may be encouraged as possible; so that, though we may contend for rights and interests, we may never cease to esteem and respect each other.

The two ships presented dismal spectacles after the battle. Crowded with the wounded and the dying, they resembled floating hospitals, sending forth groans at every roll. The brave Broke lay delirious from a wound in the head, which he is said to have received while endeavoring to prevent the slaughter of some of our men who had surrendered. In his rational intervals he always spoke in the highest terms of the courage and skill of Lawrence, and of "the gallant and masterly style" in which he brought the *Chesapeake* into action.

The wounds of Captain Lawrence rendered it impossible to remove him after the battle, and his cabin being very much shattered, he remained in the wardroom. Here he lay, attended by his own surgeon, and surrounded by his brave and suffering officers. He made no comment on the battle, nor indeed was heard to utter a word, except to make such simple requests as his necessities required. In this way he lingered through four days, in extreme bodily pain, and the silent melancholy of a proud and noble heart, and then expired. His body was wrapped in the colors of his ship and laid on the quarter-deck of the *Chesapeake,* to be conveyed to Halifax for interment.

At the time of his death he was but thirty-two years of age, nearly sixteen of which had been honorably expended in the service of his country. He was a disciplinarian of the highest order, producing perfect obedience and subordination without severity. His men became zealously devoted to him, and ready to do through affection what severity would never have compelled. He was scrupulously correct in his principles, delicate in his sense of honor; and to his extreme jealousy of reputation he fell a victim, in daring an ill-matched encounter, which prudence would have justified him in declining. In battle, where his lofty and commanding person made him conspicuous, the calm, collected courage and elevated tranquillity which he maintained in the midst of peril, imparted a confidence to every bosom. In the hour of victory he was moderate and unassuming; towards the vanquished he was gentle,

generous, and humane. But it is on the amiable qualities that adorned his private character, that his friends
will hang with the fondest remembrance,—that bland phi-
lanthropy that emanated from every look, that breathed
forth in every accent, that gave a grace to every action.
His was a general benevolence, that, like a lambent
flame, shed its cheering rays throughout the sphere of
his influence, warming and gladdening every heart, and
lighting up every countenance into smiles. But there is
one little circle on whose sacred sorrows even the eye of
sympathy dares not intrude. His brother being dead,
he was the last male branch of a family who looked up to
him as its ornament and pride. His fraternal tenderness
was the prop and consolation of two widowed sisters,
and in him their helpless offspring found a father. He
left, also, a wife and two young children, to whom he was
fervently attached. The critical situation of the former
was one of those cares which preyed upon his mind at
the time he went forth to battle. The utmost precautions had been taken by her relatives to keep from her
the knowledge of her husband's fate; their anxiety has
been relieved by the birth of a son, who, we trust, will
inherit the virtues and emulate the actions of his father.
The unfortunate mother is now slowly recovering from a
long and dangerous confinement; but has yet to learn
the heart-rending intelligence, that the infant in her arms
is fatherless.

There is a touching pathos about the death of this

5

estimable officer, that endears him more to us than if he had been successful. The prosperous conqueror is an object of admiration, but in some measure of envy; whatever gratitude we feel for his services, we are apt to think them repaid by the plaudits he enjoys. But he who falls a martyr to his country's cause excites the fulness of public sympathy. Envy cannot repine at laurels so dearly purchased, and gratitude feels that he is beyond the reach of its rewards. The last sad scene of his life hallows his memory; it remains sacred by misfortune, and honored, not by the acclamations, but the tears of his countrymen. The idea of Lawrence, cut down in the prime of his days, stretched upon his deck, wrapped in the flag of his country,—that flag which he had contributed to ennoble, and had died to defend,—is a picture that will remain treasured up in the dearest recollections of every American. His will form one of those talismanic names which every nation preserves as watchwords for patriotism and valor.

Deeply, therefore, as every bosom must lament the fall of so gallant and amiable an officer, there are some reflections consoling to the pride of friendship, and which may soothe, though they cannot prevent, the bitter tear of affection. He fell before his flag was struck. His fall was the cause, not the consequence, of defeat. He fell covered with glory, in the flower of his days, in the perfection of mental and personal endowment, and the freshness of reputation; thus leaving in every mind the full and perfect image of a hero. However we may deplore the stroke of death, his visits are occasionally well timed for his victim ; he sets a seal upon the fame of the illus, trious, fixing it beyond the reach of accident or change. And where is the son of honor, panting for distinction, who would not rather, like Lawrence, be snatched away in the brightness of youth and glory, than dwindle down to what is termed a good old age, wear his reputation to the shreds, and leave behind him nothing but the remembrance of decrepitude and imbecility ?

With feelings that swell our hearts do we notice the honors paid to the remains of the brave Lawrence at Halifax. When the ships arrived in port, a generous concern was expressed for his fate. The recollection of his humanity towards the crew of the *Peacock* was still fresh in every mind. His obsequies were celebrated with appropriate ceremonials and an affecting solemnity. His pall was supported by the oldest captains in the British service that were in Halifax; and the naval officers crowded to yield the last sad honors to a man who was late their foe, but now their foe no longer. There is a sympathy between gallant souls that knows no distinction of clime or nation. They honor in each other what they feel proud of in themselves. The group that gathered round the grave of Lawrence presented a scene worthy of the heroic days of chivalry. It was a complete triumph of the nobler feelings over the savage passions of war. We know not where most to bestow our admiration,—on the living, who showed such generous sensibility to departed virtue, or on the dead, in being worthy of such obsequies from such spirits. It is by deeds like these that we really feel ourselves subdued. The conflict of arms is ferocious, and triumph does but engender more deadly hostility; but the contest of magnanimity calls forth the better feelings, and the conquest is over the affections. We hope that in such a contest we may never be outdone; but that the present unhappy war may be continually softened and adorned by similar acts of courtesy and kindness on either part, thus sowing among present hostilities the quickening seeds of future friendship.

As to the event of this battle, deeply as we mourn the loss of so many valuable lives, we feel no further cause of lamentation. Brilliant as the victory undoubtedly was to the conquerors, our nation lost nothing of honor in the conflict. The ship was gallantly and bloodily defended to the last, and was lost, not through want of good conduct or determined bravery, but from the unavoidable chances of battle.* It was a victory "over

* In this we speak of the loyal and really American part of the crew. We have, it is true, been told of treacherous conduct among the murmurers. a number of whom, headed by the dastardly Portuguese boatswain's mate, are said to have deserted their commander at the moment of most need. As this matter will come under the scrutiny of the proper tribunal, we pass it over without further notice. If established, it will form another of the baleful disadvantages under which this battle was fought, and may serve to show the policy of admitting the leaven of foreign vagabonds among our own sound-hearted sailors.

which the conqueror mourned—so many suffered." We will not enter into any mechanical measurement of feet and inches, or any nice calculation of force; whether she had a dozen men more or less, or were able to throw a few pounds more or less of ball, than her adversary, by way of accounting for her defeat; we leave to nicer calculators to balance skill and courage against timber and old iron, and mete out victories by the square and the steelyard. The question of naval superiority, about which so much useless anxiety has been manifested of late, and which we fear will cause a vast deal of strife and ill-blood before it is put to rest, was in our opinion settled long since, in the course of the five preceding battles. From a general examination of these battles, it appears clearly to us that, under equal circumstances of force and preparation, the nations are equal on the ocean; and the result of any contest, between well-matched ships, would depend entirely on accident. This, without any charge of vanity, we may certainly claim: the British, in justice and candor, must admit as much, and it would be arrogant in us to insist on anything more.

Our officers have hitherto been fighting under superior excitement to the British. They have been eager to establish a name, and from their limited number, each has felt as if individually responsible for the reputation of the Navy. Besides, the haughty superiority with which they have at various times been treated by the enemy, had stung the feelings of the officers, and even touched the rough pride of the common sailor. They have spared no pains, therefore, to prepare for contest with so formidable a foe, and have fought with the united advantages of discipline and enthusiasm.

An equal excitement is now felt by the British. Galled by our successes, they begin to find that we are an enemy that calls for all their skill and circumspection. They have therefore resorted to a strictness of discipline, and to excessive precautions and preparations that had been neglected in their Navy, and which no other modern foe has been able to compel. Thus circumstanced, every future contest must be bloody and precarious. The question of superiority, if such an idle question is still kept up, will in all probability be shifting with the result of different battles, as either side has superior advantages or superior good fortune.

For our part, we conceive that the great purpose of our Navy is accomplished. It was not to be expected that with so inconsiderable a force we should make any impression on British power, or materially affect British commerce. We fought, not to take their ships and plunder their wealth, but to pluck some of their laurels wherewith to grace our own brows. In this we have succeeded; and thus the great mischief that our little Navy was capable of doing to Great Britain, in showing that her maritime power was vulnerable, has been effected, and is irretrievable.

The British may now swarm on our coasts—they may infest our rivers and our bays—they may destroy our ships—they may burn our docks and our ports—they may annihilate every gallant tar that fights beneath our flag—they may wreak every vengeance on our marine that their overwhelming force enables them to accomplish—and after all what have they effected? redeemed the preëminence of their flag? destroyed the naval power of this country?—no such thing. They must first obliterate from the tablets of our memories that deep-traced recollection, that we have repeatedly met them with equal force and conquered. In that inspiring idea, which is beyond the reach of mortal hand, exists the germ of future navies, future power, and future conquest. What is our Navy?—a handful of frigates; let them be destroyed; our forests can produce hundreds such. Should our docks be laid in ruins, we can rebuild them; should our gallant band of tars be annihilated, thanks to the vigorous population of our country, we can furnish thousands and thousands of such; but so long as exists the moral certainty that we have within us the spirit, the abilities, and the means of attaining naval glory,—so long the enemy, in wreaking their resentment on our present force, do but bite the stone which has been hurled at them,—the hand that hurled it remains uninjured.

———————

SINCE the publication of our biographical sketch of

this lamented officer, a letter has been put in our hands, from Commodore Bainbridge, contradicting the statement of his having dissuaded Captain Lawrence from encountering the *Shannon;* and mentioning that he did not see Captain L. for several days previous to his sailing. The hasty manner in which the biography was written, though it is a poor apology for incorrectness, may account for any errors that may occur. In fact, we did but consider ourselves as pioneers, breaking the way for more able and wary biographers who should come after us; who might diligently pursue the path we had opened, profit by the tracks we had left, and cautiously avoid the false steps we had made.

The facts respecting the battle were almost all taken from notes of a conversation with one of the officers of the *Chesapeake,* which were afterwards revised and acknowledged by him. Some, it is true, were cautiously selected from the current reports of the day, according as they bore the stamp of probability, and were supported by the concurrence of various testimony. These may occasionally be somewhat misstated, but we believe that in general they are materially correct. That any blame could ever attach for a moment to the conduct of Captain Lawrence, in encountering the *Shannon,* though superior in equipment, we never insinuated or supposed. On the contrary, we admired that zeal for the honor of his flag, and that jealousy of his own reputation, that led him, in the face of obvious disadvantages, to a battle, which men of less heroism would have declined without disgrace. The calculating, cautious-spirited commander, who warily measures the weapons, and estimates the force of his opponent, and shuns all engagements where the chances are not in his favor, may gain the reputation of prudence, but never of valor. There were sufficient chances on the side of Lawrence to exculpate him from all imputation of rashness, and sufficient perils to entitle him to the highest character for courage. He who would greatly deserve, must greatly dare, for brilliant victory is only achieved at the risk of disastrous defeat, and those laurels are ever brightest that are gathered on the very brink of danger.

T is the laudable desire of every brave man to receive the praises of his countrymen; but there is a dearer and more cherished wish that grows closer to his heart; it is to live in the recollections of those he loves and honors; to leave behind him a name, at the mention of which the bosom of friendship shall glow, the eye of affection shall brighten; which shall be a legacy of honest pride to his family, causing it to dwell on his worthy deeds and glory in his memory. The bravest soldier would not willingly expose himself to certain danger, if he thought that death were to be followed by oblivion; he might rise above the mere dread of bodily pain, but human pride shrinks from the darkness and silence of the grave.

It is the duty, and it is likewise the policy, therefore, of a nation, to pay distinguished honor to the memories of those who have fallen in its service. It is, after all, but a cheap reward for sufferings and death; but it is a reward that will prompt others to the sacrifice, when they see that it is faithfully discharged. The youthful bosom warms with emulation at the praises of departed heroes. The marble monument that bears the story of a nation's admiration and gratitude, becomes an object of ambition. Death, the great terror of warfare, ceases to be an evil when graced with such distinctions; and thus one hero may be said, like a phœnix, to spring from the ashes of his predecessor.

In the gallant young officer who is the subject of the present memoir, we shall see these observations verified; he fought with the illustrious example of his brethren before his eyes, and died with the funeral honors of Lawrence fresh in his recollection.

Lieutenant William Burrows was born in 1785, at Kinderton, near Philadelphia, the seat of his father, William Ward Burrows, Esq., of South Carolina. He was educated chiefly under the eye of his parent, who was a gentleman of accomplished mind and polished manners. It is not known whether he was intended for any particular profession; but great pains were taken to instruct him in the living languages, and at the age of thirteen he was as well acquainted with the German as with his mother tongue; he was likewise kept rigidly at the study of the French, for which, however, he showed singular aversion. The dawning of his character was pleasing and auspicious; to quickness of intellect he added an amiable disposition and generous sensibility of heart. His character, however, soon assumed more distinct and peculiar features; a shade of reserve began gradually to settle on his manners. At an age when the feelings of other chil-

dren are continually sallying forth, he seemed to hush his
into subjection. He appeared to retire within himself,
to cherish a solitary independence of mind, and to rely as
much as possible on his own resources. It seemed as if his
young imagination had already glanced forth on the rough
scene of his future life, and that he was silently preparing
himself for its vicissitudes. Nor is it improbable that
such was the case. Though little communicative of his
hopes and wishes, it was evident that his genius had taken
its bias. Even among the gentle employments and elegant
pursuits of a polite education, his family was astonished
to perceive the rugged symptoms of the sailor continually breaking forth ; and his drawing-master would sometimes surprise him neglecting the allotted task, to paint
the object of his silent adoration—a gallant ship-of-war.

On finding that such was the determined bent of his
inclinations, care was immediately taken to instruct him
in naval science. A midshipman's warrant was procured
for him in November, 1799, and in the following January
he joined the sloop-of-war *Portsmouth,* commanded by
Captain M'Neale, in which he sailed to France. This
cruise, while it confirmed his predilection for the life he
had adopted, made him acquainted with his own deficiencies. Instead of the puerile vanity and harmless
ostentation which striplings generally evince when they
first put on their uniform, and feel the importance of
command, it was with difficulty he could be persuaded to
wear the naval dress, until he had proved himself worthy

of it by his services. The same mixture of genuine diffidence and proud humility was observed in the discharge
of his duties towards his inferiors; he felt the novelty of
his situation, and shrunk from the exercise of authority
over the aged and veteran sailor, whom he considered his
superior in seamanship. On his return home, therefore,
he requested a furlough of some months, to strengthen
him in the principles of navigation. He also resumed
the study of the French language, the necessity for which
he had experienced in his late cruise, and from his knowledge of grammatical elements, joined to vigorous application, he soon learned to use it with fluency.

He was afterwards ordered on duty, and served on
board of various ships until 1803, when he was ordered
to the frigate *Constitution*, Commodore Preble. Soon
after the arrival of that ship in the Mediterranean, the
Commodore, noticing his zeal and abilities, made him an
acting lieutenant. In the course of the Tripolitan war,
he distinguished himself on various occasions by his intrepidity, particularly in one instance, when he rushed into
the midst of a mutinous body, and seized the ringleader
at the imminent hazard of his life. After his return to
the United States, in 1807, he was in different services, and
among others, as first lieutenant of the *Hornet*. While in
this situation, he distinguished himself greatly during a
violent and dangerous gale, insomuch that his brother
officers attributed the preservation of the ship entirely to
his presence of mind and consummate seamanship.

The details of a sailor's life are generally brief, and little satisfactory. We expect miraculous stories from men who rove the deep, visit every corner of the world, and mingle in storms and battles; and are mortified to find them treating these subjects with provoking brevity. The fact is, these circumstances that excite our wonder are trite and familiar to their minds. He whose whole life is a tissue of perils and adventures passes lightly over scenes at which the landsman, accustomed to the security of his fireside, shudders even in imagination. Mere bravery ceases to be a matter of ostentation, when every one around him is brave; and hair-breadth 'scapes are commonplace topics among men whose very profession consists in the hourly hazard of existence.

In seeking, therefore, after interesting anecdotes concerning those naval officers whose exploits have excited public enthusiasm, our curiosity is continually baffled by general accounts, or meagre particulars, given with the technical brevity of a log-book. We have thus been obliged to pass cursorily over several years of Burrows' seafaring life, though doubtless checkered by many striking incidents.

From what we can collect, he seems to have been a marked and eccentric character. His peculiarity, instead of being smoothed and worn down by mingling with the world, became more and more prominent, as he advanced in life. He had centred all his pride in becoming a thorough and accomplished sailor, and regarded everything else with indifference. His manners were an odd compound of carelessness and punctilio, frankness and taciturnity. He stood aloof from the familiarity of strangers, and in his contempt of what he considered fawning and profession, was sometimes apt to offend by blunt simplicity, or chill by reserve. But his character, when once known, seemed to attach by its very eccentricities, and though little studious of pleasing, he soon became a decided favorite. He had an original turn of thought and a strong perception of everything ludicrous and characteristic. Though scarcely ever seen to laugh himself, he possessed an exquisite vein of dry humor which he would occasionally indulge in the hours of hilarity, and, without moving a muscle of his own countenance, would set the table in a roar. When under the influence of this lurking drollery, everything he said and did was odd and whimsical. His replies were remarkably happy, and, heightened by the peculiarity of his manner, and the provoking gravity of his demeanor, were sources of infinite merriment to his associates. It was his delight to put on the dress of the common sailor, and explore the haunts of low life, drawing from thence traits of character and comic scenes with which he would sometimes entertain his messmates.

But with all this careless and eccentric manner, he possessed a heart full of noble qualities. He was proud of spirit, but perfectly unassuming; jealous of his own rights, but scrupulously considerate of those of others.

His friendships were strong and sincere; and he was zealous in the performance of secret and important services for those to whom he was attached. There was a rough benevolence in his disposition that manifested itself in a thousand odd ways; nothing delighted him more than to surprise the distressed with relief, and he was noted for his kindness and condescension towards the humble and dependent. His companions were full of his generous deeds, and he was the darling of the common sailors. Such was the sterling worth that lay encrusted in an unpromising exterior, and hidden from the world by a forbidding and taciturn reserve.

With such strong sensibilities and solitary pride of character, it was the lot of Burrows to be wounded in that tender part where the feelings of officers seem most assailable. In his promotion to a lieutenancy he had the mortification to find himself outranked by junior officers, some of whom he had commanded in the Tripolitan war. He remonstrated to the Navy Department, but without redress. On Mr. Hamilton's going into office, he stated to him his claims, and, impatient of the slight which he conceived he had suffered, offered to resign his commission, which, however, was not accepted. Whether the wrongs of which he complained were real or imaginary, they preyed deeply on his mind. He seemed for a time to grow careless of the world and of himself; withdrew more than ever from society, and abandoned himself to the silent broodings of a wounded spirit. Perhaps this morbid sensibility of feeling might in some measure have been occasioned by infirmity of body, his health having been broken by continual and severe duty; but it belongs to a saturnine character, like that of Burrows, to feel deeply and sorely. Men of gayer spirits and more mercurial temperament, may readily shake off vexation, or bustle it away amid the amusements and occupations of the world; but Burrows was scanty in his pleasures, limited in his resources, single in his ambition. Naval distinction was the object of all his hope and pride; it was the only light that led him on and cheered his way, and whatever intervened left him in darkness and dreariness of heart.

Finding his resignation was not accepted, and feeling temporary disgust at the service, he applied for a furlough, which, with some difficulty, he obtained. He then entered as first officer on board the merchant ship *Thomas Penrose*, Capt. Ansley, and sailed on a commercial voyage to Canton. On his return passage he was captured and carried into Barbadoes, but permitted to come home on parole. Immediately on his being exchanged, in June, 1813, he was appointed to the command of the brig *Enterprise*, at Portsmouth.

This appointment seemed to infuse new life and spirits into Burrows, and to change his whole deportment. His proper pride was gratified on having a separate command; he no longer felt like an unimportant individual, but that he had rank and station to support. He threw

6

off a great deal of his habitual reserve, became urbane
and attentive, and those who had lately looked upon him
as a mere misanthrope were delighted with the manly
frankness of his manners.

On the 1st of September, the *Enterprise* sailed from
Portsmouth on a cruise. On the 5th, early in the morning, they espied a brig inshore getting under way. They
reconnoitred her for a while to ascertain her character,
of which they were soon informed by her hoisting three
British ensigns, and firing a shot as a challenge. The
Enterprise then hauled upon a wind, stood out of the
bay, and prepared for action. A calm for some time
delayed the encounter; it was succeeded by a breeze
from the S. W., which gave our vessel the weather-gage.
After manœuvring for a while to the windward, in order
to try her sailing with the enemy, and to ascertain his
force, the *Enterprise*, about 3 P. M., shortened sail, hoisted
three ensigns, fired a gun, tacked, and ran down with an
intention to bring him to close quarters. When within
half-pistol shot the enemy gave three cheers, and commenced the action with his starboard broadside. The
cheers and the broadside were returned on our part, and
the action became general. In about five minutes after
the battle had commenced, the gallant Burrows received
a musket-ball in his body and fell; he, however, refused
to be carried below, but continued on deck through the
action. The active command was then taken by Lieutenant M'Call, who conducted himself with great skill and

coolness. The enemy was out-manœuvred and cut up; his maintopmast and topsail-yard shot away; a position gained on his starboard bow, and a raking fire kept up, until his guns were silenced and he cried for quarters, saying that as his colors were nailed to the mast, he could not haul them down. The prize proved to be his Britannic Majesty's brig *Boxer*, of 14 guns. The number of her crew is a matter of conjecture and dispute. Sixty-four prisoners were taken, seventeen of whom were wounded. How many of the dead were thrown into the sea during the action it is impossible to say;* the British return only four as killed; courtesy forbids us to question the veracity of an officer on mere presumption; but it is ever the natural wish of the vanquished to depreciate their force; and, in truth, we have seen with regret various instances of disingenuousness on the part of the enemy, in their statements of our naval encounters. But we will not enter into disputes of this kind. It is enough that the enemy entered into the battle with a bravado at the mast-head, and a confidence of success; this either implied a consciousness of his own force, or a low opinion of his antagonist; in either case he was mis-

---

* In a letter from Captain Hull to Commodore Bainbridge, he describes the state of the *Boxer* when brought into port, and observes, "We find it impossible to get at the number of killed; no papers are found by which we can ascertain it. I, however, counted ninety hammocks which were in her netting with beds in them, besides several beds without hammocks; and she had excellent accommodations for all her officers below in state-rooms, so that I have no doubt that she had one hundred men on board."

taken. It is a fruitless task to vindicate victories against the excuses of the vanquished; sufficient for the victor is the joy of his triumph, he should allow the enemy the consolation of accounting for it.

We turn gladly from such an idle discussion to notice the last moments of the worthy Burrows. There needs no elaborate pencil to impart pathos and grandeur to the death of a brave man. The simple anecdotes, given in simple terms by his surviving comrades, present more striking pictures than could be wrought up by the most refined attempts of art. "At 20 minutes past 3 р.м.," says one account, "our brave commander fell, and while lying on the deck, refusing to be carried below, raised his head and requested that *the flag might never be struck.*" In this situation he remained during the rest of the engagement, regardless of bodily pain; regardless of the life-blood fast ebbing from his wound; watching with anxious eye the vicissitudes of battle; cheering his men by his voice, but animating them still more by his glorious example. When the sword of the vanquished enemy was presented to him, we are told that he clasped his hands and exclaimed, "I am satisfied, I die contented!" He now permitted himself to be carried below, and the necessary attentions were paid to save his life, or alleviate his sufferings. His wound, however, was beyond the power of surgery, and he breathed his last within a few hours after the victory.

The commander of the *Boxer*, Captain Samuel Blythe,

was killed early in the action by a cannon-ball; had he
lived, he might have defended his ship more desperately,
but it is not probable with more success. He was an
officer of distinguished merit; having received a sword
from government for his good conduct under Sir James
L. Yeo, in the capture of Cayenne. He was also one of the
pall-bearers to our lamented Lawrence, when buried at
Halifax. It was his fate now to receive like courtesy at
the hands of his enemy. His remains, in company with
those of the brave Burrows, were brought to Portland,
where they were interred with military honors. It was a
striking and affecting sight, to behold two gallant commanders, who had lately been arrayed in deadly hostility
against each other, descending into one quiet grave, there
to mingle their dust peacefully together.

At the time of his decease Lieutenant Burrows was
but in his twenty-ninth year,—a most untimely death as
it concerned the interests of his country, and the fulness
of his own renown. Had he survived, there is little
doubt that his great professional merits, being rendered
conspicuous by this achievement, would have raised him
to importance, and enlarged the sphere of his usefulness.
And it is more than probable that those rich qualities of
heart and mind, which, chilled by neglect, had lain almost withering in the shade, being once vivified by the
quickening rays of public favor, would have sprung forth
in full luxuriance. As it is, his public actions will live
on the proud page of our naval history, and his private

worth will long flourish in the memory of his intimates, who dwell with honest warmth on the eccentric merits of this generous and true-hearted sailor.   For himself he was resigned to his premature fate; life seems never to have had much value in his eyes, and was nothing when weighed with reputation.   He had attained the bright object of his wishes, and died in the full fruition of the warrior's hope, with the shouts of victory still sounding in his ears.

N taking up the pen to commemorate another of our naval victories, we solicit the patience of our readers if we indulge in a few preliminary reflections, not strictly arising out of the subject of this memoir, though, we trust, not wholly irrelevant.

Indeed, we do not pretend to the rigid precision and dispassionate coolness of historic narrative. Excited as we are by the tone and temper of the times, and the enthusiasm that prevails around us, we cannot, if we would, repress those feelings of pride and exultation, that gush warm from the heart, when the triumphs of our Navy are the theme. Public joy is at all times contagious; but in the present lowering days of evil, it is a sight as inspiring as it is rare, to behold a whole nation breaking forth into gladness.

There is a point, however, beyond which exultation becomes insulting, and honest pride swells into vanity. When this is exceeded even success proves injurious, and, instead of begetting a proper confidence in ourselves, produces that most disgusting of all national faults, boastful arrogance. This is the evil against the

encroachments of which we would earnestly caution our
countrymen; it comes with such an open and imposing
front of worthy patriotism, and at such warm and incau-
tious moments, that it is apt to take possession of us
before we are aware. We have already noticed some
symptoms of its prevalence. We have seen many of our
papers filled with fulsome and extravagant paragraphs,
echoing the vulgar joy and coarse tauntings of the rab-
ble; these may be acceptable to the gross palates of the
mean-minded; but they must grieve the feelings of the
generous and liberal; and must lessen our triumphs in
the eyes of impartial nations. In this we behold the
striking difference between those who fight battles, and
those who merely talk about them. Our officers are
content modestly to announce their victories; to give a
concise statement of their particulars, and then drop the
subject; but then the theme is taken up by a thousand
vaunting tongues and vaunting pens; each tries to outvie
the other in extravagant applause, until the very ear of
admiration becomes wearied with excessive eulogium.

We do not know whether, in these remarks, we are not
passing censure upon ourselves, and whether we do not
largely indulge in the very weakness we condemn; but
of this we are sure, that in our rejoicings no feelings
enter insulting to the foe. We joy, indeed, in seeing the
flag of our country encircled with glory, and our nation
elevated to a dignified rank among the nations of the
earth; but we make no boastful claims to intrinsic supe-

riority, nor seek to throw sneer or stigma on an enemy, whom, in spite of temporary hostility, we honor and admire.

But, surely, if any impartial mind will consider the circumstances of the case, he will pardon our countrymen for overstepping, in the flush of unexpected and repeated success, the modest bounds of propriety. Is it a matter of surprise that, while our cheeks are yet scarce cool from the blushes—the burning blushes—of wounded pride and insulted patriotism, with which we have heard our country ridiculed and set at naught by other nations; while our ears still ring with the galling terms in which even British statesmen have derided us, as weak, pusillanimous and contemptible; while our memories are still sore with the tales of our flag insulted in every sea, and our countrymen oppressed in every port; is it a matter of surprise that we should break forth into transports at seeing these foul aspersions all suddenly brushed away —at seeing a continued series of brilliant successes flashing around the national standard, and dazzling all eyes with their excessive brightness? "Can such things be, and overcome us, like a summer cloud," without, not merely our "special wonder," but our special exultation? He who will cast his eye back, and notice how, in little more than one short year, we have suddenly sprung from peaceful insignificance to proud competition with a power whose laurels have been the slow growth of ages, will easily excuse the temporary effervescence of our feelings.

For our parts we truly declare that we revere the British nation. One of the dearest wishes of our hearts is to see a firm and well-grounded friendship established between us. But friendship can never long endure, unless founded on mutual respect and maintained with mutual independence ; and however we may deplore the present war, this double good will spring out of it, we will learn our own value and resources, and we will teach our antagonist and the world at large to know and estimate us properly. There is an obsequious deference in the minds of too many of our countrymen towards Great Britain, that not only impairs the independence of the national character, but defeats the very object they would attain. They would make any sacrifices to maintain a precarious, and patched-up, and humiliating connection with her ; but they may rest assured that the good opinion of Great Britain was never gained by servile acquiescence ; she never will think the better of a people for thinking despicably of themselves. We execrate that lowliness of spirit that would flatter her vanity, cower beneath her contumely, and meanly lay our honors at her feet. We wish not her friendship gratuitously, but to acquire it as a right ; not to supplicate it by forbearance and long-suffering, but gallantly to win and proudly to maintain it. After all, if she will not be a friend, she must be content to become a rival ; she will be obliged to substitute jealousy for contempt, and surely it is more tolerable, at any time, to be hated than despised.

Such is the kind of feeling that we avow towards Great Britain,—equally removed, we trust, from rancorous hostility on the one side, and blind partiality on the other.

Whatever we may think of the expediency or inexpediency of the present war, we cannot feel indifferent to its operations. Whenever our arms come in competition with those of the enemy, jealousy for our country's honor will swallow up every other consideration. Our feelings will ever accompany the flag of our country to battle, rejoicing in its glory—lamenting over its defeat. For there is no such thing as releasing ourselves from the consequences of the contest. He who fancies he can stand aloof in interest, and, by condemning the present war, can exonerate himself from the shame of its disasters, is wofully mistaken. Other nations will not trouble themselves about our internal wranglings and party questions; they will not ask who among us fought, or why we fought, but *how* we fought. The disgrace of defeat will not be confined to the contrivers of the war, or the party in power, or the conductors of the battle; but will extend to the whole nation, and come home to every individual. If the name of American is to be rendered honorable in the fight, we shall each participate in the honor; if otherwise, we must inevitably support our share of the ignominy. For these reasons do we watch, with anxious eye, the various fortunes of this war,—a war awfully decisive of the future character and destinies of the nation. But much as we are gladdened by the

bright gleams that occasionally break forth amid the
darkness of the times, yet joyfully, most joyfully, shall
we hail the period when the "troubled night" of war
shall be passed, and the "star of peace" again shed its
mild radiance on our country.

We have seized this opportunity to express the foregoing sentiments, because we thought that if of any
value, they might stand some chance of making an impression, when accompanied by the following memoir.
And, indeed, in writing these naval biographies, it is our
object not merely to render a small tribute of gratitude
to these intrepid champions of our honor, but to render our feeble assistance towards promoting that national feeling which their triumphs are calculated to
inspire.

Oliver Hazard Perry is the eldest son of Christopher
Raymond Perry, Esq., of the United States Navy. He
was born at Newport, Rhode Island, in August, 1785, and
being early destined for the Navy, he entered the service
in 1798, as midshipman, on board the sloop-of-war *General Greene*, then commanded by his father. When that
ship went out of commission he was transferred to a
squadron destined to the Mediterranean, where he served
during the Tripolitan war. His extreme youth prevented
his having an opportunity of distinguishing himself; but
the faithfulness and intelligence with which he discharged
the duties of his station, recommended him greatly to the
favor of his superior officers; while his private virtues,

and the manly dignity of his deportment, commanded the friendship and respect of his associates.

On returning from the Mediterranean he continued sedulously attentive to his profession, and though the reduction of the Navy, and the neglect into which it fell during an interval of peace, disheartened many of the officers, and occasioned several to resign, yet he determined to adhere to its fortunes, confident that it must at some future period rise to importance. It would be little interesting to enumerate the different vessels in which he served, or to trace his advances through the regular grades. In 1810, we find he was ordered to the United States schooner *Revenge*, as lieutenant commandant. This vessel was attached to the squadron of Commodore Rodgers, at New London, and employed in cruising in the Sound, to enforce the Embargo Act. In the following spring he had the misfortune to lose the *Revenge* on Watch Hill Reef, opposite Stoney Town. He had sailed from Newport, late in the evening, for New London, with an easterly wind, accompanied by a fog. In the morning he found himself enveloped in a thick mist, with a considerable swell going. In this situation, without any possibility of ascertaining where he was, or of guarding against surrounding dangers, the vessel was carried on the reef, and soon went to pieces. On this occasion Perry gave proofs of that admirable coolness and presence of mind for which he is remarkable. He used every precaution to save the guns and property, and was in a great

measure successful.   He got off all the crew in perfect
safety, and was himself the last to leave the wreck.   His
conduct in respect to this disaster underwent examination by a court of inquiry, at his own request, and he was
not merely acquitted of all blame, but highly applauded
for the judgment, intrepidity, and perseverance he had
displayed.   The Secretary of the Navy, Mr. Hamilton,
also wrote him a very complimentary letter on the occasion.

Shortly after this event he returned to Newport, being
peculiarly attracted thither by a tender attachment for
Miss Mason, daughter of Dr. Mason, and niece of the
Hon. Christopher Champlin of the United States Senate,
—a lovely and interesting young lady, whom he soon
after married.

At the beginning of 1812, he was promoted to the rank
of master and commander, and ordered to the command
of the flotilla of gun-boats stationed at the harbor of
New York.   He remained on this station about a year ;
during which time he employed himself diligently in dis-
ciplining his crew to serve either as landsmen or mariners, and brought his flotilla into an admirable state of
preparation for active operations.

The gun-boat service, however, is at best but an irksome employ.   Nothing can be more dispiriting for ardent and daring minds than to be obliged to skulk about
harbors and rivers, cramped up in these diminutive vessels, without the hope of exploit to atone for present

inconvenience. Perry soon grew tired of this inglorious service, and applied to the Secretary of the Navy to be ordered to a more active station, and mentioned the Lakes as the one he should prefer. His request was immediately complied with, and he received orders to repair to Sackett's Harbor, Lake Ontario, with a body of mariners to reinforce the squadron under Commodore Chauncey. So popular was he among the honest tars under his command, that no sooner was the order known than nearly the whole of the crews volunteered to accompany him.

In a few days he was ready to depart, and tearing himself from the comforts of home, and the endearments of a young and beautiful wife and blooming child, he set off at the head of a large number of chosen seamen, on his expedition to the wilderness. The rivers being completely frozen over, they were obliged to perform the journey by land, in the depth of winter. The greatest order and good humor, however, prevailed throughout the little band of adventurers, to whom the whole expedition seemed a kind of frolic, and who were delighted with what they termed a land cruise.

Not long after the arrival of Perry at Sackett's Harbor, Commodore Chauncey, who entertained a proper opinion of his merits, detached him to Lake Erie, to take command of the squadron on that station, and to superintend the building of additional vessels. The American force at that time on the Lake consisted but of several small vessels ; two of the best of which had recently been captured from the enemy in a gallant style by Captain Elliot, from under the very batteries of Malden. The British force was greatly superior, and commanded by Commodore Barclay, an able and well-tried officer. Commodore Perry immediately applied himself to increase his armament, and having ship-carpenters from the Atlantic coast, and using extraordinary exertions, two brigs of twenty guns each were soon launched at Erie, the American port on the Lake.

While the vessels were constructing, the British squadron hovered off the harbor, but offered no molestation. At length, his vessels being equipped and manned, on the 4th of August Commodore Perry succeeded in getting his squadron over the bar at the mouth of the harbor. The water on the bar was but five feet deep, and the large vessels had to be buoyed over ; this was accomplished in the face of the British, who fortunately did not think proper to make an attack. The next day he sailed in pursuit of the enemy, but returned on the 8th, without having encountered him. Being reinforced by the arrival of the brave Elliot, accompanied by several officers and eighty-nine sailors, he was enabled completely to man his squadron, and again set sail on the 12th, in quest of the enemy. On the 15th he arrived at Sandusky Bay, where the American army under General Harrison lay encamped. From thence he cruised off Malden, where the British squadron remained at anchor, under the guns of the fort. The appearance of Perry's squadron spread great alarm on shore; the women and children ran shrieking about the place, expecting an immediate attack. The Indians, we are told, looked on with astonishment, and urged the British to go out and fight. Finding the enemy not disposed to venture a battle, Commodore Perry returned to Sandusky.

Nothing of moment happened until the morning of the 10th of September. The American squadron were, at that time, lying at anchor in Put-in-Bay, and consisted of—

Brig Lawrence...Com. Perry .. ..20 guns.
 "   Niagara ....Capt. Elliot............ 20   "
 "   Caledonia...Purser M'Grath 3   "
Sch. Ariel ......Lieutenant Packet....... 4   "
 "   Scorpion ....Sailing-Master Champlin. 2   "
 "   Somers..... "   "   Almy..... 2   "   and 2 swivels.
 "   Tigress.....Lieutenant Conklin...... 1   "
 "   Porcupine ..Mid. G. Senat.......... 1   "
Sloop Trippe......Lieutenant Smith........ 1   "
                                          ――――
                                          54 guns.

At sunrise they discovered the enemy, and immediately got under way and stood for him, with a light wind at southwest. The British force consisted of—

Ship Detroit............19 guns, 1 on pivot, and 2 howitzers.
 "   Queen Charlotte ...17 "   1   "
Sch. Lady Prevost......13 "   1   "
Brig Hunter ....10 "
Sloop Little Belt........ 3 "
Sch. Chippeway .... 1 "   2 swivels.
                       ――――
                       63 guns.

At 10 A. M. the wind hauled to the southeast and brought our squadron to windward. Commodore Perry then hoisted his Union Jack, having for a motto the dying words of the valiant Lawrence, "Don't give up the ship!" It was received with repeated cheerings by the officers and crews. And now having formed his line he bore for the enemy; who likewise cleared for action, and hauled up his courses. It is deeply interesting to picture to ourselves the advances of these gallant and well-matched squadrons to a contest where the strife must be obstinate and sanguinary, and the event decisive of the fate of almost an empire.

The lightness of the wind occasioned them to approach each other but slowly, and prolonged the awful interval of suspense and anxiety that precedes a battle. This is the time when the stoutest heart beats quick, "and the boldest holds his breath;" it is the still moment of direful expectation; of fearful looking out for slaughter and destruction, when even the glow of pride and ambition is chilled for a while, and nature shudders at the awful jeopardy of existence. The very order and regularity of naval discipline heighten the dreadful quiet of the moment. No bustle, no noise prevails to distract the mind, except at intervals the shrill piping of the boatswain's whistle, or a murmuring whisper among the men, who, grouped around their guns, earnestly regard the movements of the foe, now and then stealing a wistful glance at the countenances of their commanders. In this manner did the hostile squadrons approach each other, in mute watchfulness and terrible tranquillity; when suddenly a bugle was sounded from on board the enemy's ship *Detroit*, and loud huzzas immediately burst forth from all their crews.

No sooner did the *Lawrence* come within reach of the enemies' long guns, than they opened a heavy fire upon her, which, from the shortness of her guns, she was unable to return. Commodore Perry, without waiting for his schooners, kept on his course in such gallant and determined style that the enemy supposed it was his intention to board. In a few minutes, having gained a nearer position, he opened his fire. The length of the enemies' guns, however, gave them vastly the advantage, and the *Lawrence* was excessively cut up without being able to do any great damage in return. Their shot pierced her sides in all directions, killing our men on the berth-deck and in the steerage, where they had been taken down to be dressed. One shot had nearly produced a fatal explosion; passing through the light-room it knocked the snuff of the candle into the magazine; fortunately the gunner happened to see it, and had the presence of mind to extinguish it immediately with his hand.

Indeed, it seemed to be the enemies' plan to destroy the Commodore's ship, and thus throw the squadron into confusion. For this purpose their heaviest fire was directed at the *Lawrence*, and blazed incessantly upon it from their largest vessels. Finding the hazard of his situation, Perry made sail, and directed the other vessels to follow for the purpose of closing with the foe. The tremendous fire, however, to which he was exposed, soon cut away every brace and bowline, and the *Lawrence* became unmanageable. Even in this disastrous plight she sustained the action for upwards of two hours, within canister distance, though for a great part of the time he could not get more than three guns to bear upon her antagonists. It was admirable to behold the perfect order and regularity that prevailed among her valiant and devoted crew, throughout this scene of horror. No trepidation, no confusion occurred, even for an instant; as fast as the men were wounded they were carried below, and others stept into their places; the dead remained where they fell until after the action. At this juncture the fortune of the battle trembled on a point, and the enemy believed the day their own. The *Lawrence* was reduced to a mere wreck; her decks were streaming with blood, and covered with mangled limbs and the bodies of the slain; nearly the whole of her crew was either killed or wounded; her guns were dismounted, and the Commodore and his officers helped to work the last that was capable of service.

Amidst all this peril and disaster the youthful commander is said to have remained perfectly composed, maintaining a serene and cheerful countenance, uttering no passionate or agitated expression, giving out his orders with calmness and deliberation, and inspiriting every one around him by his magnanimous demeanor.

At this crisis, finding the *Lawrence* was incapable of further service, and seeing the hazardous situation of the conflict, he formed the bold resolution of shifting his flag. Giving the ship, therefore, in charge to Lieutenant Yarnall, who had already distinguished himself by his bravery, he hauled down his union, bearing the motto of Lawrence, and taking it under his arm, ordered to be put on board of the *Niagara*, which was then in close engagement. In leaving the *Lawrence*, he gave his pilot choice either to remain on board, or accompany him; the faithful fellow told him "he'd stick by him to the last," and jumped into the boat. He went off from the ship in his usual gallant manner, standing up in the stern of the boat, until the crew absolutely pulled him down among them. Broadsides were levelled at him, and small arms discharged by the enemy, two of whose vessels were within musket-shot, and a third one nearer. His brave shipmates who remained behind, stood watching him in breathless anxiety; the balls struck around him and flew over his head in every direction; but the same special providence that seems to have watched over the youthful hero throughout this desperate battle, conducted him safely through a shower of shot, and they beheld with transport his inspiring flag hoisted at the mast-head of the *Niagara*. No sooner was he on board than Captain Elliot volunteered to put off in a boat and bring into action the schooners which had been kept astern by the lightness of the wind; the gallant offer was accepted, and Elliot left the *Niagara* to put it in execution.

About this time the Commodore saw, with infinite regret, the flag of the *Lawrence* come down. The event was unavoidable; she had sustained the whole fury of the enemy, and was rendered incapable of defence; any further show of resistance would have been most uselessly and cruelly to have provoked carnage among the relics of her brave and mangled crew. The enemy, however, were not able to take possession of her, and subsequent circumstances enabled her again to hoist her flag.

Commodore Perry now made signal for close action, and the small vessels got out their sweeps and made all sail. Finding that the *Niagara* was but little injured, he determined, if possible, to break the enemy's line. He accordingly bore up and passed ahead of the two ships and brig, giving them a raking fire from his starboard guns, and also to a large schooner and sloop from his larboard side at half-pistol shot. Having passed the whole squadron, he luffed up and laid his ship alongside the British commodore. The smaller vessels under the direction of Captain Elliot having, in the meantime, got within grape and canister distance, and keeping up a well-directed fire, the whole of the enemy struck excepting two small vessels which attempted to escape, but were taken.

The engagement lasted about three hours, and never

was victory more decisive and complete. The captured squadron, as has been shown, exceeded ours in weight of metal and number of guns. Their crews were also more numerous; ours were a motley collection, where there were some good seamen, but eked out with soldiers, volunteers, and boys, and many were on the sick-list. More prisoners were taken than we had men to guard. The loss on both sides was severe. Scarcely any of the *Lawrence's* crew escaped unhurt. Among those slain was Lieutenant Brooks, of the marines, a gay and elegant young officer, full of spirit, of amiable manners, and remarkable for his personal beauty. Lieutenant Yarnall, though repeatedly wounded, refused to quit the deck during the whole of the action. Commodore Perry, notwithstanding that he was continually in the most exposed situations of the battle, escaped uninjured; he wore an ordinary seaman's dress, which, perhaps, prevented him from being picked off by the enemies' sharpshooters. He had a younger brother with him on board the *Lawrence* as midshipman, who was equally fortunate in receiving no injury, though his shipmates fell all around him. Two Indian chiefs had been stationed in the tops of the *Detroit* to shoot down our officers, but when the action became warm, so panic-struck were they with the terrors of the scene, and the strange perils that surrounded them, that they fled precipitately to the hold of the ship, where they were found after the battle in a state of utter consternation. The bodies of several other

Indians are said to have been found the next day on the shores of the Lake, supposed to have been slain during the engagement and thrown overboard.

It is impossible to state the number of killed on board the enemy. It must, however, have been very great, as their vessels were literally cut to pieces ; and the masts of their two principal ships so shattered that the first gale blew them overboard. Commodore Barclay, the British commander, certainly did himself honor by the brave and obstinate resistance which he made. He is a fine-looking officer, of about thirty-six years of age. He has seen much service, having been desperately wounded in the battle of Trafalgar, and afterwards losing an arm in another engagement with the French. In the present battle he was twice carried below, on account of his wounds. While below the second time, his officer came down and told him that they must strike, as the ships were cut to pieces, and the men could not be kept to their guns. Commodore Barclay was then carried on deck, and after taking a view of their situation, and finding all chance of success was over, reluctantly gave orders to strike.

We have thus endeavored to lay before our readers as clear an account of this important battle as could be gathered from the scanty documents that have reached us, though sketched out, we are sensible, with a hand but little skilled in naval affairs. The leading facts, however, are all that a landsman can be expected to furnish, and we trust that this glorious affair will hereafter be recorded with more elaborate care and technical precision. There is, however, a distinctness of character about a naval victory that meets the capacity of every mind. There is such a simple unity in it; it is so well defined, so complete within itself, so rounded by space, so free from those intricacies and numerous parts that perplex us in an action on land, that the meanest intellect can fully grasp and comprehend it. And then, too, the results are so apparent. A victory on land is liable to a thousand misrepresentations ; retreat is often called falling back, and abandoning the field called taking a new position ; so that the conqueror is often defrauded of half the credit of his victory ; but the capture or destruction of a ship is not to be mistaken, and a squadron towed triumphantly into port, is a notorious fact that admits of no contradiction.

In this battle, we trust, incontrovertible proof is given, if such proof were really wanted, that the success of our Navy does not arise from chance, or superiority of force ; but from the cool, deliberate courage, the intelligent minds and naval skill of our officers, the spirit of our seamen, and the excellent discipline of our ships ; from principles, in short, which must insure a frequency of prosperous results, and give permanency to the reputation we have acquired. We have been rapidly adding trophy to trophy, and successively driving the enemy from every excuse in which he sought to shelter himself

from the humiliation of defeat; and after having perfectly
established our capability of fighting and conquering in
single ships, we have now gone further, and shown that
it is possible for us to face the foe in squadron, and van-
quish him even though superior in force.

In casting our eye over the details of this engagement,
we are struck with the prominent part which the commander takes in the contest. We realize in his dauntless
exposure and individual prowess, what we have read in
heroic story, of the warrior, streaming like a meteor
through the fight, and working wonders with his single
arm. The fate of the combat seemed to rest upon his
sword; he was the master-spirit that directed the storm
of battle, moving amid flames, and smoke, and death, and
mingling wherever the struggle was most desperate and
deadly. After sustaining in the *Lawrence* the whole
blaze of the enemy's cannonry; after fighting until all
around him was wreck and carnage; we behold him,
looking forth from his shattered deck, with unruffled
countenance, on the direful perils that environed him,
calculating with wary eye the chances of the battle, and
suddenly launching forth on the bosom of the deep, to
shift his flag on board another ship, then in the hottest
of the action. This was one of those master-strokes by
which great events are achieved, and great characters
stamped, as it were, at a single blow,—which bespeak the
rare combination of the genius to conceive, the promptness to decide, and the boldness to execute. Most com-

manders have such glorious chances for renown, some time or another, within their reach; but it requires the nerve of a hero to grasp the perilous opportunity. We behold Perry following up his daring movement with sustained energy,—dashing into the squadron of the enemy, —breaking their line,—raking starboard and larboard,— and in this brilliant style achieving a consummate victory.

But if we admire his presence of mind and dauntless valor in the hour of danger, we are no less delighted with his modesty and self-command amidst the flush of triumph. A courageous heart may carry a man stoutly through the battle, but it argues some strong qualities of head to drain unmoved the intoxicating cup of victory. The first care of Perry was to attend to the comfort of the suffering crews of both squadrons. The sick and wounded were landed as soon as possible, and every means taken to alleviate the miseries of their situation. The officers who had fallen, on both sides, were buried on Sunday morning, on an island in the Lake, with the honors of war. To the surviving officers he advanced a loan of one thousand dollars, out of his own limited purse; but, in short, his behavior in this respect is best expressed in the words of Commodore Barclay, who, with generous warmth and frankness, has declared that "the conduct of Perry towards the captive officers and men was sufficient, of itself, to immortalize him!"

The letters which he wrote announcing the intelligence

were remarkably simple and laconic. To the Secretary of the Navy he observes, "It has pleased the Almighty to give to the arms of the United States a signal victory over their enemies on this Lake. The British squadron, consisting of two ships, two brigs, one schooner, and one sloop, have this moment surrendered to the force under my command, after a sharp conflict." This has been called an imitation of Nelson's letter after the battle of the Nile; but it was choosing a noble precedent, and the important national results of the victory justified the language. Independent of the vast accession of glory to our flag, this conquest insured the capture of Detroit, the rout of the British armies, the subjugation of the whole peninsula of Upper Canada, and, if properly followed up, the triumphant success of our northern war. Well might he say "It has pleased the Almighty," when, by this achievement, he beheld immediate tranquillity restored to an immense extent of country. Mothers no longer shrunk aghast, and clasped their infants to their breasts, when they heard the shaking of the forest or the howling of the blast; the aged sire no longer dreaded the shades of night, lest ruin should burst upon him in the hour of repose, and his cottage be laid desolate by the firebrand and the scalping-knife; Michigan was rescued from the dominion of the sword, and quiet and security once more settled on the harassed frontiers, from Huron to Niagara.

But we are particularly pleased with his subsequent

letter giving the particulars of the battle. It is so chaste, so moderate and perspicuous; equally free from vaunting exultation and affected modesty; neither obtruding himself upon notice, nor pretending to keep out of sight. His own individual services may be gathered from the letter, though not expressly mentioned; indeed, where the fortune of the day depended so materially upon himself, it was impossible to give a faithful narrative without rendering himself conspicuous.

We are led to notice these letters thus particularly, because that we find the art of letter-writing is an accomplishment as rare as it is important among our military gentlemen. We are tired of the valor of the pen, and the victories of the ink-horn. There is a common French proverb, "Grand parleur, mauvais combattant," which we could wish to see introduced into our country, and engraven on the swords of our officers. We wish to see them confine themselves in their letters to simple facts, neither swaggering before battle nor vaunting afterwards. It is unwise to boast before, for the event may prove disastrous; and it is superfluous to boast afterwards, for the event speaks for itself. He who promises nothing, may with safety perform nothing, and will receive praise if he perform but little; but he who promises much will receive small credit unless he perform miracles. If a commander have done well, he may be sure the public will find it out, and their gratitude will be in proportion to his modesty. Admiration is a coin which, if left to ourselves, we lavish profusely, but we always close the hand when dunned for it.

Commodore Perry, like most of our naval officers, is yet in the prime of youth. He is of a manly and prepossessing appearance; mild and unassuming in his address, amiable in his disposition, and of great firmness and decision. Though early launched among the familiar scenes of naval life (and nowhere is familiarity more apt to be licentious and encroaching), yet the native gentility and sober dignity of his deportment always chastened, without restraining, the freedom of intimacy. It is pleasing thus to find public services accompanied by private virtues; to discover no drawbacks on our esteem, no base alloy in the man we are disposed to admire; but a character full of moral excellence, of high-minded courtesy, and pure, unsullied honor.

Were anything wanting to perpetuate the fame of this victory, it would be sufficiently memorable from the scene where it was fought. This war has been distinguished by new and peculiar characteristics. Naval warfare has been carried into the interior of a continent, and navies, as if by magic, launched from among the depths of the forest. The bosoms of peaceful lakes which, but a short time since, were scarcely navigated by man, except to be skimmed by the light canoe of the savage, have all at once been ploughed by hostile ships. The vast silence that had reigned for ages on those mighty waters, was broken by the thunder of artillery, and the affrighted savage stared with amazement from his covert, at the sudden apparition of a sea-fight amid the solitudes of the wilderness.

The peal of war has once sounded on that lake, but probably will never sound again. The last roar of cannonry that died along her shores was the expiring note of British domination. Those vast internal seas will, perhaps, never again be the separating space between contending nations; but will be embosomed within a mighty empire; and this victory, which decided their fate, will stand unrivalled and alone, deriving lustre and perpetuity from its singleness.

In future times, when the shores of Erie shall hum with busy population; when towns and cities shall brighten where now extend the dark and tangled forest; when ports shall spread their arms, and lofty barks shall ride where now the canoe is fastened to the stake; when the present age shall have grown into venerable antiquity, and the mists of fable begin to gather round its history; then will the inhabitants of Canada look back to this battle we record as one of the romantic achievements of the days of yore. It will stand first on the page of their local legends, and in the marvellous tales of the borders. The fisherman, as he loiters along the beach, will point to some half-buried cannon, corroded with the rust of time, and will speak of ocean warriors that came from the shores of the Atlantic; while the boatman, as he trims his sail to the breeze, will chant in rude ditties the name of Perry—the early hero of Lake Erie.

CAPTAIN DAVID PORTER.

AVID PORTER, the eldest son of Captain David Porter, was born in Boston on the 1st of February, 1780. His father was an officer in our navy during the Revolutionary War, and distinguished himself on various occasions by his activity, enterprise, and daring spirit. Being necessarily absent from home for the greater part of his time, the charge of his infant family devolved almost entirely on his wife. She was a pious and intelligent woman; the friend and instructor of her children, teaching them not merely by her precepts, but by her amiable and virtuous example.

Soon after the conclusion of the war, Captain Porter removed with his household to Baltimore, where he took command of the revenue-cutter *Active*. Here in the bosom of his family he would indulge in the veteran's foible of recounting past scenes of peril and adventure, and talking over the wonders and vicissitudes that checker a seafaring life. Little David would sit for hours and listen and kindle at these marvellous tales, while his father, perceiving his own love of enterprise springing up in the bosom of the lad, took every means to cherish it, and to inspire him with a passion for the sea. He at the same time gave him all the education and instruction that his limited means afforded, and being afterwards in command of a vessel in the West India trade, proposed to take him a voyage by way of initiating him into the life of a sailor. The constitution of the latter being feeble and delicate excited all the apprehensions of a tender mother, who remonstrated with maternal solicitude against exposing the puny stripling to the dangers and hardships of so rude a life. Her objections, however, were either obviated or overruled, and at the age of sixteen he sailed with his father for the West Indies, in the schooner *Eliza*. While at the port of Jeremie, in the island of St. Domingo, a press-gang endeavored to board the vessel in search for men; they were bravely repelled with the loss of several killed and wounded on both sides; one man shot down close by the side of young Porter. This affair excited considerable attention at the time. A narrative of it appeared in the public papers, and much praise was given to Captain Porter for the gallant vindication of his flag.

In the course of his second voyage, which he performed as mate of a ship, from Baltimore to St. Domingo, young Porter had a further taste of the vicissitudes of a sailor's life. He was twice impressed by the British, and each time effected his escape, but was so reduced in purse as to be obliged to work his passage home in the winter season, destitute of necessary cloth-

8

ing. In this forlorn condition he had to perform duty on a cold and stormy coast, where every spray was converted instantaneously into a sheet of ice. It would appear almost incredible that his feeble frame, little inured to hardship, could have sustained so much, were it not known how greatly the exertions of the body are supported by mental excitement.

Scarcely had he recovered from his late fatigues when he applied for admission into the Navy; and on receiving a midshipman's warrant, immediately joined the frigate *Constellation*, Commodore Truxton. In the action with the French frigate *Insurgent*, Porter was stationed in the foretop, and distinguished himself by his good conduct. Want of friends alone prevented his promotion at the time. When Commodore Barron was appointed to the command of the *Constellation*, Porter was advanced to the rank of lieutenant solely on account of his merit, having no friends or connections capable of urging his fortunes. He was ordered to join the United States schooner *Experiment*, under Captain Maley, to be employed on the West India station. During the cruise they had a long and obstinate engagement with a number of brigand barges in the Bight of Leogane, which afforded him another opportunity of bringing himself into notice. He was also frequently employed in boat expeditions to cut out vessels, in which he displayed much coolness and address. Commodore Talbot, who commanded on that station, gave him charge of the

Amphitrite, a small pilot-boat prize schooner mounting five small swivels taken from the tops of the *Constellation*, and manned with fifteen hands. Not long after taking this command he fell in with a French privateer mounting a long twelve-pounder and several swivels, having a crew of forty men, and accompanied by a prizeship and a large barge with thirty men armed with swivels. Notwithstanding the great disparity of force, Porter ordered his vessel to be laid alongside the privateer. The contest was arduous, and for some time doubtful, for in the commencement of the action he lost his rudder, which rendered the schooner unmanageable. The event, however, excused the desperateness of the attack, for after an obstinate and bloody resistance the privateer surrendered with the loss of seven killed and fifteen wounded. Not a man of Porter's crew was killed; several, however, were wounded, and his vessel was much injured. The prize was also taken, but the barge escaped. The conduct of Lieutenant Porter in this gallant little affair was highly applauded by his commander.

Shortly after his return to the United States he sailed, as first lieutenant, in the *Experiment*, commanded by Captain Charles Stewart. They were again stationed in the West Indies, and afforded great protection to the American commerce in that quarter. They had several engagements with French privateers, and were always successful, insomuch that they became the terror of those marauders of the ocean, and effectually controlled their rapacity and kept them quiet in port. The gallant and lamented Trippe was second lieutenant of the *Experiment* at the time.

When the first squadron was ordered for the Mediterranean, Porter sailed as first lieutenant of the schooner *Enterprise*, Captain Stewart. In this cruise they encountered a Tripolitan corsair of very superior force ; a severe battle ensued in which the enemy suffered great slaughter, and was compelled to surrender, while our ship received but little injury. In this brilliant action Porter acquired much reputation from the conspicuous part he acted. He afterwards served on board of different ships on the Mediterranean station, and distinguished himself by his intrepidity and zeal whenever an opportunity presented. On one occasion he commanded an expedition of boats sent to destroy some vessels laden with wheat, at anchor in the harbor of old Tripoli; the service was promptly and effectually performed ; in the engagement he received a musket-ball through his left thigh.

Shortly after recovering from his wound he was transposed from the *New York* to the *Philadelphia*, Captain Bainbridge, as first lieutenant. The frigate was then lying at Gibraltar, when he joined her in September, 1803. She soon after sailed for the blockade of Tripoli. No event took place worthy of mention until the 31st of October. Nearly a week previous to this ill-fated day, the weather had been tempestuous, which rendered it prudent to keep the ship off the land. The 31st opened with all the splendor of a Sicilian morning; the promise of a more delightful day never appeared. The land was just observed, when a sail was descried making for the harbor, with a pleasant easterly breeze. It was soon ascertained to be an armed ship of the enemy, and all sail was set in chase. After an ineffectual pursuit of several leagues, Captain Bainbridge had just given orders to haul off, when the frigate grounded. Every expedient that skill or courage could devise to float or defend her, was successfully resorted to, but in vain. The particulars of this unfortunate affair are too generally known to need a minute recital; it is sufficient to add that this noble ship and her gallant crew were surrendered to a barbarous and dastardly enemy, whose only motive in warfare is the hope of plunder. Throughout the long and dreary confinement which ensued, in the dungeons of Tripoli, Porter never suffered himself for a moment to sink into despondency; but supported the galling indignities and hardships of his situation with equanimity and even cheerfulness. A seasonable supply of books served to beguile the hours of imprisonment, and enabled him even to turn them to advantage. He closely applied himself to the study of ancient and modern history, biography, the French language, and drawing; in which art, so useful to a seaman, he has made himself a considerable proficient. He also sedulously cultivated the theory of his profession, and improved the junior officers by his frequent instructions representing the manœuvres of fleets in battle by means of small boards ingeniously arranged. He was active in promoting any plan of labor or amusement that could ameliorate the situation or dispel the gloomy reflections of his companions. By these means captivity was robbed of its heaviest evils, that dull monotony that wearies the spirits, and that mental inactivity that engenders melancholy and hypochondria.

An incident which occurred during his confinement deserves to be mentioned, as being highly creditable to Lieutenant Porter. Under the rooms occupied by the officers was a long dark passage, through which the American sailors, who were employed in public labor, frequently passed to different parts of the castle. Their conversation being repeatedly heard as they passed to and fro, some one made a small hole in the wall to communicate with them. For some days a constant intercourse was kept up, by sending down notes tied to a string. Some persons, however, indiscreetly entering into conversation with the seamen, were overheard, and information immediately carried to the Bashaw. In a few minutes the bolts of the prison door were heard to fly back with unwonted violence, and Sassi (chief officer of the castle) rushed furiously in. His features were distorted, and his voice almost inarticulate with passion. He demanded in a vehement tone of voice by whom or whose authority the wall had been opened ; when Porter advanced with a firm step and composed countenance, and replied, "I alone am responsible." He was abruptly and rudely hurried from the prison, and the gate was again closed. This generous self-devotion, while it commanded the admiration of his companions, heightened their anxiety for his fate; apprehending some act of violence from the impetuous temper and absolute power of the Bashaw. Their fears, however, were appeased by the return of Porter, after considerable detention; having been dismissed without any further severity through the intercession of the minister Mahomet Dghies, who had on previous occasions shown a friendly disposition towards the prisoners.

It is unnecessary here to dwell on the various incidents that occurred in this tedious captivity, and of the many ingenious and adventurous plans of escape, devised and attempted by our officers, in all which Porter took an active and prominent part. When peace was at length made, and they were restored to light and liberty, he embarked with his companions for Syracuse, where a court of inquiry was held on the loss of the *Philadelphia*. After an honorable acquittal he was appointed to the command of the United States brig *Enterprise*, and soon after was ordered by Commodore Rodgers to proceed to Tripoli, with permission to cruise along the shore of Bengazi, and to visit the ruins of Leptis Magna, anciently a Roman colony. He was accompanied in this expedition by some of his friends, and after a short and pleasant passage, anchored near the latter place. They passed three days in wandering among the mouldering remains of Roman taste and grandeur; and excavated in such places as seemed to promise a reward for their researches. A number of ancient coins and cameos were found, and, among other curiosities, were two statues in tolerable preservation,—the one a warrior, the other a female figure, of beautiful white marble and excellent workmanship. Verd-antique pillars, of large size, formed of a single piece, and unbroken, were scattered along the shores. Near the harbor stood a lofty and elegant building, of which Lieutenant Porter took a drawing; from its situation and form it was supposed to have been a Pharos. The awning under which the party dined was spread on the site, and among the fallen columns of a temple of Jupiter, and a zest was given to the repast by the classical ideas awakened by surrounding objects.

While in command of the *Enterprise,* and at anchor in the port of Malta, an English sailor came alongside and insulted the officers and crew by abusive language; Captain Porter overhearing the scurrilous epithets he vociferated, ordered a boatswain's mate to seize him and give him a flogging at the gangway. This well-merited chastisement excited the indignation of the Governor of Malta, who considered it a daring outrage, and gave orders that the forts should not permit the *Enterprise* to depart. No sooner was Captain Porter informed of it, than he got his vessel ready for action, weighed anchor, and with lighted matches and every man at his station, with the avowed determination of firing upon the town if attacked, sailed between the batteries and departed unmolested.

Shortly after this occurrence, in passing through the Straits of Gibraltar, he was attacked by twelve Spanish gun-boats, who either mistook, or pretended to mistake his vessel for a British brig. The calmness of the weather, the weight of their metal, and the acknowledged accuracy of their aim, made the odds greatly against him. As soon, however, as he was able to near them, they were assailed with such rapid and well-directed volleys as quickly compelled them to shear off. This affair took place in sight of Gibraltar, and in presence of several ships of the British navy; it was therefore a matter of notoriety, and spoken of in terms of the highest applause.

After an absence of five years, passed in unremitted and arduous service, Captain Porter returned to the United States, and shortly after was married to Miss Anderson, daughter of the member of Congress of that name from Pennsylvania. Being appointed to the command of the flotilla on the New Orleans station, he discharged, with faithfulness and activity, the irksome duty of enforcing the embargo and non-intercourse laws. He likewise performed an important service to his country, by ferreting out and capturing a pirate, a native of France, who, in a small well-armed schooner, had for some time infested the Chesapeake; and who, growing bolder by impunity, had committed many acts of depredation, until his maraudings became so serious as to attract the attention of Government.

While commanding on the Orleans station, the father of Captain Porter died, an officer under his command. He had lived to see the wish of his heart fulfilled, in beholding his son a skilful and enterprising sailor, rising rapidly in his profession, and in the estimation of his country.

The climate of New Orleans disagreeing with the health of Captain Porter and his family, he solicited to be ordered to some other station, and was, accordingly, appointed to the command of the *Essex* frigate, at Norfolk.

At the time of the declaration of war against England, the *Essex* was undergoing repairs at New York, and the celerity with which she was fitted for sea reflected great credit on her commander. On the 3d of July, 1812, he sailed from Sandy Hook on a cruise, which was not marked by any incident of consequence, excepting the capture of the British sloop-of-war *Alert*, Captain Laugharne. Either undervaluing the untried prowess of our tars, or mistaking the force of the *Essex*, she ran down on her weather quarter, gave three cheers and commenced an action. In a few minutes she struck her colors, being cut to pieces, with three men wounded, and seven feet water in her hold. To relieve himself from the great number of prisoners, taken in this and former prizes, Captain Porter made a cartel of the *Alert,* with orders to proceed to St. John's, Newfoundland, and thence to New York. She arrived safe, being the first ship-of-war taken from the enemy, and her flag the first British flag sent to the seat of Government during the present war.

Having returned to the United States and refitted, he again proceeded to sea, from the Delaware, on the 27th of October, 1812, and repaired, agreeably to instructions from Commodore Bainbridge, to the coast of Brazil, where different places of rendezvous had been arranged between them. In the course of his cruise on this coast he captured his Britannic Majesty's packet *Nocton,* and after taking out of her about 11,000 pounds sterling in specie, ordered her for America. Hearing of Commodore Bainbridge's victorious action with the *Java,* which would oblige him to return to port, and of the capture of the *Hornet* by the *Montague,* and learning that there was a considerable augmentation of British force on the coast, and several ships in pursuit of him, he abandoned his hazardous cruising ground, and stretched away to the southward, scouring the coast as far as Rio de la Plata. From thence he shaped his course for the Pacific Ocean, and, after suffering greatly from want of provisions, and heavy gales off Cape Horn, arrived at Valparaiso, on the 14th of March, 1813. Having victualled his ship, he ran down the coast of Chili and Perú, and fell in with a Peruvian corsair, having on board twenty-four Americans, as prisoners, the crews of two whaling ships, which she had taken on the coast of Chili. The Peruvian captain justified his conduct on the plea of being an ally of Great Britain, and the expectation likewise of a speedy war between Spain and the United States. Finding him resolved to persist in similar aggressions, Captain Porter threw all his guns and ammunition into the sea, liberated the Americans, and wrote a respectful letter to the viceroy explaining his reasons for so doing, which he delivered to the captain. He then proceeded to Lima, and luckily recaptured one of the American vessels as she was entering the port.

After this he cruised for several months in the Pacific, inflicting immense injury on the British commerce in those waters. He was particularly destructive to the shipping employed in the spermaceti whale fishery. A great number with valuable cargoes were captured; two were given up to the prisoners; three sent to Valparaiso and laid up; three sent to America; one of them he retained as a store-ship, and another he equipped with twenty guns, called her the *Essex, Jr.*, and gave the command of her to Lieutenant Downes. Most of these ships mounted several guns, and had numerous crews; and as several of them were captured by boats or by prizes, the officers and men of the *Essex* had frequent opportunities of showing their skill and courage, and of acquiring experience and confidence in naval conflict.

Having now a little squadron under his command,

Captain Porter became a complete terror in those seas. As his numerous prizes supplied him abundantly with provisions, clothing, medicine, and naval stores of every description, he was enabled for a long time to keep the sea, without sickness or inconvenience to his crew; living entirely on the enemy, and being enabled to make considerable advances of pay to his officers and crew without drawing on Government. The unexampled devastation achieved by his daring enterprises, not only spread alarm throughout the ports of the Pacific, but even occasioned great uneasiness in Great Britain. The merchants, who had any property afloat in this quarter, trembled with apprehension for its fate; the underwriters groaned at the catalogue of captures brought by every advice, while the pride of the nation was sorely incensed at beholding a single frigate lording it over the Pacific, roving about the ocean in saucy defiance of their thousand ships; revelling in the spoils of boundless wealth, and almost banishing the British flag from those regions, where it had so long waved proudly predominant.

Numerous ships were sent out to the Pacific in pursuit of him; others were ordered to cruise in the China seas, off New Zealand, Timor, and New Holland, and a frigate sent to the River La Plata. The manner in which Captain Porter cruised, however, completely baffled pursuit. Keeping in the open seas, or lurking among the numerous barren and desolate islands that form the Galapagos

group, and never touching on the American coast, he left
no traces by which he could be followed; rumor, while
it magnified his exploits, threw his pursuers at fault;
they were distracted by vague accounts of captures made
at different places, and of frigates supposed to be the
Essex hovering at the same time off different coasts and
haunting different islands.

In the meanwhile Porter, though wrapped in mystery
and uncertainty himself, yet received frequent and accu-
rate accounts of his enemies, from the various prizes
which he had taken.   Lieutenant Downes, also, who had
convoyed the prizes to Valparaiso, on his return, brought
advices of the expected arrival of Commodore Hillyar in
the *Phœbe* frigate, rating thirty-six guns, accompanied by
two sloops-of-war.   Glutted with spoil and havoc, and
sated with the easy and inglorious captures of merchant-
men, Captain Porter now felt eager for an opportunity
to meet the enemy on equal terms, and to signalize his
cruise by some brilliant achievement.   Having been
nearly a year at sea, he found that his ship would require some repairs, to enable her to face the foe; he
repaired, therefore, accompanied by several of his prizes,
to the Island of Nooaheevah, one of the Washington
group, discovered by a Captain Ingraham of Boston.
Here he landed, took formal possession of the island in
the name of the Government of the United States, and
gave it the name of Madison's Island.   He found it large,
populous, and fertile, abounding with the necessaries of

life ; the natives in the vicinity of the harbor which he had chosen received him in the most friendly manner, and supplied him with abundance of provisions. During his stay at this place he had several encounters with some hostile tribes on the island, whom he succeeded in reducing to subjection. Having calked and completely overhauled the ship, made for her a new set of water-casks, and taken on board from the prizes provisions and stores for upwards of four months, he sailed for the coast of Chili on the 12th December, 1813. Previous to sailing he secured the three prizes which had accompanied him, under the guns of a battery erected for their protection, and left them in charge of Lieutenant Gamble of the marines and twenty-one men, with orders to proceed to Valparaiso after a certain period.

After cruising on the coast of Chili without success, he proceeded to Valparaiso, in hopes of falling in with Commodore Hillyar, or, if disappointed in this wish, of capturing some merchant ships said to be expected from England. While at anchor at this port Commodore Hillyar arrived, having long been searching in vain for the *Essex*, and almost despairing of ever meeting with her. Contrary to the expectations of Captain Porter, however, Commodore Hillyar, beside his own frigate, superior in itself to the *Essex*, was accompanied by the *Cherub* sloop-of-war, strongly armed and manned. These ships, having been sent out expressly to seek for the *Essex*, were in prime order and equipment, with picked crews, and hoisted flags bearing the motto, "God and country, British sailors' best rights : *traitors offend both.*" This was in opposition to Porter's motto of "Free trade and sailors' rights," and the latter part of it suggested doubtless, by error industriously cherished, that our crews are chiefly composed of English seamen. In reply to this motto Porter hoisted at his mizzen, "God, our country, and liberty : tyrants offend them." On entering the harbor the *Phœbe* fell foul of the *Essex* in such manner as to lay her at the mercy of Captain Porter ; out of respect, however, to the neutrality of the port, he did not take advantage of her exposed situation. This forbearance was afterwards acknowledged by Commodore Hillyar, and he passed his word of honor to observe like conduct while they remained in port. They continued therefore, while in harbor and on shore, in the mutual exchange of courtesies and kind offices that should characterize the private intercourse between civilized and generous enemies. And the crews of the respective ships often mingled together and passed nautical jokes and pleasantries from one to the other.

On getting their provisions on board, the *Phœbe* and *Cherub* went off the port, where they cruised for six weeks, rigorously blockading Captain Porter. Their united force amounted to 81 guns and 500 men, in addition to which they took on board the crew of an English letter of marque lying in port. The force of the *Essex* consisted of but 46 guns, all of which, excepting six long twelves, were 32-pound carronades, only serviceable in close fighting. Her crew, having been much reduced by the manning of prizes, amounted to but 255 men. The *Essex, Jr.*, being only intended as a store-ship, mounted ten 18-pound carronades and ten short sixes, with a complement of only 60 men.

This vast superiority of force on the part of the enemy prevented all chance of encounter on anything like equal terms, unless by express covenant between the commanders. Captain Porter, therefore, endeavored repeatedly to provoke a challenge (the inferiority of his frigate to the *Phœbe* not justifying him in making the challenge himself), but without effect. He tried frequently also to bring the *Phœbe* into single action; but this Commodore Hillyar warily avoided, and always kept his ships so close together as to frustrate Captain Porter's attempts. This conduct of Commodore Hillyar has been sneered at by many as unworthy a brave officer; but it should be considered that he had more important objects to effect than the mere exhibition of individual or national prowess. His instructions were to crush a noxious foe, destructive to the commerce of his country; he was furnished with a force competent to this duty; and having the enemy once within his power, he had no right to waive his superiority, and, by meeting him on equal footing, give him a chance to conquer, and continue his work of destruction.

Finding it impossible to bring the enemy to equal

9

combat, and fearing the arrival of additional force, which he understood was on the way, Captain Porter determined to put to sea the first opportunity that should present. A rendezvous was accordingly appointed for the *Essex*, *Jr.*, and having ascertained by repeated trials that the *Essex* was a superior sailor to either of the blockading ships, it was agreed that she should let the enemy chase her off; thereby giving the *Essex, Jr.*, an opportunity of escaping.

On the next day, the 28th of March, the wind came on to blow fresh 'from the southward, and the *Essex* parted her larboard cable and dragged her starboard anchor directly out to sea. Not a moment was lost in getting sail on the ship; but perceiving that the enemy was close in with the point forming the west side of the bay, and that there was a possibility of passing to windward, and escaping to sea by superior sailing, Captain Porter resolved to hazard the attempt. He accordingly took in his top-gallant sails and braced up for the purpose; but most unfortunately, on rounding the point, a heavy squall struck the ship and carried away her main-topmast, precipitating the men who were aloft into the sea, who were drowned. Both ships now gave chase, and the crippled state of his ship left Porter no alternative but to endeavor to regain the port. Finding it impossible to get back to the common anchorage, he ran close into a small bay about three quarters of a mile to leeward of the battery, on the east of the harbor, and let go his anchor within pistol-shot of the shore. Supposing the enemy would, as formerly, respect the neutrality of the place, he considered himself secure, and thought only of repairing the damages he had sustained. The wary and menacing approach of the hostile ships, however, displaying their motto flags, and having jacks at all their masts' heads, soon showed him the real danger of his situation. With all possible despatch he got his ship ready for action, and endeavored to get a spring on his cable, but had not succeeded, when, at 54 minutes past 3 P. M., the enemy commenced an attack.

At first the *Phœbe* lay herself under his stern and the *Cherub* on his starboard bow ; but the latter soon finding herself exposed to a hot fire, bore up and ran under his stern also, where both ships kept up a severe and raking fire. Captain Porter succeeded three different times in getting springs on his cables, for the purpose of bringing his broadside to bear on the enemy, but they were as often shot away by the excessive fire to which he was exposed. He was obliged, therefore, to rely for defence against this tremendous attack merely on three long twelve-pounders, which he had run out of the stern ports, and which were worked with such bravery and skill as in half an hour to do great injury to both the enemy's ships and induce them to hale off and repair damages. It was evidently the intention of Commodore Hillyar to risk nothing from the daring courage of his antagonist, but to take the *Essex* at as cheap a rate as possible. All his manœuvres were deliberate and wary; he saw his antagonist completely at his mercy, and prepared to cut him up in the safest and surest manner. In the meantime the situation of the *Essex* was galling and provoking in the extreme ; crippled and shattered, with many killed and wounded, she lay awaiting the convenience of the enemy, to renew the scene of slaughter, with scarce a hope of escape or revenge. Her brave crew, however, in place of being disheartened, were aroused to desperation, and by hoisting ensigns in their rigging, and jacks in different parts of the ship, evinced their defiance and determination to hold out to the last.

The enemy having repaired his damages, now placed himself with both his ships, on the starboard quarter of the *Essex*, out of reach of her carronades, and where her stern guns could not be brought to bear. Here he kept up a most destructive fire, which it was not in Captain Porter's power to return; the latter, therefore, saw no hope of injuring him without getting under way and becoming the assailant. From the mangled state of his rigging he could set no other sail than the flying jib; this he caused to be hoisted, cut his cable, and ran down on both ships, with an intention of laying the *Phœbe* on board.

For a short time he was enabled to close with the enemy, and the firing on both sides was tremendous. The decks of the *Essex* were strewed with dead, and her cockpit filled with wounded ; she had been several times on fire, and was in fact a perfect wreck; still a feeble hope sprung up that she might be saved, in consequence of the *Cherub* being compelled to haul off by her crippled state; she did not return to close action again, but kept up a distant firing with her long guns. The disabled state of the *Essex*, however, did not permit her to take advantage of this circumstance; for want of sail she was unable to keep at close quarters with the *Phœbe*, who, edging off, chose the distance which best suited her long guns, and kept up a tremendous fire, which made dreadful havoc among our crew. Many of the guns of the *Essex* were rendered useless, and many had their whole crews destroyed; they were manned from those that were disabled, and one gun in particular was three times manned; fifteen men were slain at it in the course of the action, though the captain of it escaped with only a slight wound. Captain Porter now gave up all hope of closing with the enemy, but finding the wind favorable, determined to run his ship on shore, land the crew, and destroy her. He had approached within musket-shot of the shore, and had every prospect of succeeding, when in an instant the wind shifted from the land, and drove her down upon the *Phœbe*, exposing her again to a dreadful raking fire. The ship was now totally unmanageable; yet as her head was toward the enemy, and he to leeward, Captain Porter again perceived a faint hope of boarding. At this moment Lieutenant Downes of the *Essex, Jr.*, came on board to receive orders, expecting that Captain Porter would soon be a prisoner. His services could be of no avail in the deplorable state of the *Essex*, and finding, from the enemy's putting his helm up, that the last attempt at boarding would not succeed, Captain Porter directed him, after he had been ten minutes on board, to return to his own ship, to be prepared for defending and destroying her in case of attack. He took with him several of the wounded, leaving three of his boat's crew on board to make room for them. The *Cherub* kept up a hot fire on him during his return. The slaughter on board of the *Essex* now became horrible; the enemy continued to rake her, while she was unable to bring a gun to bear in return. Still her commander, with an obstinacy that bordered on desperation, persisted in the unequal and almost hopeless conflict. Every expedient that a fertile and inventive mind could suggest was resorted to, in the forlorn hope that they might yet be enabled by some lucky chance to escape from the grasp of the foe. A hawser was bent to the sheet anchor, and the anchor cut from the bows, to bring the ship's head round. This succeeded; the broadside of the *Essex* was again brought to bear; and as the enemy was much crippled and unable to hold his own, Captain Porter thought she might drift out of gunshot before she discovered that he had anchored. The hawser, however, unfortunately parted, and with it failed the last lingering hope of the *Essex*. The ship had taken fire several times during the action, but at this moment her situation was awful. She was on fire both forward and aft; the flames were bursting up each hatchway; a large quantity of powder below exploded, and word was given that the fire was near the magazine. Thus surrounded by horrors, without any chance of saving the ship, Captain Porter turned his attention to rescuing as many of his brave companions as possible. Finding his distance from the shore did not exceed three quarters of a mile, he hoped many would be able to save themselves should the ship blow up. His boats had been cut to pieces by the enemies' shot, but he advised such as could swim to jump overboard and make for shore. Some reached it, some were taken by the enemy, and some perished in the attempt; but most of this loyal and gallant crew preferred sharing the fate of their ship and their commander.

Those who remained on board now endeavored to extinguish the flames, and having succeeded, went again to the guns and kept up a firing for a few minutes; but the crew had by this time become so weakened that all further resistance was in vain. Captain Porter summoned a consultation of the officers of divisions, but was surprised to find only Acting Lieutenant Stephen Decatur M'Knight remaining; of the others some had been killed, others knocked overboard, and others carried below disabled by severe wounds. The accounts from every part of the ship were deplorable in the extreme; representing her in the most shattered and crippled condition, in imminent danger of sinking, and so crowded with the wounded that even the berth-deck could contain no more, and many were killed while under the surgeon's hands. In the meanwhile the enemy, in consequence of the smoothness of the water and his secure distance, was enabled to keep up a deliberate and constant fire, aiming with coolness and certainty as if firing at a target, and hitting the hull at every shot. At length, utterly despairing of saving the ship, Captain Porter was compelled, at 20 minutes past 6 P. M., to give the painful order to strike the colors. It is probable the enemy did not perceive that the ship had surrendered, for he continued firing; several men were killed and wounded in different parts of the ship, and Captain Porter, thinking he intended to show no quarter, was about to rehoist his flag and to fight until he sunk, when the enemy desisted his attack ten minutes after the surrender.

The foregoing account of this battle is taken almost verbatim from the letter of Captain Porter to the Secretary of the Navy. Making every allowance for its being a partial statement, this must certainly have been one of the most sanguinary and obstinately contested actions on naval record. The loss of the *Essex* is a sufficient testimony of the desperate bravery with which she was defended. Out of 255 men which comprised her crew, fifty-eight were killed; thirty-nine wounded severely; twenty-seven slightly, and thirty-one missing,—making in all 154. She was completely cut to pieces, and so covered with the dead and dying, with mangled limbs, with brains and blood, and all the ghastly images of pain and death, that the officer who came on board to take possession of her, though accustomed to scenes of slaughter, was struck with sickening horror, and fainted at the shocking spectacle.

Thousands of the inhabitants of Valparaiso were spectators of the battle, covering the neighboring heights; for it was fought so near the shore that some of the shot even struck among the citizens, who, in the eagerness of their curiosity, had ventured down upon the beach. Touched by the forlorn situation of the *Essex,* and filled with admiration at the unflagging spirit and persevering bravery of her commander and crew, a generous anxiety ran throughout the multitude for their fate; bursts of delight arose when, by any vicissitude of battle, or prompt expedient, a chance seemed to turn up in their favor; and the eager spectators were seen to wring their hands, and utter groans of sympathy, when the transient hope was defeated, and the gallant little frigate once more became an unresisting object of deliberate slaughter.

It is needless to mention particularly the many instances of individual valor and magnanimity among both the officers and common sailors of the *Essex;* their general conduct bears ample testimony to their heroism; and it will hereafter be a sufficient distinction for any man to prove that he was present in that battle. Every action that we have fought at sea has gone to destroy some envious shade which the enemy has attempted to cast on our rising reputation.   After the affair of the *Argus* and the *Pelican*, it was asserted that our sailors were brave only while successful and unhurt, but that the sight of slaughter filled them with dismay.   In this battle it has been proved that they are capable of the highest exercise of courage,—that of standing unmoved among incessant carnage, without being able to return a shot, and destitute of a hope of ultimate success.

Though, from the distance and positions which the enemy chose, this battle was chiefly fought on our part by six 12-pounders only, yet great damage was done to the assailing ships.   Their masts and yards were badly crippled, their hulls much cut up; the *Phœbe*, especially, received eighteen 12-pound shot below her water-line, some three feet under water.   Their loss in killed and wounded was not ascertained, but must have been severe; the first lieutenant of the *Phœbe* was killed, and Captain Tucker, of the *Cherub*, was severely wounded.   It was with some difficulty that the *Phœbe* and the *Essex* could be kept afloat until they anchored the next morning in the port of Valparaiso.

Much indignation has been expressed against Commodore Hillyar for his violation of the laws of nations, and of his private agreement with Captain Porter, by attacking him in the neutral waters of Valparaiso.   Waiving all discussion of these points, it may barely be observed, that his cautious attack with a vastly superior force, on a crippled ship, which, relying on his forbearance, had placed herself in a most defenceless situation, and which for six weeks previous had offered him fair fight, on advantageous terms, though it may reflect great credit on his prudence, yet certainly furnishes no triumph to a brave and generous mind. Aware, however of that delicacy which ought to be observed towards the character even of an enemy, it is not the intention of the writer to assail that of Commodore Hillyar. Indeed, his conduct after the battle entitles him to high encomium; he showed the greatest humanity to the wounded, and, as Captain Porter acknowledges, endeavored as much as lay in his power to alleviate the distresses of war by the most generous and delicate deportment towards both the officers and crew, commanding that the property of every person should be respected. Captain Porter and his crew were paroled, and permitted to return to the United States in the *Essex, Jr.*, her armament being previously taken out. On arriving off the port of New York, they were overhauled by the *Saturn razee*, the authority of Commodore Hillyar to grant a passport was questioned, and the *Essex, Jr.*, detained. Captain Porter then told the boarding officer that he gave up his parole, and considered himself a prisoner of war, and as such should use all means of escape. In consequence of this threat the *Essex, Jr.*, was ordered to remain all night under the lee of the *Saturn*, but the next morning Captain Porter put off in his boat, though thirty miles from shore; and, notwithstanding he was pursued by the *Saturn*, effected his escape and landed safely on Long Island. His reception in the United States has been such as his great services and distinguished valor deserved. The various interesting and romantic rumors that had reached this country concerning him, during his cruise in the Pacific, had excited the curiosity of the public to see this modern Sindbad; on arriving in New York his carriage was surrounded by the populace, who took out the horses, and dragged him, with shouts and acclamations, to his lodgings.

The length to which this article has already been extended, notwithstanding the brevity with which many interesting circumstances have been treated, forbids any further remarks on the character and services of Captain Porter. They are sufficiently illustrated in the foregoing summary of his eventful life, and particularly in the history of his last cruise, which was conducted with wonderful enterprise, fertility of expedient, consummate seamanship, and daring courage. In his single ship he has inflicted more injury on the commerce of the enemy than all the rest of the navy put together; not merely by actual devastation, but by the general insecurity and complete interruption which he occasioned to an extensive and invaluable branch of British trade. His last action, also, though it terminated in the loss of his frigate, can scarcely be considered as unfortunate, inasmuch as it has given a brilliancy to his own reputation, and wreathed fresh honors around the name of the American sailor.

THOMAS CAMPBELL.

T has long been deplored by authors as a lamentable truth, that they seldom receive impartial justice from the world while living. The grave seems to be the ordeal to which their names must be subjected, and from whence, if worthy of immortality, they rise with pure and imperishable lustre. Here many, who have flourished in unmerited popularity, descend into oblivion; and it may literally be said, that, "they rest from their labors, and their works do follow them." Here likewise, many an ill-starred author, after struggling with penury and neglect, and starving through a world which he has enriched by his talents, sinks to rest, and becomes a theme of universal admiration and regret. The sneers of the cynical, the detractions of the envious, the scoffings of the ignorant, are silenced at the hallowed precincts of the tomb; and the world awakens to a sense of his value, when he is removed beyond its patronage forever. Monuments are erected to his memory, books are written in his praise, and thousands will devour with avidity the biography of a man, whose life was passed unheeded before their eyes. He is like some

141

canonized saint, at whose shrine treasures are lavished, and clouds of incense offered up, though, while living, the slow hand of charity withheld the pittance that would have soothed his miseries.

But this tardiness in awarding merit its due, this preference continually shown to departed, over living authors, of perhaps superior excellence, may be attributed to a more charitable source than that of envy or ill-nature. The latter are continually before our eyes, exposed to the full glare of scrutinizing familiarity. We behold them subject to the same foibles and frailties with ourselves, and, from the constitutional delicacy of their minds, and their irritable sensibilities, prone to more than ordinary caprices. The former, on the contrary, are seen only through the magic medium of their works. We form our opinion of the whole flow of their minds, and the tenor of their dispositions, from the writings they have left behind. We witness nothing of the mental exhaustion and languor which followed these gushes of genius. We behold the stream only in the fulness of its current, and conclude that it has always been equally profound in its depth, pure in its wave, and majestic in its career.

With respect to the living writers of Europe, however, we may be said, on this side of the Atlantic, to be placed in some degree in the situation of posterity. The vast ocean that rolls between us, like a space of time, removes us beyond the sphere of personal favor, personal preju-

dice, or personal familiarity. A European work, therefore, appears before us depending simply on its intrinsic
merits. We have no private friendship, nor party purpose to serve, by magnifying the author's merits ; and, in
sober sadness, the humble state of our national literature
places us far below any feeling of national rivalship.

But, while our local situation thus enables us to exercise the enviable impartiality of posterity, it is evident
we must share likewise in one of its disadvantages. We
are in as complete ignorance respecting the biography
of most living authors of celebrity, as though they had
existed ages before our time ; and, indeed, are better informed concerning the character and lives of the authors
who have long since passed away, than of those who are
actually adding to the stores of European literature. A
proof of this assertion will be furnished in the following
sketch, which, unsatisfactory as it is, contains all the
information we can collect concerning a British poet of
rare and exquisite endowments.

THOMAS CAMPBELL was born at Glasgow, on the 27th of
September, 1777. He is the youngest son of Mr. Alexander Campbell, late merchant of Glasgow ; a gentleman
of the most unblemished integrity and amiable manners,
who united the scholar and the man of business, and,
amidst the corroding cares and sordid habits of trade,
cherished a liberal and enthusiastic love of literature.
He died at a very advanced age, in the spring of 1801,

and the event is mentioned in the "Edinburgh Magazine," with high encomiums on his moral and religious character.

It may not be uninteresting to the American reader to know that Mr. Campbell, the poet, has very near connections in this country; and, indeed, to this circumstance may be in some measure attributed the liberal sentiments he has frequently expressed concerning America. His father resided, for many years of his youth, at Falmouth, in Virginia, but returned to Europe about fifty years since. His uncle, who had accompanied his father, settled permanently in Virginia, where his family has uniformly maintained a highly respectable character. One of his sons was District Attorney under the administration of Washington, and died in 1795. He was a man of uncommon talents, and particularly distinguished for his eloquence. Robert Campbell also, a brother of the poet, settled in Virginia, where he married a daughter of the celebrated Patrick Henry. He died about the year 1808.

The genius of Mr. Campbell showed itself almost in his infancy. At the age of seven he possessed a vivacity of imagination, and a vigor of mind, surprising in such early youth. A strong inclination for poetry was already discernible in him; and, indeed, it was not more than two years after this that we are told "he began to try his wings." These bright dawnings of intellect, united to uncommon personal beauty, a winning gentleness and modesty of manners, and a generous sensibility of heart, made him an object of universal favor and admiration.

There is scarcely any obstacle more fatal to the full development and useful application of talent than an early display of genius. The extravagant caresses lavished upon it by the light and injudicious, are too apt to beget a self-confidence in the possessor, and render him impatient of the painful discipline of study; without which genius, at best, is irregular, ungovernable, and oft-times splendidly erroneous.

Perhaps there is no country in the world where this error is less frequent than in Scotland. The Scotch are a philosophical, close-thinking people. Wary and distrustful of external appearances and first impressions, stern examiners into the *utility* of things, and cautious in dealing out the dole of applause, their admiration follows tardily in the rear of their judgment, and even when they admire, they do it with peculiar rigidity of muscle. This spirit of rigorous rationality is peculiarly evident in the management of youthful genius; which, instead of meeting with enervating indulgence, is treated with a Spartan severity of education, tasked to the utmost extent of its powers, and made to undergo a long and laborious probation before it is permitted to emerge into notoriety. The consequence is, an uncommon degree of skill and vigor in their writers. They are rendered diligent by constant habits of study, powerful by science, graceful by the elegant accomplishments of the scholar, and prompt

10

and adroit in the management of their talents, by the frequent contests and exercises of the schools.

From the foregoing observations may be gathered the kind of system adopted with respect to young Campbell. His early display of genius, instead of making him the transient wonder of the drawing-room, and the *enfant gaté* of the tea-table, consigned him to the rigid discipline of the academy. At the age of seven he commenced the study of the Latin language under the care of the Rev. David Alison, a teacher of distinguished reputation in Scotland. At twelve he entered the University of Glasgow, and in the following year gained a bursary on Bishop Leighton's foundation, for a translation of one of the comedies of Aristophanes, which he executed in verse. This triumph was the more honorable, from being gained, after a hard contest, over a rival candidate of nearly twice his age, who was considered one of the best scholars in the University. His second prize exercise was the translation of a tragedy of Æschylus, likewise in verse, which he gained without opposition, as none of the students would enter the lists with him. He continued seven years in the University, during which time his talents and application were testified by yearly academical prizes. He was particularly successful in his translations from the Greek, in which language he took great delight; and on receiving his last prize for one of these performances, the Greek professor publicly pronounced it the best that had ever been produced in the University.

Moral philosophy was likewise a favorite study with Mr. Campbell; and, indeed, he applied himself to gain an intimate acquaintance with the whole circle of sciences. But though, in the prosecution of his studies, he attended the academical courses both of law and physic, it was merely as objects of curiosity, and branches of general knowledge, for he never devoted himself to any particular study with a view to prepare himself for a profession. On the contrary, his literary passion was already so strong, that he could never, for a moment, endure the idea of confining himself to the dull round of business, or engaging in the absorbing pursuits of common life.

In this he was most probably confirmed by the indulgence of a fond father, whose ardent love of literature made him regard the promising talents of his son with pride and sanguine anticipation. At one time, it is true, a part of his family expressed a wish that he should be fitted for the Church, but this was completely overruled by the rest, and he was left, without further opposition, to the impulse of his own genius and the seductions of the Muse.

After leaving the University he passed some time among the mountains of Argyleshire, at the seat of Colonel Napier, a descendant of Napier Baron Merchiston, the celebrated inventor of logarithms. It is probable that from this gentleman he first imbibed his taste and knowledge of the military art, traces of which are to be seen throughout his poems. From Argyleshire he went to Edinburgh, where the reputation he had acquired at the University gained him a favorable reception into the distinguished circle of science and literature for which that city is renowned. Among others he was particularly honored by the notice of Professors Stewart and Playfair. Nothing could be more advantageous for a youthful poet, than to commence his career under such auspices. To the expansion of mind and elevation of thought produced by the society of such celebrated men, may we ascribe, in a great measure, the philosophic spirit and moral sublimity displayed in his first production, the "Pleasures of Hope," which was written during his residence at Edinburgh. He was not more than twenty when he wrote this justly celebrated poem, and it was published in the following year.

The popularity of this work at once introduced the author to the notice and patronage of the first people of Great Britain. At first, indeed, it promised but little pecuniary advantage, as he unfortunately disposed of the copyright for an inconsiderable sum. This, however, was in some measure remedied by the liberality of his publisher, who, finding that his book ran through two editions in the course of a few months, permitted him to publish a splendid edition for himself, by which means he was enabled, in some measure, to participate in the golden harvest of his labors.

About this time the passion for German literature raged in all its violence in Great Britain, and the uni-

versal enthusiasm with which it was admired, awakened,
in the inquiring mind of our author, a desire of studying
it at the fountain-head. This, added to his curiosity to
visit foreign parts, induced him to embark for Germany
in the year 1800. He had originally fixed upon the college of Jena for his first place of residence, but on arriving at Hamburg he found, by the public prints, that a
victory had been gained by the French near Ulm, and
that Munich and the heart of Bavaria were the theatre
of an interesting war. "One moment's sensation," he
observes, in a letter to a relation in this country, "the
single hope of seeing human nature exhibited in its most
dreadful attitude, overturned my past decisions. I got
down to the seat of war some weeks before the summer
armistice of 1800, and indulged in what you will call the
criminal curiosity of witnessing blood and desolation.
Never shall time efface from my memory the recollection
of that hour of astonishment and suspended breath, when
I stood with the good monks of St. Jacob, to overlook a
charge of Klenaw's cavalry upon the French under Gren-
nier, encamped below us. We saw the fire given and
returned, and heard distinctly the sound of the French
pas de charge collecting the lines to attack in close column. After three hours' awaiting the issue of a severe
action, a park of artillery was opened just beneath the
walls of the monastery, and several wagoners, that were
stationed to convey the wounded in spring-wagons, were
killed in our sight." This awful spectacle he has de-

scribed with all the poet's fire, in his "Battle of Hohen-linden;" a poem which perhaps contains more grandeur and martial sublimity than is to be found anywhere else, in the same compass of English poetry.

Mr. Campbell afterwards proceeded to Ratisbon, where he was at the time it was taken possession of by the French, and expected, as an Englishman, to be made prisoner; but he observes, "Moreau's army was under such excellent discipline, and the behavior both of officers and men so civil, that I soon mixed among them without hesitation, and formed many agreeable acquaintances at the messes of their brigade stationed in town, to which their *chef de brigade* often invited me. This worthy man, Colonel Le Fort, whose kindness I shall ever remember with gratitude, gave me a protection to pass through the whole army of Moreau."

After this he visited different parts of Germany, in the course of which he paid one of the casual taxes on travelling; being plundered among the Tyrolese mountains, by a Croat, of his clothes, his books, and thirty ducats in gold. About midwinter he returned to Hamburg, where he remained four months, in the expectation of accompanying a young gentleman of Edinburgh in a tour to Constantinople. His unceasing thirst for knowledge, and his habits of industrous application, prevented these months from passing heavily or unprofitably. His time was chiefly employed in reading German, and making himself acquainted with the principles of Kant's philosophy; from which, however, he seems soon to have turned with distaste, to the richer and more interesting field of German belles-lettres.

While in Germany an edition of his "Pleasures of Hope" was proposed for publication in Vienna, but was forbidden by the court, in consequence of those passages which relate to Kosciusko, and the partition of Poland. Being disappointed in his projected visit to Constantinople, he returned to England in 1801, after nearly a year's absence, which had been passed much to his satisfaction and improvement, and had stored his mind with grand and awful images. "I remember," says he, "how little I valued the art of painting before I got into the heart of such impressive scenes; but in Germany I would have given anything to have possessed an art capable of conveying ideas inaccessible to speech and writing. Some particular scenes were, indeed, rather overcharged with that degree of the terrific which oversteps the sublime, and I own my flesh yet creeps at the recollection of *spring-wagons and hospitals;* but the sight of Ingolstadt in ruins, or Hohenlinden covered with fire, seven miles in circumference, were spectacles never to be forgotten."

On returning to England he visited London for the first time, where, though unprovided with a single letter of introduction, the celebrity of his writings procured him the immediate notice and attentions of the best society. His recent visit to the Continent, however, had

increased rather than gratified his desire to travel. He
now contemplated another tour, for the purpose of improving himself in the knowledge of foreign languages
and foreign manners, in the course of which he intended
to visit Italy and pass some time at Rome. From this
plan he was diverted, most probably, by an attachment
he formed to a Miss Sinclair, a distant relation, whom he
married in 1803. This change in his situation naturally
put an end to all his wandering propensities, and he
removed to Sydenham, in Kent, near London, where he
has ever since resided, devoting himself to literature, and
the calm pleasures of domestic life.

He has been enabled to indulge his love of study and
retirement more comfortably by the bounty of his sovereign, who some few years since presented him with an
annuity of 200*l.* This distinguished mark of royal favor,
so gratifying to the pride of the poet, and the loyal affections of the subject, was wholly spontaneous and unconditional. It was neither granted to the importunities of
friends at court, nor given as a *douceur* to secure the
services of the author's pen, but merely as a testimony
of royal approbation of his popular poem, the "Pleasures
of Hope." Mr. Campbell, both before and since, has
uniformly been independent in his opinions and writings.

Though withdrawn from the busy world in his retirement at Sydenham, yet the genius of Mr. Campbell, like
a true brilliant, occasionally flashed upon the public eye,
in a number of exquisite little poems, which appeared in

the periodical works of the day. Many of these he has never thought proper to rescue from their perishable repositories. But of those which he has formally acknowledged and republished, "Hohenlinden," "Lochiel," the "Mariners of England," and the "Battle of the Baltic," are sufficient of themselves, were other evidence wanting, to establish his title to the sacred name of Poet. The two last-mentioned poems we consider as two of the noblest national songs we have ever seen. They contain sublime imagery and lofty sentiments, delivered with a "gallant swelling spirit," but totally free from that hyperbole and national rhodomontade which generally disgrace this species of poetry. In the beginning of 1809 he published his second volume of poems, containing "Gertrude of Wyoming," and several smaller effusions; since which time he has produced nothing of consequence, excepting the uncommonly spirited and affecting little tale of "O'Connor's Child, or Love Lies Bleeding."

Of those private and characteristic anecdotes which display most strikingly the habits and peculiarities of a writer, we have scarcely any to furnish respecting Mr. Campbell. He is generally represented to us as being extremely studious, but at the same time social in his disposition, gentle and endearing in his manners, and extremely prepossessing in his appearance and address. With a delicate and even nervous sensibility, and a degree of self-diffidence that at times is almost painful, he shrinks from the glare of notoriety which his own works have shed around him, and seems ever deprecating criticism, rather than enjoying praise. Though his society is courted by the most polished and enlightened, among whom he is calculated to shine, yet his chief delight is in domestic life, in the practice of those gentle virtues and bland affections which he has so touchingly and eloquently illustrated in various passages of his poems.

That Mr. Campbell has by any means attained to the summit of his fame, we cannot suffer ourselves for a moment to believe. We rather look upon the works he has already produced as specimens of pure and virgin gold from a mine whose treasures are yet to be explored. It is true, the very reputation Mr. Campbell has acquired, may operate as a disadvantage to his future efforts. Public expectation is a pitiless taskmaster, and exorbitant in its demands. He who has once awakened it, must go on in a progressive ratio, surpassing what he has hitherto done, or the public will be disappointed. Under such circumstances an author of common sensibility takes up his pen with fear and trembling. A consciousness that much is expected from him deprives him of that ease of mind and boldness of imagination, which are necessary to fine writing, and he too often fails from a too great anxiety to excel. He is like some youthful soldier, who, having distinguished himself by a gallant and brilliant achievement, is ever afterward fearful of entering on a new enterprise, lest he should tarnish the laurels he has won.

We are satisfied that Mr. Campbell feels this very diffidence and solicitude from the uncommon pains he bestows upon his writings. These are scrupulously revised, modelled, and retouched over and over, before they are suffered to go out of his hands, and even then, are slowly and reluctantly yielded up to the press. This elaborate care may, at times, be carried to an excess, so as to produce fastidiousness of style, and an air of too much art and labor. It occasionally imparts to the Muse the precise demeanor and studied attire of the prude, rather than the negligent and bewitching graces of the woodland nymph. A too minute attention to finishing is likewise injurious to the force and sublimity of a poem. The vivid images which are struck off, at a single heat, in those glowing moments of inspiration, " when the soul is lifted to heaven," are too often softened down, and cautiously tamed, in the cold hour of correction. As an instance of the critical severity which Mr. Campbell exercises over his productions, we will mention a fact within our knowledge, concerning his "Battle of the Baltic." This ode, as published, consists of but five stanzas; these were all that his scrupulous taste permitted him to cull out of a large number, which we have seen in manuscript. The rest, though full of poetic fire and imagery, were timidly consigned by him to oblivion.

But though this scrupulous spirit of revision may chance to refine away some of the bold touches of his

pencil, and to injure some of its negligent graces, it is
not without its eminent advantages. While it tends to
produce a terseness of language, and a remarkable delicacy and sweetness of versification, it enables him likewise to impart to his productions a vigorous conciseness
of style, a graphical correctness of imagery, and a philosophical condensation of idea, rarely found in the popular poets of the day. Facility of writing seems to be the
bane of many modern poets ; who too generally indulge
in a ready and abundant versification, which, like a flow-
ering vine, overruns their subject, and expands through
many a weedy page. In fact, most of them seem to have
mistaken carelessness for ease, and redundance for luxuriance ; they never take pains to condense and invigorate. Hence we have those profuse and loosely written
poems, wherein the writers, either too feeble or too careless to seize at once upon their subject, prefer giving it a
chase, and hunt it through a labyrinth of verses, until it is
fairly run down and overpowered by a multitude of words.

Great, therefore, as are the intrinsic merits of Mr.
Campbell, we are led to estimate them the more highly
when we consider them as beaming forth, like the pure
lights of heaven, among the meteor exhalations and false
fires with which our literary atmosphere abounds. In an
age when we are overwhelmed by an abundance of eccentric poetry, and when we are confounded by a host of
ingenious poets of vitiated tastes and frantic fancies, it
is really cheering and consolatory to behold a writer of

Mr. Campbell's genius, studiously attentive to please, according to the established laws of criticism, as all our good old orthodox writers have pleased before; without setting up a standard, and endeavoring to establish a new sect, and inculcate some new and lawless doctrine of his own.

Before concluding this sketch, we cannot help pointing to one circumstance, which we confess has awakened a feeling of good will toward Mr. Campbell; though in mentioning it we shall do little more, perhaps, than betray our own national egotism. He is, we believe, the only British poet of eminence that has laid the story of a considerable poem in the bosom of our country. We allude to his "Gertrude of Wyoming," which describes the pastoral simplicity and innocence, and the subsequent woes of one of our little patriarchal hamlets, during the troubles of our Revolution.

We have so long been accustomed to experience little else than contumely, misrepresentation, and very witless ridicule, from the British press; and we have had such repeated proofs of the extreme ignorance and absurd errors that prevail in Great Britain respecting our country and its inhabitants, that, we confess, we were both surprised and gratified to meet with a poet sufficiently unprejudiced to conceive an idea of moral excellence and natural beauty on this side of the Atlantic. Indeed, even this simple show of liberality has drawn on the poet the censures of many narrow-minded writers, with whom liberality to this country is a crime. We are sorry to see such pitiful manifestations of hostility towards us. Indeed, we must say, that we consider the constant acrimony and traduction indulged in by the British press toward this country, to be as opposite to the interest, as it is derogatory to the candor and magnanimity of the nation. It is operating to widen the difference between two nations, which, if left to the impulse of their own feelings, would naturally grow together, and among the sad changes of this disastrous world, be mutual supports and comforts to each other.

Whatever may be the occasional collisions of etiquette and interest which will inevitably take place between two great commercial nations, whose property and people are spread far and wide on the face of the ocean ; whatever may be the clamorous expressions of hostility vented at such times by our unreflecting populace, or rather uttered in their name by a host of hireling scribblers, who pretend to speak the sentiments of the people ; it is certain that the well-educated and well-informed class of our citizens entertain a deep-rooted good will, and a rational esteem, for Great Britain. It is almost impossible it should be otherwise. Independent of those hereditary affections, which spring up spontaneously for the nation from whence we have descended, the single circumstance of imbibing our ideas from the same authors has a powerful effect in causing an attachment.

The writers of Great Britain are the adopted citizens

of our country, and, though they have no legislative voice, exercise an authority over our opinions and affections, cherished by long habit and matured by affection. In these works we have British valor, British magnanimity, British might, and British wisdom, continually before our eyes, portrayed in the most captivating colors; and are thus brought up in constant contemplation of all that is amiable and illustrious in the British character. To these works, likewise, we resort, in every varying mood of mind, or vicissitude of fortune. They are our delight in the hour of relaxation; the solemn monitors and instructors of our closet; our comforters in the gloomy seclusions of life-loathing despondency. In the season of early life, in the strength of manhood, and still in the weakness and apathy of age, it is to them we are indebted for our hours of refined and unalloyed enjoyment. When we turn our eyes to England, therefore, from whence this bounteous tide of literature pours in upon us, it is with such feelings as the Egyptian experiences, when he looks toward the sacred source of that stream, which, rising in a far distant country, flows down upon his own barren soil, diffusing riches, beauty, and fertility.*

---

* Since this biographical notice was first published, the political relations between the two countries have been changed by a war with Great Britain. The above observations, therefore, may not be palatable to those who are eager for the hostility of the pen as well as the sword. The author, indeed, was for some time in doubt whether to expunge them, as he could not prevail on himself to accommodate them to the embittered temper of

Surely it cannot be the interest of Great Britain to trifle with such feelings. Surely the good will, thus cherished among the best hearts of a country, rapidly increasing in power and importance, is of too much consequence to be scornfully neglected or surlily dashed away. It most certainly, therefore, would be both politic and honorable, for those enlightened British writers, who sway the sceptre of criticism, to expose these constant misrepresentations, and discountenance these galling and unworthy insults of the pen, whose effect is to mislead and to irritate, without serving one valuable purpose. They engender gross prejudices in Great Britain, inimical to a proper national understanding, while with us they wither all those feelings of kindness and consanguinity, that were shooting forth, like so many tendrils, to attach to us our parent country.

While, therefore, we regard the poem of Mr. Campbell with complacency, as evincing an opposite spirit to this, of which we have just complained, there are other reasons, likewise, which interest us in its favor. Among the lesser evils, incident to the infant state of our country,

the times. He determined, however, to let them remain. However the feelings he has expressed may be outraged or prostrated by the violence of warfare, they never can be totally eradicated. Besides, it should be the exalted ministry of literature to keep together the family of human nature; to calm with her "soul-subduing voice" the furious passions of warfare, and thus to bind up those ligaments which the sword would cleave asunder. The author may be remiss in the active exercise of this duty, but he will never have to reproach himself, that he has attempted to poison, with political virulence, the pure fountains of elegant literature.

we have to lament its almost total deficiency in those local associations produced by history and moral fiction. These may appear trivial to the common mass of readers; but the mind of taste and sensibility will at once acknowledge them as constituting a great source of national pride and love of country. There is an inexpressible charm imparted to every place that has been celebrated by the historian, or immortalized by the poet; a charm that dignifies it in the eyes of the stranger, and endears it to the heart of the native. Of this romantic attraction we are almost entirely destitute. While every insignificant hill and turbid stream in classic Europe has been hallowed by the visitations of the Muse, and contemplated with fond enthusiasm, our lofty mountains and stupendous cataracts awaken no poetical associations, and our majestic rivers roll their waters unheeded, because unsung.

Thus circumstanced, the sweet strains of Mr. Campbell's Muse break upon us as gladly as would the pastoral pipe of the shepherd, amid the savage solitude of one of our trackless wildernesses. We are delighted to witness the air of captivating romance and rural beauty our native fields and wild woods can assume under the plastic pencil of a master; and while wandering with the poet among the shady groves of Wyoming, or along the banks of the Susquehanna, almost fancy ourselves transported to the side of some classic stream, in the "hollow breast of Apennine." This may assist to convince many,

11

who were before slow to believe, that our country is capable of inspiring the highest poetic feelings, and furnish-
ing abundance of poetic imagery, though destitute of the
hackneyed materials of poetry ; though its groves are not
vocal with the song of the nightingale ; though no Naïads
have ever sported in its streams, nor Satyrs and Dryads
gamboled among its forests.   Wherever Nature—sweet
Nature—displays herself in simple beauty or wild magnificence, and wherever the human mind appears in new
and striking situations, neither the poet nor the philosopher can ever want subjects worthy of his genius.

Having made such particular mention of " Gertrude of
Wyoming," we will barely add one or two circumstances
connected with it, strongly illustrative of the character
of the literary author.   The story of the poem, though
extremely simple, is not sufficiently developed ; some of
the facts, particularly in the first part, are rapidly passed
over, and left rather obscure ; from which many have
inconsiderately pronounced the whole a hasty sketch,
without perceiving the elaborate delicacy with which the
parts are finished.   This defect is to be attributed entirely to the self-diffidence of Mr. Campbell.   It is his
misfortune that he is too distrustful of himself, and too
ready to listen to the opinions of inferior minds, rather
than boldly to follow the dictates of his own pure taste
and the impulses of his exalted imagination, which, if
left to themselves, would never falter or go wrong.   Thus
we are told, that when his " Gertrude " first came from

under his pen, it was full and complete; but in an evil hour he read it to some of his critical friends. Every one knows that when a man's critical judgment is consulted, he feels himself in credit bound to find fault. Various parts of the poem were of course objected to, and various alterations recommended.

With a fatal diffidence, which, while we admire we cannot but lament, Mr. Campbell struck out those parts entirely, and obliterated, in a moment, the fruit of hours of inspiration and days of labor. But when he attempted to bind together and new-model the elegant but mangled limbs of this virgin poem, his shy imagination revolted from the task. The glow of feeling was chilled, the creative powers of invention were exhausted; the parts, therefore, were slightly and imperfectly thrown together, with a spiritless pen, and hence arose that apparent want of development which occurs in some parts of the story.

Indeed, we do not think the unobtrusive, and, if we may be allowed the word, occult merits of this poem are calculated to strike popular attention, during the present passion for dashing verse and extravagant incident. It is mortifying to an author to observe, that those accomplishments which it has cost him the greatest pains to acquire, and which he regards with a proud eye, as the exquisite proofs of his skill, are totally lost upon the generality of readers; who are commonly captivated by those glaring qualities to which he attaches but little value. Most people are judges of exhibitions of force and activity of body, but it requires a certain refinement of taste and a practised eye, to estimate that gracefulness which is the achievement of labor and consummation of art. So, in writing, whatever is bold, glowing, and garish, strikes the attention of the most careless, and is generally felt and acknowledged; but comparatively few can appreciate that modest delineation of Nature, that tenderness of sentiment, propriety of language, and gracefulness of composition, that bespeak the polished and accomplished writer. Such, however, as possess this delicacy of taste and feeling, will often return to dwell, with cherishing fondness, on the " Gertrude " of Mr. Campbell. Like all his other writings, it presents virtue in its most touching and captivating forms; whether gently exercised in the " bosom scenes of life," or sublimely exerted in its extraordinary and turbulent situations. No writer can surpass Mr. Campbell in the vestal purity and amiable morality of his Muse. While he possesses the power of firing the imagination, and filling it with sublime and awful images, he excels also in those eloquent appeals to the feelings, and those elevated flights of thought, by which, while the fancy is exalted, the heart is made better.

It is now some time since he has produced any poem. Of late he has been employed in preparing a work for the press, containing critical and biographical notices of British poets from the reign of Edward III. to the present time. However much we may be gratified by such a work, from so competent a judge, still we cannot but regret that he should stoop from the brilliant track of poetic invention, in which he is so well calculated to soar, and descend into the lower regions of literature to mingle with droning critics and mousing commentators. His task should be to produce poetry, not to criticise it; for in our minds, he does more for his own fame, and for the interests of literature, who furnishes one fine verse, than he who points out a thousand beauties or detects a thousand faults.

We hope, therefore, soon to behold Mr. Campbell emerging from those dusty labors, and breaking forth in the full lustre of original genius. He owes it to his own reputation; he owes it to his own talents; he owes it to the literature of his country. Poetry has generally flowed in an abundant stream in Great Britain; but it is too apt to stray among the rocks and weeds, to expand into brawling shallows, or waste itself in turbid and ungovernable torrents. We have, however, marked a narrow, but pure and steady channel, continuing down from the earliest ages, through a line of real poets, who seem to have been sent from heaven to keep the vagrant stream from running at utter waste and random. Of this chosen number we consider Mr. Campbell; and we are happy at having this opportunity of rendering our feeble tribute of applause to a writer whom we consider an ornament to the age, an honor to his country, and one whom his country "should delight to honor."

Thomas Campbell died June 15, 1844. Soon after the

publication of the foregoing Memoir, Mr. Irving went to Europe and became personally acquainted with him. When Messrs. Harper & Brothers were about reprinting in this country the biography of the poet by Dr. Beattie, they submitted the London proof-sheets to his inspection, with a suggestion that a letter from him would be a very acceptable introduction of the work to the American people. He sent them the following reply, which seems properly to link itself with the foregoing sketch :—

MESSRS. HARPER & BROTHERS :

GENTLEMEN,—I feel much obliged to you for the perusal you have afforded me of the biography of Campbell, but fear I have nothing of importance to add to the copious details which it furnishes. My acquaintance with Campbell commenced in, I think, 1810, through his brother Archibald, a most amiable, modest, and intelligent man, but more of a mathematician than a poet. He resided at that time in New York, and had received from his brother a manuscript copy of " O'Connor's Child ; or, The Flower of Love Lies Bleeding," for which he was desirous of finding a purchaser among the American publishers. I negotiated the matter for him with a publishing house in Philadelphia, which offered a certain sum for the poem, provided I would write a biographical sketch of the author to be prefixed to a volume containing all his poetical works. To secure a good price for the poet, I wrote the sketch, being furnished with facts by his brother; it was done, however, in great haste, when I was "not in the vein," and, of course, was very slight and imperfect. It served, however, to put me at once on a friendly footing with Campbell, so that, when I met him for the first time a few years subsequently in England, he received me as an old friend. He was living at that time in his rural retreat at Sydenham. His modest mansion was fitted up in a simple style, but with a tact and taste characteristic of the occupants.

Campbell's appearance was more in unison with his writings than is generally the case with authors. He was about thirty-seven years of age; of the middle size, lightly and genteelly made; evidently of a delicate, sensitive organization, with a fine intellectual countenance and a beaming poetic eye.

He had now been about twelve years married. Mrs. Campbell still retained much of that personal beauty for which he praises her in his letters written in the early days of matrimony; and her mental qualities seemed equally to justify his eulogies,—a rare circumstance, as none are more prone to dupe themselves in affairs of the heart than men of lively imaginations. She was, in fact, a more suitable wife for a poet than poets' wives are apt to be; and for once a son of song had married a reality and not a poetical fiction.

I had considered the early productions of Campbell as brilliant indications of a genius yet to be developed, and trusted that, during the long interval which had elapsed, he had been preparing something to fulfill the public expectation; I was greatly disappointed, therefore, to find that, as yet, he had contemplated no great and sustained effort. My disappointment in this respect was shared by others, who took the same interest in his fame, and entertained the same idea of his capacity. "There he is, cooped up in Sydenham," said a great Edinburgh critic * to me, "simmering his brains to serve up a little dish of poetry, instead of pouring out a whole caldron."

Scott, too, who took a cordial delight in Campbell's poetry, expressed himself to the same effect. "What a pity is it," said he to me, "that Campbell does not give full sweep to his genius. He has wings that would bear him up to the skies, and he does, now and then, spread them grandly, but folds them up again and resumes his perch, as if afraid to launch away. The fact is, he is a bugbear to himself. The brightness of his early success is a detriment to all his future efforts. *He is afraid of the shadow that his own fame casts before him.*"

Little was Scott aware at the time that he, in truth, was a "bugbear" to Campbell. This I infer from an observation of Mrs. Campbell's in reply to an expression of regret on my part that her husband did not attempt something on a grand scale. "It is unfortunate for Campbell," said she, "that he lives in the same age with Scott

* Jeffrey.

and Byron." I asked why. "Oh," said she, "they write so much and so rapidly. Now Campbell writes slowly, and it takes him some time to get under way ; and just as he has fairly begun, out comes one of their poems, that sets the world agog and quite daunts him, so that he throws by his pen in despair,".

I pointed out the essential difference in their kinds of poetry, and the qualities which insured perpetuity to that of her husband. "You can't persuade Campbell of that," said she. "He is apt to undervalue his own works, and to consider his own little lights put out whenever they come blazing out with their great torches."

I repeated the conversation to Scott some time afterward, and it drew forth a characteristic comment.

"Pooh!" said he, good-humoredly, "how can Campbell mistake the matter so much ? Poetry goes by quality, not by bulk. My poems are mere cairngorms, wrought up, perhaps, with a cunning hand, and may pass well in the market as long as cairngorms are the fashion; but they are mere Scotch pebbles after all ; now Tom Campbell's are real diamonds, and diamonds of the first water."

I have not time at present to furnish personal anecdotes of my intercourse with Campbell, neither does it afford any of a striking nature. Though extending over a number of years, it was never very intimate. His residence in the country, and my own long intervals of absence on the Continent, rendered our meetings few and far between. To tell the truth, I was not much drawn to Campbell, having taken up a wrong notion concerning him from seeing him at times when his mind was ill at ease, and preyed upon by secret griefs. I thought him disposed to be querulous and captious, and had heard his apparent discontent attributed to jealous repining at the success of his poetical contemporaries. In a word, I knew little of him but what might be learned in the casual intercourse of general society ; whereas it required the close communion of confidential friendship to sound the depths of his character and know the treasures of excellence hidden beneath its surface. Besides, he was dogged for years by certain malignant scribblers, who took a pleasure in misrepresenting all his actions, and holding him up in an absurd and disparaging point of view. In what this hostility originated I do not know, but it must have given much annoyance to his sensitive mind, and may have affected his popularity. I know not to what else to attribute a circumstance to which I was a witness during my last visit to England. It was at an annual dinner of the Literary Fund, at which Prince Albert presided, and where was collected much of the prominent talent of the kingdom. In the course of the evening Campbell rose to make a speech. I had not seen him for years, and his appearance showed the effect of age and ill health ; it was evident, also, that his mind was obfuscated by the wine he had been drinking. He was confused and tedious in his remarks; still, there was nothing but what one would have thought would be received with indulgence, if not deference, from a veteran of his fame and standing,—a living classic. On the contrary, to my surprise, I soon observed signs of impatience in the company; the poet was repeatedly interrupted by coughs and discordant sounds, and as often endeavored to proceed; the noise at length became intolerable, and he was absolutely clamored down, sinking into his chair overwhelmed and disconcerted. I could not have thought such treatment possible to such a person at such a meeting.

Hallam, author of the "Literary History of the Middle Ages," who sat by me on this occasion, marked the mortification of the poet, and it excited his generous sympathy. Being shortly afterward on the floor to reply to a toast, he took occasion to advert to the recent remarks of Campbell, and in so doing called up in review all his eminent achievements in the world of letters, and drew such a picture of his claims upon popular gratitude and popular admiration as to convict the assembly of the glaring impropriety they had been guilty of—to soothe the wounded sensibility of the poet, and send him home to, I trust, a quiet pillow.

I mention these things to illustrate the merit of the piece of biography which you are about to lay before the American world. It is a great act of justice to the memory of a distinguished man, whose character has not been sufficiently known. It gives an insight into his domestic as well as his literary life, and lays open the springs of all his actions and the causes of all his contrariety of conduct. We now see the real difficulties he had to contend with in the earlier part of his literary career ; the worldly cares which pulled his spirit to the earth whenever it would wing its way to the skies ; the domestic afflictions, tugging at his heart-strings even in his hours of genial intercourse, and converting his very smiles into spasms ; the anxious days and sleepless nights preying upon his delicate organization, producing that morbid sensitiveness and nervous irritability which at times overlaid the real sweetness and amenity of his nature, and obscured the unbounded generosity of his heart.

The biography does more ; it reveals the affectionate considerateness of his conduct in all the domestic relations of life. The generosity with which he shared his narrow means with all the members of his family, and tasked his precarious resources to add to their relief ; his deep-felt tenderness as a husband and a father,—the source of exquisite home-happiness for a time, but ultimately of unmitigated wretchedness ; his constant and devoted friendships, which in early life were almost romantic passions, and which remained unwithered by age ; his sympathies with the distressed of every nation, class, and condition ; his love of children, that infallible sign of a gentle and amiable nature ; his sensibility to beauty

of every kind; his cordial feeling toward his literary contemporaries, so opposite to the narrow and despicable
jealousy imputed to him; above all, the crowning romance of his life, his enthusiasm in the cause of suffering
Poland, a devotion carried to the height of his poetic
temperament, and, in fact, exhausting all that poetic vein
which, properly applied, might have produced epics;
these and many more traits set forth in his biography
bring forth his character in its true light; dispel those
clouds which malice and detraction may at times have
cast over it; and leave it in the full effulgence of its
poetic glory.

This is all, gentlemen, that the hurried nature of personal occupations leaves me leisure to say on this subject. If these brief remarks will be of any service in
recommending the biography to the attention of the
American public, you are welcome to make such use of
them as you may think proper; and I shall feel satisfaction in putting on record my own recantation of the
erroneous opinion I once entertained, and may have
occasionally expressed, of the private character of an
illustrious poet, whose moral worth is now shown to
have been fully equal to his exalted genius.

Your obedient servant,

Washington Irving.

WASHINGTON ALLSTON.

I FIRST became acquainted with Washington Allston early in the spring of 1805. He had just arrived from France, I from Sicily and Naples. I was then not quite twenty-two years of age, he a little older. There was something, to me, inexpressibly engaging in the appearance and manners of Allston. I do not think I have ever been more completely captivated on a first acquaintance. He was of a light and graceful form, with large blue eyes, and black silken hair, waving and curling round a pale expressive countenance. Everything about him bespoke the man of intellect and refinement. His conversation was copious, animated, and highly graphic ; warmed by a genial sensibility and benevolence, and enlivened at times by a chaste and gentle humor. A young man's intimacy took place immediately between us, and we were much together during my brief sojourn at Rome. He was taking a general view of the place before settling himself down to his professional studies. We visited together some of the finest collections of paintings, and he taught me how to visit them to the most advantage, guiding me always to the

174

masterpieces, and passing by the others without notice. "Never attempt to enjoy every picture in a great collection," he would say, "unless you have a year to bestow upon it. You may as well attempt to enjoy every dish in a Lord Mayor's feast. Both mind and palate get confounded by a great variety and rapid succession, even of delicacies. The mind can only take in a certain number of images and impressions distinctly ; by multiplying the number you weaken each, and render the whole confused and vague. Study the choice pieces in each collection ; look upon none else, and you will afterwards find them hanging up in your memory." He was exquisitely sensible to the graceful and the beautiful, and took great delight in paintings which excelled in color ; yet he was strongly moved and roused by objects of grandeur. I well recollect the admiration with which he contemplated the sublime statue of Moses by Michael Angelo, and his mute awe and reverence on entering the stupendous pile of St. Peter's. Indeed the sentiment of veneration so characteristic of the elevated and poetic mind was continually manifested by him. His eyes would dilate ; his pale countenance would flush ; he would breathe quick, and almost gasp in expressing his feelings when excited by any object of grandeur and sublimity.

We had delightful rambles together about Rome and its environs, one of which came near changing my whole course of life. We had been visiting a stately villa, with its gallery of paintings, its marble halls, its terraced gardens set out with statues and fountains, and were returning to Rome about sunset. The blandness of the air, the serenity of the sky, the transparent purity of the atmosphere, and that nameless charm which hangs about an Italian landscape, had derived additional effect from being enjoyed in company with Allston, and pointed out by him with the enthusiasm of an artist. As I listened to him, and gazed upon the landscape, I drew in my mind, a contrast between our different pursuits and prospects. He was to reside among these delightful scenes, surrounded by masterpieces of art, by classic and historic monuments, by men of congenial minds and tastes, engaged like him in the constant study of the sublime and beautiful. I was to return home to the dry study of the law, for which I had no relish, and, as I feared, but little talent.

Suddenly the thought presented itself, "Why might I not remain here and turn painter?" I had taken lessons in drawing before leaving America, and had been thought to have some aptness, as I certainly had a strong inclination for it. I mentioned the idea to Allston, and he caught at it with eagerness. Nothing could be more feasible. We would take an apartment together. He would give me all the instruction and assistance in his power, and was sure I would succeed.

For two or three days the idea took full possession of my mind; but I believe it owed its main force to the lovely evening ramble in which I first conceived it, and to the romantic friendship I had formed with Allston. Whenever it recurred to mind, it was always connected with beautiful Italian scenery, palaces, and statues, and fountains, and terraced gardens, and Allston as the companion of my studio. I promised myself a world of enjoyment in his society, and in the society of several artists with whom he had made me acquainted, and pictured forth a scheme of life all tinted with the rainbow hues of youthful promise.

My lot in life, however, was differently cast. Doubts and fears gradually clouded over my prospect; the rainbow tints faded away; I began to apprehend a sterile reality; so I gave up the transient but delightful prospect of remaining in Rome with Allston and turning painter.

My next meeting with Allston was in America, after he had finished his studies in Italy; but as we resided in different cities we saw each other only occasionally. Our intimacy was closer some years afterwards when we were both in England. I then saw a great deal of him during my visits to London, where he and Leslie resided together. Allston was dejected in spirits from the loss of his wife, but I thought a dash of melancholy had increased the amiable and winning graces of his character. I used to pass long evenings with him and Leslie; indeed Allston, if any one would keep him company, would sit up until cock-crowing, and it was hard to break away

12

from the charms of his conversation. He was an admirable story-teller; for a ghost-story none could surpass him. He acted the story as well as told it.

I have seen some anecdotes of him in the public papers, which represent him in a state of indigence and almost despair, until rescued by the sale of one of his paintings.* This is an exaggeration. I subjoin an extract or two from his letters to me, relating to his most important pictures. The first, dated May 9, 1817, was addressed to me at Liverpool, where he supposed I was about to embark for the United States.

"Your sudden resolution of embarking for America has quite thrown me, to use a sea phrase, all aback. I have so many things to tell you of, to consult you about, &c., and am such a sad correspondent, that before I can bring my pen to do its office, 'tis a hundred to one but the vexations for which your advice would be wished, will have passed and gone. One of these subjects (and the most important) is the large picture I talked of soon beginning; the prophet Daniel interpreting the *handwriting on the wall* before Belshazzar. I have made a highly finished sketch of it, and I wished much to have your remarks on it. But as your sudden departure will deprive me of this advantage, I must beg, should any hints on the subject occur to you during your voyage, that you will favor me with them, at the same time you let me know that you are again safe in our good country.

"I think the composition the best I ever made. It contains a multitude of figures, and (if I may be allowed to say it) they are without confusion. Don't you think it a fine subject? I know not any that so happily unites the magnificent and the awful. A mighty sovereign surrounded

* *Anecdotes of Artists.*

by his whole court, intoxicated with his own state, in the midst of his revellings, palsied in a moment under the spell of a preternatural hand suddenly tracing his doom on the wall before him; his powerless limbs, like a wounded spider's, shrunk up to his body, while his heart, *compressed to a point,* is only kept from vanishing by the terrific suspense that animates it during the interpretation of his mysterious sentence. His less guilty, but scarcely less agitated queen, the panic-struck courtiers and concubines, the splendid and deserted banquet-table, the half-arrogant, half-astounded magicians, the holy vessels of the temple (shining as it were in triumph through the gloom), and the calm solemn contrast of the prophet, standing like an animated pillar in the midst, breathing forth the oracular destruction of the empire ! The picture will be twelve feet high by seventeen feet long. Should I succeed in it to my wishes, I know not what may be its fate ; but I leave the future to Providence, perhaps I may send it to America."

The next letter from Allston which remains in my possession, is dated London, 13th March, 1818. In the interim he had visited Paris, in company with Leslie and Newton; the following extract gives the result of the excitement caused by a study of the masterpieces in the Louvre :

" Since my return from Paris I have painted two pictures, in order to have something in the present exhibition at the British gallery; the subjects, the 'Angel Uriel in the Sun,' and 'Elijah in the Wilderness.' Uriel was immediately purchased (at the price I asked, 150 guineas), by the Marquis of Stafford, and the Directors of the British Institution, moreover, presented me a *donation* of a hundred and fifty pounds, as a mark of their *approbation* of the talent evinced, &c. The manner in which this was done was highly complimentary; and I can only say that it was full as gratifying as it was unexpected. As both these pictures together cost me but ten weeks, I do not regret having deducted that time from the ' Belshazzar,' to whom I have since returned with redoubled vigor. I am sorry I did not exhibit ' Jacob's Dream.' If I had dreamt of this success, I certainly would have sent it there."

Leslie, in a letter to me, speaks of the picture of Uriel seated in the sun.

" The figure is colossal, the attitude and air very noble, and the form heroic without being overcharged. In the color he has been equally successful, and with a very rich and glowing tone he has avoided *positive* colors, which would have made him too material. There is neither red, blue, nor yellow on the picture, and yet it possesses a harmony equal to the best pictures of Paul Veronese."

The picture made what is called " a decided hit," and produced a great sensation, being pronounced worthy of the old masters. Attention was immediately called to the artist. The Earl of Egremont, a great connoisseur and patron of the arts, sought him in his studio, eager for any production from his pencil. He found an admirable picture there, of which he became the glad possessor. The following is an extract from Allston's letter to me on the subject :—

" Leslie tells me he has informed you of the sale of ' Jacob's Dream.' I do not remember if you have seen it. The manner in which Lord Egremont bought it was particularly gratifying—to say nothing of the price, which is no trifle to me at present. But Leslie having told you all about it, I will not repeat it. Indeed by the account he gives me of his letter to you, he seems to have puffed me off in grand style. Well—you know I don't *bribe* him to do it, and ' if they will buckle praise upon my back,' why, I can't help it ! Leslie has just finished a very beautiful little pic-

ture of Anne Page inviting Master Slender into the house. Anne is exquisite, soft and feminine, yet arch and playful. She is all she should be.
Slender also is very happy; he is a good parody on Milton's 'linked sweetness long drawn out.' Falstaff and Shallow are seen through a window
in the background. The whole scene is very picturesque and beautifully
painted. 'Tis his best picture. You must not think this praise the 'return in kind.' I give it because I really admire the picture, and I have
not the smallest doubt that he will do great things when he is once freed
from the necessity of painting portraits."

Lord Egremont was equally well pleased with the
artist as with his works, and invited him to his noble
seat at Petworth, where it was his delight to dispense
his hospitalities to men of genius.

The road to fame and fortune was now open to Allston ; he had but to remain in England, and follow up
the signal impression he had made. Unfortunately, previous to this recent success he had been disheartened by
domestic affliction, and by the uncertainty of his pecuniary prospects, and had made arrangements to return to
America. I arrived in London a few days before his
departure, full of literary schemes, and delighted with
the idea of our pursuing our several arts in fellowship.
It was a sad blow to me to have this day-dream again
dispelled. I urged him to remain and complete his
grand painting of "Belshazzar's Feast," the study of
which gave promise of the highest kind of excellence.
Some of the best patrons of the art were equally urgent.
He was not to be persuaded, and I saw him depart with
still deeper and more painful regret than I had parted

with him in our youthful days at Rome. I think our separation was a loss to both of us—to me a grievous one. The companionship of such a man was invaluable. For his own part, had he remained in England for a few years longer, surrounded by everything to encourage and stimulate him, I have no doubt he would have been at the head of his art. He appeared to me to possess more than any contemporary the spirit of the old masters; and his merits were becoming widely appreciated. After his departure he was unanimously elected a member of the Royal Academy.

The next time I saw him was twelve years afterwards, on my return to America, when I visited him at his studio at Cambridge in Massachusetts, and found him in the gray evening of life, apparently much retired from the world; and his grand picture of "Belshazzar's Feast" yet unfinished.

To the last he appeared to retain all those elevated, refined, and gentle qualities which first endeared him to me.

Such are a few particulars of my intimacy with Allston,—a man whose memory I hold in reverence and affection, as one of the purest, noblest, and most intellectual beings that ever honored me with his friendship.

CONVERSATIONS WITH TALMA.

FROM ROUGH NOTES IN A COMMON-PLACE BOOK.

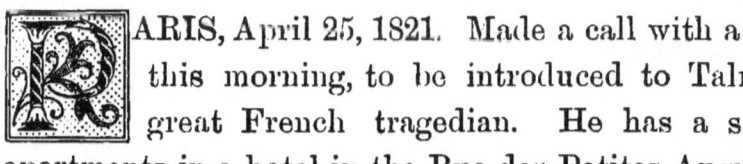ARIS, April 25, 1821. Made a call with a friend, this morning, to be introduced to Talma, the great French tragedian. He has a suite of apartments in a hotel in the Rue des Petites Augustines, but is about to build a town residence. He has also a country retreat a few miles from Paris, of which he is extremely fond, and is continually altering and improving it. He had just arrived from the country, and his apartment was rather in confusion, the furniture out of place and books lying about. In a conspicuous part of the saloon was a colored engraving of John Philip Kemble, for whom he expresses great admiration and regard.

Talma is about five feet seven or eight inches, English, in height, and somewhat robust. There is no very tragic or poetic expression in his countenance; his eyes are of a bluish gray, with, at times, a peculiar cast; his face is rather fleshy, yet flexible; and he has a short, thick neck. His manners are open, animated, and natural. He speaks English well, and is prompt, unreserved, and copious in conversation.

183

He received me in a very cordial manner, and asked if this was my first visit to Paris. I told him I had been here once before, about fourteen years since.

"Ah! that was the time of the Emperor!" cried he, with a sudden gleam of the eye.

"Yes, just after his coronation as King of Italy."

"Ah! those were the heroic days of Paris—every day some new victory! The real chivalry of France rallied round the Emperor,—the youth and talent and bravery of the nation. Now you see the courts of the Tuileries crowded by priests, and an old, worn-out nobility brought back by foreign bayonets."

He consoled himself by observing that the national character had improved under its reverses. Its checks and humiliations had made the nation more thoughtful.

"Look at the young men from the colleges," said he; "how serious they are in their demeanor. They walk together in the public promenades, conversing always on political subjects, but discussing politics philosophically and scientifically. In fact, the nation is becoming as grave as the English."

He thinks too that there is likely to be a great change in the French drama. "The public," said he, "feel greater interest in scenes that come home to common life, and in the fortunes of every-day people, than in the distresses of the heroic personages of classic antiquity. Hence they never come to the Théâtre Français, excepting to see a few great actors, while they crowd to the minor theatres to witness representations of scenes in ordinary life. "The Revolution," added he, "has caused such vivid and affecting scenes to pass before their eyes, that they can no longer be charmed by fine periods and declamation. They require character, incident, passion, life."

He seems to apprehend another revolution, and that it will be a bloody one. "The nation," said he, "that is to say, the younger part of it, the *children of the Revolution*, have such a hatred of the priests and the *noblesse*, that they would fly upon them like wolves upon sheep."

On coming away, he accompanied us to the door. In passing through the ante-chamber, I pointed to children's swords and soldiers' caps lying on a table. "Ah!" cried he, with animation, "the amusements of the children nowadays are all military. They will have nothing to play with but swords, guns, drums, and trumpets."

Such are the few brief notes of my first interview with Talma. Some time afterward I dined in company with him at Beauvillier's Restaurant. He was in fine spirits, gay and earnest by turns, and always perfectly natural and unreserved.

He spoke with pleasure of his residence in England. He liked the English. They were a noble people; but he thought the French more amiable and agreeable to live among. "The intelligent and cultivated English," he said, "are disposed to do generous actions, but the common people are not so liberal as the same class among the French; they have bitter national prejudices. If a French prisoner escaped in England, the common people would be against him. In France it was otherwise. When the fight was going on around Paris," said he, "and Austrian and other prisoners were brought in wounded, and conducted along the Boulevards, the Parisian populace showed great compassion for them, and gave them money, bread, and wine."

Of the liberality of the cultivated class of English he gave an anecdote. Two French prisoners had escaped from confinement, and made their way to a seaport, intending to get over in a boat to France. All their money, however, was exhausted, and they had not wherewithal to hire a boat. Seeing a banker's name on a door, they went in, stated their case frankly, and asked for pecuniary assistance, promising to repay it faithfully. The banker at once gave them one hundred pounds. They offered a bill, or receipt, but he declined it. "If you are not men of honor," said he, "such paper would be of no value; and if you are men of honor, there is no need of it." This circumstance was related to Talma by one of the parties thus obliged.

In the course of conversation we talked of the theatre. Talma had been a close observer of the British stage, and was alive to many of its merits. He spoke of his efforts to introduce into French acting the familiar style occasionally used by the best English tragedians; and of the difficulties he encountered in the stately declamation

and constantly recurring rhymes of French tragedy. Still
he found, he said, every familiar touch of Nature immediately appreciated and applauded by the French audience. Of Shakspeare he expressed the most exalted
opinion, and said he should like to attempt some of his
principal characters in English, could he be sure of being
able to render the text without a foreign accent. He
had represented his character of Hamlet, translated into
French, in the Théâtre Français with great success ; but
he felt how much more powerful it would be if given as
Shakspeare had written it. He spoke with admiration of
the individuality of Shakspeare's characters and the
varied play of his language, giving such a scope for familiar touches of pathos and tenderness, and natural out-
breaks of emotion and passion. "All this," he observed,
"requires quite a different style of acting from the well-
balanced verse, flowing periods, and recurring rhymes of
the French drama ; and it would, doubtless, require much
study and practice to catch the spirit of it ; and after
all," added he, laughing, "I should probably fail. Each
stage has its own peculiarities which belong to the nation, and cannot be thoroughly caught, nor perhaps
thoroughly appreciated by strangers."

[To the foregoing scanty notes were appended some
desultory observations made at the time, and suggested

by my conversations with Talma. They were intended to form the basis of some speculations on the French literature of the day, which were never carried out. They are now given very much in the rough style in which they were jotted down, with some omissions and abbreviations, but no heightenings nor additions.

The success of a translation of "Hamlet" in the Théâtre Français appears to me an era in the French drama. It is true, the play has been sadly mutilated and stripped of some of its most characteristic beauties in the attempt to reduce it to the naked stateliness of the pseudo-classic drama; but it retains enough of the wild magnificence of Shakspeare's imagination to give it an individual character on the French stage. Though the ghost of Hamlet's father does not actually tread the boards, yet it is supposed to hover about his son, unseen by other eyes; and the admirable acting of Talma conveys to the audience a more awful and mysterious idea of this portentous visitation than could be produced by any visible spectre. I have seen a lady carried fainting from the boxes, overcome by its effect on her imagination. In this translation and modification of the original play, Hamlet's mother stabs herself before the audience, a catastrophe hitherto unknown on the grand theatre, and repugnant to the French idea of classic rule.

The popularity of this play is astonishing. On the evenings of its representation the doors of the theatre are besieged at an early hour. Long before the curtain rises, the house is crowded to overflowing; and throughout the performance the audience passes from intervals of breathless attention to bursts of ungovernable applause.

The success of this tragedy may be considered one of the triumphs of what is denominated the romantic school; and another has been furnished by the overwhelming reception of "Marie Stuart," a modification of the German tragedy of Schiller. The critics of the old school are sadly alarmed at these foreign innovations, and tremble for the ancient decorum and pompous proprieties of their stage. It is true, both "Hamlet" and "Marie Stuart" have been put in the strait waistcoat of Aristotle; yet they are terribly afraid they will do mischief and set others madding. They exclaim against the apostasy of their countrymen in bowing to foreign idols, and against the degeneracy of their taste, after being accustomed from infancy to the touching beauties and harmonious numbers of "Athalie," "Polyeucte," and "Mérope," in relishing these English and German monstrosities, and that through the medium of translation. All in vain! the nightly receipts at the doors outweigh, with managers, all the invectives of the critics, and "Hamlet" and "Marie Stuart" maintain triumphant possession of the boards.

Talma assures me that it begins to be quite the fashion in France to admire Shakspeare; and those who cannot read him in English enjoy him diluted in French translations.

It may at first create a smile of incredulity that foreigners should pretend to feel and appreciate the merits of an author so recondite at times as to require commentaries and explanations even to his own countrymen; yet it is precisely writers like Shakspeare, so full of thought, of character, and passion, that are most likely to be relished, even when but partially understood. Authors whose popularity arises from beauty of diction and harmony of numbers are ruined by translation; a beautiful turn of expression, a happy combination of words and phrases, and all the graces of perfect euphony, are limited to the language in which they are written. Style cannot be translated. The most that can be done is to furnish a parallel, and render grace for grace. Who can form an idea of the exquisite beauties of Racine, when translated into a foreign tongue? But Shakspeare triumphs over translation. His scenes are so exuberant in original and striking thoughts and masterly strokes of nature, that he can afford to be stripped of all the magic of his style. His volumes are like the magician's cave in "Aladdin," so full of jewels and precious things, that he who does but penetrate for a moment may bring away enough to enrich himself.

The relish for Shakspeare, however, which, according to Talma, is daily increasing in France, is, I apprehend, but one indication of a general revolution which is taking place in the national taste. The French character, as Talma well observes, has materially changed during the last thirty years. The present generation (the " children of the Revolution," as Talma terms them), who are just growing into the full exercise of talent, are a different people from the French of the old *régime*. They have grown up in rougher times, and among more adventurous and romantic habitudes. They are less delicate in tact, but stronger in their feelings, and require more stimulating aliment. The Frenchman of the camp who has bivouacked on the Danube and the Volga; who has brought back into peaceful life the habits of the soldier; who wears fierce moustaches, swaggers in his gait, and smokes tobacco, is, of course, a different being in his literary tastes from the Frenchman of former times, who was refined but finical in dress and manners, wore powder, and delighted in perfumes and polished versification.

The whole nation, in fact, has been accustomed for years to the glitter of arms and the parade of soldiery; to tales of battles, sieges, and victories. The feverish drama of the Revolution, and the rise and fall of Napoleon, have passed before their eyes like a tale of Arabian enchantment. Though these realities have passed away, the remembrances of them remain, with a craving for the strong emotions which they excited.

This may account in some measure for that taste for the romantic which is growing upon the French nation, a taste vehemently but vainly reprobated by their critics. You see evidence of it in everything; in their paintings, in the engravings which fill their print-shops; in their songs, their spectacles, and their works of fiction. For several years it has been making its advances without exciting the jealousy of the critics; its advances being apparently confined to the lower regions of literature and the arts. The circulating libraries have been filled with translations of English and German romances, and tales of ghosts and robbers, and the theatres of the Boulevards occupied by representations of melo-dramas. Still the higher regions of literature remained unaffected, and the national theatre retained its classic stateliness and severity. The critics consoled themselves with the idea that the romances were only read by women and children, and the melo-dramas admired by the ignorant and vulgar. But the children have grown up to be men and women; and the tinge given to their imaginations in early life is now to have an effect on the forthcoming literature of the country. As yet, they depend for their romantic aliment upon the literature of other nations, especially the English and German; and it is astonishing with what promptness the Scottish novels, notwithstanding their dialects, are translated into French, and how universally and eagerly they are sought after.

In poetry, Lord Byron is the vogue; his verses are translated into a kind of stilted prose, and devoured with ecstasy, they are *si sombre!* His likeness is in every print-shop. The Parisians envelop him with melancholy and mystery, and believe him to be the hero of his own poems, or something of the vampyre order. A French poem has lately appeared in imitation of him,* the author of which has caught, in a great degree, his glowing style and deep and troubled emotions. The great success of this production insures an inundation of the same kind of poetry from inferior hands. In a little while we shall see the petty poets of France, like those of England, affecting to be moody and melancholy, each wrapping himself in a little mantle of mystery and misanthropy, vaguely accusing himself of heinous crimes, and affecting to despise the world.

That this taste for the romantic will have its way, and give a decided tone to French literature, I am strongly inclined to believe. The human mind delights in variety, and abhors monotony even in excellence. Nations, like individuals, grow sated with artificial refinements, and their pampered palates require a change of diet, even though it be for the worse. I should not be surprised, therefore, to see the French breaking away from rigid rule; from polished verse, easy narrative, the classic drama, and all the ancient delights of elegant literature, and rioting in direful romances, melo-dramatic plays, turgid prose, and glowing rough-written poetry.

Paris, 1821.

* *The Missennienes.*

13

MARGARET MILLER DAVIDSON.

[A biographical sketch of Lucretia Maria Davidson, who died on the 27th of August, 1825, just a month before her seventeenth birthday, was written by Mr. Samuel F. B. Morse, and prefixed to a collection of her poetic remains, published in 1829, under the title of "Amir Khan and other Poems."* In a notice of this volume in the "London Quarterly Review," Southey remarks : "In our own language, except in the cases of Chatterton and Kirke White, we can call to mind no instance of so early, so ardent, and so fatal a pursuit of intellectual advancement."

The biography of Margaret Miller Davidson, her no less remarkable sister, who died in 1838, four months before she had attained her sixteenth year, was prepared by Mr. Irving in 1840, and prefixed to an edition of her literary remains in 1841. The copyright was transferred to her mother, at whose request the Memoir was written, Mr. Irving reserving merely the right to publish it at any time in connection with his other writings. It has been long out of print, and is now for the first time included with his works.

In allusion to this touching narrative, the author remarks in one of his letters : "In the Spring I shall publish a biography of Miss Margaret Davidson, with her posthumous writings. She was a sister of Lucretia Davidson, whose biography you may have read,—a lovely American girl, of surprising precocity of poetical talent. The one whose biography I have just written died a year or two since. It is made up in a great degree from memorandums furnished by her mother, who is almost of as poetical a temperament as her children. The most affecting passages of the biography are quoted literally from her manuscript."—ED.]

* A more copious Memoir was afterwards written by Miss Sedgwick for *Sparks's American Biography.*

MARGARET DAVIDSON.

HE reading world has long set a cherishing value on the name of Lucretia Davidson, a lovely American girl, who, after giving early promise of rare poetic excellence, was snatched from existence in the seventeenth year of her age. An interesting biography of her by President Morse of the American Society of Arts, was published shortly after her death; another has since appeared from the classic pen of Miss Sedgwick, and her name has derived additional celebrity in Great Britain from an able article by Robert Southey, inserted some years since in the "London Quarterly Review."

An intimate acquaintance in early life with some of the relatives of Miss Davidson had caused me, while in Europe, to read with great interest everything concerning her; when, therefore, in 1838, about a year after my return to the United States, I was told, while in New York, that Mrs. Davidson, the mother of the deceased, was in the city and desirous of consulting me about a new edition of her daughter's works, I lost no time in waiting upon her. Her appearance corresponded with

the interesting idea given of her in her daughter's biography; she was feeble and emaciated, and supported by
pillows in an easy-chair, but there were the lingerings of
grace and beauty in her form and features, and her eyes
still beamed with intelligence and sensibility.

While conversing with her on the subject of her
daughter's works I observed a young girl, apparently not
more than eleven years of age, moving quietly about her;
occasionally arranging a pillow, and at the same time
listening earnestly to our conversation. There was an
intellectual beauty about this child that struck me; and
that was heightened by a blushing diffidence when Mrs.
Davidson presented her to me as her daughter Margaret.
Shortly afterwards, on her leaving the room, her mother,
seeing that she had attracted my attention, spoke of her
as having evinced the same early poetical talent that had
distinguished her sister, and as evidence, showed me
several copies of verses remarkable for such a child. On
further inquiry, I found that she had very nearly the
same moral and physical constitution, and was prone to
the same feverish excitement of the mind, and kindling
of the imagination that had acted so powerfully on the
fragile frame of her sister Lucretia. I cautioned her
mother, therefore, against fostering her poetic vein, and
advised such studies and pursuits as would tend to
strengthen her judgment, calm and regulate the sensibilities, and enlarge that common sense which is the only
safe foundation for all intellectual superstructure.

I found Mrs. Davidson fully aware of the importance of such a course of treatment, and disposed to pursue it, but saw at the same time that she would have difficulty to carry it into effect; having to contend with the additional excitement produced in the mind of this sensitive little being by the example of her sister, and the intense enthusiasm she evinced concerning her.

Three years elapsed before I again saw the subject of this memoir. She was then residing with her mother at a rural retreat in the neighborhood of New York. The interval that had elapsed had rapidly developed the powers of her mind and heightened the loveliness of her person, but my apprehensions had been verified. The soul was wearing out the body. Preparations were making to take her on a tour for the benefit of her health, and her mother appeared to flatter herself that it might prove efficacious; but when I noticed the fragile delicacy of her form, the hectic bloom of her cheek, and the almost unearthly lustre of her eye, I felt convinced that she was not long for this world; in truth, she already appeared more spiritual than mortal. We parted, and I never saw her more. Within three years afterwards a number of manuscripts were placed in my hands, as all that was left of her. They were accompanied by copious memoranda concerning her, furnished by her mother at my request. From these I have digested and arranged the following particulars, adopting in many places the original manuscript, without alteration. In fact, the nar-

rative will be found almost as illustrative of the character of the mother as of the child; they were singularly
identified in taste, feelings, and pursuits; tenderly entwined together by maternal and filial affection; they
reflected an inexpressibly touching grace and interest
upon each other by this holy relationship, and, to my
mind, it would be marring one of the most beautiful and
affecting groups in the history of modern literature, to
sunder them.

Margaret Miller Davidson, the youngest daughter of
Dr. Oliver and Mrs. Margaret Davidson, was born at the
family residence on Lake Champlain, in the village of
Plattsburgh, on the 26th of March, 1823. She evinced
fragility of constitution from her very birth. Her sister
Lucretia, whose brief poetical career has been so celebrated in literary history, was her early and fond attendant, and some of her most popular lays were composed
with the infant sporting in her arms. She used to gaze
upon her little sister with intense delight, and, remarking the uncommon brightness and beauty of her eyes,
would exclaim, "She must, she will be a poet!" The
exclamation was natural enough in an enthusiastic girl
who regarded everything through the medium of her
ruling passion; but it was treasured up by her mother,
and considered almost prophetic. Lucretia did not live
to see her prediction verified. Her brief sojourn upon
earth was over before Margaret was quite two years and
a half old; yet, to use her mother's fond expressions,

"On ascending to the skies, it seemed as if her poetic mantle fell, like a robe of light, on her infant sister."

Margaret, from the first dawnings of intellect, gave evidence of being no common child : her ideas and expressions were not like those of other children, and often startled by their precocity. Her sister's death had made a strong impression on her, and, though so extremely young, she already understood and appreciated Lucretia's character. An evidence of this, and of the singular precocity of thought and expression just noticed, occurred but a few months afterwards. As Mrs. Davidson was seated, at twilight, conversing with a female friend, Margaret entered the room with a light elastic step, for which she was remarked.

"That child never walks," said the lady ; then turning to her, "Margaret, where are you flying now ? " said she.

"To heaven ! " replied she, pointing up with her finger, "to meet my sister Lucretia, when I get my new wings."

"Your new wings ! When will you get them ? "

"Oh, soon, very soon ; and then I shall fly ! "

"She loved," says her mother, "to sit hour after hour on a cushion at my feet, her little arms resting upon my lap, and her full dark eyes fixed upon mine, listening to anecdotes of her sister's life and details of the events which preceded her death, often exclaiming, while her face beamed with mingled emotions, 'Oh mamma, I will try to fill her place ! Oh teach me to be like her !'"

Much of Mrs. Davidson's time was now devoted to her

daily instruction; noticing, however, her lively sensibility, the rapid development of her mind, and her eagerness for knowledge, her lessons were entirely oral, for she feared for the present to teach her to read, lest, by too early and severe application, she should injure her delicate frame. She had nearly attained her fourth year before she was taught to spell. Ill health then obliged Mrs. Davidson, for the space of a year, to entrust her tuition to a lady in Canada, a valued friend, who had other young girls under her care. When she returned home she could read fluently, and had commenced letters in writing. It was now decided that she should not be placed in any public seminary, but that her education should be conducted by her mother. The task was rendered delightful by the docility of the pupil; by her affectionate feelings, and quick kindling sensibilities. This maternal instruction, while it kept her apart from the world, and fostered a singular purity and innocence of thought, contributed greatly to enhance her imaginative powers, for the mother partook largely of the poetical temperament of the child; it was, in fact, one poetical spirit ministering to another.

Among the earliest indications of the poetical character in this child were her perceptions of the beauty of natural scenery. Her home was in a picturesque neighborhood, calculated to awaken and foster such perceptions. The following description of it is taken from one of her own writings : " There stood on the banks of the

Saranac a small neat cottage, which peeped forth from the surrounding foliage, the image of rural quiet and contentment. An old-fashioned piazza extended along the front, shaded with vines and honeysuckles; the turf on the bank of the river was of the richest and brighest emerald; and the wild rose and sweetbrier, which twined over the neat enclosure, seemed to bloom with more delicate freshness and perfume within the bounds of this earthly paradise. The scenery around was wildly yet beautifully romantic; the clear blue river, glancing and sparkling at its feet, seemed only as a preparation for another and more magnificent view, when the stream, gliding on to the west, was buried in the broad white bosom of Champlain, which stretched back, wave after wave in the distance, until lost in faint blue mists that veiled the sides of its guardian mountains, seeming more lovely from their indistinctness."

Such were the natural scenes which presented themselves to her dawning perceptions, and she is said to have evinced, from her earliest childhood, a remarkable sensibility to their charms. A beautiful tree, or shrub, or flower, would fill her with delight; she would note with surprising discrimination the various effects of the weather upon the surrounding landscape; the mountains wrapt in clouds; the torrents roaring down their sides in times of tempest; the "bright warm sunshine," the "cooling shower," the "pale cold moon," for such was already her poetical phraseology. A bright starlight night, also, would seem to awaken a mysterious rapture in her infant bosom, and one of her early expressions in speaking of the stars was, that they "shone like the eyes of angels."

One of the most beautiful parts of the maternal instruction was in guiding these kindling perceptions from Nature up to Nature's God.

"I cannot say," observes her mother, "at what age her religious impressions were imbibed. They seemed to be interwoven with her existence. From the very first exercise of reason she evinced strong devotional feelings, and, although she loved play, she would at any time prefer seating herself beside me, and, with every faculty absorbed in the subject, listen while I attempted to recount the wonders of Providence, and point out the wisdom and benevolence of God, as manifested in the works of creation. Her young heart would swell with rapture, and the tear would tremble in her eye, when I explained to her, that He who clothed the trees with verdure, and gave the rose its bloom, had also created her with capacities to enjoy their beauties : that the same power which clothed the mountains with sublimity, made her happiness His daily care. Thus a sentiment of gratitude and affection towards the Creator entered into all her emotions of delight at the wonders and beauties of creation."

There is nothing more truly poetical than religion when properly inculcated, and it will be found that this early piety, thus amiably instilled, had the happiest effect upon her throughout life ; elevating and ennobling her genius ; lifting her above everything gross and sordid ; attuning her thoughts to pure and lofty themes ; heightening rather than impairing her enjoyments, and at all times giving an ethereal lightness to her spirit. To use her mother's words, "she was like a bird on the wing, her fairy form scarcely seemed to touch the earth as she passed." She was at times in a kind of ecstasy from the excitement of her imagination and the exuberance of her pleasurable sensations. In such moods every object of natural beauty inspired a degree of rapture always mingled with a feeling of gratitude to the Being "who had made so many beautiful things for her." In such moods, too, her little heart would overflow with love to all around ; indeed, adds her mother, to love and be beloved was necessary to her existence. Private prayer became a habit with her at a very early age ; it was almost a spontaneous expression of her feelings, the breathings of an affectionate and delighted heart.

"By the time she was six years old," says Mrs. Davidson, "her language assumed an elevated tone, and her mind seemed filled with poetic imagery, blended with veins of religious thought. At this period I was chiefly confined to my room by debility. She was my companion and friend, and, as the greater part of my time was devoted to her instruction, she advanced rapidly in her studies. She read not only well, but elegantly. Her love of reading amounted almost to a passion, and her intelligence surpassed belief. Strangers viewed with astonishment a child little more than six years old, reading with enthusiastic delight 'Thomson's Seasons,' the 'Pleasures of Hope,' 'Cowper's Task,' the writings of Milton, Byron, and Scott, and marking, with taste and discrimination, the passages which struck her. The sacred writings were her daily studies; with her little Bible on her lap, she usually seated herself near me, and there read a chapter from the holy volume. This was a duty which she was taught not to perform lightly, and we have frequently spent two hours in reading and remarking upon the contents of a chapter."

A tendency to "lisp in numbers," was observed in her about this time. She frequently made little impromptus in rhyme, without seeming to be conscious that there was anything peculiar in the habit. On one occasion, while standing by a window at which her mother was seated, and looking out upon a lovely landscape, she exclaimed,—

> "See those lofty, those grand trees ;
> Their high tops waving in the breeze ;
> They cast their shadows on the ground,
> And spread their fragrance all around."

Her mother, who had several times been struck by little rhyming ejaculations of the kind, now handed her writing implements, and requested her to write down what she had just uttered. She appeared surprised at the request, but complied; writing it down as if it had been prose, without arranging it in a stanza, or commencing the lines with capitals; not seeming aware that she had rhymed. The notice attracted to this impromptu, however, had its effect, whether for good or for evil. From that time she wrote some scraps of poetry, or rather rhyme, every day, which would be treasured up with delight by her mother, who watched with trembling, yet almost fascinated anxiety, these premature blossomings of poetic fancy.

On another occasion, towards sunset, as Mrs. Davidson was seated by the window of her bedroom, little Margaret ran in, greatly excited, exclaiming that there was an awful thunder-gust rising, and that the clouds were black as midnight.

"I gently drew her to my bosom," says Mrs. Davidson, "and after I had soothed her agitation, she seated herself at my feet, laid her head in my lap, and gazed at the rising storm. As the thunder rolled, she clung closer to my knees, and when the tempest burst in all its fury, I felt her tremble. I passed my arms round her, but soon found it was not fear that agitated her. Her eyes kindled as she watched the warring elements, until, extending her hand, she exclaimed,—

> " 'The lightning plays along the sky,
> The thunder rolls and bursts from high !
> Jehovah's voice amid the storm
> I heard—methinks i see his form,

As riding on the clouds of even,
He spreads his glory o'er the heaven.'

This, likewise, her mother made her write down at the instant; thus giving additional impulse to this growing inclination.

I shall select one more instance of this early facility at numbers, especially as it involves a case of conscience, creditable to her early powers of self-examination. She had been reproved by her mother for some trifling act of disobedience, but aggravated her fault by attempting to justify it; she was, therefore, banished to her bedroom until she should become sensible of her error. Two hours elapsed without her evincing any disposition to yield; on the contrary, she persisted in vindicating her conduct, and accused her mother of injustice.

Mrs. Davidson mildly reasoned with her; entreated her to examine the spirit by which she was actuated; placed before her the example of our Saviour in submitting to the will of his parents; and, exhorting her to pray to God to assist her, and to give her meekness and humility, left her again to her reflections.

"An hour or two afterwards," says Mrs. Davidson, " she desired I would admit her. I sent word that, when she was in a proper frame of mind, I would be glad to see her. The little creature came in, bathed in tears, threw her arms round my neck, and sobbing violently, put into my hands the following verses :—

" 'Forgiven by my Saviour dear,
　　For all the wrongs I've done,
What other wish could I have here ?
　　Alas there yet is one.

I know my God has pardoned me,
　　I know he loves me still ;
I wish forgiven I may be
　　By her I've used so ill.

Good resolutions I have made,
　　And thought I loved my Lord :
But ah! I trusted in myself,
　　And broke my foolish word.

But give me strength, oh Lord! to trust
　　For help alone in thee ;
Thou knowest my inmost feelings best,
　　Oh teach me to obey.' "

We have spoken of the buoyancy of Margaret's feel-ings, and the vivid pleasure she received from external objects ; she entered, however, but little into the amuse-ments of the few children with whom she associated, nor did she take much delight in their society ; she was con-scious of a difference between them and herself, but scarce knew in what it consisted. Their sports seemed to divert for a while, but soon wearied her, and she would fly to a book, or seek the conversation of persons of maturer age and mind. Her highest pleasures were intellectual. She seemed to live in a world of her own creation, surrounded by the images of her own fancy.

14

Her own childish amusements had originality and freshness, and called into action the mental powers, so as to
render them interesting to persons of all ages. If at play
with her little dog or kitten, she would carry on imaginary dialogues between them; always ingenious, and
sometimes even brilliant. If her doll happened to be the
plaything of the moment, it was invested with a character exhibiting knowledge of history, and all the powers
of memory which a child can be supposed to exercise.
Whether it was Mary Queen of Scots, or her rival, Eliza-
beth, or the simple cottage maiden, each character was
maintained with propriety. In telling stories (an amusement all children are fond of) hers were always original,
and of a kind calculated to elevate the minds of the children
present, giving them exalted views of truth, honor, and integrity; and the sacrifice of all selfish feelings to the happiness of others was illustrated in the heroine of her story.

This talent for extemporaneous story-telling increased
with exercise, until she would carry on a narrative for
hours together : and in nothing was the precocity of her
inventive powers more apparent than in the discrimination and individuality of her fictitious characters, the
consistency with which they were sustained, the graphic
force of her descriptions, the elevation of her sentiments,
and the poetic beauty of her imagery.

This early gift caused her to be sought by some of the
neighbors, who would lead her unconsciously into an
exertion of her powers. Nothing was done by her from

vanity or a disposition to "show off," but she would become excited by their attention and the pleasure they seemed to derive from her narrations. When thus excited, a whole evening would be occupied by one of her stories; and when the servant came to take her home, she would observe, in the phraseology of the magazines, "the story to be continued in our next."

Between the age of six and seven she entered upon a course of English grammar, geography, history, and rhetoric, still under the direction and superintendence of her mother; but such was her ardor and application, that it was necessary to keep her in check, lest a too intense pursuit of knowledge should impair her delicate constitution. She was not required to commit her lessons to memory, but to give the substance of them in her own language and to explain their purport; thus she learnt nothing by rote, but everything understandingly, and soon acquired a knowledge of the rudiments of English education. The morning lessons completed, the rest of the day was devoted to recreation; occasionally sporting and gathering wild flowers on the banks of the Saranac; though the extreme delicacy of her constitution prevented her taking as much exercise as her mother could have wished.

In 1830 an English gentleman, who had been strongly interested and affected by the perusal of the biography and writings of Lucretia Davidson, visited Plattsburgh, in the course of a journey from Quebec to New York, to

see the place where she was born and had been buried.
While there, he sought an interview with Mrs. Davidson,
and his appearance and deportment were such as at once
to inspire respect and confidence. He had much to ask
about the object of his literary pilgrimage, but his inquiries were managed with the most considerate delicacy.
While he was thus conversing with Mrs. Davidson, the
little Margaret, then about seven years of age, came trip-
ping into the room, with a book in one hand and a pencil
in the other. He was charmed with her bright, intellectual countenance, but still more with finding that the
volume in her hand was a copy of "Thomson's Seasons,"
in which she had been marking with a pencil the passages which most pleased her. He drew her to him; his
frank, winning manner soon banished her timidity; he
engaged her in conversation, and found, to his astonishment, a counterpart of Lucretia Davidson before him.
His visit was necessarily brief; but his manners, appearance, and conversation, and, above all, the extraordinary
interest with which he had regarded her, sank deep in
the affectionate heart of the child, and inspired a friendship that remained one of her strongest attachments
through the residue of her transient existence.

The delicate state of her health this summer rendered
it advisable to take her to the Saratoga Springs, the
waters of which appeared to have a beneficial effect.
After remaining here some time, she accompanied her
parents to New York. It was her first visit to the city,

and of course fruitful of wonder and excitement; a new world seemed to open before her; new scenes, new friends, new occupations, new sources of instruction and enjoyment; her young heart was overflowing, and her head giddy with delight. To complete her happiness, she again met with her English friend, whom she greeted with as much eagerness and joy as if he had been a companion of her own age. He manifested the same interest in her that he had shown at Plattsburgh, and took great pleasure in accompanying her to many of the exhibitions and places of intellectual gratification of the metropolis, and marking their effects upon her fresh, unhackneyed feelings and intelligent mind. In company with him she, for the first and only time in her life, visited the theatre. It was a scene of magic to her, or rather, as she said, like a " brilliant dream." She often recurred to it with vivid recollection, and the effect of it upon her imagination was subsequently apparent in the dramatic nature of some of her writings.

One of her greatest subjects of regret on leaving New York, was the parting with her intellectual English friend; but she was consoled by his promising to pay Plattsburgh another visit, and to pass a few days there previous to his departure for England. Soon after returning to Plattsburgh, however, Mrs. Davidson received a letter from him saying that he was unexpectedly summoned home, and would have to defer his promised visit until his return to the United States.

It was a severe disappointment to Margaret, who had conceived for him an enthusiastic friendship remarkable in such a child. His letter was accompanied by presents of books and various tasteful remembrances, but the sight of them only augmented her affliction. She wrapped them all carefully in paper, and treasured them up in a particular drawer, where they were daily visited, and many a tear shed over them.

The excursions to Saratoga and New York had improved her health, and given a fresh impulse to her mind. She resumed her studies with great eagerness; her spirits rose with mental exercise; she soon was in one of her veins of intellectual excitement. She read, she wrote, she danced, she sang, and was for the time the happiest of the happy. In the freshness of early morning, and towards sunset, when the heat of the day was over, she would stroll on the banks of the Saranac, following its course to where it pours itself into the beautiful Bay of Cumberland in Lake Champlain. There the rich variety of scenery which bursts upon the eye; the islands, scattered like so many gems on the broad bosom of the lake; the green mountains of Vermont beyond, clothed in the atmospherical charms of our magnificent climate; all these would inspire a degree of poetic rapture in her mind, mingled with a sacred melancholy; for these were scenes which had often awakened the enthusiasm of her deceased sister Lucretia.

Her mother, in her memoranda, gives a picture of her in one of these excited moods.

"After an evening's stroll along the river bank, we seated ourselves by a window to observe the effect of the full moon rising over the waters. A holy calm seemed to pervade all nature. With her head resting on my bosom, and her eyes fixed on the firmament, she pointed to a particularly bright star, and said,—

> " 'Behold that bright and sparkling star
> Which setteth as a queen afar :
> Over the blue and spangled heaven
> It sheds its glory in the even !
>
> Our Jesus made that sparkling star
> Which shines and twinkles from afar.
> Oh ! 'twas that bright and glorious gem
> Which shone o'er ancient Bethlehem !'

"The summer passed swiftly away," continues her mother, "yet her intellectual advances seemed to outstrip the wings of time. As the autumn approached, however, I could plainly perceive that her health was again declining. The chilly winds from the lake were too keen for her weak lungs. My own health, too, was failing; it was determined, therefore, that we should pass the winter with my eldest daughter, Mrs. T——, who resided in Canada, in the same latitude, it is true, but in an inland situation. This arrangement was very gratifying to Margaret; and, had my health improved by

the change, as her own did, she would have been perfectly happy. During this period she attended to a
regular course of study, under my direction; for, though
confined wholly to my bed, and suffering extremely from
pain and debility, Heaven, in mercy, preserved my mental faculties from the wreck that disease had made of my
physical powers." The same plan as heretofore was
pursued. Nothing was learned by rote, and the lessons
were varied to prevent fatigue and distaste, though study
was always with her a pleasing duty rather than an
arduous task. After she had studied her lessons by herself she would discuss them in conversation with her
mother. Her reading was under the same guidance. "I
selected her books," says Mrs. Davidson, "with much
care, and to my surprise found that, notwithstanding her
poetical temperament, she had a high relish for history, and that she would read with as much apparent
interest an abstruse treatise that called forth the reflecting powers, as she did poetry or works of the imagination. In polite literature Addison was her favorite
author, but Shakspeare she dwelt upon with enthusiasm. She was restricted, however, to certain marked
portions of this inimitable writer; and having been told
that it was not proper for her to read the whole, such
was her innate delicacy and her sense of duty, that she
never overstepped the prescribed boundaries."

In the intervals of study she amused herself with
drawing, for which she had a natural talent, and soon

began to sketch with considerable skill. As her health had improved since her removal to Canada, she frequently partook of the favorite winter recreation of a drive in a traineau, or sleigh, in company with her sister and her brother-in-law, and completely enveloped in furs and buffalo-robes; and nothing put her in a finer flow of spirits than thus skimming along, in bright January weather, on the sparkling snow, to the merry music of the jingling sleigh-bells. The winter passed away without any improvement in the health of Mrs. Davidson; indeed she continued a helpless invalid, confined to her bed, for eighteen months; during all which time little Margaret was her almost constant companion and attendant.

"Her tender solicitude," writes Mrs. Davidson, "endeared her to me beyond any other earthly thing; although under the roof of a beloved and affectionate daughter, and having constantly with me an experienced and judicious nurse, yet the soft and gentle voice of my little darling was more than medicine to my worn-out frame. If her delicate hand smoothed my pillow, it was soft to my aching temples, and her sweet smile would cheer me in the lowest depths of despondency. She would draw for me—read to me; and often, when writing at her little table, would surprise me by some tribute of love, which never failed to operate as a cordial to my heart. At a time when my life was despaired of, she wrote the following lines while sitting at my bed:—

" ' I'll to thy arms in rapture fly,
    And wipe the tear that dims thine eye ;
    Thy pleasure will be my delight,
    Till thy pure spirit takes it flight.

When left alone—when thou art gone,
    Yet still I will not feel alone :
    Thy spirit still will hover near,
    And guard thy orphan daughter dear ! ' "

In this trying moment, when Mrs. Davidson herself had given up all hope of recovery, one of the most touching sights was to see this affectionate and sensitive child tasking herself to achieve a likeness of her mother, that it might remain with her as a memento. "How often would she sit by my bed," says Mrs. Davidson, "striving to sketch features that had been vainly attempted by more than one finished artist; and when she found that she had failed, and that the likeness could not be recognized, she would put her arms around my neck and weep, and say, ' Oh, dear mamma, I shall lose you, and not even a sketch of your features will be left me ! and if I live to be a woman, perhaps I shall even forget how you looked ! ' This idea gave her great distress, sweet lamb ! I then little thought this bosom would have been her dying pillow ! "

After being reduced to the very verge of the grave, Mrs. Davidson began slowly to recover ; but a long time elapsed before she was restored to her usual degree of health. Margaret in the meantime increased in strength and stature ; she looked fragile and delicate, but she was always cheerful and buoyant. To relieve the monotony of her life, which had been passed too much in a sick chamber, and to preserve her spirits fresh and elastic, little excursions were devised for her about the country, to Missisque Bay, St. Johns, Alburgh, Champlain, &c. The following lines, addressed to her mother on one of these occasional separations, will serve as a specimen of her compositions in this the eighth year of her age, and of the affectionate current of her feelings :—

" Farewell, dear mother ; for a while
I must resign thy plaintive smile ;
May angels watch thy couch of woe,
And joys unceasing round thee flow.

May the Almighty Father spread
His sheltering wings above thy head ;
It is not long that we must part,
Then cheer thy downcast, drooping heart.

Remember, oh, remember me,
Unceasing is my love for thee ;
When death shall sever earthly ties,
When thy loved form all senseless lies,

Oh that my soul with thine could flee,
And roam through wide eternity ;
Could tread with thee the courts of heaven,
And count the brilliant stars of even !

Farewell, dear mother ; for a while
I must resign thy plaintive smile ;
May angels watch thy couch of woe,
And joys unceasing round thee flow."

In the month of January, 1833, while still in Canada,
she was brought very low by an attack of scarlet fever,
under which she lingered many weeks, but had so far
recovered by the middle of April as to take the air in a
carriage.   Her mother, too, having regained sufficient
strength to travel, it was thought advisable, for both their
healths, to try the effect of a journey to New York. They
accordingly departed about the beginning of May, accompanied by a family party.   Of this journey, and a
sojourn of several months in New York, she kept a journal, which evinces considerable habits of observation,
but still more that kindling of the imagination which,
in the poetic mind, gives to commonplace realities the
witchery of romance. She was deeply interested by visits
to the "School for the Blind," and the "Deaf and Dumb
Asylum ;" and makes a minute of a visit of a very different nature—to Black Hawk and his fellow-chiefs, prisoners of war, who, by command of government, were
taken about through various of our cities, that they
might carry back to their brethren in the wilderness a
cautionary idea of the overwhelming power of the white
man.

"On the 25th June I saw and shook hands with the
famous Black Hawk, the Indian chief, the enemy of our

nation, who has massacred our patriots, murdered our women and helpless children! Why is he treated with so much attention by those whom he has injured? It cannot surely arise from benevolence. It must be *policy.* Be it what it may, I cannot understand it. His son, the Prophet, and others who accompanied him, interested *me* more than the chief himself. His son is no doubt a fine specimen of Indian beauty. He has a high brow, piercing black eyes, long black hair, which hangs down his back, and, upon the whole, is well suited to captivate an Indian maiden. The Prophet we found surveying himself in a looking-glass, undoubtedly wishing to show himself off to the best advantage in the fair assembly before him. The rest were dozing on a sofa, but they were awakened sufficiently to shake hands with us, and others who had the courage to approach so near them. I remember I dreamed of them the following night."

During this visit to New York, she was the life and delight of the relatives with whom she resided, and they still retain a lively recollection of the intellectual nature of her sports among her youthful companions, and of the surprising aptness and fertile invention displayed by her in contriving new sources of amusement. She had a number of playmates, nearly of her own age, and one of her projects was to get up a dramatic entertainment for the gratification of themselves and their friends. The proposal was readily agreed to, provided she would write the play. This she readily undertook, and indeed devised

and directed the whole arrangements, though she had
never been but once to a theatre, and that on her previous visit to New York.   Her little companions were
now all busily employed, under her directions, preparing
dresses and equipments; robes with trains were fitted
out for the female characters, and quantities of paper
and tinsel were consumed in making caps, helmets,
spears, and sandals.

After four or five days had been spent in these preparations, Margaret was called upon to produce the play.
"Oh!" she replied, "I have not written it yet."—"But
how is this!—Do you make the dresses first, and then
write the play to suit them?"—"Oh!" replied she, gayly,
"the writing of the play is the easiest part of the preparation; it will be ready before the dresses."   And, in
fact, in two days she produced her drama, "The Tragedy
of Alethia."   It was not very voluminous, to be sure, but
it contained within it sufficient of high character and
astounding and bloody incident to furnish out a drama
of five times its size.   A king and queen of England
resolutely bent upon marrying their daughter, the Princess Alethia, to the Duke of Ormond.   The princess
most perversely and dolorously in love with a mysterious
cavalier, who figures at her father's court under the name
of Sir Percy Lennox, but who, in private truth, is the
Spanish king, Rodrigo, thus obliged to maintain an in-
cognito on account of certain hostilities between Spain
and England.   The odious nuptials of the princess with

the Duke of Ormond proceed: she is led, a submissive victim, to the altar; is on the point of pledging her irrevocable word; when the priest throws off his sacred robe, discovers himself to be Rodrigo, and plunges a dagger into the bosom of the king. Alethia instantly plucks the dagger from her father's bosom, throws herself into Rodrigo's arms, and kills herself. Rodrigo flies to a cavern, renounces England, Spain, and his royal throne, and devotes himself to eternal remorse. The queen ends the play by a passionate apostrophe to the spirit of her daughter, and sinks dead on the floor.

The little drama lies before us, a curious specimen of the prompt talent of this most ingenious child, and by no means more incongruous in its incidents than many current dramas by veteran and experienced playwrights.

The parts were now distributed and soon learnt; Margaret drew out a play-bill, in theatrical style, containing a list of the dramatis personæ, and issued regular tickets of admission. The piece went off with universal applause; Margaret figuring, in a long train, as the princess, and killing herself in a style that would not have disgraced an experienced stage heroine.

In these, and similar amusements, her time passed happily in New York, for it was the study of the intelligent and amiable relatives, with whom she sojourned, to render her residence among them as agreeable and profitable as possible. Her visit, however, was protracted much beyond what was originally intended. As the sum-

mer advanced, the heat and restraint of the city became
oppressive; her heart yearned after her native home on
the Saranac; and the following lines, written at the time,
express the state of her feelings:—

HOME.

I WOULD fly from the city, would fly from its care,
To my own native plants and my flowerets so fair;
To the cool grassy shade, and the rivulet bright,
Which reflects the pale moon on its bosom of light.
Again would I view the old mansion so dear,
Where I sported a babe, without sorrow or fear;
I would leave this great city so brilliant and gay,
For a peep at my home on this fine summer day.
I have friends whom I love and would leave with regret,
But the love of my home, oh, 'tis tenderer yet!
There a sister reposes unconscious in death—
'Twas there she first drew and there yielded her breath—
A father I love is away from me now—
Oh could I but print a sweet kiss on his brow,
Or smooth the gray locks, to my fond heart so dear,
How quickly would vanish each trace of a tear!
Attentive I listen to pleasure's gay call,
But my own darling home, it is dearer than all.

At length, late in the month of October, the travellers
turned their faces homewards; but it was not the "darling home" for which Margaret had been longing: her
native cottage on the beautiful banks of the Saranac.
The wintry winds from Lake Champlain had been pronounced too severe for her constitution, and the family

residence had been reluctantly changed to the village of Ballston. Margaret felt this change most deeply. We have already shown the tender as well as poetical associations that linked her heart to the beautiful home of her childhood; a presentiment seemed to come over her mind that she would never see it more; a presentiment unfortunately prophetic. She was now accustomed to give prompt utterance to her emotions in rhyme, and the following lines, written at the time, remain a touching record of her feelings :—

MY NATIVE LAKE.

THY verdant banks, thy lucid stream,
Lit by the sun's resplendent beam,
Reflect each bending tree so light
Upon thy bounding bosom bright.
Could I but see thee once again,
My own, my beautiful Champlain !

The little isles that deck thy breast,
And calmly on thy bosom rest,
How often, in my childish glee,
I've sported round them, bright and free !
Could I but see thee once again,
My own, my beautiful Champlain !

How oft I've watch'd the fresh'ning shower
Bending the summer tree and flower,
And felt my little heart beat high
As the bright rainbow graced the sky.

15

Could I but see thee once again,
My own, my beautiful Champlain !

And shall I never see thee more,
My native lake, my much-loved shore ?
And must I bid a long adieu,
My dear, my infant home, to you ?
Shall I not see thee once again,
My own, my beautiful Champlain ?

Still, though disappointed in not returning to the
Saranac, she soon made herself contented at Ballston.
She was at home, in the bosom of her own family, and
reunited to her two youngest brothers, from whom she
had long been separated. A thousand little plans were
devised by her, and some few of them put in execution,
for their mutual pleasure and improvement. One of the
most characteristic of these was a " weekly paper," issued by her in manuscript, and entitled " The Juvenile
Aspirant." All their domestic occupations and amusements were of an intellectual kind. Their mornings were
spent in study ; the evenings enlivened by conversation,
or by the work of some favorite author, read aloud for
the benefit of the family circle.

As the powers of this excitable and imaginative little
being developed themselves, Mrs. Davidson felt more and
more conscious of the responsibility of undertaking to
cultivate and direct them ; yet to whom could she confide
her that would so well understand her character and constitution ? To place her in a boarding-school would sub-

ject her to increased excitement, caused by emulation, and her mind was already too excitable for her fragile frame. Her peculiar temperament required peculiar culture; it must neither be stimulated nor checked; and while her imagination was left to its free soarings, care must be taken to strengthen her judgment, improve her mind, establish her principles, and inculcate habits of self-examination and self-control. All this, it was thought, might best be accomplished under a mother's eye; it was resolved, therefore, that her education should, as before, be conducted entirely at home. "Thus she continued," to use her mother's words, "to live in the bosom of affection, where every thought and feeling was reciprocated. I strove to draw out the powers of her mind by conversation and familiar remarks upon subjects of daily study and reflection, and taught her the necessity of bringing all her thoughts, desires, and feelings under the dominion of reason; to understand the importance of self-control, when she found her inclinations were at war with its dictates. To fulfil all her duties from a conviction of right, because they were duties; and to find her happiness in the consciousness of her own integrity, and the approbation of God. How delightful was the task of instructing a mind like hers! She seized with avidity upon every new idea, for the instruction proceeded from lips of love. Often would she exclaim, 'Oh mamma! how glad I am that you are not too ill to teach me! Surely I am the happiest girl in the world!' She had read much for a child of little more than ten years of age. She was well versed in both ancient and modern history (that is to say, in the courses generally prescribed for the use of schools), Blair, Kames, and Paley had formed part of her studies. She was familiar with most of the British poets. Her command of the English language was remarkable, both in conversation and writing. She had learned the rudiments of French, and was anxious to become perfect in the language; but I had so neglected my duty in this respect after I left school, that I was not qualified to instruct her. A friend, however, who understood French, called occasionally and gave her lessons for his own amusement; she soon translated well, and such was her talent for the acquisition of languages, and such her desire to read everything in the original, that every obstacle vanished before her perseverance. She made some advances in Latin, also, in company with her brother, who was attended by a private teacher; and they were engaged upon the early books of Virgil, when her health again gave way, and she was confined to her room by severe illness. These frequent attacks upon a frame so delicate awakened all our fears. Her illness spread a gloom throughout our habitation, for fears were entertained that it would end in a pulmonary consumption." After a confinement of two months, however, she regained her usual, though at all times fragile, state of health. In the following spring, when she had just entered upon the eleventh year of her age, intelligence arrived of the death of her sister, Mrs. T., who had been resident in Canada. The blow had been apprehended from previous accounts of her extreme illness, but it was a severe shock. She had looked up to this sister as to a second mother, and as to one who, from the precarious health of her natural parent, might be called upon to fulfil that tender office. She was one, also, calculated to inspire affection; lovely in person, refined and intelligent in mind, still young in years; and with all this, her only remaining sister! In the following lines, poured out in the fulness of her grief, she touchingly alludes to the previous loss of her sister Lucretia, so often the subject of her poetic regrets, and of the consolation she had always felt in still having a sister to love and cherish her.

ON THE DEATH OF MY SISTER ANNA ELIZA.

WHILE weeping o'er our sister's tomb,
  And heaving many a heartfelt sigh,
And while in youth's bewitching bloom,
  I thought not that thou too couldst die.

When gazing on that little mound,
  Spread o'er with turf, and flowers, and mould,
I thought not that thy lovely form
  Could be as motionless and cold.

When her light, airy form was lost
  To fond affection's weeping eye;
I thought not we should mourn for thee,
  I thought not that thou too couldst die.

Yes, sparkling gem ! when thou wert here,
　From death's encircling mantle free,
Our mourning parents wiped each tear,
　And cried, "Why weep ? we still have thee."

Each tender thought on thee they turn'd;
　Each hope of joy to thee was given;
And, dwelling on each matchless charm,
　They half forgot the saint in heaven.

But thou art gone, forever gone !
　Sweet wanderer in a world of woe !
Now, unrestrain'd our grief must pour !
　Uncheck'd our mourning tears must flow.

How oft I've press'd my glowing lip
　In rapture to thy snowy brow,
And gazed upon that angel eye,
　Closed in death's chilling slumber now.

While tottering on the verge of life,
　Thine every nerve with pain unstrung,
That beaming eye was raised to heaven,—
　That heart to God for safety clung.

And when the awful moment came,
　Replete with trembling hope and fear,
Though anguish shook thy slender frame,
　Thy thoughts were in a brighter sphere.

The wreath of light, which round thee play'd,
　Bore thy pure spirit to the skies;
With thee we lost our brightest gem,
　But heaven has gain'd a glorious prize.

Oh may the bud of promise left,
    Follow the brilliant path she trod,
And of her fostering care bereft,
    Still seek and find his mother's God.

But he, the partner of her life,
    Who shared her joy and soothed her woe,
How can I heal his broken heart ?
    How bid his sorrow cease to flow ?

It's only time those wounds can heal;
    Time, from whose piercing pangs alone
The poignancy of grief can steal,
    And hush the heart's convulsive moan.

To parry the effect of this most afflicting blow, Margaret was sent on a visit to New York, where she passed a couple of months in the society of affectionate and intelligent friends, and returned home in June, recruited in health and spirits. The sight of her mother, however, though habituated to sorrow and suffering, yet bowed down by her recent bereavement, called forth her tenderest sympathies; and we consider it as illustrating the progress of the intellect and the history of the heart of this most interesting child, to insert another effusion called forth by this domestic calamity :—

TO MY MOTHER OPPRESSED WITH SORROW.

WEEP, oh my mother ! I will bid thee weep !
For grief like thine requires the aid of tears ;

But oh, I would not see thy bosom thus
Bow'd down to earth, with anguish so severe !
I would not see thine ardent feelings crush'd,
Deaden'd to all save sorrow's thrilling tone,
Like the pale flower, which hangs its drooping head
Beneath the chilling blasts of stern Æolus !
Oh I have seen that brow with pleasure flush'd,
The lightening smile around it brightly playing,
And the dark eyelids trembling with delight—
But now how chang'd !—thy downcast eye is bent,
With heavy, thoughtful glances, on the ground,
And oh, how quickly starts the tear-drop there !
It is not age which dims its wonted fire,
Or plants his lilies on thy pallid cheek,
But sorrow, keenest, darkest, biting sorrow !
When love would seek to lead thy heart from grief,
And fondly pleads one cheering look to view,
A sad, a faint sad smile one instant gleams
Athwart the brow where sorrow sits enshrined,
Brooding o'er ruins of what once was fair ;
But like departing sunset, as it throws
One farewell shadow o'er the sleeping earth
(So soon in sombre twilight to be wrapt),
Thus, thus it fades ! and sorrow more profound
Dwells on each feature where a smile, so cold,
It scarcely might be called the mockery
Of cheerful peace, but just before had been.
Long years of suffering, brighten'd not by joy,
Death and disease, fell harbingers of woe,
Must leave their impress on the human face,
And dim the fire of youth, the glow of pride ;
But oh, my mother ! mourn not thus for *her*,
The rose, just blown. transplanted to its home,

Nor weep that her angelic soul has found
A resting-place with God.
Oh let the eye of heaven-born faith disperse
The dark'ning mists of earthly grief, and pierce
The clouds which shadow dull mortality!
Gaze on the heaven of glory crown'd with light.
Where rests thine own sweet child with radiant brow,
In the same voice which charm'd her father's halls,
Chanting sweet anthems to her Maker's praise ;
And watching with delight the gentle buds
Which she had lived to mourn ; watching thine own,
My mother ! the soft unfolding blossoms,
Which, ere the breath of earthly sin could taint,
Departed to their Saviour ; there to wait
For thy fond spirit in the home of bliss !
The angel babes have found a second mother ;
But when thy soul shall pass from earth away,
The little cherubs then shall cling to thee,
And their sweet guardian welcome thee with joy,
Protector of their helpless infancy,
Who taught them how to reach that happy home.
Oh think of this, and let one heartfelt smile
Illume the face so long estranged from joy;
But may it rest not on thy brow alone,
But shed a cheering influence o'er thy heart,
Too sweet to be forgotten !   Though thy loved
And beautiful are fled from earth away,
Still there are those who loved thee—who would live
With thee alone—who weep or smile with thee.
Think of thy noble sons, and think of her
Who prays thee to be happy in the hope
Of meeting those in heaven who loved thee here,
And training those on earth, that they may live
A band of saints with thee in Paradise.

The regular studies of Margaret were now resumed, and her mother found, in attending to her instruction, a relief from the poignancy of her afflictions. Margaret always enjoyed the country, and in fine weather indulged in long rambles in the woods, accompanied by some friend, or attended by a faithful servant woman. When in the house, the versatility of her talents, her constitutional vivacity, and an aptness at coining occupation and amusement out of the most trifling incident, perpetually relieved the monotony of domestic life; while the faint gleam of health that occasionally flitted across her cheek, beguiled the anxious forebodings that had been indulged concerning her. "A strong hope was rising in my heart," says her mother, "that our frail, delicate blossom would continue to flourish, and that it was possible I might live to behold the perfection of its beauty! Alas! how uncertain is every earthly prospect! Even then the canker was concealed with the bright bud, which was eventually to destroy its loveliness! About the last of December she was again seized with a liver complaint, which, by sympathy, affected her lungs, and again awakened all our fears. She was confined to her bed, and it was not until March that she was able to sit up and walk about her room. The confinement then became irksome, but her kind and skilful physician had declared that she must not be permitted to venture out until mild weather in April." During this fit of illness her mind had remained in an unusual state of inactivity; but with the opening of spring and the faint return of health, it broke forth with a brilliancy and a restless excitability that astonished and alarmed. "In conversation," says her mother, "her sallies of wit were dazzling. She composed and wrote incessantly, or rather would have done so, had I not interposed my authority to prevent this unceasing tax upon both her mental and physical strength. Fugitive pieces were produced every day, such as 'The Shunamite,' 'Belshazzar's Feast,' 'The Nature of Mind,' 'Boabdil el Chico,' &c. She seemed to exist only in the regions of poetry." We cannot help thinking that these moments of intense poetical exaltation sometimes approached to delirium, for we are told by her mother that "the image of her departed sister Lucretia mingled in all her aspirations; the holy elevation of Lucretia's character had taken deep hold of her imagination, and in her moments of enthusiasm she felt that she held close and intimate communion with her beatified spirit."

This intense mental excitement continued after she was permitted to leave her room, and her application to her books and papers was so eager and almost impassioned, that it was found expedient again to send her on an excursion. A visit to some relatives, and a sojourn among the beautiful scenery of the Mohawk River, had a salutary effect; but on returning home she was again attacked with alarming indisposition, which confined her to her bed.

"The struggle between nature and disease," says her mother, "was for a time doubtful; she was, however, at length restored to us. With returning health, her mental labors were resumed. I reasoned and entreated, but at last became convinced that my only way was to let matters take their course. If restrained in her favorite pursuits, she was unhappy. To acquire useful knowledge was a motive sufficient to induce her to surmount all obstacles. I could only select for her a course of calm and quiet reading, which, while it furnished real food for the mind, would compose rather than excite the imagination. She read much and wrote a great deal. As for myself, I lived in a state of constant anxiety lest these labors should prematurely destroy this delicate bud."

In the autumn of 1835, Dr. Davidson made arrangements to remove his family to a rural residence near New York, pleasantly situated on the banks of the Sound, or East River, as it is commonly called. The following extract of a letter from Margaret to Moss Kent, Esq.,*

* This gentleman was an early and valued friend of the Davidson family, and is honorably mentioned by Mr. Morse for the interest he took in the education of Lucretia. The notice of Mr. Morse, however, leaves it to be supposed that Mr. Kent's acquaintance with Dr. and Mrs. Davidson was brought about by his admiration of their daughter's talents, and commenced with overtures for her instruction. The following extract of a letter from Mrs. Davidson will place this matter in a proper light, and show that these offers on the part of Mr. Kent, and the partial acceptance of them by Dr. and Mrs. Davidson, were warranted by the terms of intimacy which before existed between them. "I had the pleasure," says Mrs. Davidson, "to know Mr. Kent before my marriage, after which he frequently called at our house when visiting his sister, with whom I was

will show her anticipations and plans on this occasion :—

"*September* 20, 1835.

"We shall soon leave Ballston for New York. We are to reside in a beautiful spot upon the East River, near the Shot Tower, four miles from town, romantically called Ruremont. Will it not be delightful? Reunited to father and brothers, we must, we will be happy! We shall keep a horse and a little pleasure-wagon, to transport us to and from town. But I intend my time shall be constantly employed in my studies, which I hope I shall continue to pursue at home. I wish (and mamma concurs in the opinion that it is best) to devote this winter to the study of the Latin and French languages, while music and dancing will unbend my mind after close application to those studies, and give me that recreation

on terms of intimacy. On one of these occasions he saw Lucretia. He had often seen her when a child, but she had changed much. Her uncommon personal beauty, graceful manners, and superior intellectual endowments made a strong impression on him. He conversed with her, and examined her on the different branches which she was studying, and pronounced her a good English scholar. He also found her well read, and possessing a fund of general information. He warmly expressed his admiration of her talents, and urged me to consent that he should adopt her as his daughter, and complete her education on the most liberal plan. I so far acceded to his proposition as to permit him to place her with Mrs. Willard, and assured him I would take his generous offer into consideration. Had she lived, we should have complied with his wishes, and Lucretia would have been the child of his adoption. The pure and disinterested friendship of this excellent man continued until the day of his death. For Margaret he manifested the affection of a father, and the attachment was returned by her with all the warmth of a young and grateful heart. She always addressed him as her dear uncle Kent."

which mother deems requisite for me. If father can procure private teachers for me, I shall be saved the dreadful alternative of a boarding-school. Mother could never endure the thought of one for me, and my own aversion is equally strong. Oh! my dear uncle, you must come and see us. Come soon and stay long. Try to be with us at Christmas. Mother's health is not as good as when you was here. I hope she will be benefited by a residence in her native city,—in the neighborhood of those friends she best loves. The state of her mind has an astonishing effect upon her health."

The following letter to the same gentleman, is dated October 18, 1835: "We are now at Ruremont, and a more delightful place I never saw. The house is large, pleasant, and commodious, and the old-fashioned style of everything around it transports the mind to days long gone by, and my imagination is constantly upon the rack to burden the past with scenes transacted on this very spot. In the rear of the mansion a lawn, spangled with beautiful flowers, and shaded by spreading trees, slopes gently down to the river side, where vessels of every description are constantly spreading their white sails to the wind. In front, a long shady avenue leads to the door, and a large extent of beautiful undulating ground is spread with fruit-trees of every description. In and about the house there are so many little nooks and by-places, that sometimes I fancy it has been the resort of smugglers ; and who knows but I shall yet find their hidden treasures somewhere ? Do come and see us, my dear uncle ; but you must come soon, if you would enjoy any of the beauties of the place. The trees have already doffed their robe of green, and assumed the red and yellow of autumn, and the paths are strewed with fallen leaves. But there is loveliness even in the decay of nature. But do, do come soon, or the branches will be leafless, and the cold winds will prevent the pleasant rambles we now enjoy. Dear mother has twice accompanied me a short distance about the grounds, and indeed I think her health has improved since we removed to New York, though she is still very feeble. Her mind is much relieved, having her little family gathered once more around her. You well know how great an effect her spirits have upon her health. Oh ! if my dear mother is only in comfortable health, and you will come, I think I shall spend a delightful winter prosecuting my studies at home."

" For a short time," writes Mrs. Davidson, " she seemed to luxuriate upon the beauties of this lovely place. She selected her own room, and adjusted all her little tasteful ornaments. Her books and drawing implements were transported to this chosen spot. Still she hovered around me like my shadow. Mother's room was still her resting-place, mother's bosom her sanctuary. She sketched a plan for one or two poems which were never finished.

But her enjoyment was soon interrupted. She was again attacked by her old enemy, and though her confinement to her room was of short duration, she did not get rid of the cough. A change now came over her mind. Hitherto she had always delighted in serious conversation on heaven; the pure and elevated occupations of saints and angels in a future state had proved a delightful source of contemplation; and she would become so animated that it seemed sometimes as if she would fly to realize her hopes and joys! Now her young heart appeared to cling to life and its enjoyments, and more closely than I had ever known it. 'She was never ill.'—When asked the question, 'Margaret, how are you?' 'Well, quite well,' was her reply, when it was obvious to me, who watched her every look, that she had scarcely strength to sustain her weak frame. She saw herself the last daughter of her idolizing parents—the only sister of her devoted brothers! Life had acquired new charms, though she had always been a happy, light-hearted child."

The following lines, written about this time, show the elasticity of her spirit and the bounding vivacity of her imagination, that seemed to escape, as in a dream, from the frail tenement of clay in which they were encased :—

STANZAS.

Oh, for the pinions of a bird,
　To bear me far away,
Where songs of other lands are heard,
　And other waters play !

For some aërial car, to fly
  On through the realms of light,
To regions rife with poesy,
  And teeming with delight.

O'er many a wild and classic stream
  In ecstasy I'd bend,
And hail each ivy-covered tower
  As though it were a friend.

O'er piles where many a wintry blast
  Is swept in mournful tones,
And fraught with scenes long glided past,
  It shrieks, and sighs, and moans.

Through many a shadowy grove, and round
  Full many a cloister'd hall,
And corridors, where every step
  With echoing peal doth fall.

Enchanted with the dreariness,
  And awe-struck with the gloom,
I would wander, like a spectre,
  'Mid the regions of the tomb.

And Memory her enchanting veil
  Around my soul should twine ;
And Superstition, wildly pale,
  Should woo me to her shrine ;

I'd cherish still her witching gloom,
  Half shrinking in my dread,
But, powerless to dissolve the spell,
  Pursue her fearful tread.

16

Oh, what unmingling pleasure then
  My youthful heart would feel,
As o'er its thrilling chords each thougnt
  Of former days would steal,—

Of centuries in oblivion wrapt,
  Of forms which long were cold,
And all of terror, all of woe,
  That history's page has told.

How fondly in my bosom
  Would its monarch, Fancy, reign,
And spurn earth's meaner offices
  With glorious disdain.

Amid the scenes of past delight,
  Or misery, I'd roam :
Where ruthless tyrants swayed in might,—
  Where princes found a home ;

Where heroes have enwreathed their brows
  With chivalric renown ;
Where Beauty's hand, as Valor's meed,
  Hath twined the laurel crown.

I'd stand where proudest kings have stood,
  Or kneel where slaves have knelt,
Till wrapt in magic solitude,
  I feel what they have felt.

Oh, for the pinions of a bird,
  To waft me far away,
Where songs of other lands are heard
  And other waters play !

About this time Mrs. Davidson received a letter from the English gentleman for whom Margaret, when quite a child, had conceived such a friendship, her dear older brother, as she used to call him. The letter bore testimony to his undiminished regard. He was in good health; married to a very estimable and lovely woman; was the father of a fine little girl, and was at Havana with his family, where he kindly entreated Mrs. Davidson and Margaret to join them, being sure that a winter passed in that mild climate would have the happiest effect upon their healths. His doors, his heart, he added, were open to receive them, and his amiable consort impatient to bid them welcome. "Margaret," says Mrs. Davidson, "was overcome by the perusal of this letter. She laughed and wept alternately. One moment urged me to go; 'she was herself well, but she was sure it would cure me;' the next moment felt as though she could not leave the friends to whom she had so recently been reunited. Oh, had I gone at that time, perhaps my child might still have lived to bless me!"

During the first weeks of Margaret's residence at Ruremont, the character and situation of the place seized powerfully upon her imagination. "The curious structure of this old-fashioned house," says Mrs. Davidson, "its picturesque appearance, the varied and beautiful grounds which surrounded it, called up a thousand poetic images and romantic ideas. A long gallery, a winding staircase, a dark, narrow passage, a trap-door,

large apartments, with massive doors and heavy iron bars
and bolts, all set her mind teeming with recollections of
what she had read and imagined of old castles, banditti,
smugglers, &c. She roamed over the place in perfect
ecstasy, peopling every part with images of her own
imagination, and fancying it the scene of some foregone
event of dark and thrilling interest." There was, in fact,
some palpable material for all this spinning and weaving
of the fancy. The writer of this memoir visited Ruremont at the time it was occupied by the Davidson family.
It was a spacious, and somewhat crazy and poetical-look-
ing mansion, with large waste apartments. The grounds
were rather wild and overgrown, but so much the more
picturesque. It stood on the banks of the Sound, the
waters of which rushed, with whirling and impetuous
tides, below, hurrying on to the dangerous strait of Hell
Gate. Nor was this neighborhood without its legendary
tales. These wild and lonely shores had, in former times,
been the resort of smugglers and pirates. Hard by this
very place stood the country retreat of Ready Money
Prevost, of dubious and smuggling memory, with his
haunted tomb, in which he was said to conceal his con-
traband riches; and scarce a secret spot about these
shores but had some tradition connected with it of Kidd
the pirate and his buried treasures. All these circumstances were enough to breed thick-coming fancies in so
imaginative a brain, and the result was a drama in six
acts, entitled "The Smuggler," the scene of which was

laid at Ruremont in the old time of the Province. The play was written with great rapidity, and, considering she was little more than twelve years of age, and had never visited a theatre but once in her life, evinced great aptness and dramatic talent. It was to form a domestic entertainment for Christmas holidays ; the spacious back-parlor was to be fitted up for the theatre. In planning and making arrangements for the performance, she seemed perfectly happy, and her step resumed its wonted elasticity, though her anxious mother often detected a suppressed cough and remarked a hectic flush upon her cheek. "We now found," says Mrs. Davidson, "that private teachers were not to be procured at Ruremont, and I feared to have her enter upon a course of study which had been talked of before we came to this place. I thought she was too feeble for close mental application, while *she* was striving, by the energies of her mind and bodily exertion (which only increased the morbid excitement of her system), to overcome disease, that she feared was about to fasten itself upon her. She was the more anxious, therefore, to enter upon her studies ; and when she saw solicitude in my countenance and manner, she would fix her sweet sad eyes upon my face, as if she would read my very soul, yet dreaded to know what she might find written there. I knew and could understand her feelings ; she also understood mine ; and there seemed to be a tacit compact between us that this subject, at *present*, was forbidden ground. Her father and brothers were lulled into security by her cheerful manner and constant assertion that she was well, and considered her cough the effect of recent cold. My opinion to the contrary was regarded as the result of extreme maternal anxiety."

She accordingly went to town three times a week, to take lessons in French, music, and dancing. Her progress in French was rapid, and the correctness and elegance of her translations surprised her teachers. Her friends in the city, seeing her look so well and appear so sprightly, encouraged her to believe that air and exercise would prove more beneficial than confinement to the house. She went to town in the morning and returned in the evening in an open carriage, with her father and one of her elder brothers, each of whom was confined to his respective office until night. In this way she was exposed to the rigors of an unusually cold season ; yet she heeded them not, but returned home full of animation to join her little brothers in preparations for their holiday *fête*. Their anticipations of a joyous Christmas were doomed to sad disappointment. As the time approached, two of her brothers were taken ill. One of these, a beautiful boy about nine years of age, had been the favorite companion of her recreations, and she had taken great interest in his mental improvement. "Towards the close of 1835," says her mother, " he began to droop ; his cheek grew pale, his step languid, and his bright eye heavy. Instead of rolling the hoop, and bounding across the lawn to meet his sister on her return from the city, he drooped by the side of his feeble mother, and could not bear to be parted from her; at length he was taken to his bed, and, after lingering four months, he died. This was Margaret's first acquaintance with death. She witnessed his gradual decay almost unconsciously, but still persuaded herself 'He will, he must get well!' She saw her sweet little playfellow reclining upon my bosom during his last agonies; she witnessed the bright glow which flashed upon his long-faded cheek; she beheld the unearthly light of his beautiful eye, as he pressed his dying lips to mine and exclaimed, 'Mother! dear mother! the last hour has come!' Oh! it was indeed an hour of anguish never to be forgotten. Its effect upon her youthful mind was as lasting as her life. The sudden change from life and animation to the still unconsciousness of death, for the time almost paralyzed her. She shed no tear, but stood like a statue upon the scene of death. But when her eldest brother tenderly led her from the room, her tears gushed forth—it was near midnight, and the first thing that aroused her to a sense of what was going on around her, was the thought of my bereavement, and a conviction that it was her province to console me."

We subjoin a record, from her own pen, of her feelings on this lamentable occasion :—

ON THE CORPSE OF MY LITTLE BROTHER KENT.

BEAUTEOUS form of soulless clay !
　Image of what once was life !
Hushed is thy pulse's feeble play,
　And ceased the pangs of mortal strife.

Oh! I have heard thy dying groan,
　Have seen thy last of earthly pain ;
And while I weep that thou art gone,
　I cannot wish thee here again.

For ah ! the calm and peaceful smile
　Upon that clay-cold brow of thine,
Speaks of a spirit freed from sin,—
　A spirit joyful and divine.

But thou art gone ! and this cold clay
　Is all that now remains of thee ;
For thy freed soul hath winged its **way**
　To blessèd immortality.

That dying smile, that dying groan,
　I never, never can forget,
Till Death's cold hand hath clasped my **own,**
　His impress on my brow has set.

Those low, and sweet, and plaintive tones,
　Which o'er my heart like music swept,
And the deep, deathlike, chilling moans
　Which from thy heaving bosom crept.

Oh! thou wert beautiful and fair,
　Our loveliest and our dearest one !
No more thy pains or joys we share,
　No more—my brother, thou art gone.

Thou'rt gone !   What agony, what woe
In that brief sentence is expressed !
Oh, that the burning tears could flow,
And draw this mountain from my breast !

The anguish of the mother was still more intense, as
she saw her bright and beautiful but perishable offspring
thus, one by one, snatched away from her. "My own
weak frame," says she, "was unable longer to sustain
the effects of long watching and deep grief. I had not
only lost my lovely boy, but I felt a strong conviction
that I must soon resign my Margaret ; or, rather, that
she would soon follow me to a premature grave. Although she still persisted in the belief that she was well,
the irritating cough, the hectic flush (so often mistaken
for the bloom of health), the hurried beating of the
heart, and the drenching night-perspirations confirmed
me in this belief, and I sank under this accumulated load
of affliction. For three weeks I hovered upon the borders of the grave ; and when I arose from this bed of
pain, so feeble that I could not sustain my own weight,
it was to witness the rupture of a blood-vessel in her
lungs, caused by exertions to suppress a cough. Oh, it
was agony to see her thus ! I was compelled to conceal
every appearance of alarm, lest the agitation of her mind
should produce fatal consequences. As I seated myself
by her, she raised her speaking eyes to mine with a
mournful, inquiring gaze ; and as she read the anguish
which I could not conceal, she turned away with a look

of despair. She spoke not a word, but silence, still, death-like silence, pervaded the apartment." The best of medical aid was called in, but the physicians gave no hope; they considered it a deep-seated case of pulmonary consumption. All that could be done was to alleviate the symptoms, and protract life as long as possible, by lessening the excitement of the system. When Mrs. Davidson returned to the bedside, after an interview with the physicians, she was regarded with an anxious, searching look by the lovely little sufferer, but not a question was made. Margaret seemed fearful of receiving a discouraging reply, and "lay, all pale and still (except when agitated by the cough), striving to calm the tumult of her thoughts," while her mother seated herself by her pillow, trembling with weakness and sorrow. Long and anxious were the days and nights spent in watching over her. Every sudden movement or emotion excited the hemorrhage. "Not a murmur escaped her lips," says her mother, "during her protracted sufferings. 'How are you, love? how have you rested during the night?' 'Well, dear mamma; I have slept sweetly.' I have been night after night beside her restless couch, wiped the cold dew from her brow, and kissed her faded cheek in all the agony of grief, while she unconsciously slept on; or if she did awake, her calm sweet smile, which seemed to emanate from heaven, has, spite of my *reason*, lighted my heart with hope. Except when very ill, she was ever a bright dreamer. Her visions were usually of an unearthly cast,—about heaven and angels. She was wandering among the stars; her sainted sisters were her pioneers; her cherub brother walked hand-in-hand with her through the gardens of Paradise! I was always an early riser; but after Margaret began to decline I never disturbed her until time to rise for breakfast, a season of social intercourse in which she delighted to unite, and from which she was never willing to be absent. Often when I have spoken to her she would exclaim, 'Mother, you have disturbed the brightest visions that ever mortal was blessed with! I was in the midst of such scenes of delight! Cannot I have time to finish my dream?' And when I told her how long it was until breakfast, 'It will do,' she would say, and again lose herself in her bright imaginings; for I considered these as moments of inspiration rather than sleep. She told me it was not sleep. I never knew but one, except Margaret, who enjoyed this delightful and mysterious source of happiness; that one was her departed sister Lucretia. When awaking from these reveries, an almost ethereal light played about her eye, which seemed to irradiate her whole face. A holy calm pervaded her manner, and in truth she looked more like an angel who had been communing with kindred spirits in the world of light, than anything of a grosser nature."

How truly does this correspond with Milton's exquisite description of the heavenly influences that minister to virgin innocence:—

" A thousand liv'ried angels lackey her,
    Driving far off each thing of sin and guilt ;
And in clear dream and solemn vision,
    Tell her of things that no gross ear can hear ;
Till oft converse with heavenly habitants
Begin to cast a beam on the outward shape,
The unpolluted temple of the mind,
And turn it by degrees to the soul's essence,
Till all be made immortal."

Of the images and speculations that floated in her
mind during these half-dreams, half-reveries, we may
form an idea from the following lines, written on one
occasion after what her mother used to term her " descent into the world of reality " :—

THE JOYS OF HEAVEN.

Oh, who can tell the joy and peace
    Which souls redeemed shall know,
When all their earthly sorrows cease,
    Their pride, and pain, and woe !
Who may describe the matchless love
Which reigneth with the saints above ?

What earthly tongue can ever tell
    The pure, unclouded joy
Which in each gentle soul doth swell,
    Unmingled with alloy,
As, bending to the Lord Most High,
They sound his praises through the sky ?

Through the high regions of the air,
    On angel wings they glide,

And gaze in wondering silence there
  On scenes to us denied;
Their minds expanding every hour,
And opening like the summer flower.

Though not like them to fade away,
  To die, and bloom no more;
Beyond the reach of fell decay
  They stand in light and power;
But pure, eternal, free from care,
They join in endless praises there !

When first they leave this world of woe
  For fair, immortal scenes of light,
Angels attend them from below,
  And upward wing their joyful flight;
Where, fired with heavenly rapture's flame,
They raise on high Jehovah's name.

O'er the broad arch of heaven it peals,
  While shouts of praise unnumbered flow;
The full, sweet notes sublimely swell,
  And prostrate angels humbly bow;
Each harp is tuned to joy above,
Its theme, a Saviour's matchless love.

The dulcet voice, which here below
  Charmed with delight each listening ear,
Mixed with no lingering tone of woe,
  Swelling harmonious, soft, and clear,
Will sweetly fill the courts above,
In strains of heavenly peace and love.

The brilliant genius, which on earth
  Is struggling with disease and pain,
Will there unfold in power and light,
  Naught its bright current to restrain ;
And as each brilliant day rolls on,
'Twill find some grace till then unknown.

And as the countless years flit by,
  Their minds progressing still,
The more they know, these saints on high
  Praise more His sovereign will ;
No breath from sorrow's whirlwind blast
Around their footsteps cast.

From their high throne they gaze abroad
  On vast creation's wondrous plan,
And own the power, the might of God,
  In each resplendent work they scan ;
Though sun and moon to naught return,
Like stars these souls redeemed shall burn.

Oh! who could wish to stay below,
  If sure of such a home as this,
Where streams of love serenely flow,
  And every heart is filled with bliss ?
They praise, and worship, and adore
The Lord of heaven for evermore.

During this dangerous illness she became acquainted
with Miss Sedgwick. The first visit of that most excellent and justly distinguished person, was when Margaret
was in a state of extreme debility. It laid the foundation
of an attachment on the part of the latter which con-

tinued until her death. The visit was repeated; a correspondence afterwards took place, and the friendship of Miss Sedgwick became to the little enthusiast a source of the worthiest pride and purest enjoyment throughout the remainder of her brief existence.

At length the violence of her malady gave way to skillful remedies and the most tender and unremitting assiduity. When enabled to leave her chamber, she rallied her spirits, made great exertions to be cheerful, and strove to persuade herself that all might yet be well with her. Even her parents, with that singular self-delusion inseparable from this cruelly flattering malady, began to indulge a trembling hope that she might still be spared to them.

In the month of July her health being sufficiently re-established to bear the fatigues of travelling, she was taken by her mother and eldest brother on a tour to Dutchess county and the western part of New York. On leaving home, she wrote the following lines, expressive of the feelings called forth by the events of the few preceding months, and of a foreboding that she should never return :—

FAREWELL TO RUREMONT.

Oh ! sadly I gaze on this beautiful landscape,
　And silent and slow do the big tear-drops swell ;
And I haste to my task, while the deep sigh is breaking,
　To bid thee, sweet Ruremont, a lasting farewell.

Oh ! soft are the breezes which play round thy valley,
   And warm are the sunbeams which gild thee with light ;
All clear and serenely the deep waves are rolling,
   The sky in its radiance is dazzlingly bright.

Oh! gayly the birds 'mid thy dark vines are sporting,
   And, heaven-taught, pouring their gladness in song ;
While the rose and the lily their fair heads are bending
   To hear the soft anthems float gently along.

Full many an hour have I bent o'er thy waters,
   Or watched the light clouds with a joy-beaming eye,
Till, delighted, I longed for the eagle's swift pinions,
   To pierce the full depths of that beautiful sky.

Though wild were the fancies which dwelt in my bosom,
   Though endless the visions which swept o'er my soul,
Indulging those dreams was my dearest enjoyment,—
   Enjoyment unmingled, unchained by control !

But each garden of earth has a something of sorrow,
   A thorn in its rose, or a blight in its breeze ;
Though blooming as Eden, a shadow hangs o'er thee,
   The spirit of darkness, of pain, of disease !

Yes, Ruremont ! thy brow, in its loveliness decked,
   Is entwined with a fatal but beautiful wreath ;
For thy green leaves have shrunk at the mourner's cold touch,
   And thy pale flowers have wept in the presence of death.

Yon violets, which bloom in their delicate freshness,
   Were strewed o'er the grave of our fairest and best ;
Yon roses, which charm by their richness and fragrance,
   Have withered and died on his icy-cold breast.

The soft voice of Spring had just breathed o'er the valley,
   The sweet birds just carolled their song in her bower,
When the angel of Death in his terror swept o'er us,
   And placed in his bosom our fragile young flower.

Thus, Ruremont, we mourn not thy beauties alone,
   Thy flowers in their freshness, thy stream in its pride ;
But we leave the loved scene of our mourning and tears,—
   We leave the dear spot where our cherished one died.

The mantle of beauty thrown gracefully o'er thee,
   Must touch a soft chord in each delicate heart ;
But the tie is more sacred which bids us deplore thee,—
   Endeared by affection, 'tis harder to part.

The scene of enjoyment is ever most lovely,
   Where blissful young spirits dance mirthful and glad ;
But when Sorrow has mingled her tears with our pleasure,
   Our love is more tender, our parting more sad.

How mild is the wing of this delicate zephyr,
   Which fans in its coolness my feverish brow !
But that light wing is laden with breezes that wither,
   And check the warm current of life in its flow.

Why blight such an Eden, O spirit of terror !
   Which sweepest thy thousands each hour to the tomb ?
Why, why shouldst thou roam o'er this beautiful valley,
   And mingle thy breath with the rose's perfume?

The sun rises bright o'er the clear dancing waters,
   And tinges with gold every light waving tree,
And the young birds are singing their welcome to morning—
   Alas! they will sing it no longer for me !

17

The young buds of Summer their soft eyes are opening,
 The wild flowers are bending the pure ripples o'er ;
But I bid them farewell, and my heart is nigh breaking
 To think I shall see them and tend them no more.

I mark yonder path, where so often I've wandered,
 Yon moss-covered rock, with its sheltering tree,
And a sigh of deep sadness bursts forth to remember
 That no more its soft verdure shall blossom for me.

How often my thoughts, to these loved scenes returning,
 Shall brood o'er the past with its joy and its pain ;
Till waking at last from the long pleasing slumber,
 I sigh to behold thee, thus blooming again.

The little party was absent on its western tour about
two months. "Margaret," says her mother, "appeared
to enjoy the scenery, and everything during the journey
interested her ; but there was a sadness in her countenance, a pensiveness in her manner, unless excited by
external circumstances, which deeply affected me. She
watched every variation in my countenance ; marked
every little attention directed to herself,—such as an
alteration in her diet, dress, exposure to the changes of
weather,—yet still discovered an unwillingness to speak
of her declining health, and labored to conceal every
unfavorable symptom or change for the worse. This, of
course, imposed upon me the most painful restraint. How
heart-breaking to find that she considered my tongue as
the herald of mournful tidings, and my face as the mirror
of evil to come ! How true that self-deception seems to

be an almost invariable symptom attending this dreadful complaint! Margaret, all unconscious of the rapid strides of the destroyer, taught herself to believe that the alarming symptoms of her case existed only in the imagination of her too anxious mother. Yet knowing my experience in these matters, she still doubted and trembled and feared to ask, lest a confirmation of her vague apprehensions should be the result. She avoided the slightest allusion to the subject of her disease in any way; and in the morbid excitement of her mind it appeared to her almost like accusing her of something wrong to say she was not well."

The following letter was written by her to Miss Sedgwick, after her arrival in Dutchess County :—

LITHGOW, DUTCHESS COUNTY.

HAPPY as I am, my dear madam, in the privilege of writing to you, I cannot permit another day to pass ere I inform you of our safe arrival at one of the most lovely spots in this beautiful and healthy country. Our passage up the river was rather tedious, being debarred the pleasure of remaining upon deck, but this privation was counterbalanced by the pleasure of a few moments' conversation with dear brother, who was permitted to meet us when the boat stopped at West Point. Arrived at Poughkeepsie, brother M. procured a private carriage, which was to convey us to the end of our journey, a distance of twenty miles. The drive was delightful! The

scenery ever changing, ever beautiful! We arrived at
Lithgow without much fatigue, where a hearty welcome,
that sweetest of cordials, was awaiting us. Oh, it is a
lovely spot! I thought Ruremont the perfection of
beauty! but here I find the flowers as blooming, the
birds as gay, the air as sweet, and the prospect far more
varied and extensive. 'Tis true we have lost the beautiful East River, with its crowd of vessels sweeping
gracefully along; but here are hills crowned with the
richest foliage, valleys sprinkled with flowers, and wa-
tered with winding rivulets; and here, what we prize
more than all, a mild, salubrious air, which seems, in the
words of the divine poet, 'to bear healing in its wings.'
Dear mother bore the fatigue of our journey better than
we anticipated; and although I do not think she is permanently better, she certainly breathes more freely, and
seems altogether more comfortable, than when in the city.
Oh! how sincerely I hope that a change of air and scene
may raise her spirits and renovate her strength. She is
now in the midst of friends whom she has known and loved
for many years, and surrounded by scenes connected with
many of her earliest remembrances. Farewell, my dear
madam! Please give my love to your dear little niece;
and should you have the leisure and inclination to answer this, believe me your letter will be a source of much
gratification to your highly obliged little friend,

M. M. DAVIDSON.

Miss CATHERINE SEDGWICK,
    August, 1836.

The travellers returned to Ruremont in September. The tour had been of service to Margaret, and she endeavored to persuade herself that she was quite well. If asked about her health, her reply was, that "If her friends did not tell her she was ill, she should not, from her own feelings, suspect it." That she was, notwithstanding, dubious on this subject, was evident from her avoiding to speak about it, and from the uneasiness she manifested when it was alluded to. It was still more evident from the change that took place in her habits and pursuits; she tacitly adopted the course of conduct that had repeatedly and anxiously, but too often vainly, been urged by her mother, as calculated to allay the morbid irritability of her system. She gave up her studies, rarely indulged in writing or drawing, and contented herself with light reading, with playing a few simple airs on the piano, and with any other trivial mode of passing away the time. The want of her favorite occupations, however, soon made the hours move heavily with her. Above all things, she missed the exacting exercise of the pen, against which she had been especially warned. Her mother observed the listlessness and melancholy that were stealing over her, and hoped a change of scene might banish them. The airs from the river, too, had been pronounced unfavorable to her health; the family, therefore, removed to town. The change of residence, however, did not produce the desired effect. She became more and more dissatisfied with herself, and with the life of idleness, as she considered it, that she was leading; but still she had resolved to give the prescribed system a thorough trial. A new source of solicitude was now awakened in the bosom of her anxious mother, who read in her mournfully quiet manner and submissive silence the painful effects of compliance with her advice. There was not a murmur, however, from the lips of Margaret, to give rise to this solicitude; on the contrary, whenever she caught her mother's eye fixed anxiously and inquiringly on her, she would turn away and assume an air of cheerfulness.

Six months had passed in this inactive manner. "She was seated one day by my side," says Mrs. Davidson, "weary and restless, and scarcely knowing what to do with herself, when, marking the traces of grief upon my face, she threw her arms about my neck, and, kissing me, exclaimed, 'My dear, dear mother!' 'What is it affects you now, my child?' 'Oh, I know you are longing for something from my pen!' I saw the secret craving of the spirit that gave rise to the suggestion. 'I do, indeed, my dear, delight in the effusions from your pen, but the exertion will injure you.' 'Mamma, I *must write!* I can hold out no longer! I will return to my pen, my pencil, and my books, and shall again be happy!' I pressed her to my bosom, and cautioned her to remember she was feeble. 'Mother,' exclaimed she, 'I am well! I wish you were only as well as I am!'"

The heart of the mother was not proof against these

appeals; indeed she had almost as much need of self-denial on this subject as her child, so much did she delight in these early blossomings of her talent. Margaret was again left to her own impulses. All the frivolous expedients for what is usually termed *killing time* were discarded by her with contempt; her studies were resumed; in the sacred writings and in the pages of history she sought fitting aliment for her mind, half famished by its long abstinence; her poetical vein again burst forth, and the following lines, written at the time, show the excitement and elevation of her feelings:—

EARTH.

EARTH! thou hast naught to satisfy
  The cravings of immortal mind!
Earth! thou hast nothing pure and high,
  The soaring, struggling soul to bind.

Impatient of its long delay,
  The pinioned spirit fain would roam,
And leave this crumbling house of clay,
  To seek, above, its own bright home!

The spirit,—'t is a spark of light
  Struck from our God's eternal throne,
Which pierces through these clouds of night,
  And longs to shine where once it shone!

Earth! there will come an awful day,
  When thou shalt crumble into naught;
When thou shalt melt beneath that ray
  From whence thy splendors first were caught.

Quenched in the glories of its God,
　Yon burning lamp shall then expire ;
And flames, from heaven's own altar sent,
　Shall light the great funereal pyre.

Yes, thou must die ! and yon pure depths
　Back from thy darkened brow shall roll ;
But never can the tyrant Death
　Arrest this feeble, trusting soul.

When that great Voice, which formed thee first,
　Shall tell, surrounding world, thy doom,
Then the pure soul, enchained by thee,
　Shall rise triumphant o'er thy tomb.

Then on, still on, the unfettered mind
　Through realms of endless space shall fly ;
No earth to dim, no chain to bind,
　Too pure to sin, too great to die.

Earth ! thou hast naught to satisfy
　The cravings of immortal mind !
Earth ! thou hast nothing pure or high,
　The soaring, struggling soul to bind.

Yet is this never-dying ray
　Caught in thy cold, delusive snares,
Cased in a cell of mouldering clay,
　And bowed by woes, and pain, and cares !

Oh ! how mysterious is the bond
　Which blends the earthly with the pure,
And mingles that which death may blight
　With that which ever must endure !

Arise, my soul, from all below,
  And gaze upon thy destined home,
The heaven of heavens, the throne of God,
  Where sin and care can never come.

Prepare thee for a state of bliss,
  Unclouded by this mortal veil,
Where thou shalt see thy Maker's face,
  And dews from heaven's own air inhale.

How sadly do the sins of earth
  Deface thy purity and light,
That thus, while gazing at thyself,
  Thou shrink'st in horror at the sight.

Compound of weakness and of strength,
  Mighty, yet ignorant of thy power !
Loftier than earth, or air, or sea,
  Yet meaner than the lowliest flower.

Soaring towards heaven, yet clinging still
  To earth, by many a purer tie !
Longing to breathe a tender air,
  Yet fearing, trembling thus to die !

She was soon all cheerfulness and enjoyment. Her pen and her pencil were frequently in her hand; she occupied herself also with her needle in embroidery on canvas, and other fancy work. Hope brightened with the exhilaration of her spirits. "I now walk and ride, eat and sleep as usual," she observes in a letter to a young friend, "and although not well, have strong hopes that the opening spring, which renovates the flowers, and fields, and streams, will revive my enfeebled frame, and restore me to my wonted health." In these moods she was the life of the domestic circle, and these moods were frequent and long. And here we would observe, that though these memoirs, which are furnished principally from the recollections of an afflicted mother, may too often represent this gifted little being as a feeble invalid struggling with mortality, yet in truth her life, though a brief, was a bright and happy one. At times she was full of playful and innocent gayety; at others of intense mental exaltation; and it was the very intensity of her enjoyment that made her so often indulge in those poetic paroxysms, if we may be allowed the expression, which filled her mother with alarm. A few weeks of this intellectual excitement was followed by another rupture of a blood-vessel in the lungs, and a long interval of extreme debility. The succeeding winter was one of vicissitude. She had several attacks of bleeding at the lungs, which evidently alarmed her at the time, though she said nothing, and endeavored to repress all manifestation of her feelings. If taken suddenly, she instantly resorted to the sofa, and, by a strong effort, strove to suppress every emotion. With her eyes closed, her lips compressed, and her thin pale hand resting in that of her anxious mother, she seemed to be waiting the issue. Not a murmur would escape her lips, nor did she ever complain of pain. She would often say, by way of consolation, to her mother, "Mamma, I am highly favored. I hardly know what is meant by pain. I am sure I never, to my recollection, have felt it." The moment she was able to sit up, after one of these alarming attacks, every vestige of a sick chamber must be removed. No medicine, no cap, no bed-gown, no loose wrapper must be in sight. Her beautiful dark hair must be parted on her broad, high forehead, her dress arranged with the same care and neatness as when in perfect health; indeed she studied to banish from her appearance all that might remind her friends that her health was impaired, and, if possible, to drive the idea from her own thoughts. Her reply to every inquiry about her health was, "Well, quite well; or at least *I* feel so, though mother continues to treat me as an invalid. True I have a cold, attended by a cough, that is not willing to leave me; but when the spring returns, with its mild air and sweet blossoms, I think this cough, which alarms mother so much, will leave me."

She had, indeed, a strong desire to live; and the cause of that desire is indicative of her character. With all her retiring modesty, she had an ardent desire for literary distinction. The example of her sister Lucretia was incessantly before her; she was her leading star, and her whole soul was but to emulate her soarings into the pure regions of poetry. Her apprehensions were that she might be cut off in the immaturity of her powers. A simple, but most touching ejaculation, betrayed this feeling, as, when lying on a sofa, in one of those alarming paroxysms of her malady, she turned her eyes, full of mournful sweetness, upon her mother, and, in a low, subdued voice, exclaimed, "Oh! my dear, dear mother! *I am so young!*"

We have said that the example of her sister Lucretia was incessantly before her, and no better proof can be given of it than in the following lines, written at this time, which breathe the heavenly aspirations of her pure young spirit, in strains, to us, quite unearthly. We may have read poetry more artificially perfect in its structure, but never any more truly divine in its inspiration.

TO MY SISTER LUCRETIA.

My sister ! With that thrilling word
   What thoughts unnumbered wildly spring !
What echoes in my heart are stirred,
   While thus I touch the trembling string !

My sister ! ere this youthful mind
   Could feel the value of thine own ;
Ere this infantine heart could bind,
   In its deep cell, one look, one tone,

To glide along on memory's stream,
   And bring back thrilling thoughts of thee ;
Ere I knew aught but childhood's dream,
   Thy soul had struggled, and was free !

My sister ! with this mortal eye
   I ne'er shall see thy form again ;
And never shall this mortal ear
   Drink in the sweetness of thy strain !

Yet fancy wild and glowing love
   Reveal thee to my spirit's view,
Enwreathed with graces from above,
   And decked in heaven's own fadeless hue.

Thy glance of pure seraphic light
   Sheds o'er my heart its soft'ning ray;
Thy pinions guard my couch by night,
   And hover o'er my path by day.

I cannot weep that thou art fled ;
   For ever blends my soul with thine ;
Each thought, by purer impulse led,
   Is soaring on to realms divine.

Thy glance unfolds my heart of hearts,
   And lays its inmost recess bare ;
Thy voice a heavenly calm imparts,
   And soothes each wilder passion there.

I hear thee in the summer breeze,
   See thee in all that's pure or fair ;
Thy whisper in the murmuring trees,
   Thy breath, thy spirit everywhere.

Thine eyes, which watch when mortals sleep,
   Cast o'er my dreams a radiant hue ;
Thy tears, "such tears as angels weep,"
   Fall nightly with the glistening dew.

Thy fingers wake my youthful lyre,
   And teach its softer strains to flow ;
Thy spirit checks each vain desire,
   And gilds the low'ring brow of woe.

When fancy wings her upward flight
  On through the viewless realms of air,
Clothed in its robe of matchless light,
  I view thy ransomed spirit there !

Far from her wild delusive dreams,
  It leads my raptured soul away,
Where the pure fount of glory streams,
  And saints live on through endless day.

When the dim lamp of future years
  Sheds o'er my path its glimmering faint,
First in the view thy form appears,
  My sister, and my guardian saint !

Thou gem of light ! my leading star !
  What thou hast been, I strive to be ;
When from the path I wander far,
  Oh, turn thy guiding beam on me.

Teach me to fill thy place below,
  That I may dwell with thee above ;
To soothe, like thee, a mother's woe,
  And prove, like thine, a sister's love.

Thou wert unfit to dwell with clay,
  For sin too pure, for earth too bright !
And Death, who called thee hence away,
  Placed on his brow a gem of light !

A gem, whose brilliant glow is shed
  Beyond the ocean's swelling wave,
Which gilds the memory of the dead,
  And pours its radiance on thy grave.

When Day hath left his glowing car,
   And Evening spreads her robe of love ;
When worlds, like travellers from afar,
   Meet in the azure fields above ;

When all is still, and Fancy's realm
   Is opening to the eager view,
Mine eye full oft, in search of thee,
   Roams o'er that vast expanse of blue.

I know that here thy harp is mute,
   And quenched the bright poetic fire,
Yet still I bend my ear, to catch
   The hymnings of thy seraph lyre.

Oh ! if this partial converse now
   So joyous to my heart can be,
How must the streams of rapture flow
   When both are chainless, both are free !

When borne from earth for evermore,
   Our souls in sacred joy unite,
At God's almighty throne adore,
   And bathe in beams of endless light !

Away, away, ecstatic dream !
   I must not, dare not dwell on thee ;
My soul, immersed in life's dark stream,
   Is far too earthly to be free.

Though heaven's bright portal were unclosed,
   And angels wooed me from on high,
Too much I fear my shrinking soul
   Would cast on earth its longing eye.

Teach me to fill thy place below,
    That I may dwell with thee above ;
To soothe, like thee, a mother's woe,
    And prove, like thee, a sister's love.

It was probably this trembling solicitude about the
duration of her existence, that made her so anxious,
about this time, to employ every interval of her precarious health in the cultivation of her mental powers.
Certain it is, during the winter, checkered as it was with
repeated fits of indisposition, she applied herself to historical and other studies with an ardor that often made
her mother tremble for the consequences.

The following letters to a young female friend were
written during one of these intervals :—

"NEW YORK, *February* 26, 1837.

"NOTWITHSTANDING all the dangers which might have
befallen your letter, my dear Henrietta, it arrived safely
at its resting-place, and is now lying open before me, as
I am quietly sitting, this chill February morning, to
inform you of its safe arrival. I find I was not mistaken
in believing you too kind to be displeased at my remiss-
ness ; and I now hope that through our continued intercourse neither will have cause to complain of the other's
negligence.

"For my own part, I am always willing to assign every
reason but that of forgetfulness for a friend's silence.
Knowing how often I am obliged to claim this indulgence

foɪ myself, and how often ill health prevents me from writing to those I love, I am the more ready to frame apologies for others ; indeed I think this spirit of *charity* (if so I may call it) is necessary to the happiness of correspondents, and as I am sure you possess it, I trust we shall both glide quietly along without any of those little *jars* which so often interrupt the purest friendships. And now that my dissertation on letter-writing is at an end, I must proceed to inform you of what I fear will be a disappointment, as it breaks away all those sweet anticipations expressed in your affectionate letter. Father has concluded that we shall not return to Plattsburgh next spring, as he had once intended ; he fears the effects of the cold winds of Lake Champlain upon mother and myself, who are both delicate ; and as we have so many dear friends in and about the city, a nearer location would be pleasanter to us and to them. We now think seriously of returning to Ballston, that beautiful little village where we have already spent two delightful years ; and though in this case I must relinquish the idea of visiting my dear 'old home' and my dear *young friend*, hope points to the hour when *you* may become *my* guest, and where the charms of novelty will in some degree repay us for the delightful associations and remembrances we had hoped to enjoy. But I cannot help now and then casting a backward glance upon the beautiful scenes you describe, and wishing myself with you. A philosopher would say, 'Since you cannot enjoy what

18

you desire, turn to the pleasures you may possess, and
seek in them consolation for what you have lost;' but I
am no philosopher. . . . . .

"I will endeavor to answer your question about Mrs.
Hemans. I have read several lives of this distinguished
poetess, by different authors, and in all of them find
something new to admire in her character and venerate
in her genius! She was a woman of deep feeling, lively
fancy, and acute sensibilities; so acute, indeed, as to
have formed her chief unhappiness through life. She
mingles her own feelings with her poems so well, that in
reading *them* you read *her* character. But there is one
thing I have often remarked : the mind soon wearies in
perusing many of her pieces at *once.* She expresses
those sweet sentiments so often, and introduces the same
stream of beautiful ideas so constantly, that they sometimes degenerate into monotony. I know of no higher
treat than to read a few of her best productions, and
comment upon and feel their beauties ; but perusing her
volume is to me like listening to a strain of sweet music
repeated over and over again, until it becomes so familiar
to the ear that it loses the charm of variety.

"Now, dear H., is not this presumption in me, to criticise so exquisite an author ? But you desired my opinion, and I have given it to you without reserve.

"You desire me to send you an *original poem* for yourself. Now, my dear Hetty, this is something I am not
at present able to do for any of my friends, writing being

supposed quite injurious to persons with weak lungs. And I have still another reason. You say the effect of conveying feelings from the heart and recording them upon paper, seems to deprive them of half their warmth and ardor! Now, my dear friend, would not the effect of forming them into verse seem to render them still *less* sincere? Is not plain prose, as it slides rapidly from the pen, more apt to speak the feelings of the heart, than when an hour or two is spent in giving them rhyme and measure and all the attributes of poetry?" . . . . .

TO THE SAME.

"New York, *April* 2, 1837.

"About an hour since, my dear Henrietta, I received your token of remembrance, and commenced my answer with an act of obedience to your sovereign will; but I fear you will repent when too late, and while nodding over the closely written sheet, and peering impatiently into each crowded corner, you will secretly wish you had allowed my pen to commence its operations at a more respectful distance from the top of the page. However, the request was your own; I obey like an obedient friend, and you must abide the consequences of your rash demand. Should the first glance at my well-filled sheet be followed by a *yawn*, or its last word be welcomed with a smile, you must blame your own imprudence in bringing down upon your luckless head the accumulated nothings of a scribbler like myself. It is indeed true that we shall not return to Plattsburgh; and much as I long to revisit the home of my infancy, and the friends of my earliest remembrance, I shall be obliged to relinquish the pleasure in reality, though fancy, unshackled by earth, shall direct her pinions to the north, and linger, delighted, on the beautiful banks of the Champlain! Methinks I hear you exclaim, with impatience, ' *Fancy!* what is it? I long for something more substantial.' So do I, *ma chère,* but since I cannot hope to behold my dear native village and its dear inhabitants, with *other* eyes than those of fancy, I will e'en employ them to the best of my ability. You may be sure we do not prefer the confined and murky atmosphere of the city to the pure and health-giving breezes of the country; far from it—we are already preparing to remove, as soon as the mild influence of spring has prevailed over the chilling blasts which we still hear whistling around us; and gladly shall we welcome the day that will release us from our bondage. But there is some drawback to every pleasure—some bitter drop in almost every cup of enjoyment; and we shall taste this most keenly when we bid farewell to the delightful circle of friends who have cheered us during the solitude and confinement of this dreary winter. The New York air, so far from agreeing with us, has deprived us of every enjoyment beyond the boundaries of our own walls, and it will be hard to leave those friends who have taught us to forget the privations of ill health in the pleasure of their society. We have

chosen Ballston for our temporary home, from the hope
of seeing them oftener *there* than we could in a secluded
town, and because pure air, medicinal waters, and good
society have all combined to render it a delightful country residence; yet, with all these advantages, it can never
possess half the charms of my dear old home!

> "That dear old home, where passed my childish years,
> When fond affection wiped my infant tears!
> Where first I learned from whence my blessings came,
> And lisped, in faltering tones, a *mother's* name!

> "That *dear* old *home*, where memory fondly clings,
> Where eager fancy spreads her soaring wings;
> Around whose scenes my thoughts delight to stray,
> And pass the hours in pleasing dreams away!

> "Oh, shall I ne'er behold thy waves again,
> My native lake, my beautiful Champlain?
> Shall I no more above thy ripples bend
> In sweet communion with my childhood's friend?

> "Shall I no more behold thy rolling wave,
> The patriot's cradle, and the warrior's grave?
> Thy mountains, tinged with daylight's parting glow?
> Thy islets, mirror'd in the stream below?

> "Back! back!—thou *present*, robed in shadows lie,
> And rise, thou *past*, before my raptured eye!
> Fancy shall gild the frowning lapse between,
> And Memory's hand shall paint the glowing scene!

> "Lo! how the view beneath her pencil grows!
> The flow'ret blooms, the winding streamlet flows;

With former friends I trace my footsteps o'er,
And muse, delighted, on my own green shore !

" Alas ! it fades—the fairy dream is past !
Dissolved the veil by sportive Fancy cast.
Oh, why should thus our brightest dreams depart,
And scenes illusive cheat the longing heart ?

" Where'er through future life my steps may roam,
I ne'er shall find a spot like thee, my home ;
With all my joys the thought of *thee* shall blend,
And, joined with *thee*, shall rise my childhood's friend.

"Mother is most truly alive to all these feelings. During our first year in New York we were living a few miles from the city, at one of the loveliest situations in the world ! I think I have seldom seen a sweeter spot; but all its beauties could not divert her thoughts from our own dear *home*, and despite the superior advantages we there enjoyed, she wept to enjoy it again. But enough of this ; if I suffer my fancy to dwell longer upon these loved scenes, I shall scribble over my whole sheet, and, leaving out what I most wish to say, fill it with nothing but 'Home, home, sweet, sweet home !' as the song goes. . . . .

"*June,* 1837.

"Now for the mighty theme upon which I scarcely dare to dwell,—my visit to Plattsburgh ! Yes, my dear H., I do think, or rather I do *hope*, that such a time may come when I can at least spend a week with you. I dare not hope for a longer time, for I know I shall be disappointed. About the middle of this month brother graduates, and will leave West Point for home. He intends to visit Plattsburgh, and it will take much to wean me from my favorite plan of accompanying him. However, all is uncertain,—I must not think of it too much,—but if I do come, it will be with the hope of gaining a still greater pleasure. We are now delightfully situated. Can you not return with me, and make me a visit? What joy is like the joy of anticipation? What pleasure like those we look forward to, through a long lapse of time, and dwell upon as some bright land that we shall inhabit when the *present* shall have become the *past?* I have heard it observed that it was foolish to anticipate—that it was only increasing the pangs of disappointment. Not so ; do we not, in our most sanguine hopes, acknowledge to ourselves a fear, a doubt, an expectation of disappointment? Shall we lose the enjoyment of the present, because evil may come in future? No, no—if anticipation was not meant for a solace, an alleviation of the sorrows of life, would it have been so strongly implanted in our hearts by the great Director of all our passions? No—it is too precious! I would give up half the *reality* of joy for the sweet anticipation. Stop—I have gone too far—for indeed I could *not* resign my visit to you, though I might hope and anticipate for years !

"Just as I had written the above, father interrupted me with an invitation to ride. We have just returned from a long, delightful drive. Though Ballston cannot compare with Plattsburgh for its rich and varied scenery, still there are romantic woods and shady paths which cannot fail to delight the true lover of Nature. . . . . .

"So you do have the *blues,* eh ? I had almost said I was glad of it; but that would be too cruel—I will only say, one does not like to be alone, or in anything singular, and I too, once in a while, receive a visit from these provoking imps—are they not ? You should not have blamed Scott only (excuse me), but yourself, for selecting such a book to chase away melancholy.

"You ask me if I remember those *story-telling* days ? Indeed I do, and nothing affords me more pleasure than the recollection of those happy hours! If my memory could only retain the particulars of my last story, gladly would I resume and continue it when I meet you again. I will ease *your* heart of its fear for *mine*—your scolding did not break it. My dear H., it is not made of such brittle materials as to crack for a trifle. No, no! It would be far more prudent to save it entire for some greater occasion, and then make the crash as loud as possible—don't you think so ? Oh, nonsensical nonsense! Well—

> "'The greatest and the wisest men
> Will fool a little now and then.'

"But I believe I will not add another word, lest my pen should slide off into some new absurdity."

On the 1st of May, 1837, the family left New York for Ballston. They had scarce reached there when Mrs. Davidson had an attack of inflammatory rheumatism, which confined her to her bed, and rendered her helpless as an infant. It was Margaret's turn now to play the nurse, which she did with the most tender assiduity. The paroxysms of her mother's complaint were at first really alarming, as may be seen by the following extract of a letter from Margaret to Miss Sedgwick, written some short time afterwards :—

"We at first thought she would never revive. It was indeed a dreadful hour, my dear madam—a sad trial for poor father and myself, to watch, as we supposed, the last agonies of one so beloved as my dear mother! But the cloud has passed by, and my heart, relieved from its burden, is filled almost to overflowing, with gratitude and joy. After a few hours of dreadful suspense, reaction took place, and since then she has been slowly and steadily improving. In a few days, I hope, she will be able to ride, and breathe some of this delightful air, which cannot fail to invigorate and restore her. My own health has improved astonishingly since my coming here. I walk, and ride, and exercise as much as possible in the open air, and find it of great service to me. Oh, how much I hope to see you here! . . . . . Do, if possible, try the Ballston air once more. It has been useful to you once, it might be still more so now. You will find warm hearts to welcome you, and we will do all in our power to make your visit pleasant to you. The country does indeed look beautiful! The woods are teeming with wild flowers, and the air is full of melody. The soft, wild warbling of the birds is far more sweet to me than the most labored performances of art; *they* may weary by repetition, but what heart can resist the influence of a lovely day ushered in by the morning song of those sweet carollers! and even to sleep, as it were, by their melodious evening strain! How I wish you could be here to enjoy it with me."

The summer of 1837 was one of the happiest of her fleeting existence. For some time after the family removed to Ballston she was very much confined to the house by the illness of her mother, and the want of a proper female companion to accompany her abroad. At length a Mr. and Mrs. H., estimable and intimate friends, of a highly intellectual character, came to the village. Their society was an invaluable acquisition to Margaret. In company with them she was enabled to enjoy the healthful recreations of the country; to ramble in the woods; to take exercise on horseback, of which she was extremely fond, and to make excursions about the neighborhood; while they exerted a guardian care to prevent her, in her enthusiastic love for rural scenery, from exposing herself to anything detrimental to her health and strength. She gave herself up, for a time, to these exhilarating exercises, abstaining from her usual propensity to overtask her intellect, for she had imbibed the idea that active habits, cheerful recreations, and a holiday frame of mind would effectually reëstablish her health. As usual, in her excited moods, she occasionally carried these really healthful practices to excess, and would often, says her mother, engage, with a palpitating heart and a pulse beating at the rate of one hundred and thirty in a minute, in all the exercises usually prescribed to *preserve* health in those who are in full possession of the blessing. She was admonished of her danger by several attacks upon her lungs during the summer, but as they were of short duration she still flattered herself that she was getting well. There seemed to be almost an infatuation in her case. The exhilaration of her spirits was at times so great as almost to overpower her. Often would she stand by the window admiring a glorious sunset, until she would be raised into a kind of ecstasy; her eye would kindle; a crimson glow would mount into her cheek, and she would indulge in some of her reveries about the glories of heaven and the spirits of her deceased sisters, partly uttering her fancies aloud, until turning and catching her mother's eye fixed painfully upon her, she would throw her arms round her neck, kiss away her tears, and sink exhausted on her bosom. The excitement over, she would resume her calmness, and converse on general topics. Among her writings are fragments hastily scrawled down at this time, showing

the vague aspirations of her spirit, and her vain attempts
to grasp those shadowy images that sometimes flit across
the poetic mind.

" Oh, for a something more than this,
    To fill the void within my breast ;
A sweet reality of bliss,
    A something bright, but unexpressed.

My spirit longs for something higher
    Than life's dull stream can e'er supply ;
Something to feed this inward fire,
    This spark, which never more can die.

I'd hold companionship with all
    Of pure, of noble, or divine ;
With glowing heart adoring fall,
    And kneel at Nature's sylvan shrine.

My soul is like a broken lyre,
    Whose loudest, sweetest chord is gore ;
A note, half trembling on the wire—
    A heart that wants an echoing tone.

When shall I find this shadowy bliss,
    This shapeless phantom of the mind ?
This something words can ne'er express,
    So vague, so faint, so undefined ?

Language ! thou never canst portray
    The fancies floating o'er my soul !
Thou ne'er canst chase the clouds away
    Which o'er my changing visions roll !"

And again—

" Oh, I have gazed on forms of light,
　　Till life seemed ebbing in a tear—
Till in that fleeting space of sight
　　Were merged the feelings of a year.

And I have heard the voice of song,
　　Till my full heart gushed wild and free,
And my rapt soul would float along
　　As if on waves of melody.

But while I glowed at beauty's glance,
　　I longed to feel a deeper thrill ;
And while I heard that dying strain,
　　I sighed for something sweeter still.

I have been happy, and my soul
　　Free from each sorrow, care, regret :
Yet even in these hours of bliss
　　I longed to find them happier yet.

Oft o'er the darkness of my mind
　　Some meteor thought has glanced at will ;
'Twas bright—but ever have I sighed
　　To find a fancy brighter still.

Why are these restless, vain desires,
　　Which always grasp at something more,
To feed the spirit's hidden fires,
　　Which burn unseen—unnoticed soar ?

Well might the heathen sage have known
　　That earth must fail the soul to bind ;
That life, and life's tame joys, alone
　　Could never chain the ethereal mind."

The above, as we have before observed, are mere fragments unfinished and uncorrected, and some of the verses have a vagueness incident to the mood of mind in which they were conceived and the haste with which they were penned; but in these lofty, indefinite aspirations of a young, half-schooled, and inexperienced mind, we see the early and impatient flutterings of a poetical genius, which, if spared, might have soared to the highest regions.

In a letter written to Miss Sedgwick during the autumn, she speaks of her health as having rapidly improved. "I am no longer afflicted by the cough, and mother feels it unnecessary now to speak to me as being ill; though my health is, and probably always will be, very delicate."— "And she really did appear better," observes her mother, " and even I, who had ever been nervously alive to every symptom of her disease, was deluded by those favorable appearances, and began to entertain a hope that she might yet recover, when another sudden attack of bleeding at the lungs convinced us of the fallacy of our hopes, and warned us to take every measure to ward off the severity of the climate in the coming winter. A consultation was held between her father and our favorite physician, and the result was that she was to keep within doors. This was indeed sad, but, after an evident struggle with her own mind, she submitted, with her accustomed good sense, to the decree. All that affection could suggest was done, to prevent the effects of this seclusion on her spirits." A cheerful room was allotted to her, commanding an agreeable prospect, and communicating, by folding-doors, to a commodious parlor; the temperature of the whole apartment was regulated by a thermometer. Hither her books, writing-table, drawing implements, and fancy work were transported. When once established in these winter-quarters, she became contented and cheerful. "She read and wrote," says her mother, "and amused herself with drawing and needlework. After spending as much time as I dare permit in the more serious studies in which she was engaged, she would unbend her mind with one of Scott's delightful novels, or play with her kitten; and at evening we were usually joined by our interesting friends, Mr. and Mrs. H. It is now a melancholy satisfaction to me to believe that she could not, in her state of health, be happier or more pleasantly situated. She was always charmed with the conversation of Mr. H., and followed him through all the mazes of philosophy with the greatest delight. She read Cousin with a high zest, and produced an abstract from it which gave a convincing proof that she understood the principles there laid down; after which she gave a complete analysis of the 'Introduction to the History of Philosophy,' by the same author. Her mind must have been deeply engrossed by these studies, yet it was not visible from her manner. During this short winter she accomplished what to many would have been the labor of years, yet there was no haste, no flurry; she pursued quietly her round of occupations, always cheer-

ful. The hours flew swiftly by; not a moment lagged.
I think she never spent a more happy winter than this,
with all its varied employments.

The following extract from a letter to one of her young
friends, gives an idea of her course of reading during this
winter; and how, in her precocious mind, the playful-
ness of the child mingled with the thoughtfulness of the
woman:—

"You ask me what I am . reading. Alas! book-worm
as I am, it makes me draw a long breath to contemplate
the books I have laid out for perusal. In the first place,
I am reading 'Condillac's Ancient History,' in French,
twenty-four volumes; 'Gibbon's Decline and Fall of the
Roman Empire,' in four large volumes. I have not quite
finished 'Josephus.' In my moments of recreation I am
poring over Scott's bewitching *novels.* I wish we could
give them some other name instead of *novels,* for they
certainly should not bear the same title with the thou-
sand-and-one productions of that class daily swarming
from the press. Do you think they ought? So pure, so
pathetic, so historical, and, above all, so true to human
nature! How beautifully he mingles the sad with the
grotesque, in such a manner that the opposite feelings
they excite harmonize perfectly with each other. His
works can be read over and over again, and every time
with a growing sense of their beauties. Do you read
French? If so, I wish we could read the same works
together. It would be a great pleasure to me at least,

and our mutual remarks might benefit each other. Supposing you will be pleased to hear of my amusements, however trifling, I will venture to name one, at the risk of lowering any great opinion you may have formed of my wisdom! A pet kitten! Yes, my dear Henrietta, a sweet little creature, with a graceful shape, playful temper, white breast, and dear little innocent eyes, which completely belie the reputed disposition of a *cat*. He is neither deceitful, ferocious, nor ungrateful, but is certainly the most rational being for an irrational one, I ever saw. He is now snugly lying in my lap, watching every movement of my pen with a quiet purr of contentment. Have you such a pet? I wish you had, that we might both play with them at the same time, sunset, for instance, and while so far distant, feel that we were enjoying ourselves in the selfsame way. You ask what I think of animal magnetism? My dear Hetty, I have not troubled my head about it. I hear of it from every quarter, and mentioned so often with contempt, that I have thought of it only as an absurdity. If I understand it rightly, the leading principle is the influence of one mind upon another; there is undoubtedly such an influence, to a reasonable degree, but as to throwing one into a magnetic sleep—presenting visions before their eyes of scenes passing afar off, it seems almost too ridiculous! Still it may all be *true!* A hundred years since, what would have been our feelings to see what is now here so common, a *steam-engine*, breathing fire and smoke, gliding

19

along with the rapidity of thought, and carrying at its *black heels* a train which a hundred men would fail to move. We know not but this apparent absurdity, this magnetism, may be a great and mysterious secret, which the course of time will reveal and adapt to important purposes. . . . . . What are you studying? Do you play? Do you draw? Please tell me everything. I wish I could form some picture of you to my mind's eye. It is so tormenting to correspond with a dear friend, and have no likeness of them in our fancy. I remember everything as it used to be, but time makes great changes! Now here comes my saucy kitten, and springs upon the table before me, as if he had a perfect right there. 'What do you mean, little puss? Come, sit for your portrait.' I hope, dear H., you will fully appreciate this painting, which I consider as my *chef-d'œuvre*, and preserve it as a faithful likeness of my inimitable cat. But do forgive me so much nonsense! But I feel that to you I can rattle off anything that comes uppermost. It is near night, and the sun is setting so beautifully after the long storm, that I could not sit here much longer, even if I had a whole page to fill. How splendid the moon must look on the bright waters of the Champlain this night! Good-by, good-by—love to all from all, and believe me, now as ever,

"Your sincere friend,

"MARGARET."

The following passages from her mother's memorandums touch upon matters of more solemn interest, which occasionally occupied her young mind :—

"During the whole of the preceding summer her mind had dwelt much upon the subject of religion. Much of her time was devoted to serious reflection, self-examination, and prayer. But she evidently shunned all conversation upon the subject. It was a theme she had always conversed upon with pleasure until *now*. This not only surprised but pained me. I was a silent but close and anxious observer of the operations of her mind, and saw that, with all her apparent cheerfulness she was ill at ease ; perfect silence was however maintained on both sides until the winter commenced, and brought us more closely together. Then her young heart again reposed itself, in confiding love, upon the bosom that heretofore had shared its every thought, and the subject became one of daily discussion. I found her mind perplexed and her ideas confused by points of doctrine which she could neither understand nor reconcile with her views of the justice and benevolence of God, as exhibited in the Scriptures. Her views of the Divine character and attributes had ever been of that elevated cast, which, while they raised her mind above all grosser things, sublimated and purified her feelings and desires, and prepared her for that bright and holy communion without which she could enjoy nothing. Her faith was of that character 'which casteth out fear.' It was sweet and soothing to depend upon Jesus for salvation. It was delightful to behold, in the all-imposing majesty of God, a kind and tender father, who pitied her infirmities, and on whose justice and benevolence she could rest for time and eternity. She had, during the summer, heard much disputation on the doctrinal points, which she had silently and carefully examined, and had been shocked at the position which many professing Christians had taken; she saw much inconsistency, much bitterness of spirit, on points which she had been taught to consider not essential to salvation; she saw that the spirit of persecution and uncharitableness, which pervaded many classes of Christians, had almost totally destroyed that bond of brotherhood which ought firmly to unite the followers of the humble Saviour; and she could not reconcile these feelings with her ideas of the Christian character. Her meekness and humility led her sometimes to doubt her own state. She felt that her religious duties were but too feebly performed, and that without divine assistance all her resolutions to be more faithful were vain. She often said, ' Mamma, I am far from right. I resolve and re-resolve, and yet remain the same.' I had shunned everything that savored of controversy, knowing her enthusiasm and extreme sensibility on the subject of religion; I dreaded the excitement it might create. But I now more fully explained, as well as I was able, the simple and divine truths of the Gospel, and held up to her view the beauty and benevolence of the Father's charac-

ter, and the unbounded love which could have devised
the atoning sacrifice; and advised her at present to avoid
controversial writings, and make a more thorough examination of the Scriptures, that she might found her
principles upon the evidences to be deduced from that
groundwork of our faith, unbiased by the opinions and
prejudices of *any man.* I represented to her that,
young as she was, while in feeble health, researches into
those knotty and disputed subjects would only confuse her mind; that there was enough of plain practical religion to be gathered from the Bible; and urged
the importance of frequent and earnest prayer, which,
with God's blessing, would compose the agitation of
her mind, which I considered as essential to her inward
peace."

On one occasion, while perusing Lockhart's "Life of
Scott," with great interest, her mother ventured to sound
her feelings upon the subject of literary fame, and asked
her whether she had no ambition to have her name go
down to posterity. She took her mother's hand with
enthusiasm, kissed her cheek, and, retiring to the other
room, in less than an hour returned with the following
lines:

TO DIE AND BE FORGOTTEN.

A few short years will roll along,
  With mingled joy and pain,
Then shall I pass—a broken tone!
  An echo of a strain!

Then shall I fade away from life,
  Like cloud-tints from the sky,
When the breeze sweeps their surface o'er,
  And they are lost for aye.

The world will laugh, and weep, and sing,
  As gayly as before,
But cold and silent I shall be—
  As I have been no more.

The haunts I loved, the flowers I nursed,
  Will bloom as sweetly still,
But other hearts and other hands
  My vacant place shall fill.

And even mighty love must fail
  To bind my memory here—
Like fragrance round the faded rose,
  'Twill perish with the year.

The soul may look, with fervent hope,
  To worlds of future bliss ;
But oh, how saddening to the heart
  To be forgot in this !

How many a noble mind hath shrunk
  From death without a name ;
Hath looked beyond his shadowy realm,
  And lived and died for Fame ?

Could we not view the darksome grave
  With calmer, steadier eye,
If conscious that a world's regret
  Would seek us where we lie ?

Faith points, with mild, confiding glance,
   To realms of bliss above,
Where peace and joy and justice reign,
   And never-dying love ;

But still our earthly feelings cling
   Around this bounded spot ;
There is a something burns within
   Which will not be forgot.

It cares not for a gorgeous hearse,
   For waving torch and plume ;
For pealing hymn, funereal verse,
   Or richly sculptured tomb ;

But it would live undimmed and fresh,
   When flickering life departs ;
Would find a pure and honored grave
   Embalmed in kindred hearts.

Who would not brave a life of tears
   To win an honored name,
One sweet and heart-awakening tone
   From the silver trump of Fame ?

To be, when countless years have past,
   The good man's glowing theme ?
To be—but I—what right have I
   To this bewildering dream ?

Oh, it is vain, and worse than vain,
   To dwell on thoughts like these ;
I, a frail child, whose feeble frame
   Already knows disease !

Who, ere another spring may dawn,
    Another summer bloom,
May, like the flowers of autumn, lie
    A tenant of the tomb.

Away, away, presumptuous thought !
    I will not dwell on thee !
For what, alas ! am I to Fame,
    And what is Fame to me ?

Let all these wild and longing thoughts
    With the dying year expire,
And I will nurse within my breast
    A purer, holier fire !

Yes, I will seek my mind to win
    From all these dreams of strife,
And toil to write my name within
    The glorious Book of Life.

Then shall old Time, who, rolling on,
    Impels me towards the tomb,
Prepare for me a glorious crown,
    Through endless years to bloom.

December, 1837.

The confinement to the house, in a graduated temperature, the round of cheerful occupations, and the unremitting care taken of her, produced a visible melioration of
her symptoms. Her cough gradually subsided, the morbid irritability of her system, producing often an unnatural flow of spirits, was quieted ; as usual, she looked
forward to spring as the genial and delightful season that
was to restore her to perfect health and freedom.

Christmas was approaching, which had ever been a

time of social enjoyment in the family ; as it drew near, however, the remembrance of those lost from the fireside circle was painfully felt by Mrs. Davidson. Margaret saw the gloom on her mother's brow, and, kissing her, exclaimed, "Dear mother, do not let us waste our present happiness in useless repining. You see I am well, and you are more comfortable, and dear father is in good health and spirits. Let us enjoy the present hour, and banish vain regrets!" Having given this wholesome advice, she tripped off with a light step to prepare Christmas presents for the servants, which were to be distributed by St. Nicholas, or Santa Claus, in the old traditional way. Every animated being, rational or ir- rational, must share her liberality on that day of festivity and joy. Her Jenny, a little bay pony on which she had taken many healthful and delightful rides, must have a gayer blanket and an extra allowance of oats. "On Christmas morning," says her mother, "she woke with the first sound of the old house-clock striking the hour of five, and twining her arms round my neck (for during this winter she shared my bed), and kissing me again and again, exclaimed,—

> "'Wake, mother, wake to youthful glee,
>   The golden sun is dawning ;'

then slipping a piece of paper into my hand, she sprang out of bed, and danced about the carpet, her kitten in her arms, with all the sportive glee of childhood. When I gazed upon her young face, so bright, so animated, and beautiful, beaming with innocence and love, and thought that perhaps this was the last anniversary of her Saviour's birth she might spend on earth, I could not suppress my emotions; I caught her to my bosom in an agony of tenderness, while she, all unconscious of the nature of my feelings, returned my caresses with playful fondness." The following verses were contained in the above-mentioned paper:—

TO MY MOTHER AT CHRISTMAS.

WAKE, mother, wake to hope and glee,
  The golden sun is dawning !
Wake, mother, wake, and hail with me
  This happy Christmas morning !

Each eye is bright with pleasure's glow,
  Each lip is laughing merrily ;
A smile hath past o'er Winter's brow,
  And the very snow looks cheerily.

Hark to the voice of the awakened day,
  To the sleigh-bells gayly ringing,
While a thousand, thousand happy hearts
  Their Christmas lays are singing.

'Tis a joyous hour of mirth and love,
  And my heart is overflowing !
Come, let us raise our thoughts above,
  While pure and fresh and glowing.

'Tis the happiest day of the rolling year,
  But it comes in a robe of mourning,
Nor light, nor life, nor bloom is here
  Its icy shroud adorning.

It comes when all around is dark,
  'Tis meet it so should be,
For its joy is the joy of the happy heart,
  The spirit's jubilee.

It does not need the bloom of Spring,
  Or Summer's light and gladness,
For Love has spread her beaming wing
  O'er Winter's brow of sadness.

'Twas thus He came, beneath a cloud
  His spirit's light concealing,
No crown of earth, no kingly robe
  His heavenly power revealing.

His soul was pure, his mission love,
  His aim a world's redeeming ;
To raise the darkened soul above
  Its wild and sinful dreaming.

With all his Father's power and love,
  The cords of guilt to sever ;
To ope a sacred fount of light,
  Which flows, shall flow forever.

Then we shall hail the glorious day,
  The spirit's new creation,
And pour our grateful feelings forth,
  A pure and warm libation.

Wake, mother, wake to chastened joy,
  The golden sun is dawning !
Wake, mother, wake, and hail with me
  This happy Christmas morning.

"The last day of the year 1837 arrived. 'Mamma,' said she, 'will you sit up with me to-night until after 12 ?' I looked inquiringly. She replied, 'I wish to bid farewell to the present, and to welcome the coming year.' After the family retired, and we had seated ourselves by a cheerful fire to spend the hours which would intervene until the year 1838 should dawn upon us, she was serious, but not sad, and as if she had nothing more than usual upon her mind, took some light sewing in her hand, and so interested me by her conversation that I scarcely noticed the flight of time. At half-past 11 she handed me a book, pointing to some interesting article to amuse me, then took her seat at the writing-table, and composed the piece on the departure of the old year 1837 and the commencement of the new one 1838. When she had finished the Farewell, except the last verse, it wanted a few minutes of 12. She rested her arms in silence upon the table, apparently absorbed in meditation. The clock struck—a sort of deep thought passed over her expressive face—she remained solemn and silent until the last tone had ceased to vibrate, when she again resumed her pen and wrote. The bell had ceased. When the clock struck, I arose from my seat and stood leaning over the back of her chair, with a mind deeply solemnized by a scene so new and interesting. The words flowed rapidly from her pen, without haste or confusion, and at 1 o'clock we were quietly in bed."

We again subjoin the poem alluded to, trusting that

these effusions, which are so intimately connected with
her personal history, will be read with greater interest
when given in conjunction with the scenes and circumstances which prompted them.

ON THE DEPARTURE OF THE YEAR 1837 AND THE COM-
MENCEMENT OF 1838.

HARK ! to the house-clock's measured chime,
    As it cries to the startled ear,
" A dirge for the soul of departing Time,
    A requiem for the year ! "

Thou art passing away to the mighty past,
    Where thy countless brethren sleep,
Till the great Archangel's trumpet-blast
    Shall waken land and deep.

Oh, the lovely and beautiful things that lie
    On thy cold and motionless breast !
Oh, the tears, the rejoicings, the smiles, the sighs,
    Departing with thee to their rest.

Thou wert ushered to life amid darkness and gloom,
    But the cold icy cloud passed away,
And Spring, in her verdure and freshness and bloom,
    Touched with glory thy mantle of gray.

The flow'rets burst forth in their beauty—the trees
    In their exquisite robes were arrayed,
But thou glidest along, and the flower and the leaf
    At the sound of thy footsteps decayed.

And fairer young blossoms were blooming alone,
  And they died at the glance of thine eye,
But a life was within which should rise o'er their own,
  And a spirit thou could'st not destroy.

Thou hast folded thy pinions, thy race is complete,
  And fulfilled the Creator's behest,
Then, adieu to thee, year of our sorrows and joys,
  And peaceful and long be thy rest.

Farewell! for thy truth-written record is full,
  And the page weeps for sorrow and crime;
Farewell! for the leaf hath shut down on the past,
  And concealed the dark annals of time.

The bell! it hath ceased with its iron tongue
  To ring on the startled ear,
The dirge o'er the grave of the lost one is rung,
  All hail to the new-born year!

    All hail to the new-born year!
    To the child of hope and fear!
    He comes on his car of state,
    And weaves our web of fate;
  And he opens his robe to receive us all,
  And we live or die, and we rise or fall,
    In the arms of the new-born year!

    Hope! spread thy soaring wings!
    Look forth on the boundless sea,
  And trace thy bright and beautiful things
    On the veil of the great To Be.

Build palaces broad as the sky,
　And store them with treasures of light,
Let exquisite visions bewilder the eye,
　And illumine the darkness of night.

We are gliding fast from the buried year,
　And the present is no more ;
But, Hope, we will borrow thy sparkling gear,
　And shroud the future o'er.

Our tears and sighs shall sleep
　In the grave of the silent Past ;
We will raise up flowers—nor weep—
　That the air-hues may not last.

We will dream our dreams of joy,
　Ah ! Fear ! why darken the scene ?
Why sprinkle that ominous tear
　My beautiful visions between ?

Hath not Sorrow swift wings of her own,
　That thou must assist in her flight ?
Is not daylight too rapidly gone,
　That thou must urge onward the night ?

Ah ! leave me to fancy, to hope,
　For grief will too quickly be here ;
Ah ! leave me to shadow forth figures of light,
　In the mystical robe of the year.

'Tis true they may never assume
　The substance of pleasure—the real—
But believe me our purest of joy
　Consists in the vague—the ideal.

> Then away to the darksome cave,
>> With thy sisters, the sigh and the tear ;
> We will drink, in the crystal wave,
>> The health of the new-born year.

" She had been for some time thinking of a subject for a poem, and the next day, which was the 1st of January, came to me in great perplexity and asked my advice. I had long desired that she would direct her attention to the beautiful and sublime narratives of the Old Testament, and now proposed that she should take the Bible and examine it with that view. After an hour or two spent in research she remarked that there were many, very many subjects of deep and thrilling interest ; but, if she now should make a failure, her discouragement would be such as to prevent her from ever making another attempt. ' I am now,' she said, ' trying my wings ; I will take a lighter subject at first : if I succeed, I will then write a more perfect poem, founded upon Sacred History.' "

She accordingly took as a theme a prose tale, in a current work of the day, and wrote several pages with a flowing pen, but soon threw them by, dissatisfied. It was irksome to employ the thoughts and fancies of another, and to have to adapt her own to the plan of the author. She wanted something original. "After some farther effort," says Mrs. Davidson, " she came to me out of spirits and in tears. ' Mother,' said she, ' I must give it up after all.' I asked the reason, and then remarked that as she had already so many labors upon her hands, and was still feeble, it might be the wisest course. 'O mother,' said she, 'that is not the reason; my head and my heart are full; poetic images are crowding upon my brain, but every subject has been monopolized : "There is nothing new under the sun."' I said, 'My daughter, that others have written upon a subject is not an objection. The most eminent writers do not always choose what is new.' 'Mother, dear mother, what can I say upon a theme which has been touched by the greatest men of this or some other age?—I, a mere child; it is absurd in me to think of it.' She dropped beside me on the sofa, laid her head upon my bosom, and sobbed violently. I wiped the tears from her face, while my own were fast flowing, and strove to soothe the tumult of her mind. . . . . When we were both more calm, I said, 'Margaret, I had hoped that during this winter you would not have commenced or applied yourself to any important work ; but, if you feel in that way, I will not urge you to resign an occupation which gives you such exquisite enjoyment.'"

Mrs. Davidson then went on to show to her that, notwithstanding the number of poets that had written, the themes and materials for poetry are inexhaustible. By degrees Margaret became composed; took up a book and read. The words of her mother dwelt in her mind. In a few days she brought her mother the introduction to a projected poem to be called "Leonore." Mrs. David-

20

son was touched at finding the remarks she had made for the purpose of soothing the agitation of her daughter had served to kindle her imagination, and were poured forth with eloquence in those verses. The excitement continued, and the poem of "Leonore" was completed, corrected, and copied into her book by the 1st of March; having written her plan in prose at full length, containing about the same number of lines as the poem. "During its progress," says Mrs. Davidson, " when fatigued with writing, she would take her kitten and recline upon the sofa, asking me to relate to her some of the scenes of the last war. Accordingly I would while away our solitude by repeating anecdotes of that period ; and before " Leonore " was completed she had advanced several pages in a prose tale, the scene of which was laid upon Lake Champlain during the last war. She at the same time executed faces and figures in crayon which would not have disgraced the pencil of an artist. Her labors were truly immense. Yet a stranger coming occasionally to the house would hardly observe that she had any pressing avocations."

The following are extracts from a rough draught of a letter written to Miss Sedgwick about this time :—

My dear Madam,—

I wish I could express to you my pleasure on receiving your kind and affectionate letter. So far from considering myself neglected by your silence, I felt it a great

privilege to be permitted to write to you, and knew that
I ought not to expect a regular answer to every letter,
even while I was longing, day after day, to receive this
gratifying token of remembrance. Unless you had witnessed, I fear you would hardly believe my extravagant
delight on reading the dear little folded paper so expressive of your kind recollection. I positively danced for
joy, bestowed a thousand caresses upon everybody and
everything I loved, dreamed of you all night, and arose
next morning (with a heart full) to answer your letter;
but was prevented by indisposition, and have not been
able until now to perform a most pleasing duty by ac-
knowledging its receipt. My health during the past
winter has been much better than we had anticipated.
It is true I have been, with dear mother, entirely confined to the house; but being able to read, write, and
perform all my usual employments, I feel that I have
much more reason to be thankful for the blessings continued to me, than to repine because a few have been denied. But spring is now here in name, if not in reality;
and I can assure you my heart bounds at the thought of
once more escaping from my confinement, and breathing
the pure air of heaven, without fearing a blight or a consumption in every breeze. Spring! What pleasure does
that magic syllable convey to the heart of an invalid,
laden with sweet promises, and bringing before his mind
visions of liberty, which those who are always free cannot enjoy. Thus do I dream of summer I may never see,

and make myself happy for hours in anticipating pleasures
I may never share.   It is an idle employment, and little
calculated to sweeten disappointment.   But it has opened
to me many sources of delight otherwise unknown ; and
when out of humor with the present, I have only to send
fancy flower-gathering in the future, and I find myself
fully repaid.   Dear mother's health has also been much
better than we had feared, and her ill turns less frequent
and severe.   She sits up most of the day, walks around
the lower part of the house, and enjoys her book and her
pen as much as ever. . . . .   You speak of your intercourse with Mrs. Jameson.   It must indeed be an exquisite pleasure to be intimately associated with a mind
like hers.   I have never seen anything but extracts from
her writings, but must obtain and read them.   I suppose
the world is anxiously looking for her next volume. . . . .
We have been reading Lockhart's "Life of Scott."   Is it
not a deeply interesting work?   In what a beautiful light
it represents the character of that great and good man.
No one can read his life or his works without loving and
venerating him.   As to " the waters of Helicon," we have
but a few niggardly streams in this, our matter-of-fact village ; and father in his medical capacity has forbidden my
partaking of them as freely as I could wish.   But no matter, they have been frozen up, and will flow in "streams
more salubrious " beneath the milder sky of spring.

In all her letters we find a solicitude about her mother's

health, rather than about her own, and indeed it was difficult to say which was most precarious.

The following extract from a poem written about this time to "Her Mother on her Fiftieth Birthday," presents a beautiful portrait, and does honor to the filial hand that drew it :—

> ' Yes, mother, fifty years have fled,
>   With rapid footsteps, o'er thy head;
>   Have past with all their motley train,
>   And left thee on thy couch of pain!
>   How many smiles and sighs and tears,
>   How many hopes and doubts and fears
>   Have vanished with that lapse of years.
>
>   Oh, that we all could look, like thee,
>   Back on that dark and tideless sea,
>   And 'mid its varied records find
>   A heart at ease with all mankind,
>   A firm and self-approving mind.
>   Grief that had broken hearts less fine
>   Hath only served to strengthen thine;
>
>   Time, that doth chill the fancy's play,
>   Hath kindled thine with purer ray;
>   And stern disease, whose icy dart
>   Hath power to chill the breaking heart,
>   Hath left thine warm with love and truth
>   As in the halcyon days of youth."

The following letter was written on the 26th of March, to a female cousin resident in New York :—

DEAR KATE :—

This day I am fifteen, and you can, you will readily pardon and account for the absurd flights of my pen, by supposing that my tutelary spirits, Nonsense and Folly, have assembled around the being of their creation, and claimed the day as exclusively their own ; then I pray you to lay to their account all that I have already scribbled, and believe that, uninfluenced by these grinning deities, I can think and feel and love, as I love you, with all warmth and sincerity of heart. Do you remember how we used to look forward to sweet fifteen, as the pinnacle of human happiness, the golden age of existence ? You have but lately passed that milestone in the highway of life ; I have just reached it, but I find myself no better satisfied to stand still than before, and look forward to the continuance of my journey with the same ardent longing I felt at fourteen.

Ah, Kate, here we are, two young travellers, starting forth upon our long pilgrimage, and knowing not whither it may conduct us ! *You* some months my superior in age, and many years in acquaintance with society, in external attractions, and all those accomplishments necessary to form an elegant woman. *I*, knowing nothing of life but from books, and a small circle of friends, who love me as I love them ; looking upon the *past* as a faded dream, which I shall have time enough to study and expound when old age and sorrow come on ; upon the *present* as a nursling,—a preparative for the *future;* and upon that future, as what? a mighty whirlpool, of hopes and fears, of bright anticipations and bitter disappointments, into which I shall soon plunge, and find there, in common with the rest of the world, my happiness or misery. . . . . .

The following, to a young friend, was also written on the 26th of March :—

My Dear H.,—

You must know that winter has come and gone, and neither mother nor myself have felt a single breeze which could not force its way through the thick walls of our little dwelling. Do you not think I am looking gladly forward to April and May, as the lovely sisters who are to unlock the doors of our prison-house, and give us once more to the free enjoyment of Nature, without fearing a blight or a consumption in every breath? And now for another, and even more delightful anticipation—your visit! Are you indeed coming? And when are you coming? Do answer the first, that I may for once have the pleasure of framing delightful visions without finding them dashed to the ground by the iron hand of Reality, and the last, that I may not expect you too soon, and thus subject myself to all the bitterness of "hope deferred." Come, for I have so much to say to you, that I cannot possibly contain it until summer; and come quickly, unless you are willing to account for my wasted

time as well as your own, for I shall do little else but
dream of you and your visit until the time of your arrival.
You cannot imagine how those few words in your little
good for nothing letter have completely upset my wonted
gravity. Do not disappoint me. It is true, mother and
I are both feeble and unable to go out with you and
show you the lions of our little village, but if warm wel-
comes can atone for the want of ceremony, you shall have
them in abundance ; but it seems to me that I shall want
to pin you down in a chair, and do nothing but look at
you from morning till night. As to coming to Plattsburgh, I think if we cannot do so in the spring (which is
doubtful), we certainly shall in the course of the summer. Brother M. wrote to me yesterday, saying that he
would spend the month of August in the country, and if
nothing occurred to prevent, we would take our delightful trip by the way of Lake George. Oh, it will be so
pleasant! but my anticipations are now all bent upon a
nearer object. Do not allow a slight impediment to destroy them. We expect in May to move to Saratoga.
We shall then have a more convenient house, better society, and the benefit of a school in which I can practise
music and drawing, without being obliged to attend reg-
ularly. We shall then be a few miles nearer to you, and
at present even that seems something desirable to me. I
have read and own three volumes of "Scott's Life," and
was much disappointed to find that it was not finished
in these three, but concluded the remainder had not yet

come out. Are the five volumes all? It is indeed a deeply interesting work. I am very fond of biography, for surely there can be nothing more delightful or instructive than to trace in the infancy and youth of every noble mind the germs of its future greatness. Have you read a work called "Letters from Palmyra," by Mr. Ware of New York? I have not yet seen it, but intend to do so soon. It is written in the character of a citizen of Rome at that early period, and it is said to be a lively picture of the manners and customs of the Imperial City, and still more of the magnificence of Palmyra and its splendid queen, Zenobia. It also contains a beautiful story. I have lately been re-perusing many of Scott's novels, and intend to finish them. Was ever anything half so fascinating? Oh, how I long to have you here and tell you all these little things in person. Do write to me immediately, and tell me when we may expect you. I shall open your next with a beating heart. Do excuse all the blunders and scrawls of this hasty letter. You must receive it as a proof of friendship, for to a stranger, or one who I thought would look upon it with a cold and critical eye, I certainly should not send it. I believe you and I have entered into a tacit agreement to forgive any little mistakes which the other may chance to commit.

Croyez moi ma chère amie votre, MARGUERITE.

The spirits of this most sensitive little being became more and more excited with the opening of spring. "She watched," says her mother, "the putting forth of the tender grass and the young blossoms as the period which was to liberate her from captivity. She was pleased with everybody and everything. She loved everything in Nature, both animate and inanimate, with a warmth of affection which displayed the benevolence of her own heart. She felt that she was well, and oh! the bright dreams and imaginings, the cloudless future, presented to her ardent mind—all was sunny and gay."

The following letter is highly expressive of the state of her feelings at that period.

"A few days since, my dearest cousin, I received your affectionate letter, and if my heart smote me at the sight of the well-known superscription, you may imagine how unmercifully it thumped on reading a letter so full of affection, and so entirely devoid of reproach for my unkindly negligence. I can assure you, my dear coz., you could have found no better way of striking home to my heart the conviction of my error; and I resolved that hour, that moment, to lay my confessions at your feet, and sue for forgiveness; I knew you were too gentle to refuse. But alas for human resolves! We were that afternoon expecting brother M. Dear brother! And how could I collect my floating thoughts and curl myself up into a corner with pen, ink, and paper before me, when my heart was flying away over the sand-hills of this unromantic region to meet and embrace and welcome home the wanderer. If it can interest you, picture to yourself the little scene,—mother and I breathless with expectation, gazing from the window, in mute suspense, and listening to the "*phiz, phiz*" of the great steam-engine. Then when we caught a rapid glance of his trim little figure, how we bounded away over chairs-sofas, and kittens, to bestow in reality the greeting fancy had so often given him. Oh! what is so delightful as to welcome a friend! Well, three days have passed like a dream, and he is gone again. I am seated at my little table by the fire. Mother is sewing beside me. Puss is slumbering on the hearth, and nothing external remains to convince us of the truth of that bright sunbeam which had suddenly broken upon our quiet retreat, and departed like a vision as suddenly. When shall we have the pleasure of welcoming *you* thus, my beloved cousin? Your flying call of last summer was but an aggravation. Oh! may all good angels watch over you and all you love, shake the dew of health from their balmy wings upon your smiling home, and waft you hither, cheerful and happy, to sojourn awhile with the friends who love you so dearly! All hail to spring, the bright, the blooming, the renovating spring! Oh! I am so happy—I feel a lightness at my heart and a vigor in my frame that I have rarely felt. If I speak, my voice forms itself into a laugh. If I look forward, everything seems bright before me. If I look back, memory calls up what is pleasant, and my greatest desire is that my pen could fling a ray of sunshine over this scribbled page and infuse into your heart some of the cheerfulness of my own. I have been confined to the house all winter, as it was thought the best and only way of restoring my health. Now my symptoms are all better, and I am looking forward to next month and its blue skies with the most childish impatience. By the way, I am not to be called a child any more; for yesterday I was *fifteen!* what say you to that? I feel quite like an old woman, and think of putting on caps and spectacles next month."

It was during the same exuberance of happy feeling, with the delusive idea of confirmed health and the anticipation of bright enjoyments, that she broke forth like a bird into the following strain of melody :—

> " Oh, my bosom is throbbing with joy,
>   With a rapture too full to express ;
> From within and without I am blest,
>   And the world, like myself, I would bless.
>
> All Nature looks fair to my eye,
>   From beneath and around and above,
> Hope smiles in the clear azure sky,
>   And the broad earth is glowing with love.
>
> I stand on the threshold of life,
>   On the shore of its wide rolling sea ;
> I have heard of its storms and its strife,
>   But all things are tranquil to me.
>
> There's a veil o'er the future—'tis bright
>   As the wing of a spirit of air,
> And each form of enchantment and light
>   Is trembling in iris-hues there.

I turn to the world of affection,
  And warm, glowing treasures are mine ;
To the past, and my fond recollection
  Gathers roses from memory's shrine.

But oh, there's a fountain of joy
  More rich than a kingdom beside,
It is holy—death cannot destroy
  The flow of its heavenly tide.

'Tis the love that is gushing within,
  It would bathe the whole world in its light ;
The cold stream of time shall not quench it,
  The dark frown of woe shall not blight.

These visions of pleasure may vanish,
  These bright dreams of youth disappear,
Disappointment each air hue may banish,
  And drown each frail joy in a tear.

I may plunge in the billows of life,
  I may taste of its dark cup of woe,
I may weep, and the sad drops of grief
  May blend with the waves as they flow.

I may dream, till reality's shadow
  O'er the light form of fancy is cast ;
I may hope, until hope, too, despairing,
  Has crept—to the grave of the Past.

But though the wild waters surround me,
  Misfortune, temptation, and sin,
Though Fear be about and beyond me,
  And Sorrow's dark shadow within.

Though Age, with an icy cold finger,
  May stamp his pale seal on my brow—
Still, still in my bosom shall linger
  The glow that is warming it now.

Youth will vanish, and Pleasure, gay charmer,
  May depart on the wings of to-day,
But that spot in my heart shall grow warmer,
  As year after year rolls away."

"While her spirits were thus light and gay," says Mrs. Davidson, "from the prospect of returning health, my more mature judgment told me that those appearances might be deceptive—that even now the destroyer might be making sure his work of destruction; but she really seemed better; the cough had subsided, her step was buoyant, her face glowed with animation, her eye was bright, and love, boundless, universal love, seemed to fill her young heart. Every symptom of her disease assumed a more favorable cast. Oh, how my heart swelled with the mingled emotions of hope, doubt, and gratitude. Our hopes of her ultimate recovery seemed to be founded upon reason, yet her father still doubted the propriety of our return to Lake Champlain; and as Saratoga held out many more advantages than Ballston as a temporary residence, he decided to spend the ensuing year or two there; and then we might perhaps, without much risk, return to our much-loved and long-deserted home on the banks of the Saranac. Accordingly a house was taken and every preparation made for our removal to Saratoga

on the first of May.   Margaret was pleased with the arrangement."

The following playful extract of a letter to her brother
in New York, exhibits her feelings on the prospect of
their change of residence :—-

"I now most humbly avail myself of your most gracious
permission to scribble you a few lines in token of my everlasting love.   'This is to inform you I am very well, hoping these few lines will find you in possession of the same
blessing'—notwithstanding the blue streaks that flitted
over your pathway a few days after you left us.   Perhaps
it was occasioned by remorse at the cruelty of your parting speech, perhaps it was the reflection of a bright blue
eye upon the deep waters of your soul; but let the cause
be what it may,—'black spirits or white, blue spirits or
gray,'—I hope the effect has entirely disappeared, and
you are no longer tinged with its most doleful shadow.
A blue sky, a blue eye, or the blue dye of the violet, are
all undeniably beautiful, but this tint when transferred
from the works of Nature to the brow of man, or the
stockings of woman, becomes a thing to ridicule or weep
at.   May your spirits henceforth, my dear brother, be
preserved from this ill-omened influence, and may your
feet and ankles never be graced with garments of a hue
so repulsive.   O brother, we are all in the heat of moving;
we, I say; you will account for the use of that personal
pronoun on the authority of the old proverb, 'What a
dust we flies raise,' for, to be frank with you, I have little

or nothing to do with it, but poor mother is over head
and ears in boxes, bedclothes, carpets, straw, and discussions.   Our hall is already filled with the fruits of her
labors and perseverance, in the shape of certain blue
chests, carpet-cases, trunks, boxes, &c., all ready for a
move.   Dear mother is head, hand, and feet for the whole
machine ; our *two helps* being nothing but cranks, which
turn when you touch them, and cease their rotary movement when the force is withdrawn.   Heigho.   We miss
our good C——, with her quick invention and helpful
hand. . . . . O my dear brother, I am anticipating
so much pleasure next summer, I hope it will not all
prove a dream.   It will be so delightful when you come
up in August and bring cousin K—— with you ; tell her
I am calculating upon this pleasure with all my powers
of fore-enjoyment—tell her also that I am waiting most
impatiently for that annihilating letter of hers, and if it
does not come soon, I shall send her another cannonade,
ere she has recovered the stunning effects of the first.
Oh dear! I have written you a most dis-understandable
letter, and now you must excuse me, as I have declared
war against M——, and after mending my pen, must collect all my scattered ideas into a fleet, and launch them
for a combat upon a whole sea of ink."

"The exuberance of her spirit," says her mother, " as
the spring advanced, and she was enabled once more to
take exercise in the open air, displayed itself in everything.   Her heart was overflowing with thankfulness and

love. Every fine day in the latter part of April she either rode on horseback or drove out in a carriage. All Nature looked lovely to her; not a tree or shrub but conveyed some poetical image or moral lesson to her mind. The moment, however, that she began to take daily exercise in the open air, I again heard with agony the prophetic cough. I felt that all was over! She thought that she had taken cold, and our friends were of the same opinion. 'It was a slight cold which would vanish beneath the mild influence of spring.' I, however, feared that her father's hopes might have blinded his judgment, and upon my own responsibility consulted a skilful physician, who had on many former occasions attended her. She was not aware of my present alarm, or that the physician was now consulted. He managed in a playful manner to feel her pulse, without her suspicions. After he had left the room, 'Madam,' said he, ' it is useless to hold out any false hopes; your daughter has a seated consumption, which is, I fear, beyond the reach of medical skill. There is no hope in the case; make her as happy and as comfortable as you can; let her enjoy riding in pleasant weather, but her walks must be given up; walking is too great an exertion for her.' With an aching heart I returned to the lovely unconscious victim, and found her tying on her hat for a ramble. I gently tried to dissuade her from going. She caught my eye, and read there a tale of grief, which she could not understand, and I could not explain. As soon as I dared trust my voice,

21

I said, 'My dear Margaret, nothing has happened, only I have just been speaking with Dr. ——, respecting you, and he advises that you give up walking altogether. Knowing how much you enjoy it, I am pained to mention this, for I know that it will be a great privation.' 'Why, mamma,' she exclaimed, ' this cold is wearing off ; may I not walk then ?' 'The Doctor thinks you should make no exertion of that kind, but riding in fine weather may have a happy effect.' She stood and gazed upon my face long and earnestly ; then untied her hat and sat down, apparently ruminating upon what had passed ; she asked no questions, but an expression of thoughtfulness clouded her brow during the rest of the day. It was settled that she was to ride out in fine weather, but not to walk out at all, and in a day or two she seemed to have forgotten the circumstance altogether. The return of the cough and profuse night-perspirations too plainly told me her doom ; but I still clung to the hope, that, as she suffered no pain, she might, by tender, judicious treatment, continue yet for years. I urged her to remit her labors ; she saw how much my heart was in the request, and promised to comply with my wishes. On the first of May we removed to Saratoga. One short half hour in the railroad car completed the journey, and she arrived, fresh, cheerful, and blooming, in her appearance, such an effect had the excitement of pleasure upon her lovely face."

On the day we left Ballston she wrote a "Parting Word" to Mrs. H., who had been one of our most intimate and affectionate visitors throughout the winter, and whose husband had assisted her much in her studies of moral philosophy, as well as delighted her by his varied and instructive conversation.

A PARTING WORD TO MY DEAR MRS. H.

BALLSTON SPA, *April* 30, 1838.

AT length the awful morn hath come,
  The parting hour is nigh,
And I sit down 'mid dust and gloom,
  To bid you brief "good-bye."

Each voice to fancy's listening ear
  Repeats the doleful cry,
And the bare walls and sanded floor
  Reëcho back "good-bye."

So must it be ! but many a thought
  Comes crowding on my mind,
Of the dear friends, the happy hours,
  The joys we leave behind.

How we shall miss your cheerful face,
  Forever bright and smiling,
And your sweet voice so often heard
  Our weary hours beguiling !

How shall we miss the kindly hearts,
  Which none can know unloving,
Whose thoughts and feelings none can **read,**
  Nor find his own improving !

And he, whose converse, hour by hour,
   Hath lent old Time new pinions,
Whose hand hath drawn the shadowy veil
   From Wisdom's broad dominions.

Whose voice hath poured forth priceless gems,
   Scarce conscious that he taught,
Whose mind of broad, of loftiest reach,
   Hath showered down thought on thought.

True, we may meet with many a dear
   And cherished friend, but yet
Oft shall we cast a backward glance
   Of wistful—vain regret.

When evening spreads her sombre veil,
   To fold the slumbering earth,
When our small circle closes round
   The humble, social hearth,—

Oft shall we dream of hours gone by,
   And con these moments o'er,
Till we half bend our ears to catch
   Your footsteps at the door,
And then turn back and sigh to think
   We hear those steps no more !

But though these dismal thoughts arise,
   Hope makes me happy still;
There is a drop of comfort lurks
   In every draught of ill!

By pain and care each joy of earth
   More exquisite is made,
And when we meet, the parting grief
   Shall doubly be o'erpaid.

In disappointments deep too quick
   Our fairest prospects drown ;
Let not this hope which blooms so bright,
   Be withered at his frown !

Come, and a mother's pallid cheek
   Shall brighten at your smile,
And her poor frame, so faint and weak,
   Forget its pains the while.

Come, and a glad and happy heart
   Shall give the welcome kiss,
And puss shall purr, and frisk, and mew,
   In token of her bliss.

Come ! and behold how I improve
   In dusting—cleaning—sweeping,
And I will hear, with patient ear,
   Your lectures on house-keeping.

And now, may all good angels guard
   Your path, where'er it lie,
May peace reign monarch in your breast,
   And gladness in your eye.

And may the dews of health descend
   On him you cherish best,
To his worn frame their influence lend,
   And calm each nerve to rest!

And may we meet again ! nor feel
   The parting hour so nigh ;
Peace, love, and happiness to all,
   Once more—once more " good-bye ! "

"She interested herself," continued Mrs. Davidson, "more than I had anticipated in the arrangement of our new habitation and in forming plans of future enjoyment with our friends, when they should visit us; I exerted myself to please her taste in everything, although she was prohibited from making the slightest physical exertion herself. The house settled, then came the flower-garden, in which she spent more time than I thought prudent; but she was so happy while thus engaged, and the weather being fine, and the gardener disposed to gratify her and carry all her little plans into effect, I, like a weak mother, wanted resolution to interfere, and have always reproached myself for it, although not conscious that it was an injury at the time. Her brother had invited her to return to New York with him when he came to visit us in June, and she was now impatiently counting the days until his arrival. Her feelings are portrayed in a letter to her young friend H."

SARATOGA, June 1, 1838.

JUNE is at last with us, my dear cousin, and the blue-eyed goddess could not have looked upon the green bosom of her mother earth, attired in a lovelier or more enchanting robe. I am seated by an open window, and the breeze, laden with the perfumes of the blossoms and opening leaves, just lifts the edge of my sheet, and steals with the gentlest footsteps imaginable to fan my cheek and forehead. The grass, tinged with the deepest and freshest green, is waving beneath its influence; the birds are singing their sweetest songs; and as I look into the depths of the clear blue sky the rich tints appear to flit higher and higher as I gaze, till my eye seems searching into immeasurable distance. Oh! such a day as this, it is a luxury to breathe. I feel as if I could frisk and gambol like my kitten from the mere consciousness of life. Yet with all the loveliness around me I re-peruse your letter, and long for wings to fly from it all to the dull atmosphere and crowded highways of the city. Yes! I could then look into your eyes and I should forget the blue sky; and your smile and your voice would doubly compensate me for the loss of green trees and singing birds. There are green trees in the heart which shed a softer perfume, and birds which sing more sweetly. "Nonsense, Mag is growing sentimental;" I knew you would say so, but the streak came across me, and you have it at full length. In plainer terms, how delighted, how more than delighted I shall be when I do come! when I do come, Kate! Oh! oh! oh! What would our language be without interjections, those expressive parts of speech which say so much in so small a compass? Now I am sure you can understand from these three syllables all the pleasure, the rapture I anticipate; the meeting, the parting, all the component parts of that great whole which I denominate a visit to New York! No, not to New York! but to the few dear friends whose society will afford me all the enjoyment I expect or desire, and who, in fact, constitute all my New York.

June 2.   I had written thus far, dear Kate, when I was most agreeably interrupted by a proposal for a ride on horseback ; my sheet slid of itself into the open drawer, my hat and dress flew on as if by instinct, and in ten minutes I was galloping full speed through the streets of our little village, with father by my side.   I rode till nearly tea-time, and came home tired, tired, tired.   Oh, I ache to think of it.   My poor letter slept all night as soundly as its writer, but now that another day has dawned the very opposite of its predecessor, damp, dark, and rainy, I have drawn it forth from its receptacle, and seek to dissipate all outward gloom, by communing with one the thought of whom conveys to my mind anything but melancholy.   O Kate, Kate, in spite of your disinterested and sober advice to the contrary, I shall come, I shall soon come, just as soon as M. can and will run up for me.   Yet perhaps in the end I shall be disappointed. My happy anticipations resemble the cloudless sky of yesterday, and who knows but a stormy to-morrow may erase the brilliant tints of hope as well as those of Nature? . . . . . .   Do write quickly and tell me if I am to prepare.   If you continue to feel as when you last wrote and still advise me not to come, I shall dispose of your advice in the most approved manner, throw it to the winds, and embark armed and equipped for your city to make my destined visit, and fulfil its conditions by fair means or foul, and bring you home in triumph.   Oh ! we shall have fine times.   Oh, dear, I

blush to look back upon my sheet and see so many
I's in it.

"The time of her brother's coming drew near. He
would be with us at 9 in the morning. At 11 they were
to start. I prepared all for her departure with my own
hand, lest, should I trust it to a domestic to make the
arrangements, she would make some exertion herself.
She sat by me whilst thus engaged, relating playful
anecdotes until I urged her to retire for the night. On
going into her room an hour or two afterwards, I was
alarmed to find her in a high fever. About midnight
she was taken with bleeding at the lungs. I flew to her
father, and in a few minutes a vein was opened in her
arm. To describe our feelings at this juncture is impossible. We stood gazing at each other in mute despair.
After that shock had subsided her father retired, and I
seated myself by the bedside to watch her slumbers, and
the rising sun found me still at my post. She awoke,
pale, feeble, and exhausted by the debilitating perspira-
tion which attended her sleep. She was surprised to
find that I had not been in bed; but when she attempted
to speak I laid my finger upon her lips and desired her
to be silent. She understood my motive, and when I
bent my head to kiss her, I saw a tear upon her cheek.
I told her the necessity of perfect quiet, and the danger
which would result from agitation. Before her brother
came she desired to rise. I assisted her to do so, and he

found her quietly seated in her easy-chair, perfectly composed in manner, and determined not to increase her difficulties by giving way to feelings which must at that time have oppressed her heart. My son was greatly shocked to find her in this state. I met him and urged the importance of perfect self-possession on his part, as any sudden agitation might in her present alarming state be fatal. Poor fellow! he subdued his feelings and met her with a cheerful smile which concealed a heart almost bursting with sorrow. The propriety of her taking this jaunt had been discussed by her father and myself for a number of weeks. We both thought her too ill to leave home, but her strong desire to go, the impression she had imbibed that travelling would greatly benefit her health, and the pleading of friends in her behalf, on the ground that disappointment would have a more unfavorable effect than the journey possibly could have, all had their effect in leading us to consent. It was possible it might be of use to her, although it was at best an experiment of a doubtful nature. But this attack was decisive; yet caution must be used in breaking the matter to her in her present weak state. Her brother stayed a day or two with us, and then returned, telling her that when she was able to perform the journey, he would come again and take her with him. After he left us, she soon regained her usual strength, and in a fortnight her brother returned and took her to New York."

The anxiety of Mrs. Davidson was intense until she

received her first letter. It was written from New York, and in a cheerful vein, speaking encouragingly of her health, but showing more solicitude about the health and well-being of her mother than of her own. She continued to write frequently, giving animated accounts of scenes and persons.

The following extract relates to an excursion, in company with two of her brothers, into Westchester County, one of the pleasantest, and, until recently, the least fashionably known, regions on the banks of the Hudson.

"At 3 o'clock we were in the Sing Sing steamer, with the water sparkling below, and the sun broiling overhead. In the course of our sail a huge thunder-cloud arose, and I retreated, quite terrified, to the cabin. But it proved a refreshing shower. Oh! how sweet, how delightful the air was. When we landed at the dock, everything looked so fresh and green! We mounted into a real country vehicle, and rattled up the hill to the village inn, a quiet, pleasant little house. I was immediately shown to my room, where I stayed until tea-time, enjoying the prospect of a splendid sunset upon the mountains, and resting after the fatigues of the day. At 7 we drank tea, a meal strongly contrasted with the fashionable, meagre, unsocial city tea. The table was crowded with everything good, in the most bountiful style, and served with the greatest attention by the landlord's pretty daughter. I retired soon after tea, and slept soundly until daybreak. After breakfast we sent for a carriage to take us along the course of the Croton, to see the famous water-works; but, to our disappointment, every carriage was engaged, and we could not go. In the afternoon a party was made up to go in a boat across the river, and ascend a mountain to a singular lake upon its summit, where all the implements of fishing were provided, and a collation was prepared. In short, it was a picnic. To this we were invited, but on learning they would not return until 9 or 10 in the evening, that scheme also was abandoned. Towards night we walked around the village, looked at the tunnel, and visited the ice-cream man; and in spite of my various disappointments, I retired quite happy and pleased with my visit. The next day was Sunday, and we proposed going to the little Dutch church, a few miles distant, and hearing the service performed in Dutch; but lo! on drawing aside my curtains in the morning it rained, and we were obliged to content ourselves as well as we could until the rain was over. After dinner the sun again peeped out, as if for our especial gratification, and in a few minutes a huge country wagon, with a leathern top and two sleek horses, drew up to the door. We mounted into it, and away we rattled over the most beautiful country I ever saw. Oh! it was magnificent! Every now and then the view of the broad Hudson, with its distant hills, and the clouds resting on their summits, burst upon our view. Now we would ascend a lofty hill, clothed with forests and verdure of the most brilliant

hues; now dash down into a deep ravine, with a stream
winding and gurgling along its bed, with its tiny waves
rushing over the wheel of some rustic mill, embosomed in
its shade and solitude. Every now and then the gable-
end of some low Dutch building would present itself before us, smiling in its peaceful stillness, and conveying
to the mind a perfect picture of rural simplicity and
comfort, although, perhaps, of ignorance. At length we
paused upon the summit of a gentle hill, and judge of
my delight when I beheld below me the old Dutch
church, the quiet, secluded, beautiful little church-yard,
the running stream, the path, and the rustic bridge, the
ever-memorable scene of Ichabod's adventure with the
headless horseman. There, thought I, rushed the poor
pedagogue, his knees cramped up to his saddle-bow with
fear, his hands grasping his horse's mane, with convul-
sive energy, in the hope that the rising stream might
arrest the progress of his fearful pursuer, and allow him
to pass in safety. Vain hope! Scarce had he reached
the bridge when he heard, rattling behind him, the hoofs
of his fiendish companion. The church seemed in a
blaze to his bewildered eyes, and urging on, on, he
turned to look once more, when, horror of horrors! the
head, the fearful head, was in the act of descending upon
his devoted shoulders. Ha! ha! ha! I never laughed
so in my life. Well, we rode on through the scene of
poor Andre's capture, and dashed along the classic valleys of Sleepy Hollow. After a long and delightful

drive, we returned in time for tea. After tea we were
invited into Mrs. F.'s parlor, where, after a short time,
were collected quite a party of ladies and gentlemen.
At 9 we were served with ice-cream, wine, etc. I retired
very much pleased and very much fatigued. Early in
the morning we rose with a most brilliant sun, break-
fasted, mounted once more into the wagon, and rattled
off to the dock. Oh! that I could describe to you how
fresh and sweet the air was. I felt as if I wanted to
open my mouth wide and inhale it. We gave M. our
parting kisses, and soon found ourselves once more, after
this charming episode, approaching the mighty city.
We had a delightful sail of two or three hours, and
again rode up to dear aunt M.'s where all seemed glad
at my return. I spent the remainder of the day in resting and reading."

"In these artless epistles," continues Mrs. Davidson,
"there is much of character; for who could imagine this
constant cheerfulness, this almost forgetfulness of self,
these affectionate endeavors, by her sweetly playful account of all her employments while absent, to dispel the
grief which she knew was preying upon my mind on account of her illness. Who could conceive the pains she
took to conceal from me the ravages which disease was
daily making upon her form? She was never heard to
complain, and in her letters to me she hardly alludes to
her illness. The friends to whom I had entrusted her,
during her short period of absence, sometimes feared

that she would never be able to reach home again. Her brother told me, but not until long after her return, that on her way home she really fainted several times from debility, and that he took her from the boat to the carriage as he would have done an infant.

"On the 6th of July I once more folded to my heart this cherished object of my solicitude, but oh, the change which three short weeks had wrought in her appearance struck me forcibly. I was so wholly unprepared for it that I nearly fainted. After the excitement of the meeting (which she had evidently summoned all her fortitude to bear with composure) was over, she sat down by me, and passing her thin arm around my waist, said, 'O my dear mamma, I am home again at last; I now feel as if I never wanted to leave you again; I have had a delightful visit, my friends were all glad to see me, and have watched over me with all the kindness and care which affection could dictate; but oh, there is no place like home, and no care like a mother's care; there is something in the very air of home and in the sound of your voice, mother, which makes me happier just now than all the scenes which I have passed through in my little jaunt; oh, after all, home is the only place for a person as much out of health as I am.' I strove to suppress my emotions, while I marked her pale cheek and altered countenance. She fixed her penetrating eyes upon my face, kissed me, and drawing back to take a more full survey of the effects which pain and anxiety

had wrought in me, kissed me again and again, saying,
'she knew I had deeply felt the want of her society,
and now once more at home, she should so prize its comforts as to be in no haste to leave it again.' She was
much wasted, and could hardly walk from one room to
another; her cough was very distressing; she had no
pain, but a languor and a depression of spirits, foreign
to her nature. She struggled against this debility, and
called up all the energies of her mind to overcome it;
her constant reply to inquiries about her health, by the
friends who called, was the same as formerly, 'Well,
quite well—mother calls me an invalid, but I feel well.'
Yet to me, when alone, she talked more freely of her
symptoms, and I thought I could discern from her manner, that she had apprehensions as to the result. I had
often endeavored to acquire firmness sufficient to tell her
what was her situation, but she seemed so studiously to
avoid the disclosure, that my resolution had hitherto
been unequal to the task. But I was much surprised
one day, not long after her return from New York, by her
asking me to tell her without reserve my opinion of her
state ; the question wrung my very heart. I was wholly
unprepared for it, and it was put in so solemn a manner
that I could not evade it, were I disposed to do so. I
knew with what strong affection she clung to life and the
objects and friends which endeared it to her ; I knew
how bright the world upon which she was just entering
appeared to her young fancy, what glowing pictures she

had drawn of future usefulness and happiness. I was now called upon at one blow to crush these hopes, to destroy the delightful visions which had hovered around her from her cradle until this very period; it would be cruel and wrong to deceive her; in vain I attempted a reply to her direct and solemn appeal, and my voice grew husky; several times I essayed to speak, but the words died away on my lips; I could only fold her to my heart in silence, imprint a kiss upon her forehead, and leave the room to avoid agitating her with feelings I had no power to repress.

" The following extract from a letter to her brother in New York, dated a short time after this incident occurred, and which I never saw until after her departure, will best portray her own feelings at this period:

" 'As to my health at present, I feel as well as when you were here, and the cough is much abated; but it is evident to me that mother thinks me not so well as before I left home; I do not myself believe that I have gained anything from the visit, and in a case like mine, standing still is certainly loss, but I feel no worse. However, I have learned that feelings are no criterion of disease. Now, brother, I want to know what Dr. M—— discovered, or thought he discovered, in his examination of my lungs; father says nothing—mother, when I ask, cannot tell me, and looks so sad! Now I ask you, hoping to be answered. If you have not heard the Doctor say, I wish you would ask him, and write to me. If it is more

22

unfavorable than I anticipate, it is best I should know now; if it is the contrary, how much pain and restlessness and suspicion will be spared me by the knowledge. As to myself, I feel and know that my health is in a most precarious state, that the disease we dread has perhaps fastened upon me; but I have an impression that if I make use of the proper remedies and exercise, I may yet recover a tolerable degree of health. I do not feel that my case is incurable; I wish to know if I am wrong. I have rode on horseback twice since you left me; dear, dear brother, what a long egotistic letter I have written you; do forgive me; my heart was full, and I felt that I must unburden it. I wish you would write me a long letter. Do not let mother know at present the questions I have asked you.' . . . . .

" From this period she grew more thoughtful. There was even a solemnity in her manner which I never before observed. Her mind, as I mentioned before, had been much perplexed by some doctrinal points. To solve these doubts, I asked if I should not send for some clergyman. She said no. She had heard many discussions on these subjects, and they had always served rather to confuse than to convince her. 'I would rather converse with you alone, mother.' She then asked me if I thought it essential to salvation that she should adopt any particular creed. I felt that I was an inefficient, perhaps a blind guide, yet it was my duty not only to impart consolation, but to explain to her my own views of

the truth. I replied that I considered faith and repent-
ance only to be essential to salvation; that it was very
desirable that her mind should be settled upon some
particular mode of faith; but that I did not think it absolutely necessary that she should adopt the tenets of
any established church, and again recommended an attentive perusal of the New Testament. She expressed
her firm belief in the divinity of Christ. The perfections
of his character, its beauty and holiness excited her admiration, while the benevolence which prompted the sacrifice of himself to save a lost world filled her with the
most enthusiastic gratitude. It was a source of regret
that so much of her time had been spent in light reading, and that her writings had not been of a more decid-
edly religious character. She lamented that she had
not chosen scriptural subjects for the exercise of her
poetical talent, and said, 'Mamma, should God spare my
life, my time and talents shall for the future be devoted
to a higher and holier end.' She felt that she had trifled
with the gifts of Providence, and her self-condemnation
and grief were truly affecting. 'And must I die so young!
—my career of usefulness hardly commenced? O mother,
how sadly have I trifled with the gifts of Heaven! What
have I done which can benefit one human being?' I
folded her to my heart, and endeavored to soothe the
tumult of her feelings, bade her remember her dutiful
conduct as a daughter, her affectionate bearing as a sister and friend, and the consolation which she had af-

forded me through years of suffering! 'O my mother,'
said she, 'I have been reflecting much of late upon this
sad waste of intellect, and had marked out for myself a
course of usefulness which, should God spare my life'——
Here her emotions became too powerful to proceed. At
times she suffered much anxiety with regard to her eternal welfare, and deeply lamented her want of faithfulness
in the performance of her religious duties ; complained
of coldness and formality in her devotional exercises, and
entreated me to pray with and for her. At other times
her hope of heaven would be bright, her faith unwaver-
ing, and her devotion fervent. Yet it was evident to me
that she still cherished the hope that her life might be
prolonged. Her mother had lingered for years in a state
equally hopeless, and during that period had been enabled to attend to the moral and religious culture of her
little family. Might not the same kind Providence pro-
long *her life ?* It would be vain to attempt a description
of those seasons of deep and thrilling interest. God
alone knows in what way my own weak frame was sustained. I felt that she had been renovated and purified
by Divine Grace, and to see her thus distressed when I
thought that all the consolations of the Gospel ought to
be hers, gave my heart a severe pang. Many of our
friends now were of opinion that a change of climate
might benefit, perhaps restore her. Heretofore, when
the suggestion had been made, she shrunk from the idea
of leaving her home for a distant clime. Now her

anxiety to try the effect of a change was great, I felt that it would be vain, although I was desirous that nothing should be left untried. Feeble as she now was, the idea of her resigning the comforts of home and being subject to the fatigues of travelling in public conveyances was a dreadful one ; yet if there was a rational prospect of prolonging her life by these means, I was anxious to give them a trial. Dr. Davidson, after much deliberation on the subject, called counsel. Dr. —— came, and when, after half an hour's pleasant and playful conversation with Margaret, he joined us in the parlor, oh ! how my poor heart trembled. I hung upon the motions of his lips as if my own life depended on what they might utter. At length he spoke, and I felt as if an ice-bolt had passed through my heart. He had never thought, although he had known her many years, that a change of climate would benefit her. She had lived beyond his expectations many months, even years ; and now he was convinced, were we to attempt to take her to a Southern climate, that she would die on the passage. Make it as pleasant as possible for her at home, was his advice. He thought that a few months must terminate her life. She knew that we had confidence in the opinion of this, her favorite physician. When I had gained firmness enough to answer her questions, I again entered the room and found her composed, although she had evidently been strongly agitated, and had not brought her mind to hear her doom. Never, oh ! never to the latest hour of my

life, shall I forget the look she gave me when I met her.
What a heart-rending task was mine ! I performed it as
gently as possible. I said the Doctor thought her
strength unequal to the fatigue of the journey; that he
was not so great an advocate for change of climate as
many persons ; that he had known many cases in which
he thought it injurious, and his best advice was that we
should again ward off the severity of the winter by creating an atmosphere within our house. She mildly acqui-
esced, and the subject was dropped altogether. She
sometimes read, and frequently from mere habit held a
book in her hand when unable to digest its contents, and
within the book there usually rested a piece of paper,
upon which she occasionally marked the reflections
which arose in her mind, either in poetry or prose.

" The following fragments appear to be the very
breathings of her soul during the last few weeks of her
life—written in pencil, in a hand so weak and tremulous
that I could with difficulty decipher them word by word,
with the aid of a strong magnifying glass.

" ' Consumption ! child of woe, thy blighting breath
Marks all that's fair and lovely for thine own,
And, sweeping o'er the silver chords of life,
Blends all their music in one death-like tone.
What strange, what mystic things we are,
With spirits longing to outlive the stars.
. . . . but even in decay
Hasting to meet our brethren in the dust.

As one small dew-drop runs, another drops
To sink unnoticed in the world of waves.

Oh, it is sad to feel that when a few short years
Of life are past, we shall lie down, unpitied
And unknown, amid a careless world ;
That youth and age and revelry and grief
Above our heads shall pass, and we alone
Shall sleep ! alone shall be as we have been,
No more.' . . . .

" These are unfinished fragments, a part of which I could not decipher at all. I insert them to give an idea of the daily operations of her mind during the whole of this long summer of suffering. Her gentle spirit never breathed a murmur or complaint. I think she was rarely heard to express even a feeling of weariness. But here are a few more of those outpourings of the heart. I copy these little effusions with all their errors ; there is a sacredness about them which forbids the change even of a single letter. The first of the fragments which follow was written on a Sabbath evening in autumn, not many weeks before her death.

" ' It is autumn, the season of rapid decay,
    When the flow'rets of summer are hasting away
        From the breath of the wintry blast,
    And the buds which oped to the gazer's eye,
    And the glowing tints of the gorgeous sky,
    And the forests robed in their emerald dye,
        With their loveliest blossoms have past.

'Tis eve, and the brilliant sunset hue
Is replaced by a sky of the coldest blue,
   Untouched by a floating cloud.
And all Nature is silent, calm, and serene,
As though sorrow and suffering never had been
   On this beautiful earth abroad.
'Tis a Sabbath eve, and the longing soul
Is charmed by its quiet and gentle control
   From each wayward and wandering thought,
And it longs from each meaner affection to move,
And it soareth the troubles of earth above,
To bathe in that fountain of light and love,
   Whence our purest enjoyments are caught.'

1838.

'But winter, oh what shall thy greeting be
   From our waters, our earth, and our sky ;
What welcoming strain shall arise for thee
   As thy chariot-wheels draw nigh ?
Alas ! the fresh flowers of the spirit decay
   As thy cold, cold steps advance,
And even young Fancy is shrinking away
   From the chill of thy terrible glance ;
And Hope with her mantle of rainbow hue
   Hath fled from thy freezing eye,
And her bright train of visions are melting in air
   As thy shivering blasts sweep by.
Thy' . . . .

Oct. 1838.

     'The nature of the soul,
The spirit, what is it ? Mysterious, sublime,
   Undying, unchanging, forever the same,
It bounds lightly athwart the dark billows of time,
   And moves on unscorched by its heavenly flame.

Man owns thee, and feels thee, and knows thee divine ;
   He feels thou art his, and thou never canst die ;
He believes thee a gem from the Maker's pure shrine,
   A portion of purity holy and high.

'Tis around him, within him, the source of his life,
   Yet too weak to contemplate its glory and might ;
He trembling shrinks back to dull earth's humble strife,
   And leaves the pure atmosphere glowing with light.

Thou spark from the Deity's radiant throne,
   I know thee, yet shrink from thy greatness and power,
Thou art mine in thy splendor, I feel thee my own,
   Yet behold me as frail as the light summer flower.

I strive in my weakness to gaze on thy might,
   To trace out thy wanderings through ages to come,
Till like birds on the sea, all exhausted, at length
   I flutter back weary to earth as my home.

Like a diamond when laid in a rough case of clay,
   Which may crumble and wear from the pure gem enclosed,
But which ne'er can be lit by one tremulous ray
   From the glory-crowned star in its dark case reposed.'

"As the cool weather advanced, her decline became
more visible, and she devoted more and more of her time
to searching the Scriptures, self-examination and subjects
for reflection, and questions which were to be solved by
evidences deduced from the Bible. I found them but a
few days before her death, in the sacred volume which lay
upon the table, at which she usually sat during her hours
of retirement. She had been searching the holy book, and

overcome by the exertion, rang the bell which summoned me to her side, for no person but myself was admitted during the time set apart for her devotional exercises.

'Subjects for reflection :—

1st. The uniform usefulness of Christ's miracles.

2d. The manner in which he overthrows all the exalted hopes which the Jews entertain of a temporal kingdom, and strives to explain to them the entire spirituality of the one he has come to erect.

3d. The deep and unchangeable love for man, which must have impelled Christ to resist so many temptations and endure so many sufferings, even death, that truth might enlighten the world, and heaven and immortality become realities instead of dreams.

4th. The general thoughtlessness of man with regard to his greatest, his only interest.

5th. Christ's constant submission to the will of his Father, and the necessity of our imitating the meek and calm and gentle qualities of his character, together with that firmness of purpose and confidence in God which sustained him to the end.

6th. The necessity of so living, that we need not fear to think each day our last.

7th. The necessity of religion to soothe and support the mind on the bed of sickness.

8th. Self-examination.

9th. Is Christ mentioned expressly in Scripture as equal with God and a part?

10th. Is there sufficient ground for the doctrine of the Trinity?

11th. Did Christ come as a prophet and reformer of the world, or as a sacrifice for our sins, to appease the wrath of his Father?

12th. Is anything said of infant baptism?'

Written in November, 1838.

"About three weeks before her departure, I one morning found her in the parlor, where, as I before observed, she spent a portion of her time in retirement. I saw that she had been much agitated, and seemed weary. I seated myself by her and rested her head on my bosom, while I gently pressed my hand upon her throbbing temples, to soothe the agitation of her nerves. She kissed me again and again, and seemed as if she feared to trust her voice to speak, lest her feelings should overcome her. As I returned her caresses, she silently put a folded paper in my hand. I began to open it, when she gently laid her hand on mine, and said in a low tremulous tone, 'Not now, dear mother!' I then led her back to her room, placed her upon the sofa, and retired to examine the paper. It contained the following lines :—

TO MY MOTHER.

O MOTHER, would the power were mine
To wake the strain thou lov'st to hear,

And breathe each trembling new-born thought
  Within thy fondly listening ear,
As when in days of health and glee
My hopes and fancies wandered free.

But, mother, now a shade has past
  Athwart my brightest visions here,
A cloud of darkest gloom has wrapt
  The remnant of my brief career !
No song, no echo can I win,
The sparkling fount has died within.

The torch of earthly hope burns dim,
  And Fancy spreads her wings no more ;
And oh, how vain and trivial seem
  The pleasures that I prized before.
My soul, with trembling steps and slow,
  Is struggling on through doubt and strife,
Oh ! may it prove as time rolls on,
  The pathway to eternal life ;—
Then, when my cares and fears are o'er,
I'll sing thee as in days of yore.

I said that hope had passed from earth,
  'Twas but to fold her wings in heaven,
To whisper of the soul's new birth,
  Of sinners saved and sins forgiven.
When mine are washed in tears away,
Then shall my spirit swell my lay.

When God shall guide my soul above
By the soft cords of heavenly love,
When the vain cares of earth depart,
And tuneful voices swell my heart,

Then shall each word, each note I raise,
Burst forth in pealing hymns of praise,
And all not offered at His shrine,
Dear mother, I will place on thine.

"It was long before I could regain sufficient composure to return to her. When I did so, I found her sweetly calm, and she greeted me with a smile so full of affection, that I shall cherish the recollection of its brightness until my latest breath. It was the last piece she ever wrote, except a parody of four lines of the hymn, 'I would not live always,' which was written within the last week of her life.

"'I would not live always, thus fettered by sin,
Temptation without and corruption within,
With the soul ever dimmed by its hopes and its fears,
And the heart's holy flame ever struggling through tears.'"

Thus far, in preparing this memoir, we have availed ourselves almost entirely of copious memoranda, furnished us, at our request, by Mrs. Davidson; but when the narrator approached the closing scene of this most affecting story, the heart of the mother gave out, and she found herself totally inadequate to the task. Fortunately, Dr. Davidson had retained a copy of a letter, written by her in the midst of her affliction, to Miss Sedgwick, in reply to an epistle from that lady, expressive of the kindest sympathy, and making some inquiries relative to the melancholy event.   We subjoin that letter entire, for never have we read anything of the kind more truly eloquent or deeply affecting.

"SARATOGA SPRINGS.

"YES, my dear Miss Sedgwick; she is an angel now; calmly and sweetly she sunk to her everlasting rest, as a babe gently slumbers on its mother's bosom. I thank my Father in heaven that I was permitted to watch over her, and I trust administer to her comfort during her illness. I know, my friend, you will not expect either a very minute or connected detail of the circumstances preceding her change, from me at this time, for I am indeed bowed down with sorrow. I feel that I am truly desolate, how desolate I will not attempt to describe. Yet in the depth of grief I have consolations of the purest, most soothing and exalted nature. I would not, indeed I could not murmur, but rather bless my God that he has in the plenitude of his goodness made me, even for a brief space on earth, the honored mother of such an angel. O, my dear Miss Sedgwick, I wish you could have seen her during the last two months of her brief sojourn with us. Her meekness and patience, and her even cheerful bearing were unexampled. But when she was assured that all the tender and endearing ties which bound her to earth were about to be severed, when she saw that life and all its bright visions were fading from her eyes—that she was standing at the entrance of the dark valley which must be traversed in her way to the eternal world, the struggle was great, but brief,—she caught the hem of her Saviour's robe and meekly bowed to the mandate of her God. Since the beginning of August, I have watched this tender blossom with intense anxiety, and marked her decline with a breaking heart; and although from that time until the period of her departure, I never spent a whole night in bed, my excitement was so strong that I was unconscious of the want of sleep. O, my dear madam, the whole course of her decline was so unlike any other death-bed scene I ever witnessed; there was nothing of the gloom of a sick-chamber; a charm was in and around her; a holy light seemed to pervade everything belonging to her. There was a sacredness, if I may so express it, which seemed to tell the presence of the Divinity. Strangers felt it, all acknowledged it. Very few were admitted to her sick-room, but those few left it with an elevation of heart new, solemn, and delightful. She continued to ride out as long as the weather was mild, and even after she became too weak to walk she frequently desired to be taken into the parlor, and when there, with all her little implements of drawing and writing, her books, and even her little work-box and basket beside her; she seemed to think that by these little attempts at her usual employments, she could conceal from me, for she saw my heart was breaking, the ravages of disease and her consequent debility. The New Testament was her daily study, and a portion of every day was spent in private, in self-examination and prayer. My dear Miss

Sedgwick, how I have felt my own littleness, my total unworthiness, when compared with this pure, this high-souled, intellectual, yet timid, humble child ; bending at the altar of her God, and pleading for pardon and acceptance in his sight, and grace to assist her in preparing for eternity. As her strength wasted, she often desired me to share her hours of retirement, and converse with her and read to her, when unable to read herself. Oh! how sad, how delightful, how agonizing is the memory of the sweet and holy communion we then enjoyed. Forgive me, my friend, for thus mingling my own feelings with the circumstances you wished to know; and, oh! continue to pray that God will give me submission under this desolating stroke. She was my darling, my almost idolized child ; truly, truly, you have said, the charm of my existence. Her symptoms were extremely distressing, although she suffered no pain. A week before her departure she desired that the sacrament of the Lord's Supper might be administered to her. 'Mother,' said she, 'I do not desire it because I feel worthy to receive it ; I feel myself a sinner ; but I desire to manifest my faith in Christ by receiving an ordinance instituted by himself but a short time before his crucifixion.' The Holy Sacrament was administered by Mr. Babcock. The solemnity of the scene can be better felt than described. I cannot attempt it. After it was over, a holy calm seemed to pervade her mind, and she looked almost like a beatified spirit. The evening following she said to me,

'Mother, I have made a solemn surrender of myself to God; if it is his will, I would desire to live long enough to prove the sincerity of my profession, but his will be done; living or dying I am henceforth devoted to God.' After this, some doubt seemed to intrude, her spirit was troubled. I asked her if there was anything she desired to have done, any little arrangements to be made, anything to say which she had left unsaid, and assured her that her wishes should be sacred to me. She turned her eyes upon me with an expression so sad, so mournfully sweet: 'Mother, "when I can read my title clear to mansions in the skies," then I will think of other matters.' Her hair, which when a little child had been often cut to improve its growth, was now very beautiful, and she usually took much pains with it. During the whole course of her sickness I had taken care of it. One day, not long before her death, she said, evidently making a great effort to speak with composure, 'Mother, if you are willing I will have my hair cut off; it is troublesome; I should like it better short.' I understood her at once; she did not like to have the idea of death associated with those beautiful tresses which I had loved to braid. She would have them taken off while living. I mournfully gave my consent, and she said, 'I will not ask you, my dear mother, to do it; my friend, Mrs. F——, will be with me to-night, and she will do it for me.' The dark rich locks were severed at midnight; never shall I forget the expression of her young faded face as I entered the room.

23

'Do not be agitated, dear mamma, I am more comfortable now. Lay it away, if you please, and to-morrow I will arrange and dispose of it. Do you know that I view my hair as something sacred? It is a part of myself, which will be reunited to my body at the Resurrection.' She had sat in an easy-chair or reclined upon a sofa for several weeks.

"On Friday, the 22d of November, at my urgent entreaty, she consented to be laid upon the bed. She found it a relief, and sunk into a deep sleep, from which she was only awoke when I aroused her, to take some refreshment. When she awoke she looked and spoke like an angel, but soon dropped asleep as before. Oh! how my poor heart trembled, for I felt that it was but the precursor to her long last rest, although many of our friends thought she might yet linger some weeks. A total loss of appetite and a difficulty in swallowing prevented her from taking any nourishment throughout the day, and when we placed her in the easy-chair, at night, in order to arrange her bed, I offered her some nice food, which I had prepared, and found she could not take it. My feelings amounted almost to agony. She said, 'Do not be distressed. I will take it by and by.' I seated myself beside her, and she said, 'Surely, my dear mother, you have many consolations. You are gathering a little family in heaven to welcome you.' My heart was full; when I could speak, I said, 'Yes, my love, I feel that I am indeed gathering a little family in heaven to bid you welcome, but when they are all assembled there, how dreadful to doubt whether I may ever be permitted to join the circle.' 'Oh, hush, dear, dear mother; do not indulge such sad thoughts; the fact of your having trained this little band to inhabit that holy place is sufficient evidence to me that you will not fail to join us there.' I was with her myself that night, and a friend in the neighborhood sat up also. On Saturday morning, after I had taken half an hour's sleep, I found her quiet as a sleeping infant. I prepared her some food, and when I awoke her to take it, she said, 'Dear mother, I will try, if it is only to please you.' I fed her as I would have fed a babe. She smiled sweetly and said, 'Mother, I am again an infant.' I asked if I should read to her; she said yes, she would like to have me read a part of the Gospel of John. I did so, and then said, 'My dear Margaret, you look sweetly composed this morning. I trust all is peace within your heart.' 'Yes, mother, all is peace, sweet peace. I feel that I can do nothing for myself. I have cast my burden upon Christ.' I asked if she could rest her hopes there in perfect confidence. 'Yes,' she replied, 'Jesus will not fail me. I can trust him.' She then sank into a deep sleep, as on the preceding day. In the afternoon Mr and Mrs. H. came from Ballston; they were much affected by the change a few days had made in her appearance. I awoke her, fearing she might sleep too long, and said her friends had come. She extended her arms to them both, and kissed them, saying to Mr. H. that he

found her a late riser, and then sank to sleep again. Mrs.
H. remained with us that night. About sunset I spoke
to her. She awoke and answered me cheerfully, but observing that I was unusually depressed, she said, 'Dear
mother, I am wearing you out.' I replied, 'My child, my
beloved child, it is not that; the thought of our separation fills me with anguish.' I never shall forget the expression of her sweet face, as she replied, 'Mother, my
own dear mother, do not grieve. Our parting will not be
long; in life we were inseparable, and I feel that you cannot live without me. You will soon join me, and we shall
part no more.' I kissed her pale cheek, as I bent over
her, and finding my agitation too strong to repress, I left
the room. She soon after desired to get up; she said
she must have a coughing fit, and she could bear it better
in the chair. When there she began to cough, and her
distress was beyond description; her strength was soon
exhausted, and we again carried her to the bed. She
coughed from six until half-past ten. I then prevailed on
her to take some nutritious drink, and she fell asleep.
My husband and Mrs. H. were both of them anxious that
I should retire and get some rest, but I did not feel the
want of it; and impressed as I was with the idea that
this was the last night she would pass on earth I could
not go to bed. But others saw not the change, and to
satisfy them, I went at 12 to my room, which opened into
hers. There I sat listening to every sound. All seemed
quiet; I twice opened the door, and Mrs. F said she

slept, and had taken her drink as often as directed, and again urged me to go to bed. A little after 2 I put on my night-dress, and laid down. Between 3 and 4 Mrs. H. came in haste for ether. I pointed to the bottle, and sprang up. She said, I entreat, my dear Mrs. Davidson, that you do not rise ; there is no sensible change, only a turn of oppression. She closed the door, and I hastened to rise, when Mrs. H. came again, and said Margaret has asked for her mother. I flew—she held the bottle of ether in her own hand, and pointed to her breast. I poured it on her head and chest. She revived. 'I am better now,' said she. 'Mother, you tremble, you are cold ; put on your clothes.' I stepped to the fire, and threw on a wrapper, when she stretched out both her arms, and exclaimed, 'Mother, take me in your arms.' I raised her, and seating myself on the bed, passed my arms around her waist; her head dropped upon my bosom, and her expressive eyes were raised to mine. That look I never shall forget; it said, 'Tell me, mother, is this death?' I answered the appeal as if she had spoken. I laid my hand upon her white brow ; a cold dew had gathered there ; I spoke, 'Yes, my beloved, it is almost finished; you will soon be with Jesus.' She gave one more look, two or three short fluttering breaths, and all was over—her spirit was with its God—not a struggle or groan preceded her departure. Her father just came in time to witness her last breath. For a long half-hour I remained in the same position, with the precious form of my lifeless child upon my bosom. I closed those beautiful eyes with my own hand. I was calm. I felt that I had laid my angel from my own breast, upon the bosom of her God. Her father and myself were alone. Her Sabbath commenced in heaven. Ours was opened in deep, deep anguish. Our sons, who had been sent for, had not arrived, and four days and nights did Ellen (our young nurse, whom Margaret dearly loved), and I, watch over the sacred clay. I could not resign this mournful duty to strangers. Although no son or relative was with us in this sad and solemn hour, never did sorrowing strangers meet with more sympathy than we received in this hour of affliction, from the respected inhabitants of Saratoga. We shall carry with us through life the grateful remembrance of their kindness. And now, my dear madam, let me thank you for your kind, consoling letter; it has given me consolation. My Margaret, my now angel child, loved you tenderly. She recognized in yours a kindred mind, and I feel that her pure spirit will behold with delight your efforts to console her bereaved mother."

She departed this life on the 25th of November, 1838, aged fifteen years and eight months; her earthly remains repose in the grave-yard of the village of Saratoga.

"A few days after her departure," observes Mrs. Davidson in a memorandum, "I was searching the library in the hope of finding some further memento of my lost darling, when a packet folded in the form of a letter met my eye. It was confined with a needle and thread, instead of a seal, and secured more firmly by white sewing silk, which was passed several times around it ; the superscription was, 'For my Mother, Private.' Upon opening these papers, I found they contained the results of self-examination, from a very early period of her life until within a few days of its close. These results were noted and composed at different periods. They are some of the most interesting relics she has left, but they are of too sacred a nature to meet the public eye. They display a degree of self-knowledge and humility, and a depth of contrition, which could only emanate from a heart chastened and subdued by the power of divine grace."

We here conclude this memoir, which, for the most part, as the reader will perceive, is a mere transcript of the records furnished by a mother's heart. We shall not pretend to comment on these records ; they need no comment, and they admit no heightening. Indeed, the farther we have proceeded with our subject, the more has the intellectual beauty and the seraphic purity of the little being we have attempted to commemorate broken upon us ; and the more have we shrunk at our own unworthiness for such a task. To use one of her own exquisite expressions, she was " A spirit of heaven fettered

by the strong affections of earth;" and the whole of her
brief sojourn here seems to have been a struggle to regain her native skies.   We may apply to her a passage
from one of her own tender apostrophes, to the memory
of her sister Lucretia.

"... One who came from Heaven awhile,
    To bless the mourners here,
Their joys to hallow with her smile,
    Their sorrow with her tear.

Who joined to all the charms of earth
    The noblest gifts of Heaven,
To whom the Muses at her birth
    Their sweetest smiles had given.

Whose eye beamed forth with fancy's ray,
    And genius pure and high ;
Whose very soul had seemed to bathe
    In streams of melody.

.   .   .   .

The cheek which once so sweetly beamed
    Grew pallid with decay ;
The burning fire within consumed
    Its tenement of clay.

Death, as if fearing to destroy,
    Paused o'er her couch awhile ;
She gave a tear for those she loved,
    Then met him with a smile."

[THE residue of this volume consists of Reviews, articles from the "Knickerbocker Magazine," and the "Kaatskill Mountains," a contribution to Putnam's "Home-book of the Picturesque," published in 1850.

The Reviews of the works of Robert Treat Paine, and the Poems of Edwin C. Holland, are drawn from the "Analectic Magazine" during the period of Mr. Irving's editorship. The notice of Wheaton's "History of the Northmen" appeared in the "North American" in 1832. The review of the "Chronicle of the Conquest of Granada," a work emanating from Washington Irving, but purporting to come from the pen of Fray Antonio Agapida, an imaginary personage, was furnished to the "London Quarterly," a long time after its publication, at the instance of Murray, his publisher, who "thought the nature of the work was not sufficiently understood, and that it was considered rather as a work of fiction than one substantially of historic fact." It is needless to add that it is in no sense a laudatory review, but simply explanatory of the historical foundation of a work in which he had somewhat mystified the reader by the use of his monkish sobriquet.

The articles reproduced from "The Knickerbocker" date mainly from the year 1839. A majority of Mr. Irving's contributions to that magazine, during the two years he was engaged in writing for it, have been incorporated in "Wolfert's Roost."—ED.]

REVIEWS AND MISCELLANIES.

ROBERT TREAT PAINE.

The Works, in verse and prose, of the late ROBERT TREAT
PAINE, *Jun., Esq., with Notes. To which are prefixed
Sketches of his Life, Character, and Writings.* 8vo. pp.
464. Belcher. Boston, 1812.

IN reviewing the work before us, criticism is deprived of half its utility. However just may be
its decisions, they can be of no avail to the
author. With him the fitful scene of literary life is over;
praise can stimulate him to no new exertions, nor censure
point the way to future improvement. The only benefit,
therefore, to be derived from an examination of his merits, is to deduce therefrom instruction for his survivors,
either as to the excellences they should imitate, or the
errors they should avoid.

There is no country to which practical criticism is of
more importance than this, owing to the crude state of

native talent, and the immaturity of public taste. We are prone to all the vices of literature, from the casual and superficial manner in which we attend to it. Absorbed in politics, or occupied by business, few can find leisure, amid these strong agitations of the mind, to follow the gentler pursuits of literature, and give it that calm study and meditative contemplation necessary to discover the true principles of beauty and excellence in composition. To render criticism, therefore, more impressive, and to bring it home, as it were, to our own bosoms, it is not sufficient merely to point to those standard writers of Great Britain who should form our real models, but it is important to take those writers among ourselves who have attained celebrity, and scrutinize their characters. Authors are apt to catch and borrow the faults and beauties of neighboring authors, rather than of those removed by time or distance ; as a man is more apt to fall into the vices and peculiarities of those around him, than to form himself on the models of Roman or Grecian virtue.

This is apparent even in Great Britain, where, with all the advantages of finished education, literary society, and critical tribunals, we see her authors continually wandering away into some new and corrupt fashion of writing, rather than conforming to those orders of composition which have the sanction of time and criticism. of such be the case in Great Britain, and if even her veteran *literati* have still the need of rigorous criticism to keep them from running riot; how much more necessary is it in our country, where our literary ranks, like those of our military, are rude, undisciplined, and insubordinate. It is for these reasons that we presume with freedom, but, we trust, with candor, to examine the relics of an American poet, to do justice to his merits, but to point out his errors, as far as our judgment will allow, for the benefit of his contemporaries.

The volume before us commences with a biography of the author, written by two several hands. The style is occasionally overwrought, and swelling beyond the simplicity proper to this species of writing, but on the whole creditable to the writers. The spirit in which it is written is both friendly and candid. We cannot but admire the generous struggle between tenderness for the author's memory and a laudable determination to tell the whole truth, which occurs whenever the failings of the poet are adverted to. We applaud the frankness and delicacy with which the latter are avowed. If biography have any merit, it consists in presenting a faithful picture of the character, the habits, the whole course of living and thinking of the person who is the subject—for, otherwise, we may as well have a romance, and an ideal hero imposed on us, for our wonder and admiration.

The biography of Mr. Paine presents another of those melancholy details, too commonly furnished by literary life,—those gleams of sunshine, and days of darkness;

those moments of rapture, and periods of lingering depression; those dreams of hope, and waking hours of
black despondency.   Such is the rapid round of transient
joys and frequent sufferings that form the " be all and
the end all here," of the unlucky tribe that live by writing.
Surely, if the young imagination could ever be repressed
by sad example, these gloomy narratives would be sufficient to deter it from venturing into the fairy land of
literature—a region so precarious in its enjoyments and
fruitful in its calamities.

We find that Mr. Paine started on his career full of
ardor and confidence.   His collegiate life was gay and
brilliant.   His poetic talents had already broken forth,
and acquired him the intoxicating but dangerous meed
of early praise.   The description given of him by his
biographer, at this time, is extremely prepossessing.

> " He was graduated with the esteem of the government and the regard
> of his contemporaries.   He was as much distinguished for the opening
> virtues of his heart, as for the vivacity of his wit, the vigor of his imag-
> ination, and the variety of his knowledge.   A liberality of sentiment and
> a contempt of selfishness are usual concomitants, and in him were strik-
> ing characteristics.   Urbanity of manners and a delicacy of feeling im-
> parted a charm to his benignant temper and social disposition."

After leaving college, we begin to perceive the misfortunes which his early display of talents had entailed
upon him.   He had tasted the sweets of literary triumph,
and, as it is not the character of genius to rest satisfied
with past achievements, he longed to add fresh laurels

to those he had acquired. With this strong inclination towards a literary life, we behold him painfully endeavoring to accustom himself to mercantile pursuits, and harness his mind to the diurnal drudgery of a counting-house. The result was such as might naturally be expected. He neglected the monotonous pages of the journal and the ledger, for the magic numbers of Homer and Horace. His fancy, stimulated by restraint, repeatedly flashed forth in productions that attracted applause; he was more frequently found at the theatre than on 'change; delighted more in the society of scholars and men of taste and fancy, than of "substantial merchants," and at length abandoned the patient but comfortable realities of trade, for the splendid uncertainties of the Muse.

Our limits will not permit us to go into a minute examination of his life, which would otherwise be worthy of attention; for the habits and fortunes of an author, in this country, might yield some food for curious speculation. Unfitted for business, in a nation where every one is busy; devoted to literature, where literary leisure is confounded with idleness; the man of letters is almost an insulated being, with few to understand, less to value, and scarcely any to encourage his pursuits. It is not surprising, therefore, that our authors soon grow weary of a race which they have to run alone, and turn their attention to other callings of a more worldly and profitable nature. This is one of the reasons why the writers of this country so seldom attain to excellence. Before their genius is disciplined, and their taste refined, their talents are diverted into the ordinary channels of busy life, and occupied in what are considered its more useful purposes. In fact, the great demand for rough talent, as for common manual labor, in this country, prevents the appropriation of either mental or physical forces to elegant employments. The delicate mechanician may toil in penury, unless he devote himself to common man- ufactures, suitable to the ordinary consumption of the country; and the fine writer, if he depend upon his pen for a subsistence, will soon discover that he may starve on the very summit of Parnassus, while he sees herds of newspaper editors battening on the rank marshes of its borders.

Such is most likely to be the fate of authors by pro- fession, in the present circumstances of our country. But Mr. Paine had certainly nothing of the kind to complain of. His early prospects were extremely flattering. His productions met with a local circulation, and the poet with a degree of attention and respect highly creditable to the intelligent part of the Union where he resided.

"The qualities," says his biographer, "which had secured him esteem at the university were daily expanding, and his reputation was daily increasing. His society was eagerly sought in the most polished and refined circles; he administered compliments with great address; and no *beau* was ever a greater favorite in the *beau monde!*"

Having now confided to his pen for a support, Mr.

Paine undertook the editorship of a semi-weekly paper, devoted to Federal politics. It was conducted without diligence, and, if we may judge from the effects, without discretion ; for it drew upon him the vengeance of a mob, which attacked the house where he resided, and the resentment of a young gentleman whose father he had satirized. This youth, with an impetuosity hallowed by his filial feeling, demanded honorable satisfaction—it was denied, and the consequence was, that, in a casual rencounter, he took it, in a more degrading manner, on the person of Mr. Paine.

This was a deadly blow to the reputation of our author ; and his standing in society was still more impaired by his subsequent marriage with an actress, which produced a rupture with his father and a desertion by the fashionable world. This last is mentioned in terms of useless reprehension by his biographer. It is idle to rail at society for its laws of rank and gradations of respect. These rise, of themselves, out of the nature of things, and the moral and political circumstances in which that society is placed ; and the universal acquiescence in them by the soundest minds is a sufficient proof that they are salutary and correct. Mr. Paine should have foreseen the inevitable consequences of his union, in a society so rigid and religious, and where theatrical exhibitions had been considered so improper as for a long time to have been prohibited by law. Having foreseen the consequences, and willingly encountered them,

24

it would have been a proof of his firmness and good sense to have submitted to them without repining.

Unfortunately, Mr. Paine seems to have been deficient in that true kind of pride, which draws its support from the ample sources of conscious worth and integrity; which bears up its possessor against unmerited neglect, and induces him to persist in doing well, though certain of no approbation but his own. The moment the world neglected him, he began to neglect himself, as if he had theretofore acted right from the love of praise, rather than the love of virtue.

He contracted habits of intemperance, which, added to his natural heedlessness and want of application, rendered all the remainder of his life a scene of vicissitude. His newspaper establishment, from want of his personal attention, proved unfortunate; at the end of eighteen months he disposed of it, and became master of ceremonies of the Boston Theatre,—an anomalous office which we do not understand, but which for a time produced him a present means of subsistence. Notwithstanding the irregularity of his habits, it seems that he never exerted his talents without ample success. He was occasionally called on for orations, odes, songs, and addresses, which not only met with public applause, but with a pecuniary remuneration that is worthy of being recorded in our literary history. For his "Invention of Letters," a poem of about three hundred lines, we are told he received *fifteen hundred dollars*, exclusive of expense; and *twelve hundred* by the sale of his "Ruling Passion," a poem of about the same length. The political song of "Adams and Liberty" produced him also a profit of *seven hundred and fifty dollars.* These are sevenfold harvests, that have rarely been equalled even in the productive countries of Europe.

After a few years passed in this manner, having in some measure reformed his habits, his friends began to entertain hopes of rescuing him from this precarious mode of subsistence. They urged him to study the law, and offered him pecuniary assistance for the purpose. He listened to their advice; abandoned the theatre; applied himself diligently to legal studies; was admitted, and became a successful advocate. Business poured in upon him—his reputation rose—prospects of ease, of affluence, of substantial respectability, opened before him—but he relinquished them all with his incorrigible recklessness of mind, and relapsed into his former self-abandonment. From this time the springs of his mind seemed to have been rapidly broken down—invention languished—literary ambition was almost at an end; at the same time, an inordinate appetite for knowledge was awakened, but it was that kind of appetite which produces indigestion, rather than an invigoration of the system.

"During these last years of his life," says his biographer, "without a library, wandering from place to place, frequently uncertain where or whether he could procure a meal; his thirst and acquisition of knowledge astonishingly increased. Though frequently tormented with disease, and beset by duns and 'the law's staff-officers,' from whom, and from prison, he was frequently relieved by friendship; neither sickness nor penury abated his love of a book and of instructive conversation."

It is painful to trace the concluding history of this eccentric, contradictory, but interesting man. Broken down by penury and disease; disheartened by fancied, perhaps real, but certainly self-brought neglect; debilitated in mind and shattered in reputation, he languished into that state of nervous irritability and sickliness of thought, when the world ceases to interest and delight; when desire sinks into apathy, and " the grasshopper becomes a burden."

We cannot refrain from recurring to the picture given of him by his faithful biographer, at the outset of his career, with all the glow of youth and fancy, and the freshness of blooming reputation that graced his opening talents, and contrasting it with the following, taken in his day of premature decay and blighted intellect. The contrast is instructive and affecting; a few pages present the sad reverse of years.

" He was fed and lodged in an apartment at his father's; and in this feeble and emaciated state, walked abroad, from day to day, looking like misery personified, and pouring his lamentations into the ears of his friends, who were happy to confer those little acts of kindness which afforded to him some momentary consolation."

Even " during this period of unhoused and disconsolate

wretchedness," when the taper was fast sinking in the sock-
et, he was still capable of poetical excitement. At the request of the "Jockey Club," he undertook to write a song
for their anniversary dinner. His enfeebled imagination
faltered at the effort, until, spurred on by the last moment,
he aroused himself into a transient glow of composition,
executed the task, and then threw by the pen forever.

It is worthy of mention, that under all this accumulation of penury, despondency, and sickness, the passion
still remained for one species of amusement, which addresses itself chiefly to the imagination; or rather, perhaps, the habit remained after the passion had subsided.
He attended the theatre but two evenings before his
death. This was the last gleam of solitary pleasure; on
the following day, feeling his end approaching, he crawled
to an "attic chamber in his father's house," as to one of
those retreats—

" Where lonely want retires to die."

Here he languished until the next evening, when, in the
presence of his family and friends, he expired without a
struggle or a groan.

Such is a brief sketch of the biography of Thomas
Treat Paine,—a man calculated to flourish in the sunshine of life, but running to waste and ruin in the shade.
We have been beguiled into a more particular notice of
this part of the work from the interest which it excited,
and the strong moral picture which it presented. And

indeed the biography of authors is important in another point of view, as throwing a great light upon the state of literature and refinement of a nation. In a country where authors are few, any tract of literary anecdote, like the present, is valuable, as adding to the scanty materials from which future writers will be enabled to trace our advancement in letters and the arts. Hereafter, curiosity may be interested to gather information concerning these early adventurers in literature, not because they may have any great merit in their works, but because they were the first to adventure ; as we are curious about the early settlers of our country, not from their eminence of character, but because they were the first that settled.

In looking back upon the life of Mr. Paine, we scarcely know whether his misfortunes are to be attributed so much to his love of literature, as to his want of discretion and practical good sense. He was a man that seemed to live for the moment ; drawing but little instruction from the past, and casting but careless glances towards the future. So far as relates to him, his country stands acquitted in its literary character ; for certainly, as far as he made himself useful in his range of talents, he was amply remunerated.

The character given of him by his last biographer is highly interesting, and evinces that quick sensibility and openness to transient impressions, incident to a man more under the dominion of the fancy than the judgment.

"To speak of Mr. Paine as a man ; *hic labor, hoc opus est.* In his intercourse with the world, his earliest impressions were rarely correct. His vivid imagination, in his first interviews, undervalued or overrated almost every individual with whom he came in contact ; but when a protracted acquaintance had effaced early impressions, his judgment recovered its tone, and no man brought his associates to a fairer scrutiny, or could delineate their characteristics with greater exactness.

Nullius addictus jurare, in verba, magistri ;

and when he had once formed a deliberate opinion, without a change of circumstances, it is not known that he ever renounced it. Studious to please, he was only impatient of obtrusive folly, impertinent presumption, or idle speculation. His friendships were cordial, and his good genius soon rectified the precipitance of his enmities. To conflicting propositions he listened with attention ; heard his own opinions contested with complacency, and replied with courtesy. No root of bitterness ever quickened in his mind. If injured, he was placable ; if offended, he

> . . . . showed a hasty spark,
> And straight was cold again.

Parcere subjectis et debellare superbos

was in strict unison with the habitual elevation of his feelings. Such services as it was in his power to render to others, he performed with manly zeal; and their value was enhanced by being generally rendered where they were most needed; and through life he cherished a lively gratitude towards those from whom he had received benefits."

On his irregular habits his biographer remarks in palliation, "He sensibly felt, and clearly foresaw, the consequences of their continuous indulgence, and passed frequent resolutions of reformation; but daily embarrassments shook the resolves of his seclusion, and reform was indefinitely postponed. He urged as an excuse for delaying the Herculean task, that it was impossible to commence it while perplexed with difficulty and surrounded with distress. Instead of rising with an elastic power, and throwing the incumbent pressure from his shoulders, he succumbed under its accumulating weight, until he became insuperably recumbent; and vital action was daily precariously sustained by administering 'the extreme medicine of the constitution for its daily food.'"

We come now to the most ungracious part of our undertaking,—that of considering the literary character of the deceased. This is rendered the more delicate, from the excessive eulogiums passed on him in the enthusiasm of friendship, by his biographers, and which make us despair of yielding any praise that can approach to their ideas of his deserts.

We are told that Dryden was Mr. Paine's favorite author, and in some measure his prototype; but he appears to have admired rather than to have studied him. Like all those writers who take up some particular author as a model, a degree of bigotry has entered into his devotion, which made him blind to the faults of his original; or rather, these faults became beauties in his eyes. Such, for instance, is that propensity to far-sought allusions and forced conceits. Had he studied Dryden in connection with the literature of his day, contrasting him with the poets who preceded him, and those who were his contemporaries, Mr. Paine would have discovered that these were faults which Dryden reprobated himself. They were the lingering traces of a taste which he was himself endeavoring to abolish. Dryden was a great reformer of English poetry; not merely by improving the versification, and taming the rude roughness of the language into smoothness and harmony; but by abolishing from it those metaphysical subtleties, those strange analogies and extravagant combinations, which had been the pride and study of the old school. Thus struggling to cure others and himself of these excesses, it is not surprising that some of them still lurked about his writings; it is rather a matter of surprise that the number should be so inconsiderable.

These, however, seem to have caught the ardent and ill-regulated imagination of Mr. Paine, and to have given a tincture to the whole current of his writings. We find him continually aiming at fine thoughts, fine figures, and epigrammatic point. The censure that Johnson passes on his great prototype, may be applied with tenfold justice to him: "His delight was in wild and daring sallies of sentiment,—in the irregular and eccentric violence of wit. He delighted to tread upon the brink of meaning, where light and darkness begin to mingle; to approach the precipice of absurdity, and hover over the abyss of unideal vacancy." His verses are often so dizened out with embroidery, that the subject-matter is lost in the ornament—the idea is confused by the illustration; or rather, instead of one plain, distinct idea being presented

to the mind, we are bewildered with a score of simili-
tudes. Such, for instance, is the case with the following
passage, taken at random, and which is intended to be
descriptive of misers :—

> "In life's dark cell, pale burns their glimmering soul:
> A rush-light warms the winter of the pole.
> To chill and cheerless solitude confined,
> No spring of virtue thaws the ice of mind.
> They creep in blood, as frosty streamlets flow,
> And freeze with life, as dormice sleep in snow.
> Like snails they bear their dungeons on their backs,
> And shut out light—to save a window-tax !"

His figures and illustrations are often striking and
beautiful, but too often far-fetched and extravagant. He
had always plenty at command, and, indeed, every
thought that he conceived drew after it a cluster of similes. Among these he either had not the talent to dis-
criminate, or the self-denial to discard. Everything that
entered his mind was transferred to his page ; trope followed trope ; illustration was heaped on illustration,
ornament outvied ornament, until what at first promised
to be fine, ended in being tawdry.

Of his didactic poems, one of the most prominent is
the "Ruling Passion." It contains many passages of
striking merit, but is loaded with epithet, and distorted
by constant straining after epigram and eccentricity.
The author seems never content unless he be sparkling ;
the reader is continually perplexed to know what he

means, and sometimes disappointed, when he does find out, to discover that he means so little. It is one of the properties of poetic genius to give consequence to trifles. By a kind of magic power, it swells things up beyond their natural dimensions, and decks them out with a splendor of dress and coloring that completely hides their real insignificance. Pigmy thoughts that crept in prose, start up into gigantic size in poetry; and strutting in lofty epithets, inflated with hyperbole, and glittering with fine figures, are apt to take the imagination by surprise and dazzle the judgment. The steady eye of scrutiny, however, soon penetrates the glare; and when the thought has shrunk back to its real dimensions, what appeared to be oracular, turns out to be a truism.

As an instance of this we will quote the following passage :—

> "Heroes and bards, who nobler flights have won
> Than Cæsar's eagles, or the Mantuan swan,
> From eldest era share the common doom;
> The sun of glory shines but on the tomb.
> Firm as the Mede, the stern decree subdues
> The brightest pageant of the proudest Muse.
> Man's noblest powers could ne'er the law revoke,
> Though Handel harmonized what Chatham spoke;
> Though tuneful Morton's magic genius graced
> The Hyblean melody of Merry's taste!

> "Time, the stern censor, talisman of fame,
> With rigid justice portions praise and shame :

And, while his laurels, reared where genius grew,
'Mid wide oblivion's lava bloom anew;
Oft will his chymic fire, in distant age
Elicit spots, unseen on ancient page.
So the famed sage, who plunged in Ætna's flame,
'Mid pagan deities enshrined his name ;
Till from the iliac mountain's crater thrown,
The Martyr's sandal cost the God his crown."—*P.* 187.

Here the simple thought conveyed in this gorgeous page, as far as we can rake it out from among the splendid rubbish, is this, that fame is tested by time ; a truth, than which scarcely any is more familiar, and which the author, from the resemblance of the fourth line, and the tenor of those which preceded it, had evidently seen much more touchingly expressed in the elegy of Gray.

The characters in this poem, which are intended to exemplify a ruling passion, are trite and commonplace. The pedant, the deluded female, the fop, the old maid, the miser, are all hackneyed subjects of satire, and are treated in a hackneyed manner. If these old dishes are to be served up again, we might at least expect that the sauces would be new. It is evident Mr. Paine drew his characters from books rather than from real life. His fop flourishes the cane and snuff-box as in the days of Sir Fopling Flutter. His old maid is sprigged and behooped, and hides behind her fan according to immemorial usage ; and in his other characters we trace the same family likeness that marks the descendants of the heroes and heroines of ancient British poetry.

The following description of the Savoyard is sprightly and picturesque, though, unfortunately for the author, it reminds us of the Swiss peasant of Goldsmith, and forces upon us the contrast between that sparkling poetry which dazzles the fancy, and those simple, homefelt strains, which sink to the heart, and are treasured up there :—

> " To fame unknown, to happier fortune born,
> The blithe Savoyard hails the peep of morn,
> And while the fluid gold his eye surveys,
> The hoary glaciers fling their diamond blaze;
> Geneva's broad lake rushes from its shores,
> Arve gently murmurs, and the rough Rhone roars.
> 'Mid the cleft Alps, his cabin peers from high,
> Hangs o'er the clouds, and perches on the sky.
> O'er fields of ice, across the headlong flood,
> From cliff to cliff he bounds in fearless mood;
> While, far beneath, a night of tempest lies,
> Deep thunder mutters, harmless lightning flies;
> While, far above, from battlements of snow,
> Loud torrents tumble on the world below;
> On rustic reed he wakes a merrier tune,
> Than the lark warbles on the ' Ides of June.'
> Far off let glory's clarion shrilly swell;
> He loves the music of his pipe as well.
> Let shouting millions crown the hero's head,
> And Pride her tessellated pavement tread,
> More happy far, this denizen of air
> Enjoys what Nature condescends to spare;

> His days are jocund, undisturbed his nights,
> His spouse contents him and his mule delights."—*P.* 184.

The conclusion of this very descriptive passage partakes lamentably of the bathos. We cannot but smile at the last line, where he has paid the conjugal feelings of his hero but a sorry compliment, making him more delighted with his mule than with the wife of his bosom.

The "Invention of Letters" is another poem, where the author seems to have exerted the full scope of his talents. It shows that adroitness in the tricks of composition, that love for meretricious ornament, and at the same time that amazing store of imagery and illustration, which characterize this writer. We see in it many fine flights of thought, and brave sallies of the imagination, but at the same time a superabundance of the luscious faults of poetry; and we rise from it with augmented regret that so rich and prolific a genius had not been governed by a purer taste. The following eulogium of Faustus is a fair specimen of the author's beauties and defects :—

> " Egyptian shrubs, in hands of cook or priest,
> A king could mummy, or enrich a feast;
> Faustus, great shade! a nobler leaf imparts,
> Embalms all ages, and preserves all arts.
>   The ancient scribe, employed by bards divine,
> With faltering finger traced the lingering line.
> So few the scrivener's dull profession chose,
> With tedious toil each tardy transcript rose;
> And scarce the Iliad, penned from oral rhyme,
> Grew with the bark that bore its page sublime.

But when the press, with fertile womb supplies
The useful sheet, on thousand wings it flies;
Bound to no climate, to no age confined,
The pinioned volume spreads to all mankind.

    No sacred power the Cadmean art could claim,
O'er time to triumph, and defy the flame:
In one sad day a Goth could ravage more
Than ages wrote, or ages could restore.

    The Roman helmet, or the Grecian lyre,
A realm might conquer, or a realm inspire;
Then sink, oblivious, in the mouldering dust,
With those who blessed them, and with those who curst.
What guide had then the lettered pilgrim led
Where Plato moralized, where Cæsar bled?
What page had told, in lasting record wrought,
The world who butchered, or the world who taught?

    Thine was the mighty power, immortal sage!
To burst the cerements of each buried age.
Through the drear sepulchre of sunless Time,
Rich with the trophied wrecks of many a clime,
Thy daring genius broke the pathless way,
And brought the glorious relics forth to day."—*P.* **165.**

Of the lyrical poetry of Mr. Paine we can but give the same mixed opinion. It sometimes comes near being very fine, at other times is bombastic, and too often is obscure by far-fetched metaphors. The enthusiasm which is the life and spirit of this kind of poetry, certainly allows great license to the imagination, and permits the poet to use bolder figures and stronger exaggerations than any other species of serious composition; but he should be wary that he be not carried too far by the fervor of his feelings, and that he run not into obscurity and extravagance. In listening to lyrical poetry, we have to depend entirely on the ear to comprehend the subject; and as verse follows verse without allowing time for meditation, it is next to impossible for the auditor to extricate the meaning, if it be entangled in metaphor. The thoughts, therefore, should be clear and striking, and the figures, however lofty and magnificent, yet of that simple kind that flash at once upon the mind.

The following stanza is one of those that come near being extremely beautiful. The versification is swelling and melodious, and captivates the ear with the luxury of sound; the imagery is sublime, but the meaning a little obscure.

> " The sea is valor's charter,
>   A nation's wealthiest mine:
> His foaming caves when ocean bares,
>   Not pearls, but heroes shine;
> Aloft they mount the midnight surge,
>   Where shipwrecked spirits roam,
> And oft the knell is heard to swell,
>   Where bursting billows foam.
> Each storm a race of heroes rears,
>   To guard their native home."—*P.* 275.

The ode entitled " Rise, Colubmia," possesses more simplicity than most of his poems. Several of the verses are deserving of much praise, both for the sentiment and the composition.

" Remote from realms of rival fame,
    Thy bulwark is thy mound of waves;
The sea, thy birthright, thou must claim,
    Or, subject, yield the soil it laves.

Nor yet, though skilled, delight in arms;
    Peace, and her offspring Arts, be thine;
The face of Freedom scarce has charms,
    When on her cheeks no dimples shine.

While Fame, for thee, her wreath entwines,
    To bless, thy nobler triumph prove;
And, though the eagle haunts thy pines,
    Beneath thy willows shield the dove.

.   .   .   .

Revered in arms, in peace humane,
    No shore nor realm shall bound thy sway;
While all the virtues own thy reign,
    And subject elements obey ! "

The ode of "Spain, Commerce, and Freedom," is a mere conflagration of fancy. What shall we say to such a " melting hot—hissing hot" stanza as the following?—

" Bright Day of the world! dart thy lustre afar !
    Fire the north with thy heat! gild the south with thy splendor!
With thy glance light the torch of redintegrant war,
    Till the dismembered earth effervesce and regender.
        Through each zone may'st thou roll,
        Till thy beams at the Pole
Melt Philosophy's Ice in the sea of the soul ! "

We have unwarily exceeded our intended limits in this

25

article, and must now bring it to a conclusion. From the examination which we have given Mr. Paine's writings, we can by no means concur in the opinion that he is an author on whom the nation should venture its poetic claims. His natural requisites were undoubtedly great, and had they been skilfully managed, might have raised him to an enviable eminence. He possessed a brilliant imagination, but not great powers of reflection. He thinks often acutely, seldom profoundly; indeed, there was such a constant wish to be ingenious and pungent, that he was impatient of the regular flow of thought and feeling, and seemed dissatisfied with every line that did not contain a paradox, a simile, or an apothegm. There appears also to have been an indistinctness in his conceptions; his mind teemed with vague ideas, with shadows of thought, which he could not accurately embody, and the consequence was a frequent want of precision in his writings. He had read much and miscellaneously; and having a tenacious memory, was enabled to illustrate his thoughts by a thousand analogies and similes, drawn from books, and often to enrich his poems with the thoughts of others. Indeed, his acquired treasures were often a disadvantage; not having a simple, discriminating taste, he could not select from among them; and being a little ostentatious of his wealth, was too apt to pour it in glittering profusion upon his page.

If we have been too severe in our animadversions on this author's faults, we can only say that the high encomiums of his biographers, and the high assumptions of the author himself, which are evident from the style of his writings, obliged us to judge of him by an elevated standard. Mr. Paine ventured in the lofty walks of composition, and appears continually to have been measuring himself with the masters of the art. His biographers have even hinted at placing him "on the same shelf with the prince of English rhyme," and thus, in a manner, have invited a less indulgent examination than, perhaps, might otherwise have been given.

If, however, we are unjust in our censures, a little while will decide their futility. To the living every hour of reputation is important, as adding one hour of enjoyment to existence; but the fame of the dead, to be valuable, must be permanent; and it is in nowise impaired, if for a year or two the misrepresentations of criticism becloud its lustre.

We assure the biographers of Mr. Paine that we heartily concur with them in the wish to see one of our native poets rising to equal excellence with the immortal bards of Great Britain; but we do not feel any restless anxiety on the subject. We wait with hope, but we wait with patience. Of all writers a great poet is the rarest. Britain, with all her patronage of literature, with her standing army of authors, has through a series of ages produced but a very, very few who deserve the name. Can it, then, be a matter of surprise, or should it be of humiliation, that, in our country, where the literary ranks are so scanty, the incitements so small, and the advantages so inconsiderable, we should not yet have produced a master in the art? Let us rest satisfied; as far as the intellect of the nation has been exercised, we have furnished our full proportion of ordinary poets, and some that have even risen above mediocrity; but a really great poet is the production of a century.

EDWIN C. HOLLAND.

Odes, Naval Songs, and other occasional Poems. By EDWIN
C. HOLLAND, ESQ., Charleston.

 SMALL volume, with the above title, has been
handed to us, with a request that it might be
criticised. Though we do not profess the art
and mystery of reviewing, and are not ambitious of being
either wise or facetious at the expense of others, yet we
feel a disposition to notice the present work, because
it is a specimen of one branch of literature at present
very popular throughout our country, and also because
the author, who, we understand, is quite young, gives
proof of very considerable poetical talent and is in great
danger of being spoiled.

We apprehend, from various symptoms about his work,
that he has for some time past received great honors
from circles of literary ladies and gentlemen, and that he
has great facility at composition—we find, moreover, that
he has written for public papers under the signature of
"Orlando;" and above all, that a prize has been awarded
to one of his poems, in a kind of poetical lottery, cun-
ningly devised by an "eminent bookseller."

These, we must confess, are melancholy disadvantages to start withal ; and many a youthful poet of great promise has been utterly ruined by misfortunes of much inferior magnitude. We trust, however, that in the present case they are not without remedy, and that the author is not so far gone in the evil habit of publishing, as to be utterly beyond reclaim. Still we feel the necessity of extending immediate relief, from a hint he gives us on the cover of his book, that the present poems are " presented merely as specimens of his manner, and comprise but a *very small portion*" of those he has on hand. This information really startled us ; we beheld in imagination a mighty mass of odes, songs, sonnets, and acrostics, impending in awful volume over our heads, and threatening every instant to flutter down, like a theatrical snow-storm of white paper. To avert so fearful an *avalanche* have we hastened to take pen in hand, determined to risk the author's displeasure, by giving him good advice, and to deliver him, if possible, uninjured out of the hands both of his admirers and his patron.

The main piece of advice we would give him is, to lock up all his remaining writings, and to abstain most abstemiously from publishing for some years to come. We know that this will appear very ungracious counsel, and we have not very great hope that it will be adopted. We are well aware of the eagerness of young authors to hurry into print, and that the Muse is too fond of present pay, and " present pudding," to brook voluntarily the postponement of reward. Besides, this early and exuberant foliage of the mind is peculiar to warm sensibilities and lively fancies, in which the principles of fecundity are so strong as to be almost irrepressible. The least ray of popular admiration sets all the juices in motion, produces a bursting forth of buds and blossoms, and a profusion of vernal and perishable vegetation. But there is no greater source of torment to a writer than the flippancies of his juvenile Muse. The sins and follies of his youth arise in loathsome array, to disturb the quiet of his maturer years, and he is perpetually haunted by the spectres of the early murders he has perpetrated on good English and good sense.

We have no intention to discourage Mr. Holland from his poetic career. On the contrary, it is in consequence of the good opinion we entertain of his genius, that we are solicitous that it should be carefully nurtured, wholesomely disciplined, and trained up to full and masculine vigor, rather than dissipated and enfeebled by early excesses. We think we can discern in his writings strong marks of amiable, and generous, and lofty sentiment, of ready invention, and great brilliancy of expression. These are as yet obscured by a false, or rather puerile taste, which time and attention will improve, but it is necessary that time and attention should be employed. Were his faults merely those of mediocrity we should despair, for there is no such thing as fermenting a dull mind into anything like poetic inspiration; but we think the effervescence of this writer's fancy will at a future day settle down into something substantially excellent. Rising genius always shoots forth its rays from among clouds and vapors, but these will gradually roll away and disappear, as it ascends to its steady and meridian lustre.

One thing which pleases us in the songs in this collection is, that they have more originality than we commonly meet with in our national songs. We begin to think that it is a much more difficult thing to write a good song than to fight a good battle ; for our tars have achieved several splendid victories in a short space of time ; but, notwithstanding the thousand pens that have been drawn forth in every part of the Union, we do not recollect a single song of really sterling merit that has been written on the occasion. Nothing is more offensive than a certain lawless custom which prevails among our patriotic songsters, of seizing upon the noble songs of Great Britain, mangling and disfiguring them, with pens more merciless than Indian scalping-knives, and then passing them off for American songs. This may be an idea borrowed from the custom of our savage neighbors, of adopting prisoners into their families, and so completely taking them to their homes and hearts, as almost to consider them as children of their own begetting. At any rate, it is a practice worthy of savage life and savage ideas of property. We have witnessed such horrible distortions of sense and poetry ; we have seen the fine members of an elegant stanza so mangled and wrenched, in order to apply it to this country, that our very hearts ached with sympathy and vexation. We are continually annoyed with the figure of poor Columbia, an honest, awkward, dowdy sort of dame, thrust into the place of Britannia, and made to wield the trident and "rule the waves," and play off a thousand clumsy ceremonies before company, as maladroitly as a worthy tradesman's wife enacting a fine lady or a tragedy queen.

Besides, there is in this a pitifulness of spirit, an appearance of abject poverty of mind, that would be degrading if it really belonged to the nation. Nay, more, there is a positive dishonesty in it. We may, if we choose, plunder the bodies of our enemies, whom we have fairly conquered in the field of battle ; and we may strut about, uncouthly arrayed in their garments, with their coats swinging to our heels, and their boots " a world too wide for our shrunk shanks," but the same privilege does not extend to literature ; and however our puny poetasters may flaunt for a while in the pilfered garbs of their gigantic neighbors, they may rest assured that if there should be a tribunal hereafter to try the crimes of authors, they will be considered as mere poetical highwaymen, and condemned to swing most loftily for their offences.

It is really insulting to tell this country, as some of these varlets do, that she " needs no bulwarks, no towers along the steep," when there is a cry from one end of the

Union to the other for the fortifying our seaports and the defence of our coast, and when every post brings us intelligence of the enemy depredating in our bays and rivers ; and it is still more insulting to tell her that " her home is on the deep," which, if it really be the case, only proves that at present she is turned out of doors. No, if we really must have national songs, let them be of our own manufacturing, however coarse. We would rather hear our victories celebrated in the merest doggerel that sprang from native invention, than beg, borrow, or steal from others, the thoughts and words in which to express our exultation. By tasking our own powers, and relying entirely on ourselves, we shall gradually improve and rise to poetical independence ; but this practice of appropriating the thoughts of others, of getting along by contemptible shifts and literary larcenies, prevents native exertion, and produces absolute impoverishment. It is in literature as in the accumulation of private fortune ; the humblest beginning should not dishearten ; much may be done by persevering industry or spirited enterprise ; but he who depends on borrowing will never grow rich, and he who indulges in theft will ultimately come to the gallows.

We are glad to find that the writer before us is innocent of these enormous sins against honesty and good sense ; but we would warn him against another evil, into which young writers, and young men, are very prone to fall—we mean bad company. We are apprehensive that

the companions of his literary leisure have been none of
the most profitable, and that he has been trifling too
much with the fantastic gentry of the Della Cruscan
school, revelling among flowers and hunting butterflies,
when he should have been soberly walking, like a dute-
ous disciple, in the footsteps of the mighty masters of his
art. We are led to this idea from seeing in his poems
the portentous names of "the blue-eyed Myra," and
"Rosa Matilda," and from reading of "lucid vests veiling
snowy breasts," and "satin sashes," and "sighs of rosy
perfume," and "trembling eve-star beam, through some
light cloud's glory seen" (which, by the bye, is a rhyme
very much like that of "muffin and dumpling"), and—

> "The sweetest of perfumes that languishing flies
> Like a kiss on the nectarous morning-tide air."

Now all this kind of poetry is rather late in the day—
the fashion has gone by. A man may as well attempt to
figure as a fine gentleman in a pea-green silk coat, and
pink satin breeches, and powdered head, and paste
buckles, and sharp-toed shoes, and all the finery of Sir
Fopling Flutter, as to write in the style of Della Crusca.
Gifford has long since brushed away all this trum-
pery.

We think also the author has rather perverted his
fancy by reading the amatory effusions of Moore; which,
whatever be the magic of their imagery and versification,
breathe a spirit of heartless sensuality and soft voluptu-

ousness beneath the tone of vigorous and virtuous manhood.

This rhapsodizing about " brilliant pleasures," and
" hours of bliss," and " humid eyelids," and " ardent
kisses," is, after all, mighty cold-blooded, silly stuff. It
may do to tickle the ears of love-sick striplings and romantic milliners ; but one verse describing pure domestic affection, or tender innocent love, from the pen of
Burns, speaks more to the heart than all the meretricious
rhapsodies of Moore.

We doubt if in the whole round of rapturous scenes,
dwelt on with elaborate salacity by the modern Ana-
creon, one passage can be found, combining equal eloquence of language, delicacy of imagery, and impassioned
tenderness, with the following picture of the interview
and parting of two lovers :—

> " How sweetly bloomed the gay, green birk,
>   How rich the hawthorn's blossom;
> As underneath their fragrant shade
>   I clasped her to my bosom!
> The golden hours, on angel wings,
>   Flew o'er me and my dearie :
> For dear to me, as light and life,
>   Was my sweet Highland Mary.
>
> " Wi' mony a vow, and locked embrace,
>   Our parting was fu' tender;
> And pledging aft to meet again,
>   We tore oursel's asunder ;

But oh ! fell death's untimely frost,
    That nipt my flower sae early !
Now green's the sod, and cauld's the clay,
    That wraps my Highland Mary.

" O pale, pale now those rosy lips,
    I aft hae kissed sae fondly!
And closed for aye the sparkling glance
    That dwelt on me sae kindly!
And mouldering now in silent dust
    That heart that lo'ed me dearly!
But still within my bosom's core
    Shall live my Highland Mary."

Throughout the whole of the foregoing stanzas we would remark the extreme simplicity of the language, the utter absence of all false coloring, of those "roseate hues," and "ambrosial odors," and "purple mists," that steam from the pages of our voluptuous poets, to intoxicate the weak brains of their admirers. Burns depended on the truth and tenderness of his ideas, on that deep-toned feeling which is the very soul of poetry. To use his own admirably descriptive words,—

' His rural loves are Nature's sel,
    Nae bombast spates o' nonsense swell;
Nae *snap conceits*, but that *sweet spell*,
        O' witchin' love,
    That charm, that can the strongest quell,
        The sternest move."

But the chief fault which infests the style of the poems before us, is a passion for hyperbole, and for the glare of extravagant images and flashing phrases. This taste for

gorgeous finery and violent metaphor prevails throughout our country, and is characteristic of the early efforts
of literature. Our national songs are full of ridiculous exaggeration, and frothy rant and commonplace bloated up
into fustian. The writers seem to think that huge words
and mountainous figures constitute the sublime. Their
puny thoughts are made to sweat under loads of cum-
brous imagery, and now and then they are so wrapt up
in conflagrations, and blazes, and thunders and lightnings,
that, like Nick Bottom's hero, they seem to have " slipt
on a brimstone shirt, and are all on fire ! "

We would advise these writers, if they wish to see
what is really grand and forcible in patriotic minstrelsy,
to read the national songs of Campbell, and the " Ban-
nock-Burn " of Burns, where there is the utmost grandeur of thought conveyed in striking but perspicuous
language. It is much easier to be fine than correct in
writing. A rude and imperfect taste always heaps on
decoration, and seeks to dazzle by a profusion of brilliant incongruities. But true taste evinces itself in pure
and noble simplicity, and a fitness and chasteness of ornament. The Muses of the ancients are described as
beautiful females, exquisitely proportioned, simply attired, with no ornaments but the diamond clasps that
connected their garments ; but were we to paint the Muse
of one of our popular poets, we should represent her as a
pawnbroker's widow, with rings on every finger, and
loaded with borrowed and heterogeneous finery.

One cause of the epidemical nature of our literary errors, is the proneness of our authors to borrow from each other, and thus to interchange faults, and give a circulation to absurdities. It is dangerous always for a writer to be very studious of contemporary publications, which have not passed the ordeal of time and criticism. He should fix his eye on those models which have been scrutinized, and of the faults and excellences of which he is fully apprised. We think we can trace, in the popular songs of the volume before us, proofs that the author has been very conversant with the works of Robert Treat Paine, a late American writer of very considerable merit, but who delighted in continued explosions of fancy and glitter of language. As we do not censure wantonly, or for the sake of finding fault, we shall point to one of the author's writings, on which it is probable he most values himself, as it is the one which publicly received the prize in the Bookseller's Lottery. We allude to "The Pillar of Glory." We are likewise induced to notice this particularly, because we find it going the rounds of the Union,—strummed at pianos, sang at concerts, and roared forth lustily at public dinners. Having this universal currency, and bearing the imposing title of "Prize Poem," which is undoubtedly equal to the "Tower Stamp," it stands a great chance of being considered abroad as a prize production of one of our Universities, and at home as a standard poem, worthy the imitation of all tyros in the art.

The first stanza is very fair, and indeed is one of those passages on which we found our good opinion of the author's genius. The last line is really noble.

> " Hail to the heroes whose triumphs have brightened
>   The darkness which shrouded America's name !
> Long shall their valor in battle that lightened,
>   Live in the brilliant escutcheons of fame !
>   Dark where the torrents flow,
>   And the rude tempests blow,
>   The stormy-clad Spirit of Albion raves ;
>   Long shall she mourn the day,
>   When in the vengeful fray,
>   Liberty walked, like a god, on the waves."

The second stanza, however, sinks from this vigorous and perspicuous tone. We have the "halo and lustre of story" *curling* round the "wave of the ocean ;" a mixture of ideal and tangible objects wholly inadmissible in good poetry. But the great mass of sin lies in the third stanza, where the writer rises into such a glare and confusion of figure as to be almost incomprehensible.

> " The pillar of glory, the sea that enlightens,
>   Shall last till eternity rocks on its base !
> The splendor of fame its waters that brightens,
>   Shall follow the footsteps of time in his race !
>   Wide o'er the stormy deep,
>   Where the rude surges sweep,
>   Its lustre shall circle the brows of the brave !
>   Honor shall give it light,
>   Triumph shall keep it bright,
>   Long as in battle we meet on the wave ! "

We confess that we were sadly puzzled to understand the nature of this ideal pillar, that seemed to have set the sea in a blaze, and was to last " till eternity rocks on its base," which we suppose is, according to a vulgar phrase, " forever and a day after." Our perplexity was increased by the cross light from the " splendor of fame," which, like a foot-boy with a lantern, was to jog on after the footsteps of Time ; who it appears was to run a race against himself on the water—and as to the other lights and gleams that followed, they threw us into complete bewilderment. It is true, after beating about for some time, we at length landed on what we suspected to be the author's meaning; but a worthy friend of ours, who read the passage with great attention, maintains that this pillar of glory which enlightened the sea can be nothing more nor less than a light-house.

We do not certainly wish to indulge in improper or illiberal levity. It is not the author's fault that his poem has received a prize, and been elevated into unfortunate notoriety. Were its faults matters of concernment merely to himself, we should barely have hinted at them ; but the poem has been made, in a manner, a national poem, and in attacking it we attack generally that prevailing taste among our poetical writers for excessive ornament, for turgid extravagance, and vapid hyperbole. We wish in some small degree to counteract the mischief that may be done to national literature by eminent booksellers crowning inferior effusions as prize poems, setting them

26

to music, and circulating them widely through the country. We wish also, by a little good-humored rebuke, to stay the hurried career of a youth of talent and promise, whom we perceive lapsing into error, and liable to be precipitated forward by the injudicious applauses of his friends.

We therefore repeat our advice to Mr. Holland, that he abstain from further publication until he has cultivated his taste and ripened his mind. We earnestly exhort him rigorously to watch over his youthful Muse ; who, we suspect, is very spirited and vivacious, subject to quick excitement, of great pruriency of feeling, and a most uneasy inclination to breed. Let him in the meanwhile diligently improve himself in classical studies, and in an intimate acquaintance with the best and simplest British poets, and the soundest British critics. We do assure him that really fine poetry is exceedingly rare, and not to be written copiously nor rapidly. Middling poetry may be produced in any quantity ; the press groans with it, the shelves of circulating libraries are loaded with it ; but who reads merely middling poetry ? Only two kinds can possibly be tolerated,—the very good or the very bad,—one to be read with enthusiasm, the other to be laughed at.

We have in the course of this article quoted him rather unfavorably, but it was for the purpose of general criticism, not individual censure ; before we conclude, it is but justice to give a specimen of what we consider his best manner. The following stanzas are taken from elegiac lines on the death of a young lady. The comparison of a beautiful female to a flower is obvious and frequent in poetry, but we think it is managed here with uncommon delicacy and consistency, and great novelty of thought and manner :—

> " There was a flower of beauteous birth,
>   Of lavish charms, and chastened dye;
> It smiled upon the lap of earth,
>   And caught the gaze of every eye.

> " The vernal breeze, whose step is seen
>   Imprinted in the early dew,
> Ne'er brushed a flower of brighter beam,
>   Or nursed a bud of lovelier hue!

> " It blossomed not in dreary wild,
>   In darksome glen, or desert bower,
> But grew, like Flora's fav'rite child,
>   In sunbeam soft and fragrant shower.

> " The graces loved with chastened light
>   To flush its pure celestial bloom,
> And all its blossoms were so bright,
>   It seemed not formed to die so soon.

> " Youth round the flow'ret ere it fell
>   In armor bright was seen to stray,
> And beauty said, *her* magic spell
>   Should keep its perfume from decay.

"The parent-stalk from which it sprung,
    Transported as its halo spread,
  In holy umbrage o'er it hung,
    And tears of heaven-born rapture shed.

"Yet, fragile flower! thy blossom bright,
    Though guarded by a magic spell,
  Like a sweet beam of evening light,
    In lonely hour of tempest fell.

"The death-blast of the winter air,
    The cold frost and the night-wind came,
  They nipt thy beauty once so fair!—
    It shall not bloom on earth again!"

From a general view of the poems of Mr. Holland, it is evident that he has the external requisites for poetry in abundance,—he has fine images, fine phrases, and ready versification; he must only learn to think with fulness and precision, and he will write splendidly. As we have already hinted, we consider his present productions but the blossoms of his genius, and like blossoms they will fall and perish; but we trust that after some time of silent growth and gradual maturity, we shall see them succeeded by a harvest of rich and highly flavored fruit.

History of the Northmen, or Danes and Normans.   London.
8vo.   1831.

E are misers in knowledge as in wealth.   Open inexhaustible mines to us on every hand, yet we return to grope in the exhausted stream of past opulence, and sift its sands for ore ; place us in an age when history pours in upon us like an inundation and the events of a century are crowded into a lustre, yet we tenaciously hold on to the scanty records of foregone times, and often neglect the all-important present to discuss the possibility of the almost forgotten past.

It is worthy of remark that this passion for the antiquated and the obsolete appears to be felt with increasing force in this country.   It may be asked, what sympathies can the native of a land, where everything is in its youth and freshness, have with the antiquities of the ancient hemisphere ?   What inducement can he have to turn from the animated scene around him, and the brilliant perspective that breaks upon his imagination, to wander among the mouldering monuments of the olden world, and to call up its shadowy lines of kings and warriors from the dim twilight of tradition?—

> " Why seeks he, with unwearied toil,
>   Through death's dark walls to urge his way,
>   Reclaim his long-asserted spoil,
>   And lead oblivion into day ?"

We answer, that he is captivated by the powerful charm of contrast. Accustomed to a land where everything is bursting into life, and history itself but in its dawning, antiquity has, in fact, for him the effect of novelty; and the fading but mellow glories of the past, which linger in the horizon of the Old World, relieve the eye, after being dazzled with the rising rays which sparkle up the firmament of the New.

It is a mistake, too, that the political faith of a republican requires him, on all occasions, to declaim with bigot heat against the stately and traditional ceremonials, the storied pomps and pageants of other forms of government; or even prevents him from, at times, viewing them with interest, as matters worthy of curious investigation. Independently of the themes they present for historical and philosophical inquiry, he may regard them with a picturesque and poetical eye, as he regards the Gothic edifices rich with the elaborate ornaments of a gorgeous and intricate style of architecture, without wishing to exchange therefor the stern but proud simplicity of his own habitation; or, as he admires the romantic keeps and castles of chivalrous and feudal times, without desiring to revive the dangerous customs and warlike days in which they originated. To him the whole pageantry of emperors and kings, and nobles, and titled knights, is, as it were, a species of poetical machinery, addressing itself to his imagination, but no more affecting his faith than does the machinery of the heathen mythology affect the orthodoxy of the scholar who delights in the strains of Homer and Virgil, and wanders with enthusiasm among the crumbling temples and sculptured deities of Greece and Rome; or do the fairy mythology of the East, and the demonology of the North, impair the Christian faith of the poet or the novelist who interweaves them in his fictions.

We have been betrayed into these remarks, in considering the work before us, where we find one of our countrymen, and a thorough republican, investigating with minute attention some of the most antiquated and dubious tracts of European history, and treating of some of its exhausted and almost forgotten dynasties; yet evincing throughout the enthusiasm of an antiquarian, the liberality of a scholar, and the enlightened toleration of a citizen of the world.

The author of the work before us, Mr. Henry Wheaton, has for some years filled the situation of Chargé d'Affaires at the court of Denmark. Since he has resided at Copenhagen, he has been led into a course of literary and historic research, which has ended in the production of the present history of those Gothic and Teutonic people, who, inhabiting the northern regions of Europe, have so often and so successfully made inroads into other countries, more genial in climate and abundant in wealth. A considerable part of his book consists of what may be called conjectural or critical history, relating to remote and obscure periods of time, previous to the introduction of Christianity, historiography, and the use of Roman letters among those northern nations. At the outset, therefore, it assumes something of an austere and antiquarian air, which may daunt and discourage that class of readers who are accustomed to find history carefully laid out in easy rambling walks through agreeable landscapes, where just enough of the original roughness is left to produce the picturesque and romantic. Those, however, who have the courage to penetrate the dark and shadowy boundary of our author's work, grimly beset with hyperborean horrors, will find it resembling one of those enchanted forests described in northern poetry,—embosoming regions of wonder and delight, for such as have the hardihood to achieve the adventure. For our own part, we have been struck with the variety of adventurous incidents crowded into these pages, and with the abundance of that poetical material which is chiefly found in early history; while many of the rude traditions of the Normans, the Saxons, and the Danes have come to us with the captivating charms of early association, recalling the marvellous tales and legends that have delighted us in childhood.

The first seven chapters may be regarded as preliminary to the narrative, or, more strictly, historical part of the book. They trace the scanty knowledge possessed by Greek and Roman antiquity of the Scandinavian North; the earliest migrations from that quarter to the west, and south, and east of Europe; the discovery of Iceland by the Norwegians; with the singular circumstances which rendered that barren and volcanic isle, where ice and fire contend for mastery, the last asylum of Pagan faith and Scandinavian literature. In this wild region they lingered until the Latin alphabet superseded the Runic character, when the traditionary poetry and oral history of the North were consigned to written records, and rescued from that indiscriminate destruction which overwhelmed them on the Scandinavian continent.

The government of Iceland is described by our author as being more properly a patriarchal aristocracy than a republic; and he observes that the Icelanders, in consequence of their adherence to their ancient religion, cherished and cultivated the language and literature of their ancestors, and brought them to a degree of beauty and. perfection which they never reached in the Christianized countries of the North, where the introduction of the learned languages produced feeble and awkward, though classical imitation, instead of graceful and national originality.

When, at the end of the tenth century, Christianity was at length introduced into the island, the national literature, though existing only in oral tradition, was full blown, and had attained too strong and deep a root in the affections of the people to be eradicated, and had given a charm and value to the language with which it was identified. The Latin letters, therefore, which accompanied the introduction of the Romish religion, were merely adapted to designate the sounds heretofore expressed by Runic characters, and thus contributed to preserve in Iceland the ancient language of the North, when exiled from its parent countries of Scandinavia. To this fidelity to its ancient tongue, the rude and inhospitable shores of Iceland owe that charm which gives them an inexhaustible interest in the eyes of the antiquary, and endears them to the imagination of the poet. " The popular superstitions," observes our author, " with which the mythology and poetry of the North are interwoven, continued still to linger in the sequestered glens of this remote island."

The language in itself appears to have been worthy of this preservation, since we are told that "it bears in its internal structure a strong resemblance to the Latin and Greek, and even to the ancient Persian and Sanscrit, and rivals in copiousness, flexibility, and energy, every modern tongue."

Before the introduction of letters, all Scandinavian knowledge was perpetuated in oral tradition by their Skalds, who, like the rhapsodists of ancient Greece, and the bards of the Celtic tribes, were at once poets and his-

torians. We boast of the encouragement of letters and
literary men in these days of refinement; but where are
they more honored and rewarded than they were among
these barbarians of the North? The Skalds, we are told,
were the companions and chroniclers of kings, who entertained them in their trains, enriched them with rewards, and sometimes entered the lists with them in
trials of skill in their art. They in a manner bound
country to country, and people to people, by a delightful
link of union, travelling about as wandering minstrels,
from land to land, and often performing the office of ambassadors between hostile tribes. While thus applying
the gifts of genius to their divine and legitimate ends, by
calming the passions of men, and harmonizing their feelings into kindly sympathy, they were looked up to with
mingled reverence and affection, and a sacred character
was attached to their calling. Nay, in such estimation
were they held, that they occasionally married the
daughters of princes, and one of them was actually
raised to a throne in the fourth century of the Christian
era.

It is true the Skalds were not always treated with
equal deference, but were sometimes doomed to experience the usual caprice that attends upon royal patronage. We are told that Canute the Great retained several
at his court, who were munificently rewarded for their
encomiastic lays. One of them having composed a short
poem in praise of his sovereign, hastened to recite it to

him, but found him just rising from table, and surrounded by suitors.

" The impatient poet craved an audience of the king for his lay, assuring him it was ' very short.' The wrath of Canute was kindled, and he answered the Skald with a stern look, — ' Are you not ashamed to do what none but yourself has dared, — to write a short poem upon me ? — unless by the hour of dinner to-morrow you produce a *drapa* above thirty strophes long on the same subject, your life shall pay the penalty.' The inventive genius of the poet did not desert him ; he produced the required poem, which was of the kind called *Tog-drapa*, and the king liberally rewarded him with fifty marks of silver.

" Thus we perceive how the flowers of poetry sprung up and bloomed amidst eternal ice and snows. The arts of peace were successfully cultivated by the free and independent Icelanders. Their Arctic isle was not warmed by a Grecian sun, but their hearts glowed with the fire of freedom. The natural divisions of the country by icebergs and lava streams insulated the people from each other, and the inhabitants of each valley and each hamlet formed, as it were, an independent community. These were again reunited in the general national assembly of the Althing, which might not be unaptly likened to the Amphictyonic council or Olympic games, where all the tribes of the nation convened to offer the common rites of their religion, to decide their mutual differences, and to listen to the lays of the Skald, which commemorated the exploits of their ancestors. Their pastoral life was diversified by the occupation of fishing. Like the Greeks, too, the sea was their element, but even their shortest voyages bore them much farther from their native shores than the boasted expedition of the Argonauts. Their familiarity with the perils of the ocean, and with the diversified manners and customs of foreign lands, stamped their national character with bold and original features, which distinguished them from every other people.

" The power of oral tradition, in thus transmitting, through a succession of ages, poetical or prose compositions of considerable length, may appear almost incredible to civilized nations accustomed to the art of writing. But it is well known, that even after the Homeric poems had been reduced to writing, the rhapsodists who had been accustomed to recite them could readily repeat any passage desired. And we have, in our own times, among the Servians, Calmucks, and other barbarous and semi-barbarous nations, examples of heroic and popular poems of great length thus preserved and handed down to posterity. This is more especially the case where there is a perpetual order of men, whose exclusive employment it is to learn and repeat, whose faculty of the memory is thus improved and carried to the highest pitch of perfection, and who are relied upon as historiographers to preserve the national annals. The interesting scene presented this day in every Icelandic family, in the long nights of winter, is a living proof of the existence of this ancient custom. No sooner does the day close, than the whole patriarchal family, domestics and all, are seated on their couches in the principal apartment, from the ceiling of which the reading and working lamp is suspended; and one of the family, selected for that purpose, takes his seat near the lamp, and begins to read some favorite Saga, or it may be the works of Klopstock and Milton (for these have been translated in Icelandic), whilst all the rest attentively listen, and are at the same time engaged in their respective occupations. From the scarcity of printed books in this poor and sequestered country, in some families the Sagas are recited by those who have committed them to memory, and there are still instances of itinerant orators of this sort, who gain a livelihood during the winter by going about, from house to house, repeating the stories they have thus learnt by heart."

The most prominent feature of Icelandic verse, according to our author, is its alliteration. In this respect it resembles the poetry of all rude periods of society. That of the eastern nations, the Hebrews and the Persians, is full of this ornament; and it is found even

among the classic poets of Greece and Rome. These
observations of Mr. Wheaton are supported by those of
Dr. Henderson,* who states that the fundamental rule
in Icelandic poetry required that there should be three
words in every couplet having the same initial letter, two
of which should be in the former hemistich, and one in
the latter. The following translation from Milton is
furnished as a specimen : —

> *V*id that *V*illu diup
> *V*ard annum slæga,
> *B*öloerk *B*idleikat
> *B*armi vitis â.

> " Into this wild abyss the wary Fiend
> Stood on the brink of Hell and looked."

As a specimen of the tales related by the Skalds, we
may cite that of Sigurd and the beauteous Brynhilda, a
royal virgin, who is described as living in a lonely castle,
encircled by magic flames.

In the Teutonic lay, Brynhilda is a mere mortal virgin; but in the Icelandic poem she becomes a Valkyria,
one of those demi-divinities, servants of Odin or Woden
in the Gothic mythology, who were appointed to watch
over the fate of battle, and were, as their name betokens,
selectors of the slain. They were clothed in armor, and
mounted on fleet horses, with drawn swords, and mingled

---

* *Henderson's Iceland.* Edinb., 1819. Appendix III.

in the shock of battle, choosing the warrior-victims, and conducting them to Valhalla, the hall of Odin, where they joined the banquet of departed heroes, in carousals of mead and beer.

The first interview of the hero and heroine is wildly romantic. Sigurd, journeying toward Franconia, sees a flaming light upon a lofty mountain; he approaches it, and beholds a warrior in full armor asleep upon the ground. On removing the helmet of the slumberer, he discovers the supposed knight to be an Amazon. Her armor clings to her body, so that he is obliged to separate it with his sword. She then arises from her death-like sleep, and apprises him that he has broken the spell by which she lay entranced. She had been thrown into this lethargic state by Odin, in punishment for having disobeyed his orders. In a combat between two knights, she had caused the death of him who should have had the victory.

This romantic tale has been agreeably versified by William Spencer, an elegant and accomplished genius, who has just furnished the world with sufficient proofs of his talents to cause regret that they did not fall to the lot of a more industrious man. We subjoin the fragments of his poem cited by our author.

"Oh, strange is the bower where Brynhilda reclines,
Around it the watch-fire high bickering shines!
Her couch is of iron, her pillow a shield,
And the maiden's chaste eyes are in deep slumber sealed;

Thy charm, dreadful Odin, around her is spread,
From thy wand the dread slumber was poured on her head.
Oh, whilom in battle so bold and so free,
Like a *Vikingr* victorious she roved o'er the sea.
The love-lighting eyes, which are fettered by sleep,
Have seen the sea-fight raging fierce o'er the deep ;
And 'mid the dread wounds of the dying and slain,
The tide of destruction poured wide o'er the plain.

"Who is it that spurs his dark steed at the fire ?
Who is it, whose wishes thus boldly aspire
To the chamber of shields, where the beautiful maid
By the spell of the mighty All-Father is laid ?
It is Sigurd the valiant, the slayer of kings,
With the spoils of the Dragon, his gold and his rings."

BRYNHILDA.

.   .   .   .

"Like a Virgin of the Shield I roved o'er the sea,
My arm was victorious, my valor was free.
By prowess, by Runic enchantment and song,
I raised up the weak, and I beat down the strong;
I held the young prince 'mid the hurly of war,
My arm waved around him the charmed scimitar;
I saved him in battle, I crowned him in hall,
Though Odin and Fate had foredoomed him to fall:
Hence Odin's dread curses were poured on my head;
He doomed the undaunted Brynhilda to wed.
But I vowed the high vow which gods dare not gainsay,
That the boldest in warfare should bare me away:
And full well I knew that thou, Sigurd, alone
Of mortals the boldest in battle hast shone;

I knew that none other the furnace could stem
(So wrought was the spell, and so fierce was the flame),
Save Sigurd the glorious, the slayer of kings,
With the spoils of the Dragon, his gold and his rings."

The story in the original runs through several cantos, comprising varied specimens of those antique Gothic compositions, which, to use the words of our author,—

"are not only full of singularly wild and beautiful poetry, and lively pictures of the manners and customs of the heroic age of the ancient North, its patriarchal simplicity, its deadly feuds, and its fanciful superstition, peopling the earth, air, and waters with deities, giants, genii, nymphs, and dwarfs ; but there are many exquisite touches of the deepest pathos, to which the human heart beats in unison in every age and in every land."

Many of these hyperborean poems, he remarks, have an Oriental character and coloring in their subjects and imagery, their mythology and their style, bearing internal evidence of their having been composed in remote antiquity, and in regions less removed from the cradle of the human race than the Scandinavian North. "The oldest of this fragmentary poetry," as he finely observes, "may be compared to the gigantic remains, the wrecks of a more ancient world, or to the ruins of Egypt and Hindostan, speaking a more perfect civilization, the glories of which have long since departed."

Our author gives us many curious glances at the popular superstitions of the North, and those poetic and mythic fictions which pervaded the great Scandinavian

27

family of nations. The charmed armor of the warrior; the dragon who keeps a sleepless watch over buried treasure; the spirits or genii that haunt the rocky tops of mountains or the depths of quiet lakes; and the elves or vagrant demons which wander through forests, or by lonely hills; these are found in all the popular superstitions of the North. Ditmarus Blefkenius tells us that the Icelanders believed in domestic spirits, which woke them at night to go and fish; and that all expeditions to which they were thus summoned were eminently fortunate. The water-sprites, originating in Icelandic poetry, may be traced throughout the north of Europe. The Swedes delight to tell of the *Strömkerl,* or boy of the stream, who haunts the glassy brooks that steal gently through green meadows, and sits on the silver waves at moonlight, playing his harp to the elves who dance on the flowery margin. Scarcely a rivulet in Germany also but has its *Wasser-nixe,* or water-witches, all evidently members of the great northern family.

Before we leave this enchanted ground, we must make a few observations on the Runic characters, which were regarded with so much awe in days of yore, as locking up darker mysteries and more potent spells than the once redoubtable hieroglyphics of the Egyptians. The Runic alphabet, according to our author, consists properly of sixteen letters. Northern tradition attributes them to Odin, who, perhaps, brought them into Scandinavia, but they have no resemblance to any of the alphabets of Central Asia. Inscriptions in these characters are still to be seen on rocks and stone monuments in Sweden, and other countries of the North, containing Scandinavian verses in praise of their ancient heroes. They were also engraved on arms, trinkets, amulets, and utensils, and sometimes on the bark of trees, and on wooden tablets, for the purpose of memorials or of epistolary correspondence. In one of the Eddaic poems, Odin is represented as boasting the magic power of the Runic rhymes to heal diseases and counteract poison; to spell-bind the arms of an enemy; to lull the tempest; to stop the career of witches through the air; to raise the dead, and extort from them the secrets of the world of spirits. The reader who may desire to see the letters of this all-potent alphabet, will find them in Mallet's "Northern Antiquities."

In his sixth chapter, Mr. Wheaton gives an account of the religion of Odin, and his migration, with a colony of Scythian Goths, from the banks of the Tanais, in Asia, to the peninsula of Scandinavia, to escape the Roman legions. Without emulating his minute and interesting detail, we will merely and briefly state some of the leading particulars, and refer the curious reader to the pages of his book.

The expedition of this mythological hero is stated to have taken place about seventy years before the Christian era, when Pompey the Great, then consul of Rome, finished the war with Tigranes and Mithridates, and carried

his victorious arms throughout the most important parts
of Asia.   We quote a description of the wonderful vessel
Skidbladner, the ship of the gods, in which he made the
voyage :—

" *Skidbladner*," said one of the genii, when interrogated by Gangler,
" is one of the best ships, and most curiously constructed. It was built by
certain dwarfs, who made a present of it to Freyn. It is so vast that there
is room to hold all the deities, with their armor. As soon as the sails are
spread, it directs its course, with a favorable breeze, wherever they desire
to navigate; and when they wish to land, such is its marvellous construction, that it can be taken to pieces, rolled up, and put in the pocket."
"That is an excellent ship, indeed," replied Gangler, "and must have
required much science and magic art to construct."—*P.* 118.

With this very convenient, portable, and pocketable
ship, and a crew of Goths of the race of Sviar, called by
Tacitus Suiones, the intrepid Odin departed from Scythia,
to escape the domination of the Romans, who were spreading themselves over the world.   He took with him also
his twelve pontiffs, who were at once priests of religion
and judges of the law.   Whenever sea or river intervened,
he launched his good ship *Skidbladner*, embarked with his
band, and sailed merrily over ; then landing, and pocket-
ing the transport, he again put himself at the head of his
crew, and marched steadily forward.   To add to the facil-
ities of these primitive emigrants, Odin was himself a seer
and a magician.   He could look into futurity ; could strike
his enemies with deafness, blindness, and sudden panic;
could blunt the edge of their weapons, and render his

own warriors invisible. He could transform himself into
bird, beast, fish, or serpent, and fly to the most distant
regions, while his body remained in a trance. He could,
with a single word, extinguish fire, control the winds, and
bring the dead to life. He carried about with him an
embalmed and charmed head, which would reply to his
questions, and give him information of what was passing
in the remotest lands. He had, moreover, two most gifted
and confidential ravens, who had the gift of speech, and
would fly, on his behests, to the uttermost parts of the
earth. We have only to believe in the supernatural powers of such a leader, provided with such a ship, and such
an oracular head, attended by two such marvellously
gifted birds, and backed by a throng of stanch and stal-
wart Gothic followers, and we shall not wonder that he
found but little difficulty in making his way to the peninsula of Scandinavia, and in expelling the aboriginal inhabitants, who seem to have been but a diminutive and
stunted race; although there are not wanting fabulous
narrators, who would fain persuade us there were giants
among them. They were gradually subdued and reduced
to servitude, or driven to the mountains, and subsequently
to the desert wilds and fastnesses of Norrland, Lapland,
and Finland, where they continued to adhere to that form
of polytheism called Fetishism, or the adoration of birds
and beasts, stocks and stones, and all the animate and
inanimate works of creation.

As to Odin, he introduced into his new dominions the

religion he had brought with him from the banks of the
Tanais; but, like the early heroes of most barbarous
nations, he was destined to become himself an object of
adoration; for though to all appearance he died, and was
consumed on a funeral pile, it was said that he was translated to the blissful abode of Godheim, there to enjoy
eternal life. In process of time it was declared, that,
though a mere prophet on earth, he had been an incarnation of the Supreme Deity, and had returned to the
sacred hall of Valhalla, the paradise of the brave, where,
surrounded by his late companions in arms, he watched
over the deeds and destinies of the children of men.

The primitive people who had been conquered by Odin
and his followers, seem to have been as diminutive in
spirit as in form, and withal a rancorous race of little
vermin, whose expulsion from their native land awakens
but faint sympathy; yet candor compels us to add, that
their conquerors are not much more entitled to our
esteem, although their hardy deeds command our admiration. The author gives a slight sketch of the personal
peculiarities which discriminated both, extracted from an
Eddaic poem, and which is worthy of notice, as accounting, as far as the authority is respected, for some of the
diversities in feature and complexion of the Scandinavian
races.

"The slave caste, descended from the aboriginal Finns, were distinguished from their conquerors by black hair and complexion. . . . .
The caste of freemen and freeholders, lords of the soil which they cul-

tivated, and descended from the Gothic conquerors, had reddish hair
fair complexion, and all the traits which peculiarly mark that famous
race, ... while the caste of the illustrious Jarls and the Hersen,
earls and barons, were distinguished by still fairer hair and skin, and
by noble employments and manners : from these descended the kingly
race, skilled in Runic science, in manly exercises, and the military art."

The manners, customs, and superstitions of these northern people, which afterwards, with various modifications,
pervaded and stamped an indelible character on so great
a part of Europe, deserve to be more particularly mentioned ; and we give a brief view of them, chiefly taken
from the work of our author, and partly from other
sources. The religion of the early Scandinavians taught
the existence of a Supreme Being, called Thor, who ruled
over the elements, purified the air with refreshing showers, dispensed health and sickness, wielded the thunder
and lightning, and with his celestial weapon, the rainbow,
launched unerring arrows at the evil demons. He was
worshipped in a primitive but striking manner, amidst
the solemn majesty of Nature, on the tops of mountains,
in the depths of primeval forests, or in those groves
which rose like natural temples on islands surrounded by
the dark waters of lonely and silent lakes. They had,
likewise, their minor deities, or genii, whom we have
already mentioned, who were supposed to inhabit the
sun, the moon, and stars,—the regions of the air, the
trees, the rocks, the brooks, and mountains of the earth,
and to superintend the phenomena of their respective

elements.   They believed, also, in a future state of torment for the guilty, and of voluptuous and sensual enjoyment for the virtuous.

This primitive religion gave place to more complicated
beliefs.   Odin, elevated, as we have shown, into a divinity,
was worshipped as the Supreme Deity, and with him was
associated his wife Freya; from these are derived our
Odensday—Wodensday or Wednesday—and our Freytag,
or Friday.   Thor, from whom comes Thursday, was now
more limited in his sway, though he still bent the rainbow, launched the thunderbolt, and controlled the seasons.   These three were the principal deities, and held
assemblies of those of inferior rank and power.   The
mythology had also its devil, called Loke, a most potent
and malignant spirit, and supposed to be the cause of all
evil.

By degrees the religious rites of the northern people
became more artificial and ostentatious; they were performed in temples, with something of Asiatic pomp.   Festivals were introduced of symbolical and mystic import,
at the summer and the winter solstice, and at various
other periods; in which were typified, not merely the
decline and renovation of Nature and the changes of the
seasons, but the epochs in the moral history of man.   As
the ceremonials of religion became more dark and mysterious, they assumed a cruel and sanguinary character;
prisoners taken in battle were sacrificed by the victors,
subjects by their kings, and sometimes even children by

their parents. Superstition gradually spread its illusions over all the phenomena of Nature, and gave each some occult meaning: oracles, lots, auguries, and divination gained implicit faith; and soothsayers read the decrees of fate in the flight of birds, the sound of thunder, and the entrails of the victim. Every man was supposed to have his attendant spirit, his destiny, which it was out of his power to avert, and his appointed hour to die;—Odin, however, could control or alter the destiny of a mortal, and defer the fatal hour. It was believed, also, that a man's life might be prolonged if another would devote himself to death in his stead.

The belief in magic was the natural attendant upon these superstitions. Charms and spells were practised, and the Runic rhymes, known but to the gifted few, acquired their reputation among the ignorant multitude, for an all-potent and terrific influence over the secrets of Nature and the actions and destinies of man.

As war was the principal and the only noble occupation of these people, their moral code was suitably brief and stern. After profound devotion to the gods, valor in war was inculcated as the supreme virtue, cowardice as the deadly sin. Those who fell gloriously in war were at once transported to Valhalla, the airy hall of Odin, there to partake of the eternal felicities of the brave. Fighting and feasting, which had constituted their fierce joys on earth, were lavished upon them in this supernal abode. Every day they had combats in the listed field,—the rush of steeds, the flash of swords, the shining of lances, and all the maddening tumult and din of battle;—helmets and bucklers were riven,—horses and riders overthrown, and ghastly wounds exchanged; but at the setting of the sun all was over; victors and vanquished met unscathed in glorious companionship around the festive board of Odin in Valhalla's hall, where they partook of the ample banquet, and quaffed full horns of beer and fragrant mead. For the just who did not die in fight, a more peaceful but less glorious elysium was provided,—a resplendent golden palace, surrounded by verdant meads and shady groves and fields of spontaneous fertility.

The early training of their youth was suited to the creed of this warlike people. In the tender days of childhood they were gradually hardened by athletic exercises, and nurtured through boyhood in difficult and daring feats. At the age of fifteen they were produced before some public assemblage, and presented with a sword, a buckler, and a lance; from that time forth they mingled among men, and were expected to support themselves by hunting or warfare. But though thus early initiated in the rough and dangerous concerns of men, they were prohibited all indulgence with the softer sex until matured in years and vigor.

Their weapons of offence were bow and arrow, battle-axe and sword; and the latter was often engraved with some mystic characters, and bore a formidable and vaunting name.

The helmets of the common soldiery were of leather, and their bucklers leather and wood; but warriors of rank had helmets and shields of iron and brass, sometimes richly gilt and decorated; and they wore coats of mail, and occasionally plated armor.

A young chieftain of generous birth received higher endowments than the common class. Beside the hardy exercise of the chase and the other exercises connected with the use of arms, he was initiated betimes into the sacred science of the Runic writing, and instructed in the ancient lay, especially if destined for sovereignty, as every king was the pontiff of his people. When a prince had attained the age of eighteen, his father usually gave him a small fleet and a band of warriors, and sent him on some marauding voyage, from which it was disgraceful to return with empty hands.

Such was the moral and physical training of the Northmen, which prepared them for that wide and wild career of enterprise and conquest which has left its traces along all the coasts of Europe, and thrown communities and colonies, in the most distant regions, to remain themes of wonder and speculation in after ages. Actuated by the same roving and predatory spirit which had brought their Scythian ancestors from the banks of the Tanais, and rendered daring navigators by their experience along the stormy coasts of the North, they soon extended their war-like roamings over the ocean, and became complete maritime marauders, with whom piracy at sea was equivalent to chivalry on shore, and a freebooting cruise to a heroic enterprise.

For a time, the barks in which they braved the dangers of the sea, and infested the coasts of England and France, were mere canoes, formed from the trunks of trees, and so light as readily to be carried on men's shoulders, or dragged along the land. With these they suddenly swarmed upon a devoted coast, sailing up the rivers, shifting from stream to stream, and often making their way back to the sea by some different river from that they had ascended. Their chiefs obtained the appellation of sea-kings, because, to the astonished inhabitants of the invaded coasts, they seemed to emerge suddenly from the ocean, and when they had finished their ravages, to retire again into its bosom as to their native home; and they were rightly named, in the opinion of the author of "A Northern Saga," seeing that their lives were passed upon the waves, and "they never sought shelter under a roof, or drained their drinking-horn at a cottage-fire."

Though plunder seemed to be the main object of this wild ocean chivalry, they had still that passion for martial renown which grows up with the exercise of arms, however rude and lawless, and which in them was stimulated by the songs of the Skalds.

We are told that they were " sometimes seized with a sort of frenzy, a *furor Martis*, produced by their excited imaginations dwelling upon the images of war and glory, and perhaps increased by those potations of stimulating

liquors in which the people of the North, like other un-
civilized tribes, indulged to great excess. When this
madness was upon them, they committed the wildest ex-
travagances, attacked indiscriminately friends and foes,
and even waged war against the rocks and trees. At
other times they defied each other to mortal combat in
some lonely and desert isle."

Among the most renowned of these early sea-kings was
Ragnar Lodbrok, famous for his invasion of Northumbria, in England, and no less famous in ancient Sagas for
his strange and cruel death. According to those poetic
legends, he was a king of Denmark, who ruled his realms
in peace without being troubled with any dreams of conquest. His sons, however, were roving the seas with
their warlike followers, and after a time tidings of their
heroic exploits reached his court. The jealousy of Ragnar was excited, and he determined on an expedition that
should rival their achievements. He accordingly ordered
the "Arrow," the signal of war, to be sent through his
dominions, summoning his "champions" to arms. He
had ordered two ships of immense size to be built, and
in them he embarked with his followers. His faithful
and discreet queen, Aslauga, warned him of the perils to
which he was exposing himself, but in vain. He set sail
for the north of England, which had formerly been invaded by his predecessors. The expedition was driven
back to port by a tempest. The queen repeated her
warnings and entreaties, but finding them unavailing, she

gave him a magical garment that had the virtue to render the wearer invulnerable.

"Ragnar again put to sea, and was at last shipwrecked on the English coast. In this emergency his courage did not desert him, but he pushed forward with his small band to ravage and plunder. Ella collected his forces to repel the invader. Ragnar, clothed with the enchanted garment he had received from his beloved Aslauga, and armed with the spear with which he had slain the guardian serpent of Thora, four times pierced the Saxon ranks, dealing death on every side, whilst his own body was invulnerable to the blows of his enemies. His friends and champions fell one by one around him, and he was at last taken prisoner alive. Being asked who he was, he preserved an indignant silence. Then King Ella said,— 'If this man will not speak, he shall endure so much the heavier punishment for his obduracy and contempt.' So he ordered him to be thrown into the dungeon full of serpents, where he should remain till he told his name. Ragnar, being thrown into the dungeon, sat there a long time before the serpents attacked him ; which being noticed by the spectators, they said he must be a brave man indeed whom neither arms nor vipers could hurt. Ella, hearing this, ordered his enchanted vest to be stripped off, and soon afterwards, the serpents clung to him on all sides. Then Ragnar said, 'How the young cubs would roar if they knew what the old boar suffers !' and expired with a laugh of defiance."—*pp.* 152, 153.

The death-song of Ragnar Lodbrok will be found in an appendix to Henderson's "Iceland," both in the original and in a translation. The version, however, which is in prose, conveys but faintly the poetic spirit of the original. It consists of twenty-nine stanzas, most of them of nine lines, and contains, like the death-song of a warrior among the American Indians, a boastful narrative of his expeditions and exploits. Each stanza bears the same burden :

> "Hiuggom ver med hiarvi."

> "We hewed them with our swords."

Lodbrok exults that his achievements entitle him to admission among the gods; predicts that his children shall avenge his death; and glories that no sigh shall disgrace his exit. In the last stanza he hails the arrival of celestial virgins sent to invite him to the Hall of Odin, where he shall join the assembly of heroes, sit upon a lofty throne, and quaff the mellow beverage of barley. The last strophe of this death-song is thus rendered by Mr. Wheaton :—

> "Cease my strain! I hear Them call
> Who bid me hence to Odin's hall !
> High seated in their blest abodes,
> I soon shall quaff the drink of gods.
> The hours of Life have glided by,—
> I fall! but laughing will I die!
> The hours of Life have glided by,—
> I fall ! but laughing will I die !"

The sons of Ragnar, if the Sagas may be believed, were not slow in revenging the death of their parent. They were absent from home on warlike expeditions at the time, and did not hear of the catastrophe until after their return to Denmark. Their first tidings of it were from the messengers of Ella, sent to propitiate their hostility. When the messengers entered the royal hall, they found the sons of Ragnar variously employed. Sigurdɪ Snakeseye was playing at chess with his brother Huitserk the Brave ; while Björn Ironside was polishing the handle of his spear in the middle pavement of the hall. The messengers approached to where Ivar, the other brother, was sitting, and, saluting him with due reverence, told him they were sent by King Ella to announce the death of his royal father.

"As they began to unfold their tale, Sigurdr and Huitserk dropped their game, carefully weighing what was said. Björn stood in the midst of the hall, leaning on his spear ; but Ivar diligently inquired by what means, and by what kind of death, his father had perished ; which the messengers related, from his first arrival in England till his death. When, in the course of their narrative, they came to the words of the dying king, 'How the young whelps would roar if they knew their father's fate !' Björn grasped the handle of his spear so fast that the prints of his fingers remained ; and when the tale was done, dashed the spear in pieces. Huitserk pressed the chess-board so hard with his hands, that they bled.

"Ivar changed color continually, now red, now black, now pale, whilst he struggled to suppress his kindling wrath.

"Huitserk the Brave, who first broke silence, proposed to begin their revenge by the death of the messengers ; which Ivar forbade, commandng them to go in peace, wherever they would, and if they wanted any·thing they should be supplied.

"Their mission being fulfilled, the delegates, passing through the hall, went down to their ships ; and the wind being favorable, returned safely to their king. Ella, hearing from them how his message had been received by the princes, said that he foresaw that of all the brothers, Ivar or none was to be feared."—*pp.* 188, 189.

The princes summoned their followers, launched their fleets, and attacked King Ella in the spring of 867.

"The battle took place at York, and the Anglo-Saxons were entirely routed. The sons of Ragnar inflicted a cruel and savage retaliation on Ella for his barbarous treatment of their father.

"After this battle, Northumbria appears no more as a Saxon kingdom, and Ivar was made king over that part of England which his ancestors had possessed, or into which they had made repeated incursions."—*pp.* 189, 190.

Encouraged by the success that attended their enterprises in the northern seas, the Northmen now urged their adventurous prows into more distant regions, besetting the southern coasts of France with their fleets of light and diminutive barks. Charlemagne is said to have witnessed the inroad of one of their fleets from the windows of his palace, in the harbor of Narbonne; upon which he lamented the fate of his successors, who would have to contend with such audacious invaders. They entered the Loire, sacked the city of Nantes, and carried their victorious arms up to Tours. They ascended the Garonne, pillaged Bordeaux, and extended their incursion even to Toulouse. They also entered the Seine in 845, ravaging its banks, and pushing their enterprise to the very gates of Paris, compelled the monarch Charles to take refuge in the monastery of St. Denis, where he was fain to receive the piratical chieftain, Regnier, and to pay him a tribute of 7000 pounds of silver, on condition of his evacuating his capital and kingdom. Regnier,

28

besides immense booty, carried back to Denmark, as trophies of his triumph, a beam from the abbey of St. Germain, and a nail from the gate of Paris; but his followers spread over their native country a contagious disease which they had contracted in France.

Spain was, in like manner, subject to their invasions. They ascended the Guadalquivir, attacked the great city of Seville, and demolished its fortifications, after severe battles with the Moors, who were then sovereigns of that country, and who regarded these unknown invaders from the sea as magicians, on account of their wonderful daring and still more wonderful success. As the author well observes, " The contrast between these two races of fanatic barbarians, the one issuing forth from the frozen regions of the North, the other from the burning sands of Asia and Africa, forms one of the most striking pictures presented by history."

The Straits of Gibraltar being passed by these rovers of the North, the Mediterranean became another region for their exploits. Hastings, one of their boldest chieftains, and father of that Hastings who afterwards battled with King Alfred for the sovereignty of England, accompanied by Björn Ironside and Sydroc, two sons of Ragnar Lodbrok, undertook an expedition against Rome, the capital of the world, tempted by accounts of its opulence and splendor, but not precisely acquainted with its site. They penetrated the Mediterranean with a fleet of one hundred barks, and entered the port of Luna in Tuscany, an ancient city, whose high walls and towers and stately edifices made them mistake it for imperial Rome.

" The inhabitants were celebrating the festival of Christmas in the cathedral, when the news was spread among them of the arrival of a fleet of unknown strangers. The church was instantly deserted, and the citizens ran to shut the gates, and prepared to defend their town. Hastings sent a herald to inform the count and bishop of Luna that he and his band were Northmen, conquerors of the Franks, who designed no harm to the inhabitants of Italy, but merely sought to repair their shattered barks. In order to inspire more confidence, Hastings pretended to be weary of the wandering life he had so long led, and desired to find repose in the bosom of the Christian Church. The bishop and the count furnished the fleet with the needful succor ; Hastings was baptized ; but still his Norman followers were not admitted within the city walls. Their chief was then obliged to resort to another stratagem ; he feigned to be dangerously ill ; his camp resounded with the lamentations of his followers ; he declared his intention of leaving the rich booty he had acquired to the Church, provided they would grant him sepulture in holy ground. The wild howl of the Normans soon announced the death of their chieftain. The inhabitants followed the funeral procession to the Church, but at the moment they were about to deposit his apparently lifeless body, Hastings started up from his coffin, and, seizing his sword, struck down the officiating bishop. His followers instantly obeyed this signal of treachery ; they drew from under their garments their concealed weapons, massacred the clergy and others who assisted at the ceremony, and spread havoc and consternation throughout the town. Having thus become master of Luna, the Norman chieftain discovered his error, and found that he was still far from Rome, which was not likely to fall so easy a prey. After having transported on board his barks the wealth of the city, as well as the most beautiful women, and the young men capable of bearing arms or of rowing, he put to sea, intending to return to the North.

" The Italian traditions as to the destruction of this city resemble more nearly the romance of 'Romeo and Juliet,' than the history of the Scandinavian adventurer. According to these accounts, the prince of Luna was inflamed with the beauty of a certain young empress, then travelling in company with the emperor her husband. Their passion was mutual, and the two lovers had recourse to the following stratagem, in order to accomplish their union. The empress feigned to be grievously sick ; she was believed to be dead ; her funeral obsequies were duly celebrated ; but she escaped from the sepulchre, and secretly rejoined her lover. The emperor had no sooner heard of their crime, than he marched to attack the residence of the ravisher, and avenged himself by the entire destruction of the once flourishing city of Luna. The only point of resemblance between these two stories consists in the romantic incident of the destruction of the city by means of a feigned death, a legend which spread abroad over Italy and France."

The last and greatest of the sea-kings, or pirate heroes of the North, was Rollo, surnamed Ferus Fortis, the Lusty Boar or Hardy Beast, from whom William the Conqueror comes in lineal, though not legitimate, descent. Our limits do not permit us to detail the early history of this warrior, as selected by our author from among the fables of the Norman chronicles, and the more simple, and, he thinks, more veritable narratives in the Icelandic Sagas. We shall merely state that Rollo arrived with a band of Northmen, all fugitive adventurers, like himself, upon the coast of France ; ascended the Seine to Rouen, subjugated the fertile province then called Neustria ; named it Normandy from the Northmen, his followers, and crowned himself first Duke.

"Under his firm and vigorous rule, the blessings of order and peace were restored to a country which had so long and so cruelly suffered from the incursions of the northern adventurers. He tolerated the Christians in their worship, and they flocked in crowds to live under the dominion of a Pagan and barbarian, in preference to their own native and Christian prince (Charles the Simple), who was unwilling or incapable to protect them."

Rollo established in his duchy of Normandy a feudal aristocracy, or rather it grew out of the circumstances of the country. His followers elected him duke, and he made them counts and barons and knights. The clergy also pressed themselves into his great council or parliament. The laws were reduced to a system by men of acute intellect, and this system of feudal law was subsequently transplanted by William the Conqueror into England, as a means of consolidating his power and establishing his monarchy.

"Rollo is said also to have established the Court of Exchequer as the supreme tribunal of justice; and the perfect security afforded by the admirable system of police established in England by King Alfred is likewise attributed to the legislation of the first Duke of Normandy."—*P.* 252.

Trial by battle, or judicial combat, was a favorite appeal to God by the warlike nations of Scandinavia, as by most of the barbarous tribes who established themselves on the ruin of the Roman empire. It had fallen into disuse in France, but was revived by Rollo in Normandy, although the clergy were solicitous to substitute the ordeal of fire and water, which brought controversies within their control. The fierce Norman warriors disdained this clerical mode of decision, and strenuously insisted on the appeal to the sword. They afterwards, at the Conquest, introduced the trial by combat into England, where it became a part of the common law.*

A spirit of chivalry and love of daring adventure, a romantic gallantry towards the sex, and a zealous devotion, were blended in the character of the Norman knights. These high and generous feelings they brought with them into England, and bore with them in their crusades into the Holy Land. Poetry also continued to be cherished

---

* A statue or effigy of Rollo, over a sarcophagus, is still to be seen in the cathedral at Rouen, with a Latin inscription, stating that he was converted to Christianity in 913, and died in 917, and that his bones were removed to this spot from their place of original sepulture, in A. D. 1063. The ancient epitaph, in rhyming monkish Latin, has been lost, except the following lines :—

> Dux Normanorum
>   Cunctorum,
> Norma Bonorum.
> Rollo, Ferus fortis,
> Quem gens Normanica mortis
> Invocat articulo,
> Clauditur hoc tumulo.

Imitation.

> Rollo, that hardy Boar
>   Renowned of yore,
> Of all the Normans Duke :
> Whose name with dying breath
>   In article of death,
> All Norman knights invoke ;
>   That mirror of the bold,
>   This tomb doth hold.

and cultivated among them, and the Norman troubadour succeeded to the Scandinavian skald. The Dukes of Normandy and Anglo-Norman kings were practisers as well as patrons of this delightful art; and Henry I., surnamed Beauclerc, and Richard Cœur de Lion, were distinguished among the poetical composers of their day.

"The Norman minstrel," to quote the words of our author, "appropriated the fictions they found already accredited among the people for whom they versified. The British King Arthur, his fabled knights of the Round Table, and the enchanter Merlin, with his wonderful prophecies ; the Frankish monarch Charlemagne and his paladins ; and the rich inventions of Oriental fancy borrowed from the Arabs and the Moors."— *P.* 262.

We have thus cursorily accompanied our author in his details of the origin and character, the laws and superstitions, and primitive religion, and also of the roving expeditions and conquests of the Northmen ; and we give him credit for the judgment and candor and careful research with which he has gleaned and collated his interesting facts from the rubbish of fables and fictions with which they were bewildered and obscured.

Another leading feature in his work is the conversion of the Northmen, and the countries from which they came, to the Christian faith. An attempt to condense or analyze this part of his work would lead us too far, and do injustice to the minuteness and accuracy of his details. We must, for like reasons, refer the reader to the work itself for the residue of its contents. We shall merely remark, that he goes over the same ground with the English historians, Hume, Turner, Lingard, and Palgrave, gleaning from the original authorities whatever may have been omitted by them. He has also occasionally corrected some errors into which they have fallen, through want of more complete access or more critical attention to the Icelandic sagas and the Danish and Swedish historians, who narrated the successful invasion of England by the Danes, under Canute, and its final conquest by William of Normandy.

We shall take leave of our author with some extracts from the triumphant invasion of William, premising a few words concerning his origin and early history. Robert Duke of Normandy, called Robert the Magnificent by his flatterers, but more commonly known as Robert the Devil, from his wild and savage nature, had an amour with Arlette, the daughter of a tanner or currier of Falaise, in Normandy. The damsel gave birth to a male child, who was called William. While the boy was yet in childhood, Robert the Devil resolved to expiate his sins by a pilgrimage to the Holy Land; and compelled his counts and barons to swear fealty to his son. "Par ma foi," said Robert, "je ne vous laisserai point sans seigneur. J'ai un petit bâtard qui grandira s'il plait à Dieu. Choisissez le dès ce présent, et je le saiserai devant vous de ce duché comme mon successeur." The Norman lords placed their hands between the hands of the child, and swore fidelity to him according to feudal usage. Robert the Devil set out on his pious pilgrimage, and died at Nice. The right of the boy William was contested by Guy, Count of Burgundy, and other claimants, but he made it good with his sword, and then confirmed it by espousing Matilda, daughter of the Count of Flanders.

On the death of Edward the Confessor, King of England, Harold, from his fleetness surnamed Harefoot, one of the bravest nobles of the realm, assumed the crown, to the exclusion of Edgar Atheling, the lawful heir. It was said that Edward had named Harold to succeed him. William Duke of Normandy laid claim to the English throne. We have not room in this review to investigate his title, which was little more than bare pretension. He alleged that Edward the Confessor had promised to bequeath to him the crown; but his chief reliance was upon his sword. Harold, while yet a subject, had fallen by accident within the power of William, who had obtained from him, by cajolery and extortion, an oath, sworn on certain sacred relics, not to impede him in his plans to gain the English crown.

William prepared an expedition in Normandy, and published a war-ban, inviting adventurers of all countries to join him in the invasion of England, and partake the pillage. He procured a consecrated banner from the Pope under the promise of a portion of the spoil, and embarked a force of nearly sixty thousand men on board four hundred vessels and above a thousand boats.

"The ship which bore William preceded the rest of the fleet, with the consecrated banner of the Pope displayed at the mast-head, its many-colored sails embellished with the lions of Normandy, and its prow adorned with the figure of an infant archer bending his bow and ready to let fly his arrow."

William landed his force at Pevensey, near Hastings, on the coast of Sussex, on the 28th of September, 1066; and we shall state from the Norman chronicles some few particulars of this interesting event, not included in the volume under review.   The archers disembarked first,—they had short vestments and cropped hair; then the horsemen, armed with coats of mail, caps of iron, straight two-edged swords, and long powerful lances; then the pioneers and artificers, who disembarked, piece by piece, the materials for three wooden towers, all ready to be put together. The Duke was the last to land, for, says the chronicle, "there was no opposing enemy."   King Harold was in Northumbria, repelling an army of Norwegian invaders.

As William leaped on shore, he stumbled and fell upon his face.   Exclamations of foreboding were heard among his followers; but he grasped the earth with his hands, and raising them filled with it towards the heavens, "Thus," cried he, "do I seize upon this land, and by the splendor of God, as far as it extends, it shall be mine." His ready wit thus converted a sinister accident into a favorable omen.   Having pitched his camp and reared his wooden towers near to the town of Hastings, he sent forth his troops to forage and lay waste the country; nor were even the churches and cemeteries held sacred to which the English had fled for refuge.

Harold was at York, reposing after a victory over the Norwegians, in which he had been wounded, when he heard of this new invasion. Undervaluing the foe, he set forth instantly with such force as he could muster, though a few days' delay would have brought great reinforcements. On his way he met a Norman monk, sent to him by William, with three alternatives: 1. To abdicate in his favor. 2. To refer their claims to the decision of the Pope. 3. To determine them by single combat. Harold refused all three, and quickened his march; but finding, as he drew nearer, that the Norman army was thrice the number of his own, he intrenched his host seven miles from their camp, upon a range of hills, behind a rampart of palisades and osier hurdles.

The impending night of the battle was passed by the Normans in warlike preparations, or in confessing their sins and receiving the sacrament, and the camp resounded with the prayers and chantings of priests and friars. As to the Saxon warriors, they sat round their camp-fires, carousing horns of beer and wine, and singing old national war-songs.

At an early hour in the morning of the 14th of October, Odo, Bishop of Bayeux, and bastard brother of the Duke, being the son of his mother Arlette, by a burgher of Falaise, celebrated mass, and gave his benediction to the Norman army. He then put a hauberk under his cassock,

mounted a powerful white charger, and led forth a brigade of cavalry; for he was as ready with the spear as
with the crosier, and for his fighting and other turbulent propensities, well merited his surname of Odo the
Unruly.

The army was formed into three columns;—one composed of mercenaries from the countries of Boulogne and
Ponthieu; the second of auxiliaries from Brittany and
elsewhere; the third of Norman troops, led by William
in person. Each column was preceded by archers in
light quilted coats instead of armor, some with long bows,
and others with cross-bows of steel. Their mode of fighting was to discharge a flight of arrows, and then retreat
behind the heavy armed troops. The Duke was mounted
on a Spanish steed, around his neck were suspended some
of the relics on which Harold had made oath, and the
consecrated standard was borne at his side.

William harangued his soldiers, reminding them of the
exploits of their ancestors, the massacre of the Northmen
in England, and, in particular, the murder of their brethren the Danes. But he added another and a stronger excitement to their valor: " Fight manfully, and put all to
the sword; and if we conquer, we shall all be rich. What
I gain, you gain; what I conquer, you conquer; if I gain
the land, it is yours." We shall give, in our author's
own words, the further particulars of this decisive
battle, which placed a Norman sovereign on the English
throne.

"The spot which Harold had selected for this ever-memorable contest was a high ground, then called Senlac, nine miles from Hastings, opening to the south, and covered in the rear by an extensive wood. He posted his troops on the declivity of the hill in one compact mass, covered with their shields, and wielding their enormous battle-axes. In the centre the royal standard, or gonfanon, was fixed in the ground, with the figure of an armed warrior, worked in thread of gold, and ornamented with precious stones. Here stood Harold, and his brothers Gurth and Leofwin, and around them the rest of the Saxon army, every man on foot.

"As the Normans approached the Saxon intrenchments, the monks and priests who accompanied their army retired to a neighboring hill to pray, and observe the issue of the battle. A Norman warrior, named Taillefer, spurred his horse in front of the line, and, tossing up in the air his sword, which he caught again in his hand, sang the national song of Charlemagne and Roland;—the Normans joined in the chorus and shouted, 'Dieu aide! Dieu aide!' They were answered by the Saxons, with the adverse cry of 'Christ's rood! the holy rood!'

"The Norman archers let fly a shower of arrows into the Saxon ranks. Their infantry and cavalry advanced to the gates of the redoubts, which they vainly endeavored to force. The Saxons thundered upon their armor, and broke their lances with the heavy battle-axe, and the Normans retreated to the division commanded by William. The Duke then caused his archers again to advance, and to direct their arrows obliquely in the air, so that they might fall beyond and over the enemy's rampart. The Saxons were severely galled by the Norman missiles, and Harold himself was wounded in the eye. The attack of the infantry and men-at-arms again commenced with the cries of 'Nôtre-Dame! Dieu aide! Dieu aide!' But the Normans were repulsed, and pursued by the Saxons to a deep ravine, where their horses plunged and threw the riders. The *mêlée* was here dreadful, and a sudden panic seized the invaders, who fled from the field, exclaiming that their duke was slain. William rushed before the fugitives, with his helmet in hand, menacing and even striking them with his lance, and shouting with a loud voice : 'I am still alive, and with the help of God I still shall conquer!' The men-at-arms once more returned to attack the redoubts, but they were again repelled by the impregnable phalanx of the Saxons. The Duke now resorted to the stratagem of ordering a thousand horse to advance, and then suddenly retreat, in the hope of drawing the enemy from his intrenchments. The Saxons fell into the snare, and rushed out with their battle-axes slung about their necks, to pursue the flying foe. The Normans were joined by another body of their own army, and both turned upon the Saxons, who were assailed on every side with swords and lances, whilst their hands were employed in wielding their enormous battle-axes. The invaders now rushed through the broken ranks of their opponents into the intrench-ments, pulled down the royal standard, and erected in its place the papal banner. Harold was slain, with his brothers Gurth and Leofwin. The sun declined in the western horizon, and with his retiring beams sunk the glory of the Saxon name.

"The rest of the companions of Harold fled from the fatal field, where the Normans passed the night, exulting over their hard-earned victory. The next morning, William ranged his troops under arms, and every man who passed the sea was called by name, according to the muster-roll drawn up before their embarkation at St. Valery. Many were deaf to that call. The invading army consisted originally of nearly sixty thousand men, and of these one fourth lay dead on the field. To the fortunate survivors was allotted the spoil of the vanquished Saxons, as the first-fruits of their victory; and the bodies of the slain, after being stripped, were hastily buried by their trembling friends. According to one narra-tive, the body of Harold was begged by his mother as a boon from Will-iam, to whom she offered as a ransom its weight in gold. But the stern and pitiless conqueror ordered the corpse of the Saxon king to be buried on the beach, adding, with a sneer, 'He guarded the coast while he lived, let him continue to guard it now he is dead.' Another account represents that two monks of the monastery of Waltham, which had been founded by the son of Godwin, humbly approached the Norman, and offered him ten marks of gold for permission to bury their king and benefactor. They were unable to distinguish his body among the heaps of slain, and sent for Harold's mistress, Editha, surnamed 'the Fair' and 'the Swan's Neck,' to assist them in the search. The features of the Saxon monarch were recognized by her whom he had loved, and his body was interred at Waltham, with regal honors, in the presence of several Norman earls and knights."

We have reached the conclusion of Mr. Wheaton's interesting volume, yet we are tempted to add a few words more from other sources. We would observe that there are not wanting historians who dispute the whole story of Harold having fallen on the field of battle. "Years afterwards," we are told by one of the most curiously learned of English scholars, "when the Norman yoke pressed heavily upon the English, and the battle of Hastings had become a tale of sorrow, which old men narrated by the light of the embers, until warned to silence by the sullen tolling of the curfew," there was an ancient anchorite, maimed and scarred and blind of an eye, who led a life of penitence and seclusion in a cell near the Abbey of St. John at Chester. This holy man was once visited by Henry I., who held a long and secret discourse with him, and on his death-bed he declared to the attendant monks that he was Harold.* According to this account, he had been secretly conveyed from the field of battle to a castle, and thence to this sanctuary; and the finding and burying of his corpse by the tender Editha is supposed to have

---

* Palgrave, *Hist. Eng.*, Chap. XV.

been a pious fraud. The monks of Waltham, however, stood up stoutly for the authenticity of their royal relics. They showed a tomb, inclosing a mouldering skeleton, the bones of which still bore the marks of wounds received in battle, while the sepulchre bore the effigies of the monarch, and this brief but pathetic epitaph: "*Hic jacet Harold infelix.*"

For a long time after the eventful battle of the Conquest, it is said that traces of blood might be seen upon the field, and, in particular, upon the hills to the southwest of Hastings, whenever a light rain moistened the soil. It is probable they were discolorations of the soil, where heaps of the slain had been buried. We have ourselves seen broad and dark patches on the hill-side of Waterloo, where thousands of the dead lay mouldering in one common grave, and where, for several years after the battle, the rank green corn refused to ripen, though all the other part of the hill was covered with a golden harvest.

William the Conqueror, in fulfilment of a vow, caused a monastic pile to be erected on the field, which, in commemoration of the event, was called the "Abbey of Battle." The architects complained that there were no springs of water on the site. "Work on! work on!" replied he, jovially; "if God but grant me life, there shall flow more good wine among the holy friars of this convent, than there does clear water in the best monastery of Christendom."

The abbey was richly endowed, and invested with archiepiscopal jurisdiction. In its archives was deposited a roll, bearing the names of the followers of William, among whom he had shared the conquered land. The grand altar was placed on the very spot where the banner of the hapless Harold had been unfurled, and here prayers were perpetually to be offered up for the repose of all who had fallen in the contest. "All this pomp and solemnity," adds Mr. Palgrave, "has passed away like a dream! The perpetual prayer has ceased forever; the roll of battle is rent; the escutcheons of the Norman lineages are trodden in the dust. A dark and reedy pool marks where the abbey once reared its stately towers, and nothing but the foundations of the choir remain for the gaze of the idle visitor, and the instruction of the moping antiquary."

29

CONQUEST OF GRANADA.

Review of a Chronicle of the Conquest of Granada, from the
*MSS. of Fray Antonio Agapida.**

HERE are a few places scattered about this "working-day world" which seem to be elevated above its dull prosaic level, and to be clothed with the magic lights and tints of poetry. They possess a charmed name, the very mention of which, as if by fairy power, conjures up splendid scenes and pageants of the past; summons from "death's dateless night" the shadows of the great and good, the brave and beautiful, and fills the mind with visions of departed glory. Such is preëminently the case with Granada, one of the most classical names in the history of latter ages. The very nature of the country and the climate contributes to bewitch the fancy. The Moors, we are told, while in possession of the land, had wrought it up to a wonderful degree of prosperity. The hills were

* *Note by the Author.* This review, published in the *London Quarterly Review* for 1830, was written by the author at the request of his London publisher, to explain the real nature of his work, and its claim to historic truth.

450

clothed with orchards and vineyards, the valleys embroidered with gardens, and the plains covered with waving grain. Here were seen in profusion the orange, the citron, the fig, the pomegranate, and the silk-producing mulberry. The vine clambered from tree to tree, the grapes hung in rich clusters about the peasant's cottage, and the groves were rejoiced by the perpetual song of the nightingale. In a word, so beautiful was the earth, so pure the air, and so serene the sky of this delicious region, that the Moors imagined the paradise of their prophet to be situate in that part of the heaven which overhung their kingdom of Granada.

But what has most contributed to impart to Granada a great and permanent interest, is the ten years' war of which it was the scene, and which closed the splendid drama of Moslem domination in Spain. For nearly eight centuries had the Spaniards been recovering, piece by piece, and by dint of the sword, that territory which had been wrested from them by their Arab invaders in little more than as many months. The kingdom of Granada was the last stronghold of Moorish power, and the favorite abode of Moorish luxury. The final struggle for it was maintained with desperate valor; and the compact nature of the country, hemmed in by the ocean and by lofty mountains, and the continual recurrence of the names of the same monarchs and commanders throughout the war, give to it a peculiar distinctness, and an almost epic unity.

But though this memorable war had often been made the subject of romantic fiction, and though the very name possessed a spell upon the imagination, yet it had never been fully and distinctly treated. The world at large had been content to receive a strangely perverted idea of it, through Florian's romance of " Gonsalvo of Cordova ;" or through the legend, equally fabulous, entitled " The Civil Wars of Granada," by Ginez Perez de la Hita, the pretended work of an Arabian contemporary, but in reality a Spanish fabrication.* It had been woven over with love-tales and scenes of sentimental gallantry, totally opposite to its real character ; for it was, in truth, one of the sternest of those iron contests which have been sanctified by the title of " holy wars." In fact, the genuine nature of the war placed it far above the need of any amatory embellishments. It possessed sufficient interest in the striking contrast presented by the combatants, of Oriental and European creeds, costumes, and manners ; and in the hardy and hair-brained enterprises, the romantic adventures, the picturesque forages through mountain regions, the daring assaults and surprisals of cliff-built castles and cragged fortresses, which succeeded

---

* The following censure on the work of La Hita is passed by old Padre Echevarria, in his *Paseos por Granada*, or *Walks through Granada*. " Esta es una historia toda fabulosa, cuyo autor se ignora, por mas que corra con el nombre de alguno, llena de cuentos y quimeras, en la que apenas si hallarán seis verdades, y estas desfiguradas." Such is the true character of a work which has hitherto served as a fountain of historic fact concerning the conquest of Granada.

each other with a variety and brilliancy beyond the scope of mere invention.

The time of the contest also contributed to heighten the interest. It was not long after the invention of gunpowder, when fire-arms and artillery mingled the flash, smoke, and thunder of modern warfare with the steely splendor of ancient chivalry, and gave an awful magnificence and terrible sublimity to battle; and when the old Moorish towers and castles, that for ages had frowned defiance to the battering-rams and catapults of classic tactics, were toppled down by the lombards of the Spanish engineers. It was one of those cases in which history rises superior to fiction. The author seems to have been satisfied of this fact, by the manner in which he has constructed the present work. The idea of it, we are told, was suggested to him while in Spain, occupied upon his "History of the Life and Voyages of Columbus." The application of the great navigator to the Spanish sovereigns, for patronage to his project of discovery, was made during their crusade against the Moors of Granada, and continued throughout the residue of that war. Columbus followed the court in several of its campaigns, mingled occasionally in the contest, and was actually present at the grand catastrophe of the enterprise, the surrender of the metropolis. The researches of Mr. Irving, in tracing the movements of his hero, led him to the various chronicles of the reign of Ferdinand and Isabella. He became deeply interested in the details of the war, and was induced, while collecting materials for the biography he had in hand, to make preparation also for the present history. He subsequently made a tour in Andalusia, visited the ruins of the Moorish towns, fortresses, and castles, and the wild mountain passes and defiles which had been the scenes of the most remarkable events of the war; and passed some time in the ancient palace of the Alhambra, once the favorite abode of the Moorish monarchs in Granada. It was then, while his mind was still excited by the romantic scenery around him, and by the chivalrous and poetical associations which throw a moral interest over every feature of Spanish landscape, that he completed these volumes.

His great object appears to have been, to produce a complete and authentic body of facts relative to the war in question, but arranged in such a manner as to be attractive to the reader for mere amusement. He has, therefore, diligently sought for his materials among the ancient chronicles, both printed and in manuscript, which were written at the time by eye-witnesses, and, in some instances, by persons who had actually mingled in the scenes recorded. These chronicles were often diffuse and tedious, and occasionally discolored by the bigotry, superstition, and fierce intolerance of the age; but their pages were illumined, at times, with scenes of high emprize, of romantic generosity, and heroic valor, which flashed upon the reader with additional splendor, from the surrounding darkness. It has been the study of the author to bring forth these scenes in their strongest light; to arrange them in clear and lucid order; to give them somewhat of a graphic effect, by connecting them with the manners and customs of the age in which they occurred, and with the splendid scenery amidst which they took place; and thus, while he preserved the truth and chronological order of events, to impart a more impressive and entertaining character to his narrative, than regular histories are accustomed to possess. By these means his chronicle, at times, wears almost the air of romance; yet the story is authenticated by frequent reference to existing documents, proving that he has substantial foundation for his most extraordinary incidents.

There is, however, another circumstance, by which Mr. Irving has more seriously impaired the *ex-facie* credibility of his narrative. He has professed to derive his materials from the manuscripts of an ancient Spanish monk, Fray Antonio Agapida, whose historical productions are represented as existing in disjointed fragments, in the archives of the Escurial and other conventual libraries. He often quotes the very words of the venerable friar; particularly when he bursts forth in exaggerated praises of the selfish policy or bigot zeal of Ferdinand; or chants, "with pious exultation, the united triumphs of the cross and the sword." This friar is manifestly a mere fiction—a stalking-horse, from behind which the author launches his satire at the intolerance of that persecuting age, and at the errors, the inconsistencies, and the self-delusions of the singular medley of warriors, saints, politicians, and adventurers engaged in that holy war. Fray Antonio, however, may be considered as an incarnation of the blind bigotry and zealot extravagance of the " good old orthodox Spanish chroniclers ; " and, in fact, his exaggerated sallies of loyalty and religion are taken, almost word for word, from the works of some one or other of the monkish historians. Still, though this fictitious personage has enabled the author to indulge his satirical vein at once more freely and more modestly, and has diffused over his page something of the quaintness of the cloister, and the tint of the country and the period, the use of such machinery has thrown a doubt upon the absolute verity of his history; and it will take some time before the general mass of readers become convinced that the pretended manuscript of Fray Antonio Agapida is, in truth, a faithful digest of actual documents.

The chronicle opens with the arrival of a Spanish cavalier at Granada, with a demand of arrears of tribute, on the part of Ferdinand and Isabella, from Muley Aben Hassan, the Moorish king. This measure is well understood to have been a crafty device of Ferdinand. The tribute had become obsolete, and he knew it would be indignantly refused ; but he had set his heart on driving the Moors out of their last Spanish dominions, and he now sought a cause of quarrel.

" Muley Aben Hassan received the cavalier in state, seated on a magnificent divan, and surrounded by the officers of his court, in the Hall of

Ambassadors, one of the most sumptuous apartments of the Alhambra. When De Vera had delivered his message, a haughty and bitter smile curled the lip of the fierce monarch. 'Tell your sovereigns,' said he, 'that the kings of Granada who used to pay tribute in money to the Castilian crown are dead. Our mint at present coins nothing but blades of scimitars and heads of lances."—Vol. I. p. 10.

The fiery old Moslem had here given a very tolerable pretext for immediate war; yet King Ferdinand forbore to strike the blow. He was just then engaged in a contest with Portugal, the cause of which Mr. Irving leaves unnoticed, as irrelevant to his subject. It is, however, a curious morsel of history, involving the singular and romantic fortunes of the fair Juana of Castile, by many considered the rightful heir to the crown. It is illustrative, also, of the manners of the age of which this chronicle peculiarly treats, and of the character and policy of the Spanish sovereign who figures throughout its pages; a brief notice of it, therefore, may not be unacceptable.

Henry IV. of Castile, one of the most imbecile of kings and credulous of husbands, had lived for five years in sterile wedlock with his queen, a gay and buxom princess of Portugal, when, at length, she rejoiced him by the birth of the Infanta Juana. The horn of the king was, of course, exalted on this happy occasion, but the whisper was diligently circulated about the court, that he was indebted for the tardy honors of paternity to the good offices of Don Beltran de Cuevas, Count of Ledesma, a youthful and gallant cavalier, who had enjoyed the peculiar favor and intimacy of the queen. The story soon took wind, and became a theme of popular clamor. Henry, however, with the good easy faith, or passive acquiescence of an imbecile mind, continued to love and honor his queen, and to lavish favors on her paramour, whom he advanced in rank, making him his prime minister, and giving him the title of Duke of Albuquerque. Such blind credulity is not permitted, in this troublesome world, to kings more than to common men. The public were furious ; civil commotions took place ; Henry was transiently deposed, and was only reinstated in his royal dignity, on signing a treaty, by which he divorced his wife, disowned her child, and promised to send them both to Portugal. His connubial faith ultimately revived, in defiance of every trial, and on his death-bed he recognized the Infanta Juana as his daughter and legitimate successor. The public, however, who will not allow even kings to be infallible judges in cases of the kind, persisted in asserting the illegitimacy of the Infanta ; and gave her the name of *La Beltranaja*, in allusion to her supposed father, Don Beltran.* No judicial investigation took place, but the question was decided as a point of faith, or a notorious fact ; and the youthful princess, though of great beauty and merit, was set aside, and the crown adjudged to her father's sister, the renowned Isabella.

* Pulgar, *Chron. de los Reyes Católicos*, c. 1, note **A.**

It should be observed, however, that the charge of illegitimacy is maintained principally by Spanish writers; the Portuguese historians reject it as a calumny. Even the classic Mariana expresses an idea that it might have been an invention or exaggeration, founded on the weakness of Henry IV. and the amorous temperament of his queen,* and artfully devised to favor the views of the crafty Ferdinand, who laid claim to the crown as the rightful inheritance of his spouse, Isabella.

Young, beautiful, and unfortunate, the discarded princess was not long in want of a champion in that heroic age. Her mother's brother, the brave Alonzo V. of Portugal, surnamed *el Lidiador*, or the Combatant, from his exploits against the Moors of Africa, stepped forward as her vindicator, and marched into Spain at the head of a gallant army, to place her on the throne. He asked her hand in marriage, and it was yielded. The espousals were publicly solemnized at Placentia, but were not consummated, the consanguinity of the parties obliging them to wait for a dispensation from the Pope.

All the southern provinces of Castile, with a part of Galicia, declared in favor of Juana, and town after town yielded to the arms or the persuasion of Alonzo, as he advanced. The majority of the kingdom, however, rallied round the standard of Ferdinand and Isabella. The latter assembled their warrior nobles at Valladolid, and

* Mariana, lib. xxii. c. 20.

amidst the chivalrous throng that appeared glittering in
arms was Don Beltran, Duke of Albuquerque, the surmised father of Juana. His predicament was singular
and delicate. If, in truth, the father of Juana, natural
affection called upon him to support her interests; if
she were not his child, then she had an unquestionable
right to the crown, and it was his duty, as a true cavalier, to support her claim. It is even said that he had
pledged himself to Alonzo, to stand forth in loyal adherence to the virgin queen; but when he saw the array of
mailed warriors and powerful nobles that thronged round
Ferdinand and Isabella, he trembled for his great estates,
and tacitly mingled with the crowd.* The gallant inroad
of Alonzo into Spain was attended with many vicissitudes; he could not maintain his footing against the
superior force of Ferdinand, and being defeated in a decisive battle, between Zamora and Toro, was obliged to
retire from Castile. He conducted his beautiful and yet
virgin bride into Portugal, where she was received as
queen with great acclamations. There leaving her in
security, he repaired to France, to seek assistance from
Louis XI. During this absence, Pope Sixtus IV. granted
the dispensation for his marriage. It was cautiously
worded, and secretly given, that it might escape the
knowledge of Ferdinand, until carried into effect. It
authorized the king of Portugal to marry any relative

* Pulgar, part ii. cap. xxii.

not allied to him in the first degree of consanguinity, but avoided naming the bride.*

The negotiation of Alonzo at the court of France was protracted during many weary months, and was finally defeated by the superior address of Ferdinand. He returned to Portugal, to forget his vexations in the arms of his blooming bride; but even here he was again disappointed by the crafty intrigues of his rival. The pliant pontiff had been prevailed upon to issue a patent bull, overruling his previous dispensation, as having been obtained without naming both of the persons to be united in marriage, and as having proved the cause of wars and bloodshed.† The royal pair were thus obliged to meet in the relations of uncle and niece, instead of husband and wife. Peace was finally negotiated by the intervention of friends, on the condition that Donna Juana should either take the veil and become a nun, or should be wedded to Don Juan, the infant son and heir of Ferdinand and Isabella, as soon as he should arrive at a marriageable age. This singular condition, which would place her on the throne from which she had been excluded, has been adduced as a proof of her legitimate right.

Alonzo V. was furious, and rejected the treaty; but Donna Juana shrunk from being any longer the cause of war and bloodshed, and determined to devote herself to celibacy and religion. All the entreaties of the king were

---

* Zurita, *Annales.*　　　　　　† Zurita.

of no avail; she took the irrevocable vows, and, exchanging her royal robes for the humble habit of a Franciscan nun, entered the convent of Santa Clara, with all the customary solemnities; not having yet completed her nineteenth year, and having been four years a virgin wife. All authors concur in giving her a most amiable and exemplary character; and Garibay says " she was named, for her virtues, *La Excellenta,* and left a noble example to the world. Her retirement," he adds, " occasioned great affliction to King Alonzo, and grief to many others, who beheld so exquisite a lady reduced to such great humility." *

The king, in a transport of tender melancholy, took a sudden resolution, characteristic of that age, when love and chivalry and religion were strangely intermingled. Leaving his capital on a feigned pretence, he repaired to a distant city, and there, laying aside his royal state, set forth on a pilgrimage to Jerusalem, attended merely by a chaplain and two grooms. He had determined to renounce the pomp, and glories, and vanities of the world; and, after humbling himself at the holy sepulchre, to devote himself to a religious life. He sent back one of his attendants, with letters, in which he took a tender leave of Donna Juana, and directed his son to assume the crown. His letters threw the court into great affliction; his son was placed on the throne, but several of the an-

* Garibay, *Compend. Hist.,* lib. xxxv. cap. 19.

cient courtiers set out in pursuit of the pilgrim king. They overtook him far on his journey, and prevailed on him to return and resume his sceptre, which was dutifully resigned to him by his son. Still restless and melancholy, Alonzo afterwards undertook a crusade for the recovery of the holy sepulchre, and proceeded to Italy with a fleet and army ; but was discouraged from the enterprise by the coldness of Pope Pius II. He then returned to Portugal ; and his love melancholy reviving in the vicinity of Donna Juana, he determined, out of a kind of romantic sympathy, to imitate her example, and to take the habit of St. Francis. His sadness and depression, however, increased to such a degree as to overwhelm his forces, and he died, in 1481, at Cintra, in the chamber in which he was born.*

We cannot close the brief record of this romantic story without noticing the subsequent fortunes of Donna Juana. She resided in the monastery of Santa Anna, with the seclusion of a nun, but the state of a princess. The fame of her beauty and her worth drew suitors to the cloisters ; and her hand was solicited by the youthful king of Navarre, Don Francisco Phebus, surnamed the Handsome. His courtship, however, was cut short by his sudden death, in 1483, which was surmised to have been caused by poison.† For six-and-twenty years did the royal nun continue shut up in holy seclusion from the world. The

---

* Faria y Sousa, *Hist. Portugal*, p. iii. cap. xiii.
† Abarca, *Reyes de Aragon*, Rey. 30, cap. 2.

desire of youth and the pride of beauty had long passed away, when suddenly, in 1505, Ferdinand himself, her ancient enemy, the cause of all her sorrows and disappointments, appeared as a suitor for her hand. His own illustrious queen, the renowned Isabella, was dead, and had bequeathed her hereditary crown of Castile to their daughter, for whose husband, Philip I., he had a jealous aversion. It was supposed that the crafty and ambitious monarch intended, after marrying Juana, to revive her claim to that throne, from which his own hostility had excluded her. His conduct in this instance is another circumstance strongly in favor of the lawful right of Juana to the crown of Castile. The vanity of the world, however, was dead in the tranquil bosom of the princess, and the grandeur of a throne had no longer attraction in her eyes. She rejected the suit of the most politic and perfidious of monarchs; and, continuing faithful to her vows, passed the remainder of her days in the convent of Santa Anna, where she died in all the odor of holiness, and of immaculate and thrice-proved virginity, which had passed unscorched even through the fiery ordeal of matrimony.

To return to Mr. Irving's narrative. Ferdinand having successfully terminated the war with Portugal, and seated himself and Isabella firmly on the throne of Castile, turned his attention to his contemplated project—the conquest of Granada. His plan of operations was characteristic of his cautious and crafty nature. He determined to proceed step by step, taking town after town, and fortress after fortress, before he attempted the Moorish capital. "I will pick out the seeds of this pomegranate one by one," said the wary monarch, in allusion to Granada,—the Spanish name both for the kingdom and the fruit. The intention of the Catholic sovereign did not escape the eagle eye of old Muley Aben Hassan. Being, however, possessed of great treasures, and having placed his territories in a warlike posture, and drawn auxiliary troops from his allies, the princes of Barbary, he felt confident in his means of resistance. His subjects were fierce of spirit, and stout of heart—inured to the exercises of war, and patient of fatigue, hunger, thirst, and nakedness. Above all, they were dexterous horsemen, whether heavily armed and fully appointed, or lightly mounted *a la geneta*, with merely lance and target. Adroit in all kinds of stratagems, impetuous in attack, quick to disperse, prompt to rally and to return like a whirlwind to the charge, they were considered the best of troops for daring inroads, sudden scourings, and all kinds of partisan warfare. In fact, they have bequeathed their wild and predatory spirit to Spain; and her bandaleros, her contrabandistas, and her guerrillas, her marauders of the mountain, and scamperers of the plain, may all be traced back to the belligerent era of the Moors.

The truce which had existed between the Catholic sovereign and the king of Granada contained a singular

30

clause, characteristic of the wary and dangerous situation of the two neighboring nations, with respect to each other. It permitted either party to make sudden inroads and assaults upon towns and fortresses, provided they were done furtively and by stratagem, without display of banner or sound of trumpet, or regular encampment, and that they did not last above three days. This gave rise to frequent enterprises of a hardy and adventurous character, in which castles and strongholds were taken by surprise, and carried sword in hand. Monuments of these border scourings, and the jealous watchfulness awakened by them, may still be seen by the traveller in every part of Spain, but particularly in Andalusia. The mountains which formed the barriers of the Christian and Moslem territories are still crested with ruined watch-towers, where the helmed and turbaned sentinels kept a look-out on the Vega of Granada, or the plains of the Guadalquivir. Every rugged pass has its dismantled fortress, and every town and village, and even hamlet, the mountain or valley, its strong tower of defence. Even on the beautiful little stream of the Guadayra, which now winds peacefully among flowery banks and groves of myrtles and oranges, to throw itself into the Guadalquivir, the Moorish mills, which have studded its borders for centuries, have each its battlemented tower, where the miller and his family could take refuge until the foray which swept the plains, and made hasty sack and plunder in its career, had passed away. Such was the situation of Moor and Spaniard in those days, when the sword and spear hung ready on the wall of every cottage, and the humblest toils of husbandry were performed with the weapon close at hand.

The outbreaking of the war of Granada is in keeping with this picture. The fierce old king, Muley Aben Hassan, had determined to anticipate his adversary, and strike the first blow. The fortress of Zahara was the object of his attack ; and the description of it may serve for that of many of those old warrior towns which remain from the time of the Moors, built, like eagle-nests, among the wild mountains of Andalusia.

"This important post was on the frontier, between Ronda and Medina Sidonia, and was built on the crest of a rocky mountain, with a strong castle perched above it, upon a cliff so high that it was said to be above the flight of birds or drift of clouds. The streets, and many of the houses, were mere excavations, wrought out of the living rock. The town had but one gate, opening to the west, and defended by towers and bulwarks. The only ascent to this cragged fortress was by roads cut in the rock, and so rugged as in many places to resemble broken stairs. Such was the situation of the mountain fortress of Zahara, which seemed to set all attack at defiance, insomuch that it had become so proverbial throughout Spain, that a woman of forbidding and inaccessible virtue was called a Zahareña. But the strongest fortress and sternest virtue have their weak points, and require unremitting vigilance to guard them : let warrior and dame take warning from the fate of Zahara."

Muley Aben Hassan made a midnight attack upon this fortress during a howling wintry storm, which had driven the very sentinels from their posts. He scaled the walls, and gained possession of both town and castle before the garrison were roused to arms. Such of the inhabitants as made resistance were cut down, the rest were taken prisoners, and driven, men, women, and children, like a herd of cattle, to Granada.

The capture of Zahara was as an electric shock to the chivalry of Spain. Among those roused to action was Don Rodrigo Ponce de Leon, Marquis of Cadiz, who is worthy of particular notice as being the real hero of the war. Florian has assigned this honor, in his historical romance, to Gonsalvo of Cordova, surnamed the Great Captain, who, in fact, performed but an inferior part in these campaigns. It was in the subsequent war of Italy that he acquired his high renown. Rodrigo Ponce de Leon is a complete exemplification of the Spanish cavalier of the olden time. Temperate, chaste, vigilant, and valorous; kind to his vassals, frank towards his equals, faithful and loving to his friends, terrible, yet magnanimous to his enemies; contemporary historians extol him as the mirror of chivalry, and compare him to the immortal Cid. His ample possessions extended over the most fertile parts of Andalusia, including many towns and fortresses. A host of retainers, ready to follow him to danger or to death, fed in his castle hall, which waved with banners taken from the Moors. His armories glittered with helms and cuirasses, and weapons of all kinds, ready burnished for use, and his stables were filled with hardy steeds trained to a mountain scamper. This ready preparation arose not merely from his residence on the Moorish border; he had a formidable foe near at hand, in Juan de Guzman, Duke of Medina Sidonia, one of the most wealthy of Spanish nobles. We shall notice one or two particulars of his earlier life, which our author has omitted, as not within the scope of his chronicle, but which would have given additional interest to some of its scenes. An hereditary feud subsisted between these two noblemen; and as Ferdinand and Isabella had not yet succeeded in their plan of reducing the independent and dangerous power of the nobles of Spain, the whole province of Andalusia was convulsed by their strife. They waged war against each other like sovereign princes, regarding neither the authority of the crown nor the welfare of the country. Every fortress and castle became a stronghold of their partisans, and a kind of club law prevailed over the land, like the *faust recht* once exercised by the robber counts of Germany. The sufferings of the province awakened the solicitude of Isabella, and brought her to Seville, where, seated on a throne in a great hall of the Alcazar or Moorish palace, she held an open audience to receive petitions and complaints. The nobles of the province hastened to do her homage. The Marquis of Cadiz alone did not appear. The Duke of Medina Sidonia accused him of having been treasonably in the interest of Portugal, in the late war of the succession ; of exercising tyrannical sway over certain royal domains ; of harassing the subjects of the crown with his predatory bands, and keeping himself aloof in warlike defiance, in his fortified city of Xeres. The continued absence of the marquis countenanced these charges, and they were reiterated by the relations and dependants of the Duke, who thronged and controlled the ancient city of Seville. The indignation of the queen was roused, and she determined to reduce the supposed rebel by force of arms. Tidings of these events were conveyed to Ponce de Leon, and roused him to vindicate his honor with frankness and decision. He instantly set off from Xeres, attended by a single servant. Spurring across the country, and traversing the hostile city, he entered the palace by a private portal, and penetrating to the apartment of the queen, presented himself suddenly before her.

" Behold me here, most potent sovereign !" exclaimed he, "to answer any charge in person. I come not to accuse others, but to vindicate myself ; not to deal in words, but in deeds. It is said that I hold Xeres and Alcala fortified and garrisoned, in defiance of your authority : send and take possession of them, for they are yours. Do you require my patrimonial hereditaments ? From this chamber I will direct their surrender ; and here I deliver up my very person into your power. As to the other charges, let investigation be made ; and if I stand not clear and loyal, impose on me whatever pain or penalty you may think proper to inflict." *

Isabella saw in the intrepid frankness of the marquis strong proof of innocence, and declared, that had she

* Pulgar, c. lxx., &c.

thought him guilty, his gallant confidence would have insured her clemency. She took possession of the fortresses surrendered, but caused the duke to give up equally his military posts, and to free Seville from these distracting contests, ordered either chief to dwell on his estate. Such was the feud betwixt these rival nobles at the time when the old Moorish king captured and sacked Zahara.

The news of this event stirred up the warrior spirit of Ponce de Leon to retaliation. He sent out his scouts, and soon learnt that the town of Alhama was assailable. "This was a large, wealthy, and populous place, which, from its strong position on a rocky height, within a few leagues of the Moorish capital, had acquired the appellation of the 'Key of Granada.'" The marquis held conference with the most important commanders of Andalusia, excepting the Duke of Medina Sidonia, his deadly foe, and concerted a secret march through the mountain passes to Alhama, which he surprised and carried. We forbear to follow the author in his detail of this wild and perilous enterprise, the success of which struck deep consternation in the Moors of Granada. The exclamation of "Ay de mi, Alhama!—Woe is me, Alhama!" was in every mouth. It has become the burden of a mournful Spanish ballad, supposed of Moorish origin, which has been translated by Lord Byron.

The Marquis of Cadiz and his gallant companions, now in possession of Alhama, were but a handful of men, in

the heart of an enemy's country, and were surrounded
by a powerful army, led by the fierce King of Granada.
They despatched messengers to Seville and Cordova,
describing their perilous situation, and imploring aid.
Nothing could equal the anguish of the Marchioness of
Cadiz on hearing of the danger of her lord. She looked
round in her deep distress for some powerful noble, competent to raise the force requisite for his deliverance. No
one was so competent as the Duke of Medina Sidonia.
To many, however, he would have seemed the last person
to whom to apply; but she judged of him by her own
high and generous mind, and did not hesitate. The event
showed how well noble spirits understand each other.

"He immediately despatched a courteous letter to the marchioness,
assuring her that, in consideration of the request of so honorable and
estimable a lady, and to rescue from peril so valiant a cavalier as her
husband, whose loss would be great, not only to Spain, but to all Christendom, he would forego the recollection of all past grievances and hasten
to his relief. The duke wrote at the same time to the alcaydes of his
towns and fortresses, ordering them to join him forthwith at Seville, with
all the force they could spare from their garrisons. He called on all the
chivalry of Andalusia to make a common cause in the rescue of those
Christian cavaliers; and he offered large pay to all volunteers who would
resort to him with horses, armor, and provisions. Thus all who could be
incited by honor, religion, patriotism, or thirst of gain, were induced to
hasten to his standard; and he took the field with an army of five thousand horse and fifty thousand foot."

Ferdinand was in church at Medina del Campo when
he heard of the achievement and the peril of his gallant

cavaliers, and set out instantly to aid in person in their rescue. He wrote to the Duke of Medina Sidonia to pause for him on the frontier; but it was a case of life and death: the duke left a message to that effect for his sovereign, and pressed on his unceasing march. He arrived just in time, when the garrison, reduced to extremity by incessant skirmishes and assaults, and the want of water, and resembling skeletons rather than living men, were on the point of falling into the hands of the enemy. Muley Aben Hassan, who commanded the siege in person, tore his beard when his scouts brought him word of their arrival.

"They had seen from the heights the long columns and flaunting banners of the Christian army approaching through the mountains. To linger would be to place himself between two bodies of the enemy. Breaking up his camp, therefore, in all haste, he gave up the siege of Alhama, and hastened back to Granada; and the last clash of his cymbals scarce died upon the ear from the distant hills, before the standard of the Duke of Medina Sidonia was seen emerging in another direction from the defiles of the mountains. . . . . . It was a noble and gracious sight to behold the meeting of those two ancient foes, the Duke of Medina Sidonia and the Marquis of Cadiz. When the marquis beheld his magnanimous deliverer approaching, he melted into tears: all past animosities only gave the greater poignancy to present feelings of gratitude and admiration; they clasped each other in their arms; and, from that time forward, were true and cordial friends."

Having duly illustrated these instances of chivalrous hardihood and noble magnanimity, the author shifts his scene from the Christian camp to the Moslem hall, and gives us a peep into the interior of the Alhambra, and the domestic policy of the Moorish monarchs. The old King of Granada was perplexed, not merely with foreign wars, but with family feuds, and seems to have evinced a kind of tiger character in both. He had several wives, two of whom were considered as sultanas, or queens. One, named Ayxa, was of Moorish origin, and surnamed *La Horra*, or *The Chaste*, from the purity of her manners. Fatima, the other, had been originally a Christian captive, and was called, from her beauty, *Zoroya*, or *The Light of Dawn*. The former had given birth to his eldest son, Abdalla, or Boabdil, commonly called *El Chico*, or *The Younger;* and the latter had brought him two sons. Zoroya abused the influence that her youth and beauty gave her over the hoary monarch, inducing him to repudiate the virtuous Ayxa, and exciting his suspicions against Boabdil to such a degree that he determined upon his death. It was the object of Zoroya, by these flagitious means, to secure the succession for one of her own children.

"The Sultana Ayxa was secretly apprised of the cruel design of the old monarch. She was a woman of talents and courage, and, by means of her female attendants, concerted a plan for the escape of her son. A faithful servant was instructed to wait below the Alhambra, in the dead of the night, on the banks of the river Darro, with a fleet Arabian courser. The sultana, when the castle was in a state of deep repose, tied together the shawls and scarfs of herself and her female attendants, and lowered the youthful prince from the tower of Comares. He made his way in safety down the steep rocky hill to the banks of the Darro, and, throwing himself on the Arabian courser, was thus spirited off to the city of Guadix. Here he lay for some time concealed, until, gaining adherents, he fortified himself in the place, and set his tyrant father at defiance. Such was the commencement of those internal feuds which hastened the downfall of Granada. The Moors became separated into two hostile factions, headed by the father and the son, and several bloody encounters took place between them ; yet they never failed to act with all their separate force against the Christians, as a common enemy."

It is proper in this place to remark, that the present chronicle gives an entirely different character to Boabdil from that by which he is usually described. It says nothing of his alleged massacre of the Abencerrages, nor of the romantic story of his jealous persecution and condemnation of his queen, and her vindication in combat by Christian knights. The massacre, in fact, if it really did take place, was the deed of his tiger-hearted father ; the story of the queen is not to be found in any contemporary chronicle, either Spanish or Arabian, and is considered by Mr. Irving as a mere fabrication. Boabdil appears to have been sometimes rash, at other times irresolute, but never cruel.

As a specimen of the predatory war that prevailed about the borders, we would fain make some extracts from a foray of the old Moorish king into the lands of the Duke of Medina Sidonia, who had foiled him before Alhama ; but this our limits forbid. It ends triumphantly for Muley Hassan ; and Boabdil el Chico, in consequence, found it requisite for his popularity to strike some signal blow that might eclipse the brilliant exploits of the rival king, his father. He was in the flower of his age, and renowned at joust and tourney, but as yet unproved in the field of battle. He was encouraged to make a daring inroad into the Christian territories by the father of his favorite sultana, Ali Atar, alcayde of Loxa, a veteran warrior, ninety years of age, whose name was the terror of the borders.

"Boabdil assembled a brilliant army of nine thousand foot and seven hundred horse, comprising the most illustrious and valiant of the Moorish chivalry. His mother, the Sultana Ayxa La Horra, armed him for the field, and gave him her benediction as she girded his cimetar to his side. His favorite wife, Morayma, wept as she thought of the evils that might befall him. 'Why dost thou weep, daughter of Ali Atar?' said the high-minded Ayxa; 'these tears become not the daughter of a warrior, nor the wife of a king. Believe me, there lurks more danger for a monarch within the strong walls of a palace, than within the frail curtains of a tent. It is by perils in the field that thy husband must purchase security on his throne.' But Morayma still hung upon his neck, with tears and sad forebodings; and when he departed from the Alhambra, she betook herself to her mirador, which looks out over the Vega, whence she watched the army as it passed in shining order along the road that leads to Loxa ; and every burst of warlike melody that came swelling on the breeze was answered by a gush of sorrow. . . . .

"At Loxa, the royal army was reinforced by old Ali Atar, with the chosen horsemen of his garrison, and many of the bravest warriors of the border towns. The people of Loxa shouted with exultation when they beheld Ali Atar armed at all points, and once more mounted on his Barbary steed, which had often borne him over the borders. The veteran warrior, with nearly a century of years upon his head, had all the fire and animation of a youth at the prospect of a foray, and careered from rank to rank with the velocity of an Arab of the desert. The populace watched the army as it paraded over the bridge, and wound into the passes of the mountains; and still their eyes were fixed upon the pennon of Ali Atar, as if it bore with it an assurance of victory."

The enemy has scarcely had a day's ravage in the Christian land, when the alarm-fires give notice that the Moor is over the border. Our limits do not permit us to give this picture of the sudden rising of a frontier in those times of Moorish inroad. We pass on to the scene of action, when the hardy Count de Cabra came up with the foe, having pressed fearlessly forward at the head of a handful of household troops and retainers.

" The Moorish king descried the Spanish forces at a distance, although a slight fog prevented his seeing them distinctly and ascertaining their numbers. His old father-in-law, Ali Atar, was by his side, who, being a veteran marauder, was well acquainted with all the standards and armorial bearings of the frontiers. When the king beheld the ancient and long-disused banner of Cabra emerging from the mist, he turned to Ali Atar, and demanded whose ensign it was. The old borderer was for once at a loss, for the banner had not been displayed in battle in his time. 'Sire,' replied he, after a pause, 'I have been considering that standard, but do not know it. It appears to be a dog, which is a device borne by the towns of Baeza and Ubeda. If it be so, all Andalusia is in movement against you; for it is not probable that any single commander or community would venture to attack you. I would advise you, therefore, to retire.'

"The Count of Cabra, in winding down the hill towards the Moors, found himself on a much lower station than the enemy. He therefore ordered, in all haste, that his standard should be taken back, so as to gain the vantage-ground. The Moors, mistaking this for a retreat, rushed impetuously towards the Christians.   The latter, having gained the height proposed, charged down upon them at the same moment, with the battle-cry of 'Santiago !' and, dealing the first blows, laid many of the Moorish cavaliers in the dust.

"The Moors, thus checked in their tumultuous assault, were thrown into confusion, and began to give way,—the Christians following hard upon them.   Boabdil el Chico endeavored to rally them.   'Hold! hold! for shame!' cried he ; 'let us not fly, at least until we know our enemy !'   The Moorish chivalry was stung by this reproof, and turned to make front, with the valor of men who feel that they are fighting under their monarch's eye.   At this moment, Lorenzo de Porres, alcayde of Luque, arrived with fifty horse and one hundred foot, sounding an Italian trumpet from among a copse of oak-trees, which concealed his force. The quick ear of old Ali Atar caught the note.   'That is an Italian trumpet,' said he to the king ; 'the whole world seems in arms against your majesty !'   The trumpet of Lorenzo de Porres was answered by that of the Count de Cabra in another direction ; and it seemed to the Moors as if they were between two armies.   Don Lorenzo, sallying from among the oaks, now charged upon the enemy.   The latter did not wait to ascertain the force of this new foe.   The confusion, the variety of alarms, the attacks from opposite quarters, the obscurity of the fog, all conspired to deceive them as to the number of their adversaries.   Broken and dismayed, they retreated fighting ; and nothing but the presence and remonstrances of the king prevented their retreat from becoming a headlong flight."

The skirmishing retreat lasted for about three leagues; but on the banks of the Mingonzalez the rout became complete.   The result is related by a fugitive from the field :—

"The sentinels looked out from the watch-towers of Loxa, along the valley of the Xenil, which passes through the mountains.   They looked, to behold the king returning in triumph, at the head of his shining host, laden with the spoil of the unbeliever. They looked, to behold the standard of their warlike idol, the fierce Ali Atar, borne by the chivalry of Loxa, ever foremost in the wars of the border.

"In the evening of the 21st of April, they descried a single horseman, urging his faltering steed along the banks of the river. As he drew near, they perceived, by the flash of arms, that he was a warrior; and, on nearer approach, by the richness of his armor and the caparison of his steed, they knew him to be a warrior of rank.

"He reached Loxa faint and aghast; his Arabian courser covered with foam, and dust, and blood, panting and staggering with fatigue, and gashed with wounds. Having brought his master in safety, he sank down and died, before the gate of the city. The soldiers at the gate gathered round the cavalier, as he stood, mute and melancholy, by his expiring steed. They knew him to be the gallant Cidi Caleb, nephew of the chief alfaqui of the albaycen of Granada. When the people of Loxa beheld this noble cavalier thus alone, haggard and dejected, their hearts were filled with fearful forebodings.

"'Cavalier,' said they, 'how fares it with the king and army!' He cast his hand mournfully towards the land of the Christians. 'There they lie!' exclaimed he; 'the heavens have fallen upon them! all are lost—all dead!'

"Upon this there was a great cry of consternation among the people, and loud wailings of women; for the flower of the youth of Loxa were with the army. An old Moorish soldier, scarred in many a border battle, stood leaning on his lance by the gateway. 'Where is Ali Atar?' demanded he eagerly. 'If he still live, the army cannot be lost.'

"'I saw his turban cleft by the Christian sword,' replied Cidi Caleb. 'His body is floating in the Xenil.'

"When the soldier heard these words, he smote his breast and threw dust upon his head; for he was an old follower of Ali Atar."

The unfortunate Boabdil was conducted a captive to Vaena, a frontier town among the mountains; and the ruined towers of the old time-worn castle are still pointed out to the traveller in which he was held in honorable durance by the hardy Count de Cabra. Ferdinand at length liberated him, on stipulation of an ample tribute and vassalage, with military service to the Castilian crown. It was his policy to divide the Moors, by fomenting a civil war between the two rival kings; and his foresight was justified by the result. The factions of the father and the son broke forth again with redoubled fury, and Moor was armed against Moor, instead of uniting against the common foe.

Muley Aben Hassan became infirm through vexation as well as age, and blindness was added to his other calamities. He had, however, a brother, named Abdalla, but generally called El Zagal, or the Valiant, younger, of course, than himself, yet well stricken in years, who was alike distinguished for cool judgment and fiery courage, and for most of the other qualities which form an able general. This chief, whose martial deeds run through the present history, became the ruler of his brother's realm, and was soon after raised by acclamation to the throne, even before the ancient king's decease, which shortly followed, and not without suspicion of foul play. The civil war, which had commenced between father and son, was kept up between uncle and nephew. The latter, though vacillating and irresolute, was capable of being suddenly aroused to prompt and vigorous measures. The voice of the multitude, changeful as the winds, fluctuated between El Chico and El Zagal, according as either was successful; and in depicting the frequent, and almost ludicrous vicissitudes of their power and popularity, the author has indulged a quiet vein of satire on the capricious mutability of public favor.

The varied and striking scenes of daring foray and mountain maraud, of military pomp and courtly magnificence, which occur throughout the work, make selection difficult. The following extract shows the splendor of a Spanish camp, and the varied chivalry assembled from different Christian powers:

"Great and glorious was the style with which the Catholic sovereigns opened another year's campaign of this eventful war. It was like commencing another act of a stately and heroic drama, where the curtain rises to the inspiring sound of martial melody, and the whole stage glitters with the array of warriors and the pomp of arms. The ancient city of Cordova was the place appointed by the sovereigns for the assemblage of the troops ; and, early in the spring of 1486, the fair valley of the Guadalquivir resounded with the shrill blast of trumpet and the impatient neighing of the war-horse. In this splendid era of Spanish chivalry, there was a rivalship among the nobles, who most should distinguish himself by the splendor of his appearance and the number and equipments of his feudal followers. . . . . . Sometimes they passed through the streets of Cordova at night, in cavalcade, with great numbers of lighted torches, the rays of which, falling upon polished armor, and nodding plumes, and silken scarfs, and trappings of golden embroidery, filled all beholders with admiration. But it was not the chivalry of Spain alone which thronged the streets of Cordova. The fame of this war had spread throughout Christendom ; it was considered a kind of crusade, and Catholic knights from all parts hastened to signalize themselves in so holy a

31

cause.   There were several valiant chevaliers from France, among whom
the most distinguished was Gaston du Léon, seneschal of Toulouse.   With
him came a gallant train, well armed and mounted, and decorated with
rich surcoats and penaches of feathers.   These cavaliers, it is said,
eclipsed all others in the light festivities of the court.   They were devoted
to the fair ; but not after the solemn and passionate manner of the
Spanish lovers ; they were gay, gallant, and joyous in their amours,
and captivated by the vivacity of their attacks.   They were at first held
in light estimation by the grave and stately Spanish knights, until
they made themselves to be respected by their wonderful prowess in the
field.

   "The most conspicuous of the volunteers, however, who appeared in
Cordova on this occasion, was an English knight, of royal connection.
This was the Lord Scales, Earl of Rivers, related to the Queen of England,
wife of Henry VII.   He had distinguished himself, in the preceding year,
at the battle of Bosworth Field, where Henry Tudor, then Earl of Rich-
mond, overcame Richard III.   That decisive battle having left the country at peace, the Earl of Rivers, retaining a passion for warlike scenes,
repaired to the Castilian court, to keep his arms in exercise in a campaign against the Moors.   He brought with him a hundred archers, all
dexterous with the long-bow and the cloth-yard arrow ; also two hundred
yeomen, armed *cap-a-pie*, who fought with pike and battle-axe,—men
robust of frame, and of prodigious strength.   The worthy Padre Fray
Antonio Agapida describes this stranger knight and his followers with
his accustomed accuracy and minuteness.   'This cavalier,' he observes,
'was from the island of England, and brought with him a train of his
vassals ; men who had been hardened in certain civil wars which had
raged in their country.   They were a comely race of men, but too fair
and fresh for warriors,—not having the sunburnt, martial hue of our old
Castilian soldiery.   They were huge feeders, also, and deep carousers ;
and could not accommodate themselves to the sober diet of our troops,
but must fain eat and drink after the manner of their own country.   They
were often noisy and unruly, also, in their wassail ; and their quarter of
the camp was prone to be a scene of loud revel and sudden brawl.   They

were withal of great pride ; yet it was not like our inflammable Spanish pride ; they stood not much upon the *pundonor* and high punctillo, and rarely drew the stiletto in their disputes ; but their pride was silent and contumelious. Though from a remote and somewhat barbarous island, they yet believed themselves the most perfect men upon earth ; and magnified their chieftain, the Lord Scales, beyond the greatest of our grandees. With all this, it must be said of them that they were marvellous good men in the field, dexterous archers, and powerful with the battle-axe. In their great pride and self-will, they always sought to press in the advance, and take the post of danger, trying to outvie our Spanish chivalry. They did not rush forward fiercely, or make a brilliant onset, like the Moorish and Spanish troops, but they went into the fight deliberately, and persisted obstinately, and were slow to find out when they were beaten. Withal, they were much esteemed, yet little liked, by our soldiery, who considered them stanch companions in the field, yet coveted but little fellowship with them in the camp. Their commander, the Lord Scales, was an accomplished cavalier, of gracious and noble presence, and fair speech. It was a marvel to see so much courtesy in a knight brought up so far from our Castilian court. He was much honored by the king and queen, and found great favor with the fair dames about the court ; who, indeed, are rather prone to be pleased with foreign cavaliers. He went always in costly state, attended by pages and esquires, and accompanied by noble young cavaliers of his country, who had enrolled themselves under his banner, to learn the gentle exercise of arms. In all pageants and festivals, the eyes of the populace were attracted by the singular bearing and rich array of the English earl and his train, who prided themselves in always appearing in the garb and manner of their country ; and were, indeed, something very magnificent, delectable, and strange to behold.'"

Ferdinand led this gallant army to besiege Loxa, a powerful city on the Moorish frontier, before which he had formerly been foiled. The assault was made in open day, by a detachment which had been thrown in the advance, and which was bravely and fiercely met and repelled by the Moors.

"At this critical juncture, King Ferdinand emerged from the mountains with the main body of the army, and advanced to an eminence commanding a full view of the field of action. By his side was the noble English cavalier, the Earl of Rivers. This was the first time he had witnessed a scene of Moorish warfare. He looked with eager interest at the chance-medley fight before him,—the wild career of cavalry, the irregular and tumultuous rush of infantry, and Christian helm and Moorish turban intermingling in deadly struggle. His high blood mounted at the sight; and his very soul was stirred within him by the confused war-cries, the clangor of drums and trumpets, and the reports of arquebuses, that came echoing up the mountains. Seeing the king was sending a reinforcement to the field, he entreated permission to mingle in the affray, and fight according to the fashion of his country. His request being granted, he alighted from his steed. He was merely armed *en blanco;* that is to say, with morion, backpiece, and breastplate; his sword was girded by his side, and in his hand he wielded a powerful battle-axe. He was followed by a body of his yeomen, armed in like manner, and by a band of archers, with bows made of the tough English yew-tree. The earl turned to his troops, and addressed them briefly and bluntly, according to the manner of his country. 'Remember, my merry men all,' said he, 'the eyes of strangers are upon you; you are in a foreign land, fighting for the glory of God and the honor of merry old England!' A loud shout was the reply. The earl waved his battle-axe over his head. 'St. George for England!' cried he ; and, to the inspiring sound of this old English war-cry, he and his followers rushed down to the battle, with manly and courageous hearts.

"The Moors were confounded by the fury of these assaults, and gradually fell back upon the bridge ; the Christians followed up their advantage, and drove them over it tumultuously. The Moors retreated into the suburbs, and Lord Rivers and his troops entered with them pell-mell, fighting in the streets and in the houses. King Ferdinand came up to the scene of action with his royal guard, and the infidels were all driven within the city walls. Thus were the suburbs gained by the hardihood of the English lord, without such an event having been premeditated."

Various striking events marked the progress of the war,—ingenious and desperate manœuvres on the part of El Zagal, and persevering success in the well-judged policy of Ferdinand. A spell of ill-fortune seemed to surround the old Moorish king ever since the suspicious death of his brother and predecessor, Muley Aben Hassan, which was surmised to have been effected through his connivance; and his popularity sunk with his versatile subjects. The Spaniards at length laid siege to the powerful city of Baza, the key to all the remaining possessions of El Zagal. The peril of the Moorish kingdom of Granada resounded now throughout the East. The Grand Turk, Bajazet II., and his deadly foe the Grand Soldan of Egypt, or of Babylon, as he is termed by the old chroniclers, suspended their bloody feuds to check this ruinous war. A singular embassy from the latter of these potentates now entered the Spanish camp.

"While the holy Christian army was beleaguering the infidel city of Baza, there rode into the camp one day two reverend friars of the order of Saint Francis. One was of portly person and authoritative air. He bestrode a goodly steed, well conditioned and well caparisoned; while his companion rode behind him upon a humble hack, poorly accoutred, and, as he rode, he scarcely raised his eyes from the ground but maintained a meek and lowly air. The arrival of two friars in the camp was not a matter of much note; for in these holy wars the church militant continually mingled in the affray, and helmet and cowl were always seen together; but it was soon discovered that these worthy saints errant were from a far country, and on a mission of great import. They were, in truth, just arrived from the Holy Land, being two of the saintly men who kept vigil over the sepulchre of our blessed Lord at Jerusalem. He of the tall and portly form and commanding presence, was Fray Antonio Millan, prior of the Franciscan convent in the Holy City. He had a full and florid countenance, a sonorous voice, and was round, and swelling, and copious, in his periods, like one accustomed to harangue, and to be listened to with deference. His companion was small and spare in form, pale of visage, and soft, and silken, and almost whispering, in speech. 'He had a humble and lowly way,' says Agapida; 'evermore bowing the head, as became one of his calling. Yet he was one of the most active, zealous, and effective brothers of the convent; and, when he raised his small black eye from the earth, there was a keen glance out of the corner, which showed that, though harmless as a dove, he was nevertheless as wise as a serpent.' These holy men had come, on a momentous embassy, from the Grand Soldan of Egypt, who, as head of the whole Moslem sect, considered himself bound to preserve the kingdom of Granada from the grasp of unbelievers. He despatched, therefore, these two holy friars, with letters to the Castilian sovereigns, insisting that they should desist from this war, and reinstate the Moors of Granada in the territory of which they had been dispossessed; otherwise, he threatened to put to death all the Christians beneath his sway, to demolish their convents and temples, and to destroy the holy sepulchre."

It may not be uninteresting to remark that Christopher Columbus, in the course of his tedious solicitation to the Spanish court, was present at this siege; and it is surmised that, in conversations with these diplomatic monks, he was first inspired with that zeal for the recovery of the holy sepulchre which, throughout the remainder of his life, continued to animate his fervent and enthusiastic spirit, and beguile him into magnificent schemes and speculations. The ambassadors of the Soldan, meantime, could produce no change in the resolution of Ferdinand. Baza yielded after more than six months' arduous siege, and was followed by the surrender of most of the fortresses of the Alpuxarra Mountains; and at length the fiery El Zagal, tamed by misfortunes and abandoned by his subjects, surrendered his crown to the Christian sovereigns for a stipulated revenue or productive domain.

Boabdil el Chico remained the sole and unrivalled sovereign of Granada, the vassal of the Christian sovereigns, whose assistance had supported him in his wars against his uncle. But he was now to prove the hollow-hearted friendship of the politic Ferdinand. Pretences were easily found where a quarrel was already predetermined, and he was presently required to surrender the city and crown of Granada. A ravage of the Vega enforced the demand, and the Spanish armies laid siege to the metropolis. Ferdinand had fulfilled his menace; he had picked out the seeds of the pomegranate. Every town and fortress had successively fallen into his hand, and the city of Granada stood alone. He led his desolating armies over this paradise of a country, and left scarcely a living animal or a green blade on the face of

the land,—and Granada, the queen of gardens, remained
a desert. The history closes with the last scene of this
eventful contest,—the surrender of the Moorish capital:—

"Having surrendered the last symbol of power, the unfortunate Boabdil continued on towards the Alpuxarras, that he might not behold the
entrance of the Christians into his capital. His devoted band of cavaliers
followed him in gloomy silence ; but heavy sighs burst from their bosoms,
as shouts of joy and strains of triumphant music were borne on the breeze
from the victorious army. Having rejoined his family, Boabdil set forward with a heavy heart for his allotted residence, in the valley of Por-
chena. At two leagues' distance, the cavalcade, winding into the skirts
of the Alpuxarras, ascended an eminence commanding the last view of
Granada. As they arrived at this spot, the Moors paused involuntarily to
take a farewell gaze at their beloved city, which a few steps more would
shut from their sight forever. Never had it appeared so lovely in their
eyes. The sunshine, so bright in that transparent climate, lighted up
each tower and minaret, and rested gloriously upon the crowning battlements of the Alhambra ; while the Vega spread its enamelled bosom of
verdure below, glistening with the silver windings of the Xenil. The
Moorish cavaliers gazed with a silent agony of tenderness and grief upon
that delicious abode, the scene of their loves and pleasures. While they
yet looked, a light cloud of smoke burst forth from the citadel; and,
presently, a peal of artillery, faintly heard, told that the city was taken
possession of, and the throne of the Moslem kings was lost forever. The
heart of Boabdil, softened by misfortunes and overcharged with grief,
could no longer contain itself. 'Allah achbar ! God is great !' said he ;
but the words of resignation died upon his lips, and he burst into a flood
of tears. His mother, the intrepid Sultana Ayxa la Horra, was indignant
at his weakness. 'You do well,' said she, 'to weep like a woman for what
you failed to defend like a man !' The vizier, Aben Comixa, endeavored
to console his royal master. 'Consider, sire,' said he, 'that the most signal misfortunes often render men as renowned as the most prosperous

achievements, provided they sustain them with magnanimity.' The unhappy monarch, however, was not to be consoled. His tears continued
to flow. 'Allah achbar!' exclaimed he, 'when did misfortunes ever equal
mine!' From this circumstance, the hill, which is not far from Padul,
took the name of Feg Allah Achbar ; but the point of view commanding
the last prospect of Granada is known among Spaniards by the name of
el ultimo suspiro del Moro, or 'the last sigh of the Moor.'"

Here ends the "Chronicle of the Conquest of Granada,"
for here the author lets fall the curtain. We shall,
however, extend our view a little further. The rejoicings
of the Spanish sovereigns were echoed at Rome, and
throughout Christendom. The venerable chronicler,
Pedro Abarca, assures us that King Henry VII. of England celebrated the conquest by a grand procession to St.
Paul's, where the Chancellor pronounced an eloquent
eulogy on King Ferdinand, declaring him not only a glorious captain and conqueror, but also entitled to a seat
among the Apostles.*

The pious and politic monarch governed his new kingdom with more righteousness than mercy. The Moors
were at first a little restive under the yoke ; there were
several tumults in the city, and a quantity of arms were
discovered in a secret cave. Many of the offenders were
tried, condemned, and put to death, some being quar-
tered, others cut in pieces ; and the whole mass of infidel
inhabitants was well sifted, and purged of upwards of

* Abarca, *Anales de Aragon,* p. 30.

forty thousand delinquents. This system of wholesome purgation was zealously continued by Fray Francisco (afterwards Cardinal) Ximenes, who, seconded by Fernando de Talavera, Archbishop of Granada, and clothed in the terrific power of the Inquisition, undertook the conversion of the Moors. We forbear to detail the various modes—sometimes by blandishment, sometimes by rigor, sometimes exhorting, sometimes entreating, sometimes hanging, sometimes burning—by which the hard hearts of the infidels were subdued, and above fifty thousand coaxed, teased, and terrified into baptism.

One act of Ximenes has been the subject of particular regret. The Moors had cultivated the sciences while they lay buried in Europe, and were renowned for the value of their literature. Ximenes, in his bigoted zeal to destroy the Koran, extended his devastation to the indiscriminate destruction of their works, and burnt five thousand manuscripts on various subjects, some of them very splendid copies, and others of great intrinsic worth, sparing a very few, which treated chiefly of medicine. Here we shall pause, and not pursue the subject to the further oppression and persecution, and final expulsion, of these unhappy people ; the latter of which events is one of the most impolitic and atrocious recorded in the pages of history.

Centuries have elapsed since the time ot this chivalrous and romantic struggle, yet the monuments of it still remain, and the principal facts still linger in the popular traditions and legendary ballads with which the country abounds. The likenesses of Ferdinand and Isabella are multiplied, in every mode, by painting and sculpture, in the churches, and convents, and palaces of Granada. Their ashes rest in sepulchral magnificence in the royal chapel of the cathedral, where their effigies in alabaster lie side by side before a splendid altar, decorated in relief with the story of their triumph. The anniversary of the surrender of the capital is still kept up by *fêtes*, and ceremonies, and public rejoicings. The standard of Ferdinand and Isabella is again unfurled and waved to the sound of trumpets. The populace are admitted to rove all day about the halls and courts of the Alhambra, and to dance on its terraces; the ancient alarm-bell resounds at morn, at noon, and at nightfall; great emulation prevails among the damsels to ring a peal,—it is a sign they will be married in the course of the opening year. But this commemoration is not confined to Granada alone. Every town and village of the mountains on the Vega has the anniversary of its deliverance from Moorish thraldom; when ancient armor, and Spanish and Moorish dresses, and unwieldy arquebuses, from the time of the Conquest, are brought forth from their repositories—grotesque processions are made—and sham battles, celebrated by peasants, arrayed as Christians and Moors, in which the latter are sure to be signally defeated, and sometimes, in the ardor and illusion of the moment, soundly rib-roasted.

In traversing the mountains and valleys of the ancient kingdom, the traveller may trace with wonderful distinctness the scenes of the principal events of the war. The muleteer, as he lolls on his pack-saddle, smoking his cigar or chanting his popular romance, pauses to point out some wild, rocky pass, famous for the bloody strife of infidel and Christian, or some Moorish fortress butting above the road, or some solitary watch-tower on the heights, connected with the old story of the Conquest. Gibralfaro, the warlike hold of Hamet el Zegri, formidable even in its ruins, still frowns down from its rocky height upon the streets of Malaga. Loxa, Alhama, Zahara, Ronda, Guadix, Baza, have all their Moorish ruins, rendered classic by song and story. The "Last sigh of the Moor" still lingers about the height of Padul; the traveller pauses on the arid and thirsty summit of the hill, commanding a view over the varied bosom of the Vega, to the distant towers of Granada. A humble cabin is erected by the wayside, where he may obtain water to slake his thirst, and the very rock is pointed out whence the unfortunate Boabdil took his last look, and breathed the last farewell, to his beloved Alhambra.

Every part of Granada itself retains some memorial of the taste and elegance, the valor and voluptuousness, of the Moors, or some memento of the strife that sealed their downfall. The fountains which gush on every side are fed by the aqueducts once formed by Moslem hands; the Vega is still embroidered by the

gardens they planted, where the remains of their ingenious irrigation spread the verdure and freshness of a
northern climate under the cloudless azure of a southern sky. But the pavilions that adorned these gardens
—and where, if romances speak true, the Moslem heroes
solaced themselves with the loves of their Zaras, their
Zaidas, and their Zelindas—have long since disappeared.
The orange, the citron, the fig, the vine, the pomegranate, the aloe, and the myrtle, shroud and overwhelm
with Oriental vegetation the crumbling ruins of towers
and battlements. The Vivarrambla, once the scene of
chivalric pomp and splendid tourney, is degraded to a
market-place; the Gate of Elvira, from whence so many
a shining array of warriors passed forth to forage the
land of the Christians, still exists, but neglected and dismantled, and tottering to its fall. The Alhambra rises
from amidst its groves, the tomb of its former glory.
The fountains still play in its marble halls, and the
nightingale sings among the roses of its gardens; but the
halls are waste and solitary; the owl hoots from its
battlements, the hawk builds in its warrior towers, and
bats flit about its royal chambers. Still the fountain
is pointed out where the gallant Abencerrages were put
to death; the mirador, where Morayma sat and wept
the departure of Boabdil, and watched for his return;
and the broken gateway, from whence the unfortunate
monarch issued forth to surrender his fortress and his
kingdom; and which, at his request, was closed up,

never to be entered by mortal footstep. At the time when the French abandoned this fortress, after its temporary occupation a few years since, the tower of the gateway was blown up; the walls were rent and shattered by the explosion, and the folding-doors hurled into the garden of the convent of Los Martiros. The portal, however was closed up with stones, by persons who were ignorant of the tradition connected with it, and thus the last request of poor Boabdil continued unwittingly to be performed. In fact, the story of the gateway, though recorded in ancient chronicle, has faded from general recollection, and is only known to two or three ancient inhabitants of the Alhambra, who inherit it, with other local traditions, from their ancestors.

LETTER TO THE EDITOR OF "THE KNICKER-BOCKER,"

ON COMMENCING HIS MONTHLY CONTRIBUTIONS.

SIR: I have observed that as a man advances in life, he is subject to a kind of plethora of the mind, doubtless occasioned by the vast accumulation of wisdom and experience upon the brain. Hence he is apt to become narrative and admonitory, that is to say, fond of telling long stories, and of doling out advice, to the small profit and great annoyance of his friends. As I have a great horror of becoming the oracle, or, more technically speaking, the "bore," of the domestic circle, and would much rather bestow my wisdom and tediousness upon the world at large, I have always sought to ease off this surcharge of the intellect by means of my pen, and hence have inflicted divers gossiping volumes upon the patience of the public. I am tired, however, of writing volumes; they do not afford exactly the relief I require; there is too much preparation, arrangement, and parade in this set form of coming before the public. I am growing too indolent and unambitious for anything that requires labor or display. I have thought, therefore, of securing to myself a snug corner in some periodical work, where I might, as it were, loll at my ease in my elbow-chair, and chat sociably with the public, as with an old friend, on any chance subject that might pop into my brain.

In looking around, for this purpose, upon the various excellent periodicals with which our country abounds, my eye was struck by the title of your work,—"THE KNICKERBOCKER." My heart leaped at the sight.

DIEDRICH KNICKERBOCKER, sir, was one of my earliest and most valued friends, and the recollection of him is associated with some of the pleasantest scenes of my youthful days. To explain this, and to show how I came into possession of sundry of his posthumous works, which I have from time to time given to the world, permit me to relate a few particulars of our early intercourse. I give them with the more confidence, as I know the interest you take in that departed worthy, whose name and effigy are stamped upon your title-page, and as they will be found important to the better understanding and relishing divers communications I may have to make to you.

My first acquaintance with that great and good man,— for such I may venture to call him, now that the lapse of some thirty years has shrouded his name with venerable antiquity, and the popular voice has elevated him to the rank of the classic historians of yore — my first acquaintance with him was formed on the banks of the

Hudson, not far from the wizard region of Sleepy Hollow. He had come there in the course of his researches among the Dutch neighborhoods for materials for his immortal history. For this purpose, he was ransacking the archives of one of the most ancient and historical mansions in the country. It was a lowly edifice, built in the time of the Dutch dynasty, and stood on a green bank overshadowed by trees, from which it peeped forth upon the Great Tappan Zee, so famous among early Dutch navigators. A bright pure spring welled up at the foot of the green bank; a wild brook came babbling down a neighboring ravine, and threw itself into a little woody cove, in front of the mansion. It was indeed as quiet and sheltered a nook as the heart of man could require in which to take refuge from the cares and troubles of the world; and as such, it had been chosen in old times by Wolfert Acker, one of the privy councillors of the renowned Peter Stuyvesant.

This worthy but ill-starred man had led a weary and worried life throughout the stormy reign of the chivalric Peter, being one of those unlucky wights with whom the world is ever at variance, and who are kept in a continual fume and fret by the wickedness of mankind. At the time of the subjugation of the province by the English, he retired hither in high dudgeon; with the bitter determination to bury himself from the world, and live here in peace and quietness for the remainder of his days. In token of this fixed resolution, he inscribed over his

32

door the favorite Dutch motto, "Lust in Rust" (pleasure in repose). The mansion was thence called "Wolfert's Rust,"—Wolfert's Rest; but in process of time the name was vitiated into Wolfert's Roost, probably from its quaint cockloft look, or from its having a weathercock perched on every gable. This name it continued to bear long after the unlucky Wolfert was driven forth once more upon a wrangling world, by the tongue of a termagant wife; for it passed into a proverb through the neighborhood, and has been handed down by tradition, that the cock of the roost was the most hen-pecked bird in the country.

This primitive and historical mansion has since passed through many changes and trials, which it may be my lot hereafter to notice. At the time of the sojourn of Diedrich Knickerbocker, it was in possession of the gallant family of the Van Tassels, who have figured so conspicuously in his writings. What appears to have given it peculiar value in his eyes, was the rich treasury of historical facts here secretly hoarded up, like buried gold; for it is said that Wolfert Acker, when he retreated from New Amsterdam, carried off with him many of the records and journals of the province, pertaining to the Dutch dynasty; swearing that they should never fall into the hands of the English. These, like the lost books of Livy, had baffled the research of former historians; but these did I find the indefatigable Diedrich diligently deciphering. He was already a sage in years and experience, I but an idle stripling; yet he did not despise my youth and ignorance, but took me kindly by the hand, and led me gently into those paths of local and traditional lore which he was so fond of exploring. I sat with him in his little chamber at the Roost, and watched the antiquarian patience and perseverance with which he deciphered those venerable Dutch documents, worse than Herculanean manuscripts. I sat with him by the spring, at the foot of the green bank, and listened to his heroic tales about the worthies of the olden time,—the paladins of New Amsterdam. I accompanied him in his legendary researches about Tarrytown and Sing-Sing, and explored with him the spell-bound recesses of Sleepy Hollow. · I was present at many of his conferences with the good old Dutch burghers and their wives, from whom he derived many of those marvellous facts not laid down in books or records, and which give such superior value and authenticity to his history over all others that have been written concerning the New Netherlands.

But let me check my proneness to dilate upon this favorite theme; I may recur to it hereafter. Suffice it to say, the intimacy thus formed continued for a considerable time; and in company with the worthy Diedrich, I visited many of the places celebrated by his pen. The currents of our lives at length diverged. He remained at home to complete his mighty work, while a vagrant fancy led me to wander about the world. Many, many years elapsed before I returned to the parent soil. In the interim, the venerable historian of the New Netherlands had been gathered to his fathers, but his name had risen to renown. His native city, that city in which he so much delighted, had decreed all manner of costly honors to his memory. I found his effigy imprinted upon new-year cakes, and devoured with eager relish by holiday urchins; a great' oyster-house bore the name of " Knickerbocker Hall"; and I narrowly escaped the pleasure of being run over by a Knickerbocker omnibus!

Proud of having associated with a man who had achieved such greatness, I now recalled our early intimacy with tenfold pleasure, and sought to revisit the scenes we had trodden together. The most important of these was the mansion of the Van Tassels, the Roost of the unfortunate Wolfert. Time, which changes all things, is but slow in its operations upon a Dutchman's dwelling. I found the venerable and quiet little edifice much as I had seen it during the sojourn of Diedrich. There stood his elbow-chair in the corner of the room he had occupied; the old-fashioned Dutch writing-desk at which he had pored over the chronicles of the Manhattoes; there was the old wooden chest, with the archives left by Wolfert Acker, many of which, however, had been fired off as wadding from the long duck-gun of the Van Tassels. The scene around the mansion was still the same; the green bank; the spring beside which I had listened to the legendary narratives of the historian; the wild brook babbling down to the woody cove, and the overshadowing locust-trees, half shutting out the prospect of the Great Tappan Zee.

As I looked round upon the scene, my heart yearned at the recollection of my departed friend, and I wistfully eyed the mansion which he had inhabited, and which was fast mouldering to decay. The thought struck me to arrest the desolating hand of Time; to rescue the historic pile from utter ruin, and to make it the closing scene of my wanderings,—a quiet home, where I might enjoy "lust in rust" for the remainder of my days. It is true, the fate of the unlucky Wolfert passed across my mind; but I consoled myself with the reflection that I was a bachelor, and that I had no termagant wife to dispute the sovereignty of the Roost with me.

I have become possessor of the Roost! I have repaired and renovated it with religious care, in the genuine Dutch style, and have adorned and illustrated it with sundry relics of the glorious days of the New Netherlands. A venerable weathercock, of portly Dutch dimensions, which once battled with the wind on the top of the Stadt-House of New Amsterdam, in the time of Peter Stuyvesant, now erects its crest on the gable end of my edifice; a gilded horse, in full gallop, once the weathercock of the great Vander Heyden Palace of Albany, now glitters in the sunshine, and veers with every breeze, on the peaked turret over my portal; my sanctum sanctorum is the chamber once honored by the illustrious Diedrich, and it is from his elbow-chair, and his identical old Dutch writing-desk, that I pen this rambling epistle.

Here then have I set up my rest, surrounded by the recollections of earlier days, and the mementos of the historian of the Manhattoes, with that glorious river before me, which flows with such majesty through his works, and which has ever been to me a river of delight.

I thank God I was born on the banks of the Hudson! I think it an invaluable advantage to be born and brought up in the neighborhood of some grand and noble object in Nature,—a river, a lake, or a mountain. We make a friendship with it,—we in a manner ally ourselves to it for life. It remains an object of our pride and affections, a rallying-point, to call us home again after all our wanderings. "The things which we have learned in our childhood," says an old writer, "grow up with our souls, and unite themselves to it." So it is with the scenes among which we have passed our early days; they influence the whole course of our thoughts and feelings; and I fancy I can trace much of what is good and pleasant in my own heterogeneous compound to my early companionship with this glorious river. In the warmth of my youthful enthusiasm, I used to clothe it with moral attributes, and almost to give it a soul. I admired its frank, bold, honest character; its noble sincerity and perfect truth. Here was no specious, smiling surface, covering the dangerous sand-bar or perfidious rock; but a stream deep as it was broad, and bearing with honorable faith the bark that trusted to its waves. I gloried in its simple, quiet, majestic, epic flow; ever straightforward. Once indeed, it turns aside for a moment, forced from its course by opposing mountains; but it struggles bravely through them, and immediately resumes its straightforward march. Behold, thought I, an emblem of a good man's course through life; ever simple, open, and direct; or if, overpowered by adverse circumstances, he deviate into error, it is but momentary; he soon recovers his onward and honorable career, and continues it to the end of his pilgrimage.

Excuse this rhapsody into which I have been betrayed by a revival of early feelings. The Hudson is, in a manner, my first and last love; and after all my wanderings, and seeming infidelities, I return to it with a heartfelt preference over all the other rivers in the world. I seem to catch new life, as I bathe in its ample billows, and inhale the pure breezes of its hills. It is true, the romance of youth is past that once spread illusions over every scene. I can no longer picture an Arcadia in every green valley, nor a fairy-land among the distant mountains, nor a peerless beauty in every villa gleaming among the trees; but, though the illusions of youth have faded from the landscape, the recollections of departed years and departed pleasures shed over it the mellow charm of evening sunshine.

Permit me then, Mr. Editor, through the medium of your work, to hold occasional discourse from my retreat with the busy world I have abandoned. I have much to say about what I have seen, heard, felt, and thought, through the course of a varied and rambling life, and some lucubrations that have long been encumbering my portfolio; together with divers reminiscences of the venerable historian of the New Netherlands, that may not be unacceptable to those who have taken an interest in his writings, and are desirous of anything that may cast a light back upon our early history. Let your readers rest assured of one thing, that, though retired from the world, I am not disgusted with it; and that if, in my communings with it, I do not prove very wise, I trust I shall at least prove very good-natured.

Which is all at present, from

Yours, etc.,

GEOFFREY CRAYON.

SLEEPY HOLLOW.

BY GEOFFREY CRAYON, GENT.

AVING pitched my tent, probably for the remainder of my days, in the neighborhood of Sleepy Hollow, I am tempted to give some few particulars concerning that spellbound region; especially as it has risen to historic importance under the pen of my revered friend and master, the sage historian of the New Netherlands. Besides, I find the very existence of the place has been held in question by many, who, judging from its odd name, and from the odd stories current among the vulgar concerning it, have rashly deemed the whole to be a fanciful creation, like the Lubber Land of mariners. I must confess there is some apparent cause for doubt, in consequence of the coloring given by the worthy Diedrich to his descriptions of the Hollow, who, in this instance, has departed a little from his usually sober if not severe style; beguiled, very probably, by his predilection for the haunts of his youth, and by a certain lurking taint of romance, whenever anything connected with the Dutch was to be described. I shall endeavor to make up for this amiable error, on the part of my vener-

able and venerated friend, by presenting the reader with
a more precise and statistical account of the Hollow;
though I am not sure that I shall not be prone to lapse,
in the end, into the very error I am speaking of, so potent
is the witchery of the theme.

I believe it was the very peculiarity of its name, and
the idea of something mystic and dreamy connected with
it, that first led me, in my boyish ramblings, into Sleepy
Hollow. The character of the valley seemed to answer
to the name : the slumber of past ages apparently reigned
over it; it had not awakened to the stir of improvement,
which had put all the rest of the world in a bustle. Here
reigned good old long-forgotten fashions : the men were
in homespun garbs, evidently the product of their own
farms, and the manufacture of their own wives ; the
women were in primitive short gowns and petticoats,
with the venerable sun-bonnets of Holland origin. The
lower part of the valley was cut up into small farms :
each consisting of a little meadow and cornfield ; an
orchard of sprawling, gnarled apple-trees ; and a garden,
where the rose, the marigold, and the hollyhock were
permitted to skirt the domains of the capacious cabbage,
the aspiring pea, and the portly pumpkin. Each had its
prolific little mansion, teeming with children : with an old
hat nailed against the wall for the house-keeping wren ;
a motherly hen, under a coop on the grass-plot, clucking
to keep around her a brood of vagrant chickens ; a cool
stone well, with the moss-covered bucket suspended to

the long balancing-pole, according to the antediluvian
idea of hydraulics; and its spinning-wheel humming
within doors, the patriarchal music of home manufacture.

The Hollow at that time was inhabited by families
which had existed there from the earliest times, and
which, by frequent intermarriage, had become so interwoven as to make a kind of natural commonwealth. As
the families had grown larger, the farms had grown
smaller, every new generation requiring a new subdi-
vision, and few thinking of swarming from the native
hive. In this way that happy golden mean had been
produced, so much extolled by the poets, in which there
was no gold and very little silver. One thing which
doubtless contributed to keep up this amiable mean, was
a general repugnance to sordid labor. The sage inhabitants of Sleepy Hollow had read in their Bible, which
was the only book they studied, that labor was originally
inflicted upon man as a punishment of sin; they regarded
it, therefore, with pious abhorrence, and never humiliated
themselves to it but in cases of extremity. There seemed,
in fact, to be a league and covenant against it, throughout
the Hollow, as against a common enemy. Was any one
compelled by dire necessity to repair his house, mend his
fences, build a barn, or get in a harvest, he considered it
a great evil, that entitled him to call in the assistance
of his friends. He accordingly proclaimed a "bee," or
rustic gathering; whereupon all his neighbors hurried to
his aid, like faithful allies; attacked the task with the

desperate energy of lazy men, eager to overcome a job; and when it was accomplished, fell to eating and drinking, fiddling and dancing, for very joy that so great an amount of labor had been vanquished, with so little sweating of the brow.

Yet let it not be supposed that this worthy community was without its periods of arduous activity. Let but a flock of wild pigeons fly across the valley, and all Sleepy Hollow was wide awake in an instant. The pigeon season had arrived! Every gun and net was forthwith in requisition. The flail was thrown down on the barn-floor; the spade rusted in the garden; the plough stood idle in the furrow; every one was to the hill-side and stubble-field at daybreak, to shoot or entrap the pigeons, in their periodical migrations.

So, likewise, let but the word be given that the shad were ascending the Hudson, and the worthies of the Hollow were to be seen launched in boats upon the river; setting great stakes, and stretching their nets, like gigantic spider-webs, half across the stream, to the great annoyance of navigators. Such are the wise provisions of Nature, by which she equalizes rural affairs. A laggard at the plough is often extremely industrious with the fowling-piece and fishing-net; and whenever a man is an indifferent farmer, he is apt to be a first-rate sportsman. For catching shad and wild pigeons, there were none throughout the country to compare with the lads of Sleepy Hollow.

As I have observed, it was the dreamy nature of the name that first beguiled me, in the holiday rovings of boyhood, into this sequestered region. I shunned, however, the populous parts of the Hollow, and sought its retired haunts, far in the foldings of the hills, where the Pocantico "winds its wizard stream," sometimes silently and darkly, through solemn woodlands; sometimes sparkling between grassy borders, in fresh green meadows; sometimes stealing along the feet of ragged heights, under the balancing sprays of beech and chestnut trees. A thousand crystal springs, with which this neighborhood abounds, sent down from the hill-sides their whimpering rills, as if to pay tribute to the Pocantico. In this stream I first essayed my unskilful hand at angling. I loved to loiter along it, with rod in hand, watching my float as it whirled amid the eddies, or drifted into dark holes, under twisted roots and sunken logs, where the largest fish are apt to lurk. I delighted to follow it into the brown recesses of the woods; to throw by my fishing-gear and sit upon rocks beneath towering oaks and clambering grape-vines; bathe my feet in the cool current, and listen to the summer breeze playing among the tree-tops. My boyish fancy clothed all Nature around me with ideal charms, and peopled it with the fairy beings I had read of in poetry and fable. Here it was I gave full scope to my incipient habit of day-dreaming, and to a certain propensity to weave up and tint sober realities with my own whims and imaginings, which has sometimes made life a little too much like an Arabian tale to me, and this "working-day world " rather like a region of romance.

The great gathering place of Sleepy Hollow, in those days, was the church. It stood outside of the Hollow, near the great highway, on a green bank, shaded by trees, with the Pocantico sweeping round it and emptying itself into a spacious mill-pond. At that time the Sleepy Hollow church was the only place of worship for a wide neighborhood. It was a venerable edifice, partly of stone and partly of brick,—the latter having been brought from Holland, in the early days of the Province, before the arts in the New Netherlands could aspire to such a fabrication. On a stone above the porch were inscribed the names of the founders, Frederick Filipsen, —a mighty man of the olden time, who got the better of the native savages, subdued a great tract of country by dint of trinkets, tobacco, and *aqua vitœ*, and established his seat of power at Yonkers,—and his wife, Katrina Van Courtlandt, of the no less heroic line of the Van Courtlandts of Croton, who in like manner subdued and occupied a great part of the Highlands.

The capacious pulpit, with its wide-spreading sounding-board, was likewise an early importation from Holland ; as also the communion-table, of massive form and curious fabric. The same might be said of a weathercock, perched on top of the belfry, and which was considered orthodox in all windy matters, until a small pragmatical rival was set up on the other end of the church, above the chancel. This latter bore, and still bears, the initials of Frederick Filipsen, and assumed great airs in consequence. The usual contradiction ensued that always exists among church weathercocks, which can never be brought to agree as to the point from which the wind blows, having doubtless acquired, from their position, the Christian propensity to schism and controversy.

Behind the church, and sloping up a gentle acclivity, was its capacious burying-ground, in which slept the earliest fathers of this rural neighborhood. Here were tombstones of the rudest sculpture; on which were inscribed, in Dutch, the names and virtues of many of the first settlers, with their portraitures curiously carved in similitude of cherubs. Long rows of gravestones, side by side, of similar names but various dates, showed that generation after generation of the same families had followed each other, and been garnered together in this last gathering place of kindred.

Let me speak of this quiet graveyard with all due reverence, for I owe it amends for the heedlessness of my boyish days. I blush to acknowledge the thoughtless frolic with which, in company with other whipsters, I have sported within its sacred bounds, during the intervals of worship,—chasing butterflies, plucking wild flowers, or vying with each other who could leap over the tallest tombstones,—until checked by the stern voice of the sexton.

The congregation was, in those days, of a really rural character. City fashions were as yet unknown, or unregarded, by the country people of the neighborhood. Steamboats had not as yet confounded town with country. A weekly market-boat from Tarrytown, the *Farmer's Daughter*, navigated by the worthy Gabriel Requa, was the only communication between all these parts and the metropolis. A rustic belle in those days considered a visit to the city in much the same light as one of our modern fashionable ladies regards a visit to Europe,— an event that may possibly take place once in the course of a lifetime, but to be hoped for rather than expected. Hence the array of the congregation was chiefly after the primitive fashions existing in Sleepy Hollow; or if, by chance, there was a departure from the Dutch sun-bonnet, or the apparition of a bright gown of flowered calico, it caused quite a sensation throughout the church. As the dominie generally preached by the hour, a bucket of water was providently placed on a bench near the door, in summer, with a tin cup beside it, for the solace of those who might be athirst, either from the heat of the weather or the drought of the sermon.

Around the pulpit, and behind the communion-table, sat the elders of the church, reverend, gray-headed, leathern-visaged men, whom I regarded with awe, as so many apostles. They were stern in their sanctity, kept a vigilant eye upon my giggling companions and myself, and shook a rebuking finger at any boyish device to relieve the tediousness of compulsory devotion. Vain, however, were all their efforts at vigilance. Scarcely had the preacher held forth for half an hour, in one of his interminable sermons, than it seemed as if the drowsy influence of Sleepy Hollow breathed into the place : one by one the congregation sank into slumber; the sanctified elders leaned back in their pews, spreading their handkerchiefs over their faces, as if to keep off the flies ; while the locusts in the neighboring trees would spin out their sultry summer notes, vying with the sleep-pro voking tones of the dominie.

I have thus endeavored to give an idea of Sleepy Hollow and its church, as I recollect them to have been in the days of my boyhood. It was in my stripling days, when a few years had passed over my head, that I revisited them, in company with the venerable Diedrich. I shall never forget the antiquarian reverence with which that sage and excellent man contemplated the church. It seemed as if all his pious enthusiasm for the ancient Dutch dynasty swelled within his bosom at the sight. The tears stood in his eyes as he regarded the pulpit and the communion-table ; even the very bricks that had come from the mother-country seemed to touch a filial chord within his bosom. He almost bowed in deference to the stone above the porch, containing the names of Frederick Filipsen and Katrina Van Courtlandt, regarding it as the linking together of those patronymic names once so famous along the banks of the Hudson ; or rather

33

as a key-stone, binding that mighty Dutch family connection of yore, one foot of which rested on Yonkers, and
the other on the Croton.   Nor did he forbear to notice
with admiration the windy contest which had been
carried on since time immemorial, and with real Dutch
perseverance, between the two weathercocks; though I
could easily perceive he coincided with the one which
had come from Holland.

Together we paced the ample church-yard. With deep
veneration would he turn down the weeds and brambles
that obscured the modest brown gravestones, half sunk
in earth, on which were recorded, in Dutch, the names of
the patriarchs of ancient days, — the Ackers, the Van
Tassels, and the Van Warts.   As we sat on one of the
tombstones, he recounted to me the exploits of many of
these worthies; and my heart smote me, when I heard of
their great doings in days of yore, to think how heed-
lessly I hadonce sported over their graves.

From the church the venerable Diedrich proceeded in
his researches up the Hollow.   The genius of the place
seemed to hail its future historian.   All Nature was alive
with gratulation.   The quail whistled a greeting from
the cornfield; the robin carolled a song of praise from
the orchard; the loquacious cat-bird flew from bush to
bush, with restless wing, proclaiming his approach in
every variety of note, and anon would whisk about and
perk inquisitively into his face, as if to get a knowledge
of his physiognomy; the woodpecker, also, tapped a tat-

too on the hollow apple-tree, and then peered knowingly round the trunk to see how the great Diedrich relished his salutation; while the ground-squirrel scampered along the fence, and occasionally whisked his tail over his head by way of a huzza!

The worthy Diedrich pursued his researches in the valley with characteristic devotion; entering familiarly into the various cottages, and gossiping with the simple folk, in the style of their own simplicity. I confess my heart yearned with admiration, to see so great a man, in his eager quest after knowledge, humbly demeaning himself to curry favor with the humblest; sitting patiently on a three-legged stool, patting the children, and taking a purring grimalkin on his lap, while he conciliated the good-will of the old Dutch housewife, and drew from her long ghost-stories, spun out to the humming accompaniment of her wheel.

His greatest treasure of historic lore, however, was discovered in an old goblin-looking mill, situated among rocks and water-falls, with clanking wheels, and rushing streams, and all kinds of uncouth noises. A horseshoe, nailed to the door to keep off witches and evil spirits, showed that this mill was subject to awful visitations. As we approached it, an old negro thrust his head, all dabbled with flour, out of a hole above the water-wheel, and grinned, and rolled his eyes, and looked like the very hobgoblin of the place. The illustrious Diedrich fixed upon him, at once, as the very one to give him that invaluable kind of information, never to be acquired from books. He beckoned him from his nest, sat with him by the hour on a broken mill-stone, by the side of the water-fall, heedless of the noise of the water and the clatter of the mill; and I verily believe it was to his conference with this African sage, and the precious revelations of the good dame of the spinning-wheel, that we are indebted for the surprising though true history of "Ichabod Crane and the Headless Horseman," which has since astounded and edified the world.

But I have said enough of the good old times of my youthful days; let me speak of the Hollow as I found it, after an absence of many years, when it was kindly given me once more to revisit the haunts of my boyhood. It was a genial day as I approached that fated region. The warm sunshine was tempered by a slight haze, so as to give a dreamy effect to the landscape. Not a breath of air shook the foliage. The broad Tappan Sea was without a ripple, and the sloops, with drooping sails, slept on its glassy bosom. Columns of smoke, from burning brushwood, rose lazily from the folds of the hills, on the opposite side of the river, and slowly expanded in mid-air. The distant lowing of a cow, or the noontide crowing of a cock, coming faintly to the ear, seemed to illustrate, rather than disturb, the drowsy quiet of the scene.

I entered the Hollow with a beating heart. Contrary to my apprehensions, I found it but little changed. The march of intellect, which had made such rapid strides along every river and highway, had not yet, apparently, turned down into this favored valley. Perhaps the wizard spell of ancient days still reigned over the place, binding up the faculties of the inhabitants in happy contentment with things as they had been handed down to them from yore. There were the same little farms and farm-houses, with their old hats for the house-keeping wren; their stone wells, moss-covered buckets, and long balancing-poles. There were the same little rills, whimpering down to pay their tributes to the Pocantico; while that wizard stream still kept on its course, as of old, through solemn woodlands and fresh green meadows; nor were there wanting joyous holiday boys, to loiter along its banks, as I had done; throw their pin-hooks in the stream, or launch their mimic barks. I watched them with a kind of melancholy pleasure, wondering whether they were under the same spell of the fancy that once rendered this valley a fairy-land to me. Alas! alas! to me everything now stood revealed in its simple reality. The echoes no longer answered with wizard tongues; the dream of youth was at an end; the spell of Sleepy Hollow was broken!

I sought the ancient church on the following Sunday. There it stood, on its green bank, among the trees; the Pocantico swept by it in a deep dark stream, where I had so often angled; there expanded the mill-pond, as of old, with the cows under the willows on its margin, knee-deep in water, chewing the cud, and lashing the flies from their sides with their tails. The hand of improvement, however, had been busy with the venerable pile. The pulpit, fabricated in Holland, had been superseded by one of modern construction, and the front of the semi-Gothic edifice was decorated by a semi-Grecian portico. Fortunately, the two weathercocks remained undisturbed on their perches, at each end of the church, and still kept up a diametrical opposition to each other on all points of windy doctrine.

On entering the church the changes of time continued to be apparent. The elders round the pulpit were men whom I had left in the gamesome frolic of their youth, but who had succeeded to the sanctity of station of which they once had stood so much in awe. What most struck my eye was the change in the female part of the congregation. Instead of the primitive garbs of homespun manufacture and antique Dutch fashion, I beheld French sleeves, French capes, and French collars, and a fearful fluttering of French ribbons.

When the service was ended I sought the churchyard in which I had sported in my unthinking days of boyhood. Several of the modest brown stones, on which were recorded, in Dutch, the names and virtues of the patriarchs, had disappeared, and had been succeeded by others of white marble, with urns, and wreaths, and scraps of English tombstone poetry, marking the intrusion of taste, and literature, and the English language, in this once unsophisticated Dutch neighborhood.

As I was stumbling about among these silent yet eloquent memorials of the dead, I came upon names familiar to me,—of those who had paid the debt of Nature during the long interval of my absence. Some I remembered, my companions in boyhood, who had sported with me on the very sod under which they were now mouldering; others, who in those days had been the flower of the yeomanry, figuring in Sunday finery on the church-green ; others, the white-haired elders of the sanctuary, once arrayed in awful sanctity around the pulpit, and ever ready to rebuke the ill-timed mirth of the wanton stripling, who, now a man, sobered by years and schooled by vicissitudes, looked down pensively upon their graves.   "Our fathers," thought I, "where are they?—and the prophets, can they live forever?"

I was disturbed in my meditations by the noise of a troop of idle urchins, who came gambolling about the place where I had so often gambolled.   They were checked, as I and my playmates had often been, by the voice of the sexton, a man staid in years and demeanor. I looked wistfully in his face ; had I met him anywhere else I should probably have passed him by without remark ; but here I was alive to the traces of former times, and detected in the demure features of this guardian of the sanctuary the lurking lineaments of one of the very playmates I have alluded to.   We renewed our acquaintance.   He sat down beside me, on one of the tombstones over which we had leaped in our juvenile sports, and we talked together about our boyish days, and held edifying discourse on the instability of all sublunary things, as instanced in the scene around us. He was rich in historic lore, as to the events of the last thirty years and the circumference of thirty miles, and from him I learned the appalling revolution that was taking place throughout the neighborhood. All this I clearly perceived he attrib·uted to the boasted march of intellect, or rather to the all-pervading influence of steam. He bewailed the times when the only communication with town was by the weekly market-boat, the *Farmer's Daughter*, which, under the pilotage of the worthy Gabriel Requa, braved the perils of the Tappan Sea. Alas! Gabriel and the *Farmer's Daughter* slept in peace. Two steamboats now splashed and paddled up daily to the little rural port of Tarrytown. The spirit of speculation and improvement had seized even upon that once quiet and unambitious little dorp. The whole neighborhood was laid out into town lots. Instead of the little tavern below the hill, where the farmers used to loiter on market-days, and indulge in cider and gingerbread, an ambitious hotel, with cupola and verandas, now crested the summit, among churches built in the Grecian and Gothic styles, showing the great increase of piety and polite taste in the neighborhood. As to Dutch dresses and sun-bonnets, they were no longer tolerated, or even thought of; not a farmer's daughter but now went to town for the fashions;

nay, a city milliner had recently set up in the village, who threatened to reform the heads of the whole neighborhood.

I had heard enough! I thanked my old playmate for his intelligence, and departed from the Sleepy Hollow church with the sad conviction that I had beheld the last lingerings of the good old Dutch times in this once favored region. If anything were wanting to confirm this impression, it would be the intelligence which has just reached me, that a bank is about to be established in the aspiring little port just mentioned. The fate of the neighborhood is, therefore, sealed. I see no hope of averting it. The golden mean is at an end. The country is suddenly to be deluged with wealth. The late simple farmers are to become bank directors, and drink claret and champagne; and their wives and daughters to figure in French hats and feathers; for French wines and French fashions commonly keep pace with paper money. How can I hope that even Sleepy Hollow may escape the general awakening? In a little while I fear the slumber of ages will be at an end; the strum of the piano will succeed to the hum of the spinning-wheel; the trill of the Italian opera to the nasal quaver of Ichabod Crane; and the antiquarian visitor to the Hollow, in the petulance of his disappointment, may pronounce all that I have recorded of that once spell-bound region a fable.

GEOFFREY CRAYON.

NATIONAL NOMENCLATURE.

To the Editor of " The Knickerbocker :"

IR,—I am somewhat of the same way of think-ing, in regard to names, with that profound philosopher, Mr. Shandy the elder, who main-tained that some inspired high thoughts and heroic aims, while others entailed irretrievable meanness and vulgar-ity; insomuch that a man might sink under the insignifi-cance of his name, and be absolutely " Nicodemused into nothing." I have ever, therefore, thought it a great hard-ship for a man to be obliged to struggle through life with some ridiculous or ignoble " *Christian* name," as it is too often falsely called, inflicted on him in infancy, when he could not choose for himself; and would give him free liberty to change it for one more to his taste, when he had arrived at years of discretion.

I have the same notion with respect to local names. Some at once prepossess us in favor of a place; others repel us, by unlucky associations of the mind; and I have known scenes worthy of being the very haunt of poetry and romance, yet doomed to irretrievable vulgar-ity by some ill-chosen name, which not even the magic numbers of a Halleck or a Bryant could elevate into poetical acceptation.

This is an evil unfortunately too prevalent throughout our country. Nature has stamped the land with features of sublimity and beauty; but some of our noblest mountains and loveliest streams are in danger of remaining forever unhonored and unsung, from bearing appellations totally abhorrent to the Muse. In the first place, our country is deluged with names taken from places in the Old World, and applied to places having no possible affinity or resemblance to their namesakes. This betokens a forlorn poverty of invention, and a second-hand spirit, content to cover its nakedness with borrowed or cast-off clothes of Europe.

Then we have a shallow affectation of scholarship; the whole catalogue of ancient worthies is shaken out from the back of Lempriere's "Classical Dictionary," and a wide region of wild country sprinkled over with the names of the heroes, poets, and sages of antiquity, jumbled into the most whimsical juxtaposition. Then we have our political god-fathers, — topographical engineers, perhaps, or persons employed by government to survey and lay out townships. These, forsooth, glorify the patrons that give them bread; so we have the names of the great official men of the day scattered over the land, as if they were the real "salt of the earth," with which it was to be seasoned. Well for us is it when these official great men happen to have names of fair ac-

ceptation; but woe unto us should a Tubbs or a Potts be
in power; we are sure, in a little while, to find Tubbs-
villes and Pottsylvanias springing up in every direction.

Under these melancholy dispensations of taste and
loyalty, therefore, Mr. Editor, it is with a feeling of
dawning hope that I have lately perceived the attention
of persons of intelligence beginning to be awakened on
this subject.   I trust if the matter should once be taken
up, it will not be readily abandoned.   We are yet young
enough, as a country, to remedy and reform much of
what has been done, and to release many of our rising
towns and cities, and our noble streams, from names calculated to vulgarize the land.

I have, on a former occasion, suggested the expediency
of searching out the original Indian names of places, and
wherever they are striking and euphonious, and those by
which they have been superseded are glaringly objec-
tionable, to restore them.   They would have the merit of
originality, and of belonging to the country; and they
would remain as relics of the native lords of the soil,
when every other vestige had disappeared.   Many of
these names may easily be regained, by reference to old
title-deeds, and to the archives of States and counties.
In my own case, by examining the records of the county
clerk's office, I have discovered the Indian names of
various places and objects in the neighborhood, and have
found them infinitely superior to the trite, poverty-
stricken names which had been given by the settlers.   A

beautiful pastoral stream, for instance, which winds for many a mile through one of the loveliest little valleys in the State, has long been known by the commonplace name of the "Saw-mill River." In the old Indian grants it is designated as the Neperan. Another, a perfectly wizard stream, which winds through the wildest recesses of Sleepy Hollow, bears the humdrum name of Mill Creek; in the Indian grants it sustains the euphonious title of the Pocantico.

Similar researches have released Long Island from many of those paltry and vulgar names which fringed its beautiful shores,—their Cow Bays, and Cow Necks, and Oyster Ponds, and Musquito Coves, which spread a spell of vulgarity over the whole island, and kept persons of taste and fancy at a distance.

It would be an object worthy the attention of the historical societies, which are springing up in various parts of the Union, to have maps executed of their respective States or neighborhoods, in which all the local Indian names should, as far as possible, be restored. In fact, it appears to me that the nomenclature of the country is almost of sufficient importance for the foundation of a distinct society; or rather, a corresponding association of persons of taste and judgment, of all parts of the Union. Such an association, if properly constituted and composed, comprising especially all the literary talent of the country, though it might not have legislative power in its enactments, yet would have the all-pervading power of the Press; and the changes in nomenclature which it might dictate, being at once adopted by elegant writers in prose and poetry, and interwoven with the literature of the country, would ultimately pass into popular currency.

Should such a reforming association arise, I beg to recommend to its attention all those mongrel names that have the adjective *New* prefixed to them, and pray they may be one and all kicked out of the country. I am for none of these second-hand appellations, that stamp us a second-hand people, and that are to perpetuate us a new country to the end of time. Odds my life! Mr. Editor, I hope and trust we are to live to be an old nation, as well as our neighbors, and have no idea that our cities, when they shall have attained to venerable antiquity, shall still be dubbed *New* York and *New* London, and *new* this and *new* that, like the Pont Neuf (the New Bridge) at Paris, which is the oldest bridge in that capital, or like the Vicar of Wakefield's horse, which continued to be called "the colt" until he died of old age.

Speaking of New York, reminds me of some observations which I met with some time since, in one of the public papers, about the name of our State and city. The writer proposes to substitute for the present names, those of the State of Ontario and the City of Manhattan. I concur in his suggestion most heartily. Though born and brought up in the city of New York, and though I love every stick and stone about it, yet I do not, nor ever did, relish its name. I like neither its sound nor its significance. As to its *significance*, the very adjective *new* gives to our great commercial metropolis a second-hand character, as if referring to some older, more dignified, and important place, of which it was a mere copy; though in fact, if I am rightly informed, the whole name commemorates a grant by Charles II. to his brother, the Duke of York, made in the spirit of royal munificence, of a tract of country which did not belong to him. As to the *sound*, what can you make of it either in poetry or prose? New York! Why, sir, if it were to share the fate of Troy itself; to suffer a ten years' siege, and be sacked and plundered; no modern Homer would ever be able to elevate the name to epic dignity.

Now, sir, Ontario would be a name worthy of the Empire State. It bears with it the majesty of that internal sea which washes our northwestern shore. Or, if any objection should be made, from its not being completely embraced within our boundaries, there is the Mohegan, one of the Indian names for that glorious river, the Hudson, which would furnish an excellent State appellation. So also New York might be called Manhatta, as it is named in some of the early records, and Manhattan used as the adjective. Manhattan, however, stands well as a substantive, and "Manhattanese," which I observe Mr. Cooper has adopted in some of his

writings, would be a very good appellation for a citizen
of the commercial metropolis.

A word or two more, Mr. Editor, and I have done.
We want a national name. We want it poetically, and
we want it politically. With the poetical necessity of
the case I shall not trouble myself. I leave it to our
poets to tell how they manage to steer that collocation
of words, "The United States of North America," down
the swelling tide of song, and to float the whole raft out
upon the sea of heroic poesy. I am now speaking of the
mere purposes of common life. How is a citizen of this
republic to designate himself? As an American? There
are two Americas, each subdivided into various empires,
rapidly rising in importance. As a citizen of the United
States? It is a clumsy, lumbering title, yet still it is
not distinctive; for we have now the United States of
Central America, and Heaven knows how many "United
States" may spring up under the Proteus changes of
Spanish America.

This may appear matter of small concernment; but
any one that has travelled in foreign countries must be
conscious of the embarrassment and circumlocution sometimes occasioned by the want of a perfectly distinct and
explicit national appellation. In France, when I have
announced myself as an American, I have been supposed
to belong to one of the French colonies; in Spain, to be
from Mexico, or Peru, or some other Spanish American
country. Repeatedly have I found myself involved in a

long geographical and political definition of my national identity.

Now, sir, meaning no disrespect to any of our coheirs of this great quarter of the world, I am for none of this coparceny in a name, that is to mingle us up with the riff-raff colonies and off-sets of every nation of Europe. The title of American may serve to tell the quarter of the world to which I belong, the same as a Frenchman or an Englishman may call himself a European; but I want my own peculiar national name to rally under. I want an appellation that shall tell at once, and in a way not to be mistaken, that I belong to this very portion of America, geographical and political, to which it is my pride and happiness to belong; that I am of the Anglo-Saxon race which founded this Anglo-Saxon empire in the wilderness; and that I have no part or parcel with any other race or empire, Spanish, French, or Portuguese, in either of the Americas. Such an appellation, sir, would have magic in it. It would bind every part of the confederacy together, as with a key-stone; it would be a passport to the citizen of our republic throughout the world.

We have it in our power to furnish ourselves with such a national appellation, from one of the grand and eternal features of our country; from that noble chain of mountains which formed its backbone, and ran through the "old confederacy," when it first declared our national independence. I allude to the Appalachian or Alleghany

34

mountains. We might do this without any very incon-venient change in our present titles. We might still use the phrase "The United States," substituting Appalachia, or Alleghania (I should prefer the latter) in place of America. The title of Appalachian, or Alleghanian, would still announce us as Americans, but would specify us as citizens of the Great Republic. Even our old national cypher of U. S. A. might remain unaltered, designating the United States of Alleghania.

These are crude ideas, Mr. Editor, hastily thrown out, to elicit the ideas of others, and to call attention to a subject of more national importance than may at first be supposed.

Very respectfully yours,

GEOFFREY CRAYON.

DESULTORY THOUGHTS ON CRITICISM.

"Let a man write never so well, there are nowadays a sort of persons they call critics, that, egad, have no more wit in them than so many hobby-horses; but they'll laugh at you, sir, and find fault, and censure things, that, egad, I'm sure they are not able to do themselves; a sort of envious persons, that emulate the glories of persons of parts, and think to build their fame by calumniation of persons that, egad, to my knowledge, of all persons in the world, are in nature the persons that do as much despise all that, as—a—In fine, I'll say no more of 'em!"

REHEARSAL.

LL the world knows the story of the tempest-tossed voyager, who, coming upon a strange coast, and seeing a man hanging in chains, hailed it with joy as the sign of a civilized country. In like manner we may hail, as a proof of the rapid advancement of civilization and refinement in this country, the increasing number of delinquent authors daily gibbeted for the edification of the public.

In this respect, as in every other, we are "going ahead" with accelerated velocity, and promising to outstrip the superannuated countries of Europe. It is really astonishing to see the number of tribunals incessantly springing up for the trial of literary offences. Indepen-

531

dent of the high courts of Oyer and Terminer, the great quarterly reviews, we have innumerable minor tribunals, monthly and weekly, down to the Pie-poudre courts in the daily papers ; insomuch that no culprit stands so little chance of escaping castigation as an unlucky author, guilty of an unsuccessful attempt to please the public.

Seriously speaking, however, it is questionable whether our national literature is sufficiently advanced to bear this excess of criticism; and whether it would not thrive better if allowed to spring up, for some time longer, in the freshness and vigor of native vegetation. When the worthy Judge Coulter, of Virginia, opened court for the first time in one of the upper counties, he was for enforcing all the rules and regulations that had grown into use in the old, long-settled counties. " This is all very well," said a shrewd old farmer ; " but let me tell you, Judge Coulter, you set your coulter too deep for a new soil."

For my part, I doubt whether either writer or reader is benefited by what is commonly called criticism. The former is rendered cautious and distrustful ; he fears to give way to those kindling emotions, and brave sallies of thought, which bear him up to excellence ; the latter is made fastidious and cynical ; or rather, he surrenders his own independent taste and judgment, and learns to like and dislike at second hand.

Let us, for a moment, consider the nature of this thing called criticism, which exerts such a sway over the literary world. The pronoun *we*, used by critics, has a most imposing and delusive sound. The reader pictures to himself a conclave of learned men, deliberating gravely and scrupulously on the merits of the book in question; examining it page by page, comparing and balancing their opinions, and when they have united in a conscientious verdict, publishing it for the benefit of the world: whereas the criticism is generally the crude and hasty production of an individual, scribbling to while away an idle hour, to oblige a bookseller, or to defray current expenses. How often is it the passing notion of the hour, affected by accidental circumstances; by indisposition, by peevishness, by vapors or indigestion, by personal prejudice or party feeling. Sometimes a work is sacrificed because the reviewer wishes a satirical article; sometimes because he wants a humorous one; and sometimes because the author reviewed has become offensively celebrated, and offers high game to the literary marksman.

How often would the critic himself, if a conscientious man, reverse his opinion, had he time to revise it in a more sunny moment; but the press is waiting, the printer's devil is at his elbow, the article is wanted to make the requisite variety for the number of the review, or the author has pressing occasion for the sum he is to receive for the article; so it is sent off, all blotted and blurred, with a shrug of the shoulders, and the consolatory ejaculation, "Pshaw! curse it! it's nothing but a review!"

The critic, too, who dictates thus oracularly to the world, is perhaps some dingy, ill-favored, ill-mannered varlet, who, were he to speak by word of mouth, would be disregarded, if not scoffed at; but such is the magic of types; such the mystic operation of anonymous writing; such the potential effect of the pronoun *we*, that his crude decisions, fulminated through the press, become circulated far and wide, control the opinions of the world, and give or destroy reputation.

Many readers have grown timorous in their judgments since the all-pervading currency of criticism. They fear to express a revised, frank opinion about any new work, and to relish it honestly and heartily, lest it should be condemned in the next review, and they stand convicted of bad taste. Hence they hedge their opinions, like a gambler his bets, and leave an opening to retract, and retreat, and qualify, and neutralize every unguarded expression of delight, until their very praise declines into a faintness that is damning.

Were every one, on the contrary, to judge for himself, and speak his mind frankly and fearlessly, we should have more true criticism in the world than at present. Whenever a person is pleased with a work, he may be assured that it has good qualities. An author who pleases a variety of readers, must possess substantial powers of pleasing; or, in other words, intrinsic merits; for otherwise we acknowledge an effect and deny the cause. The reader, therefore, should not suffer himself to be readily shaken from the conviction of his own feelings by the sweeping censures of pseudo-critics. The author he has admired may be chargeable with a thousand faults; but it is nevertheless beauties and excellences that have excited his admiration; and he should recollect that taste and judgment are as much evinced in the perception of beauties among defects, as in a detection of defects among beauties. For my part, I honor the blessed and blessing spirit that is quick to discover and extol all that is pleasing and meritorious. Give me the honest bee, that extracts honey from the humblest weed, but save me from the ingenuity of the spider, which traces its venom even in the midst of a flower-garden.

If the mere fact of being chargeable with faults and imperfections is to condemn an author, who is to escape? The greatest writers of antiquity have, in this way, been obnoxious to criticism. Aristotle himself has been accused of ignorance; Aristophanes of impiety and buffoonery; Virgil of plagiarism, and a want of invention; Horace of obscurity; Cicero has been said to want vigor and connection, and Demosthenes to be deficient in nature, and in purity of language. Yet these have all survived the censures of the critic, and flourished on to a glorious immortality. Every now and then, the world is startled by some new doctrines in matters of taste, some levelling attacks on established creeds; some sweeping denunciations of whole generations or schools of writers, as they are called, who had seemed to be embalmed and canonized in public opinion. Such has been the case, for instance, with Pope, and Dryden, and Addison; who for a time have almost been shaken from their pedestals, and treated as false idols.

It is singular, also, to see the fickleness of the world with respect to its favorites. Enthusiasm exhausts itself, and prepares the way for dislike. The public is always for positive sentiments, and new sensations. When wearied of admiring, it delights to censure; thus coining a double set of enjoyments out of the same subject. Scott and Byron are scarce cold in their graves, and already we find criticism beginning to call in question those powers which held the world in magic thraldom. Even in our own country, one of its greatest geniuses has had some rough passages with the censors of the press; and instantly criticism begins to unsay all that it has repeatedly said in his praise; and the public are almost led to believe that the pen which has so often delighted them is absolutely destitute of the power to delight!

If, then, such reverses in opinion as to matters of taste can be so readily brought about, when may an author feel himself secure? Where is the anchoring-ground of popularity, when he may thus be driven from his moorings, and foundered even in harbor? The reader, too, when is he to consider himself safe in admiring, when he sees long-established altars overthrown, and his household deities dashed to the ground?

There is one consolatory reflection. Every abuse carries with it its own remedy or palliation. Thus the excess of crude and hasty criticism, which has of late prevailed throughout the literary world, and threatened to overrun our country, begins to produce its own antidote. Where there is a multiplicity of contradictory paths, a man must make his choice; in so doing, he has to exercise his judgment, and that is one great step to mental independence. He begins to doubt all, where all differ, and but one can be in the right. He is driven to trust his own discernment, and his natural feelings; and here he is most likely to be safe. The author, too, finding that what is condemned at one tribunal is applauded at another, though perplexed for a time, gives way at length to the spontaneous impulse of his genius, and the dictates of his taste, and writes in the way most natural to himself. It is thus that criticism, which by its severity may have held the little world of writers in check, may, by its very excess, disarm itself of its terrors, and the hardihood of talent become restored.

COMMUNIPAW.

To the Editor of " The Knickerbocker:"

IR,—I observe with pleasure that you are per-forming, from time to time, a pious duty, imposed upon you, I may say, by the name you have adopted as your titular standard, in following in the footsteps of the venerable *Knickerbocker*, and gleaning every fact concerning the early times of the Manhattoes, which may have escaped his hand. I trust, therefore, a few particulars, legendary and statistical, concerning a place which figures conspicuously in the early pages of his history, will not be unacceptable. I allude, sir, to the ancient and renowned village of Communipaw, which, according to the veracious Diedrich, and to equally veracious tradition, was the first spot where our ever-to-be-lamented Dutch progenitors planted their standard, and cast the seeds of empire, and from whence subsequently sailed the memorable expedition under Oloffe the Dreamer, which landed on the opposite island of Manhatta, and founded the present city of New York, —the city of dreams and speculations.

Communipaw, therefore, may truly be called the parent of New York; yet it is an astonishing fact, that though immediately opposite to the great city it has produced, from whence its red roofs and tin weathercocks can actually be descried peering above the surrounding apple orchards, it should be almost as rarely visited, and as little known by the inhabitants of the metropolis, as if it had been locked up among the Rocky Mountains. Sir, I think there is something unnatural in this, especially in these times of ramble and research, when our citizens are antiquity-hunting in every part of the world. Curiosity, like charity, should begin at home; and I would enjoin it on our worthy burghers, especially those of the real Knickerbocker breed, before they send their sons abroad, to wonder and grow wise among the remains of Greece and Rome, to let them make a tour of ancient Pavonia, from Weehawk even to the Kills, and meditate, with filial reverence, on the moss-grown mansions of Communipaw.

Sir, I regard this much-neglected village as one of the most remarkable places in the country. The intelligent traveller, as he looks down upon it from the Bergen Heights, modestly nestled among its cabbage-gardens. while the great flaunting city it has begotten is stretching far and wide on the opposite side of the bay, the intelligent traveller, I say, will be filled with astonishment; not, sir, at the village of Communipaw, which in truth is a very small village, but at the almost incredible fact that so small a village should have produced so great a

ity.　It looks to him, indeed, like some squat little
dame with a tall grenadier of a son strutting by her side;
or some simple-hearted hen that has unwittingly hatched
out a long-legged turkey.

But this is not all for which Communipaw is remarkable.　Sir, it is interesting on another account.　It is to
the ancient Province of the New Netherlands, and the
classic era of the Dutch dynasty, what Herculaneum and
Pompeii are to ancient Rome and the glorious days of
the Empire.　Here everything remains in *statu quo*, as
it was in the days of Oloffe the Dreamer, Walter the
Doubter, and the other worthies of the golden age; the
same broad-brimmed hats and broad-bottomed breeches;
the same knee-buckles and shoe-buckles; the same close
quilled caps, and linsey-woolsey short-gowns and petticoats; the same implements and utensils, and forms and
fashions; in a word, Communipaw at the present day is
a picture of what New Amsterdam was before the conquest.　The "intelligent traveller," aforesaid, as he
treads its streets, is struck with the primitive character
of everything around him.　Instead of Grecian temples
for dwelling-houses, with a great column of pine boards
in the way of every window, he beholds high, peaked
roofs, gable-ends to the street, with weathercocks at
top, and windows of all sorts and sizes,—large ones for
the grown-up members of the family, and little ones for
the little folk.　Instead of cold marble porches, with
close-locked doors, and brass knockers, he sees the doors

hospitably open; the worthy burgher smoking his pipe on the old-fashioned stoop in front, with his "vrouw" knitting beside him; and the cat and her kittens at their feet, sleeping in the sunshine.

Astonished at the obsolete and "old-world" air of everything around him, the intelligent traveller demands how all this has come to pass. Herculaneum and Pompeii remain, it is true, unaffected by the varying fashions of centuries; but they were buried by a volcano and preserved in ashes. What charmed spell has kept this wonderful little place unchanged, though in sight of the most changeful city in the universe? Has it, too, been buried under its cabbage-gardens, and only dug out in modern days for the wonder and edification of the world? The reply involves a point of history, worthy of notice and record, and reflecting immortal honor on Communipaw.

At the time when New Amsterdam was invaded and conquered by British foes, as has been related in the history of the venerable Diedrich, a great dispersion took place among the Dutch inhabitants. Many, like the illustrious Peter Stuyvesant, buried themselves in rural retreats in the Bowerie; others, like Wolfert Acker, took refuge in various remote parts of the Hudson; but there was one stanch, unconquerable band, that determined to keep together, and preserve themselves, like seed-corn, for the future fructification and perpetuity of the Knickerbocker race. These were headed by one Garret Van Horne, a gigantic Dutchman, the Pelayo of

the New Netherlands. Under his guidance, they retreated across the bay, and buried themselves among the
marshes of ancient Pavonia, as did the followers of Pelayo among the mountains of Asturias, when Spain was
overrun by its Arabian invaders.

The gallant Van Horne set up his standard at Communipaw, and invited all those to rally under it who were
true Nederlanders at heart, and determined to resist all
foreign intermixture or encroachment. A strict non-
intercourse was observed with the captured city; not a
boat ever crossed to it from Communipaw, and the English language was rigorously tabooed throughout the village and its dependencies. Every man was sworn to
wear his hat, cut his coat, build his house, and harness
his horses, exactly as his father had done before him;
and to permit nothing but the Dutch language to be
spoken in his household.

As a citadel of the place, and a stronghold for the
preservation and defence of everything Dutch, the gallant Van Horne erected a lordly mansion, with a chimney
perched at every corner, which thence derived the aris-
tocratical name of " The House of the Four Chimneys."
Hither he transferred many of the precious relics of New
Amsterdam, — the great round-crowned hat that once
covered the capacious head of Walter the Doubter, and
the identical shoe with which Peter the Headstrong
kicked his pusillanimous councillors down stairs. Saint
Nicholas, it is said, took this loyal house under his espe-

cial protection; and a Dutch soothsayer predicted that, as long as it should stand, Communipaw would be safe from the intrusion either of Briton or Yankee.

In this house would the gallant Van Horne and his compeers hold frequent councils of war, as to the possibility of re-conquering the Province from the British; and here would they sit for hours, nay days together, smoking their pipes, and keeping watch upon the growing city of New York; groaning in spirit whenever they saw a new house erected, or ship launched, and persuading themselves that Admiral Van Tromp would one day or other arrive, to sweep out the invaders with the broom which he carried at his mast-head.

Years rolled by, but Van Tromp never arrived. The British strengthened themselves in the land, and the captured city flourished under their domination. Still, the worthies of Communipaw would not despair; something or other, they were sure, would turn up, to restore the power of the Hogen Mogens, the Lord States General; so they kept smoking and smoking, and watching and watching, and turning the same few thoughts over and over in a perpetual circle, which is commonly called deliberating. In the meantime, being hemmed up within a narrow compass, between the broad bay and the Bergen hills, they grew poorer and poorer, until they had scarce the wherewithal to maintain their pipes in fuel during their endless deliberations.

And now must I relate a circumstance which will call

for a little exertion of faith on the part of the reader ; but
I can only say that if he doubts it he had better not utter
his doubts in Communipaw, as it is among the religious
beliefs of the place.   It is, in fact, nothing more nor less
than a miracle, worked by the blessed Saint Nicholas,
for the relief and sustenance of this loyal community.

It so happened, in this time of extremity, that in the
course of cleaning the House of the Four Chimneys, by
an ignorant housewife, who knew nothing of the historic
value of the relics it contained, the old hat of Walter the
Doubter, and the executive shoe of Peter the Headstrong, were thrown out of doors as rubbish.   But mark
the consequence.   The good Saint Nicholas kept watch
over these precious relics, and wrought out of them a
wonderful providence.

The hat of Walter the Doubter, falling on a stercora-
ceous heap of compost, in the rear of the house, began
forthwith to vegetate.   Its broad brim spread forth
grandly, and exfoliated, and its round crown swelled, and
crimped, and consolidated, until the whole became a prodigious cabbage, rivalling in magnitude the capacious
head of the Doubter.   In a word, it was the origin of that
renowned species of cabbage, known by all Dutch epi-
cures by the name of the Governor's Head, and which is
to this day the glory of Communipaw.

On the other hand, the shoe of Peter Stuyvesant, being thrown into the river, in front of the house, gradually
hardened, and concreted, and became covered with bar-

nacles, and at length turned into a gigantic oyster; being the progenitor of that illustrious species, known throughout the gastronomical world by the name of the Governor's Foot.

These miracles were the salvation of Communipaw. The sages of the place immediately saw in them the hand of Saint Nicholas, and understood their mystic significacation. They set to work, with all diligence, to cultivate and multiply these great blessings; and so abundantly did the gubernatorial hat and shoe fructify and increase, that in a little time great patches of cabbages were to be seen extending from the village of Communipaw quite to the Bergen Hills; while the whole bottom of the bay in front became a vast bed of oysters. Ever since that time, this excellent community has been divided into two great classes, those who cultivate the land, and those who cultivate the water. The former have devoted themselves to the nurture and edification of cabbages, rearing them in all their varieties; while the latter have formed parks and plantations, under water, to which juvenile oysters are transplanted from foreign parts, to finish their education.

As these great sources of profit multiplied upon their hands, the worthy inhabitants of Communipaw began to long for a market, at which to dispose of their superabundance. This gradually produced, once more, an intercourse with New York; but it was always carried on by the old people and the negroes; never would they

35

permit the young folks, of either sex, to visit the city, lest they should get tainted with foreign manners, and bring home foreign fashions. Even to this day, if you see an old burgher in the market, with hat and garb of antique Dutch fashion, you may be sure he is one of the old unconquered race of the "bitter blood," who maintain their stronghold at Communipaw.

In modern days, the hereditary bitterness against the English has lost much of its asperity, or rather has become merged in a new source of jealousy and apprehension. I allude to the incessant and wide-spreading irruptions from New England. Word has been continually brought back to Communipaw, by those of the community who return from their trading voyages in cabbages and oysters, of the alarming power which the Yankees are gaining in the ancient city of New Amsterdam; elbowing the genuine Knickerbockers out of all civic posts of honor and profit; bargaining them out of their hereditary homesteads; pulling down the venerable houses, with crowstep gables, which have stood since the time of the Dutch rule, and erecting, instead, granite stores and marble banks; in a word, evincing a deadly determination to obliterate every vestige of the good old Dutch times.

In consequence of the jealousy thus awakened, the worthy traders from Communipaw confine their dealings, as much as possible, to the genuine Dutch families. If they furnish the Yankees at all, it is with inferior articles. Never can the latter procure a real "Governor's Head," or " Governor's Foot," though they have offered extravagant prices for the same, to grace their table on the annual festival of the New England Society.

But what has carried this hostility to the Yankees to the highest pitch, was an attempt made by that all-pervading race to get possession of Communipaw itself. Yes, sir; during the late mania for land speculation, a daring company of Yankee projectors landed before the village, stopped the honest burghers on the public highway, and endeavored to bargain them out of their hereditary acres; displayed lithographic maps, in which their cabbage-gardens were laid out into town lots; their oyster-parks into docks and quays; and even the "House of the Four Chimneys" metamorphosed into a bank, which was to enrich the whole neighborhood with paper money.

Fortunately, the gallant Van Hornes came to the rescue, just as some of the worthy burghers were on the point of capitulating. The Yankees were put to the rout, with signal confusion, and have never since dared to show their faces in the place. The good people continue to cultivate their cabbages, and rear their oysters; they know nothing of banks, nor joint-stock companies, but treasure up their money in stocking-feet, at the bottom of the family chest, or bury it in iron pots, as did their fathers and grandfathers before them.

As to the "House of the Four Chimneys," it still remains in the great and tall family of the Van Hornes. Here are to be seen ancient Dutch corner cupboards,

chests of drawers, and massive clothes-presses, quaintly
carved, and carefully waxed and polished; together with
divers thick, black-letter volumes, with brass clasps,
printed of yore in Leyden and Amsterdam, and handed
down from generation to generation, in the family, but
never read. They are preserved in the archives, among
sundry old parchment deeds, in Dutch and English,
bearing the seals of the early governors of the province.

In this house, the primitive Dutch holidays of Paas
and Pinxter are faithfully kept up; and New-Year celebrated with cookies and cherry-bounce; nor is the festival of the blessed Saint Nicholas forgotten, when all the
children are sure to hang up their stockings, and to have
them filled according to their deserts; though it is said
the good saint is occasionally perplexed, in his nocturnal
visits, which chimney to descend.

Of late this portentous mansion has begun to give
signs of dilapidation and decay. Some have attributed
this to the visits made by the young people to the city,
and their bringing thence various modern fashions; and
to their neglect of the Dutch language, which is gradually
becoming confined to the older persons in the community.
The house, too, was greatly shaken by high winds during
the prevalence of the speculation mania, especially at the
time of the landing of the Yankees. Seeing how myste-
riously the fate of Communipaw is identified with this
venerable mansion, we cannot wonder that the older and
wiser heads of the community should be filled with dis-

may whenever a brick is toppled down from one of the chimneys, or a weathercock is blown off from a gable-end.

The present lord of this historic pile, I am happy to say, is calculated to maintain it in all its integrity. He is of patriarchal age, and is worthy of the days of the patriarchs. He has done his utmost to increase and multiply the true race in the land. His wife has not been inferior to him in zeal, and they are surrounded by a goodly progeny of children and grandchildren, and great-grandchildren, who promise to perpetuate the name of Van Horne until time shall be no more. So be it! Long may the horn of the Van Hornes continue to be exalted in the land! Tall as they are, may their shadows never be less! May the "House of the Four Chimneys" remain for ages the citadel of Communipaw, and the smoke of its chimneys continue to ascend, a sweet-smelling incense in the nose of Saint Nicholas!

With great respect, Mr. Editor,

Your ob't servant,

HERMANUS VANDERDONK.

CONSPIRACY OF THE COCKED HATS.

To the Editor of " The Knickerbocker : "

SIR,—I have read, with great satisfaction, the valuable paper of your correspondent, Mr. Hermanus Vanderdonk (who, I take it, is a descendant of the learned Adrian Vanderdonk, one of the early historians of the Nieuw-Nederlands), giving sundry particulars, legendary and statistical, touching the venerable village of Communipaw, and its fate-bound citadel, the "House of the Four Chimneys." It goes to prove, what I have repeatedly maintained, that we live in the midst of history, and mystery, and romance ; and that there is no spot in the world more rich in themes for the writer of historic novels, heroic melodramas, and rough-shod epics, than this same business-looking city of the Manhattoes and its environs. He who would find these elements, however, must not seek them among the modern improvements and modern people of this moneyed metropolis, but must dig for them, as for Kidd the pirate's treasures, in out-of-the-way places, and among the ruins of the past.

Poetry and romance received a fatal blow at the overthrow of the ancient Dutch dynasty, and have ever since been gradually withering under the growing domination of the Yankees. They abandoned our hearths when the old Dutch tiles were superseded by marble chimney-pieces; when brass andirons made way for polished grates, and the crackling and blazing fire of nut-wood gave place to the smoke and stench of Liverpool coal; and on the downfall of the last gable-end house, their requiem was tolled from the tower of the Dutch church in Nassau Street, by the old bell that came from Holland. But poetry and romance still live unseen among us, or seen only by the enlightened few who are able to contemplate this city and its environs through the medium of tradition, and clothed with the associations of foregone ages.

Would you seek these elements in the country, Mr. Editor, avoid all turnpikes, railroads, and steamboats, those abominable inventions by which the usurping Yankees are strengthening themselves in the land, and subduing everything to utility and commonplace. Avoid all towns and cities of white clapboard palaces, and Grecian temples, studded with "Academies," "Seminaries," and "Institutes," which glisten along our bays and rivers; these are the strongholds of Yankee unsurpation; but if haply you light upon some rough, rambling road, winding between stone fences, gray with moss, and overgrown with elder, poke-berry, mullen, and sweetbrier, with here and there a low, red-roofed, whitewashed farmhouse, cowering among apple and cherry trees; an old stone church, with elms, willows, and button-woods as old-looking as itself, and tombstones almost buried in their own graves; and, peradventure, a small log school-house, at a cross-road, where the English is still taught with a thickness of the tongue, instead of a twang of the nose; should you, I say, light upon such a neighborhood, Mr. Editor, you may thank your stars that you have found one of the lingering haunts of poetry and romance.

Your correspondent, sir, has touched upon that sublime and affecting feature in the history of Communipaw, the retreat of the patriotic band of Nederlanders, led by Van Horne, whom he justly terms the Pelayo of the New Netherlands. He has given you a picture of the manner in which they ensconced themselves in the "House of the Four Chimneys," and awaited with heroic patience and perseverance the day that should see the flag of the Hogen Mogens once more floating on the fort of New Amsterdam.

Your correspondent, sir, has but given you a glimpse over the threshold; I will now let you into the heart of the mystery of this most mysterious and eventful village. Yes, sir, I will now

"unclasp a secret book;
And to your quick conceiving discontents,
I'll read you matter deep and dangerous,
As full of peril and adventurous spirit,

As to o'er walk a current, roaring loud,
On the unsteadfast footing of a spear."

Sir, it is one of the most beautiful and interesting facts connected with the history of Communipaw, that the early feeling of resistance to foreign rule, alluded to by your correspondent, is still kept up. Yes, sir, a settled, secret, and determined conspiracy has been going on for generations among this indomitable people, the descendants of the refugees from New Amsterdam, the object of which is to redeem their ancient seat of empire, and to drive the losel Yankees out of the land.

Communipaw, it is true, has the glory of originating this conspiracy; and it was hatched and reared in the "House of the Four Chimneys;" but it has spread far and wide over ancient Pavonia, surmounted the heights of Bergen, Hoboken, and Weehawk, crept up along the banks of the Passaic and the Hackensack, until it pervades the whole chivalry of the country, from Tappan Slote, in the North, to Piscataway, in the South, including the pugnacious village of Rahway, more heroically denominated Spank-town.

Throughout all these regions, a great "in-and-in confederacy" prevails; that is to say, a confederacy among the Dutch families, by dint of diligent and exclusive intermarriage, to keep the race pure, and to multiply. If ever, Mr. Editor, in the course of your travels between Spank-town and Tappan Slote, you should see a cosey, low-eaved farmhouse, teeming with sturdy, broad-built little urchins, you may set it down as one of the breeding-places of this grand secret confederacy, stocked with the embryo deliverers of New Amsterdam.

Another step in the progress of this patriotic conspiracy is the establishment, in various places within the ancient boundaries of the Nieuw-Nederlands, of secret, or rather mysterious, associations, composed of the genuine sons of the Nederlanders, with the ostensible object of keeping up the memory of old times and customs, but with the real object of promoting the views of this dark and mighty plot, and extending its ramifications throughout the land.

Sir, I am descended from a long line of genuine Neder-landers, who, though they remained in the city of New Amsterdam after the conquest, and throughout the usurpation, have never in their hearts been able to tolerate the yoke imposed upon them. My worthy father, who was one of the last of the cocked hats, had a little knot of cronies, of his own stamp, who used to meet in our wainscoted parlor, round a nut-wood fire, talk over old times, when the city was ruled by its native burgomasters, and groan over the monopoly of all places of power and profit by the Yankees. I well recollect the effect upon this worthy little conclave when the Yankees first insti-tuted their New-England Society, held their "national festival," toasted their "father-land," and sang their for-eign songs of triumph within the very precincts of our ancient metropolis. Sir, from that day, my father held the smell of codfish and potatoes, and the sight of pumpkin-pie, in utter abomination; and whenever the annual dinner of the New-England Society came round, it was a sore anniversary for his children. He got up in an ill humor, grumbled and growled throughout the day, and not one of us went to bed that night without having had his jacket well trounced, to the tune of "The Pilgrim Fathers."

You may judge, then, Mr. Editor, of the exultation of all true patriots of this stamp, when the Society of Saint Nicholas was set up among us, and intrepidly established, cheek by jole, alongside of the society of the invaders. Never shall I forget the effect upon my father and his little knot of brother groaners, when tidings were brought them that the ancient banner of the Manhattoes was actually floating from the window of the City Hotel. Sir, they nearly jumped out of their silver-buckled shoes for joy. They took down their cocked hats from the pegs on which they had hanged them, as the Israelites of yore hung their harps upon the willows, in token of bondage, clapped them resolutely once more upon their heads, and cocked them in the face of every Yankee they met on the way to the banqueting-room.

The institution of this society was hailed with transport throughout the whole extent of the New Netherlands; being considered a secret foothold gained in New Amsterdam, and a flattering presage of future triumph.

Whenever that society holds its annual feast, a sympathetic hilarity prevails throughout the land ; ancient Pavonia sends over its contributions of cabbages and oysters ; the "House of the Four Chimneys" is splendidly illuminated, and the traditional song of Saint Nicholas, the mystic bond of union and conspiracy, is chanted with closed doors, in every genuine Dutch family.

I have thus, I trust, Mr. Editor, opened your eyes to some of the grand, moral, poetical, and political phenomena with which you are surrounded. You will now be able to read the "signs of the times." You will now understand what is meant by those "Knickerbocker Halls," and "Knickerbocker Hotels," and "Knickerbocker Lunches," that are daily springing up in our city, and what all these "Knickerbocker Omnibuses" are driving at. You will see in them so many clouds before a storm ; so many mysterious but sublime intimations of the gathering vengeance of a great though oppressed people. Above all, you will now contemplate our bay and its portentous borders with proper feelings of awe and admiration. Talk of the Bay of Naples, and its volcanic mountain ! Why, sir, little Communipaw, sleeping among its cabbage-gardens, "quiet as gunpowder," yet with this tremendous conspiracy brewing in its bosom, is an object ten times as sublime (in a moral point of view, mark me,) as Vesuvius in repose, though charged with lava and brimstone, and ready for an eruption.

Let me advert to a circumstance connected with this theme, which cannot but be appreciated by every heart of sensibility. You must have remarked, Mr. Editor, on summer evenings, and on Sunday afternoons, certain grave, primitive-looking personages, walking the Battery, in close confabulation, with their canes behind their backs, and ever and anon turning a wistful gaze toward the Jersey shore. These, sir, are the sons of Saint Nicholas, the genuine Nederlanders; who regard Communipaw with pious reverence, not merely as the progenitor, but the destined regenerator, of this great metropolis. Yes, sir; they are looking with longing eyes to the green marshes of ancient Pavonia, as did the poor conquered Spaniards of yore toward the stern mountains of Asturias, wondering whether the day of deliverance is at hand. Many is the time, when, in my boyhood, I have walked with my father and his confidential compeers on the Battery, and listened to their calculations and conjectures, and observed the points of their sharp cocked hats ever more turned toward Pavonia. Nay, sir, I am convinced that at this moment, if I were to take down the cocked hat of my lamented father from the peg on which it has hung for years, and were to carry it to the Battery, its centre point, true as the needle to the pole, would turn to Communipaw.

Mr. Editor, the great historic drama of New Amsterdam is but half acted. The reigns of Walter the Doubter

William the Testy, and Peter the Headstrong, with the rise, progress, and decline of the Dutch dynasty, are but so many parts of the main action, the triumphant catastrophe of which is yet to come. Yes, sir! the deliverance of the New Nederlands from Yankee domination will eclipse the far-famed redemption of Spain from the Moors, and the oft-sung Conquest of Granada will fade before the chivalrous triumph of New Amsterdam. Would that Peter Stuyvesant could rise from his grave to witness that day!

Your humble servant,

ROLOFF VAN RIPPER.

P. S.—Just as I had concluded the foregoing epistle, I received a piece of intelligence which makes me tremble for the fate of Communipaw. I fear, Mr. Editor, the grand conspiracy is in danger of being countermined and counteracted by those all-pervading and indefatigable Yankees. Would you think it, sir! one of them has actually effected an entry in the place by covered way; or, in other words, under cover of the petticoats. Finding every other mode ineffectual, he secretly laid siege to a Dutch heiress, who owns a great cabbage-garden in her own right. Being a smooth-tongued varlet, he easily prevailed on her to elope with him, and they were privately married at Spank-town! The first notice the good people of Communipaw had of this awful event, was a lithographed map of the cabbage-garden laid out in town lots, and advertised for sale! On the night of the wedding, the main weathercock of the "House of the Four Chimneys" was carried away in a whirlwind! The greatest consternation reigns throughout the village!

LETTER FROM GRANADA.

To the Editor of " The Knickerbocker : "

IR,—The following letter was scribbled to a friend during my sojourn in the Alhambra, in 1828. As it presents scenes and impressions noted down at the time, I venture to offer it for the consideration of your readers. Should it prove acceptable, I may from time to time give other letters, written in the course of my various ramblings, and which have been kindly restored to me by my friends.

Yours,   G. C.

GRANADA, 1828.

MY DEAR ———— :

Religious festivals furnish, in all Catholic countries, occasions of popular pageant and recreation ; but in none more so than in Spain, where the great end of religion seems to be to create holidays and ceremonials. For two days past, Granada has been in a gay turmoil with the great annual fête of Corpus Christi. This most eventful and romantic city, as you well know, has ever been the rallying-point of a mountainous region, studded with small towns and villages. Hither, during the time that Granada was the splendid capital of a Moorish kingdom, the Moslem youth repaired from all points to participate in chivalrous festivities; and hither the Spanish populace, at the present day, throng from all parts of the surrounding country, to attend the festivals of the Church.

As the populace like to enjoy things from the very commencement, the stir of Corpus Christi began in Granada on the preceding evening. Before dark, the gates of the city were thronged with the picturesque peasantry from the mountain villages, and the brown laborers from the Vega, or vast fertile plain. As the evening advanced, the Vivarrambla thickened and swarmed with a motley multitude. This is the great square in the centre of the city, famous for tilts and tourneys during the times of Moorish domination, and incessantly mentioned in all the old Moorish ballads of love and chivalry. For several days the hammer had resounded throughout this square. A gallery of wood had been erected all round it, forming a covered way for the grand procession of Corpus Christi. On this eve of the ceremonial, this gallery was a fashionable promenade. It was brilliantly illuminated, bands of music were stationed in balconies on the four sides of the square, and all the fashion and beauty of Granada, and all its population that could boast a little finery of apparel, together with the *majos* and *majas*, the beaux and belles of the villages, in their

36

gay Andalusian costumes, thronged this covered walk, anxious to see and to be seen. As to the sturdy peasantry of the Vega, and such of the mountaineers as did not pretend to display, but were content with hearty enjoyment, they swarmed in the centre of the square; some in groups, listening to the guitar and the traditional ballad; some dancing their favorite *boléro;* some seated on the ground, making a merry though frugal supper; and some stretched out for their night's repose.

The gay crowd of the gallery dispersed gradually toward midnight; but the centre of the square resembled the bivouac of an army; for hundreds of the peasantry —men, women, and children—passed the night there, sleeping soundly on the bare earth, under the open canopy of heaven. A summer's night requires no shelter in this genial climate; and with a great part of the hardy peasantry of Spain, a bed is a superfluity which many of them never enjoy, and which they affect to despise. The common Spaniard spreads out his manta, or mule-cloth, or wraps himself in his cloak, and lies on the ground, with his saddle for a pillow.

The next morning I revisited the square at sunrise. It was still strewed with groups of sleepers; some were reposing from the dance and revel of the evening; others had left their villages after work, on the preceding day, and having trudged on foot the greater part of the night, were taking a sound sleep to freshen them for the festivities of the day. Numbers from the mountains, and the remote villages of the plain, who had set out in the night, continued to arrive, with their wives and children. All were in high spirits; greeting each other, and exchanging jokes and pleasantries. The gay tumult thickened as the day advanced. Now came pouring in at the city gates, and parading through the streets, the deputations from the various villages, destined to swell the grand procession. These village deputations were headed by their priests, bearing their respective crosses and banners, and images of the blessed Virgin, and of patron saints; all which were matters of great rivalship and jealousy among the peasantry. It was like the chivalrous gatherings of ancient days, when each town and village sent its chiefs, and warriors, and standards, to defend the capital, or grace its festivities.

At length all these various detachments congregated into one grand pageant, which slowly paraded round the Vivarrambla, and through the principal streets, where every window and balcony was hung with tapestry. In this procession were all the religious orders, the civil and military authorities, and the chief people of the parishes and villages: every church and convent had contributed its banners, its images, its relics, and poured forth its wealth, for the occasion. In the centre of the procession walked the archbishop, under a damask canopy, and surrounded by inferior dignitaries and their dependants. The whole moved to the swell and cadence of numerous bands of music, and, passing through the midst of a countless yet silent multitude, proceeded onward to the cathedral.

I could not but be struck with the changes of times and customs, as I saw this monkish pageant passing through the Vivarrambla, the ancient seat of modern pomp and chivalry. The contrast was indeed forced upon the mind by the decorations of the square. The whole front of the wooden gallery erected for the procession, extending several hundred feet, was faced with canvas, on which some humble though patriotic artist had painted, by contract, a series of the principal scenes and exploits of the Conquest, as recorded in chronicle and romance. It is thus the romantic legends of Granada mingle themselves with everything, and are kept fresh in the public mind.

Another great festival at Granada, answering in its popular character to our Fourth of July, is *El Dia de la Toma,* " The Day of the Capture ;" that is to say, the anniversary of the capture of the city by Ferdinand and Isabella. On this day all Granada is abandoned to revelry. The alarm-bell on the Terre de la Campana, or watch-tower of the Alhambra, keeps up a clangor from morn till night ; and happy is the damsel that can ring that bell ; it is a charm to secure a husband in the course of the year.

The sound, which can be heard over the whole Vega, and to the top of the mountains, summons the peasantry to the festivities. Throughout the day the Alhambra is thrown open to the public. The halls and courts of the Moorish monarchs resound with the guitar and castanet, and gay groups, in the fanciful dresses of Andalusia, perform those popular dances which they have inherited from the Moors.

In the meantime a grand procession moves through the city. The banner of Ferdinand and Isabella, that precious relic of the Conquest, is brought forth from its depository, and borne by the Alferez Mayor, or grand standard-bearer, through the principal streets. The portable camp-altar, which was carried about with them in all their campaigns, is transported into the chapel royal, and placed before their sepulchre, where their effigies lie in monumental marble. The procession fills the chapel. High mass is performed in memory of the Conquest; and at a certain part of the ceremony the Alferez Mayor puts on his hat and waves the standard above the tomb of the conquerors.

A more whimsical memorial of the Conquest is exhibited on the same evening at the theatre, where a popular drama is performed, entitled "Ave Maria." This turns on the oft-sung achievement of Hernando del Pulgar, surnamed *El de las Hazañas*, "He of the Exploits," the favorite hero of the populace of Granada.

During the time that Ferdinand and Isabella besieged the city, the young Moorish and Spanish knights vied with each other in extravagant bravados. On one occasion Hernando del Pulgar, at the head of a handful of

youthful followers, made a dash into Granada at the dead
of the night, nailed the inscription of Ave Maria, with
his dagger, to the gate of the principal mosque, as a token
of having consecrated it to the Virgin, and effected his
retreat in safety.

While the Moorish cavaliers admired this daring exploit, they felt bound to revenge it. On the following
day, therefore, Tarfe, one of the stoutest of the infidel
warriors, paraded in front of the Christian army, dragging the sacred inscription of Ave Maria at his horse's
tail. The cause of the Virgin was eagerly vindicated by
Garcilaso de la Vega, who slew the Moor in single combat, and elevated the inscription of Ave Maria, in devotion and triumph, at the end of his lance.

The drama founded on this exploit is prodigiously
popular with the common people. Although it has been
acted time out of mind, and the people have seen it repeatedly, it never fails to draw crowds, and so completely
to engross the feelings of the audience, as to have almost
the effect on them of reality. When their favorite Pulgar
strides about with many a mouthy speech, in the very
midst of the Moorish capital, he is cheered with enthusiastic bravos ; and when he nails the tablet of Ave
Maria to the door of the mosque, the theatre absolutely
shakes with shouts and thunders of applause. On the
other hand, the actors who play the part of the Moors
have to bear the brunt of the temporary indignation of
their auditors ; and when the infidel Tarfe plucks down

the tablet to tie it to his horse's tail, many of the people absolutely rise in fury, and are ready to jump upon the stage to revenge this insult to the Virgin.

Beside this annual festival at the capital, almost every village of the Vega and the mountains has its own anniversary, wherein its own deliverance from the Moorish yoke is celebrated with uncouth ceremony and rustic pomp.

On these occasions, a kind of resurrection takes place of ancient Spanish dresses and armor,—great two-handed swords, ponderous arquebuses, with match-locks, and other weapons and accoutrements, once the equipments of the village chivalry, and treasured up from generation to generation since the time of the Conquest. In these hereditary and historical garbs, some of the most sturdy of the villagers array themselves as champions of the faith, while its ancient opponents are represented by another band of villagers, dressed up as Moorish warriors. A tent is pitched in the public square of the village, within which is an altar and an image of the Virgin. The Spanish warriors approach to perform their devotions at this shrine, but are opposed by the infidel Moslems, who surround the tent. A mock fight succeeds, in the course of which the combatants sometimes forget that they are merely playing a part, and exchange dry blows of grievous weight; the fictitious Moors, especially, are apt to bear away pretty evident marks of the pious zeal of their antagonists. The contest, however, invariably terminates in favor of the good cause. The Moors are defeated and taken prisoners. The image of the Virgin, rescued from thraldom, is elevated in triumph ; and a grand procession succeeds, in which the Spanish conquerors figure with great vainglory and applause, and their captives are led in chains, to the infinite delight and edification of the populace. These annual festivals are the delight of the villagers, who expend considerable sums in their celebration. In some villages they are occasionally obliged to suspend them for want of funds ; but when times grow better, or they have been enabled to save money for the purpose, they are revived with all their grotesque pomp and extravagance.

To recur to the exploit of Hernando del Pulgar. However extravagant and fabulous it may seem, it is authenticated by certain traditional usages, and shows the vainglorious daring that prevailed between the youthful warriors of both nations, in that romantic war. The mosque thus consecrated to the Virgin was made the cathedral of the city after the Conquest ; and there is a painting of the Virgin beside the royal chapel, which was put there by Hernando del Pulgar. The lineal representative of the hair-brained cavalier has the right, to this day, to enter the church, on certain occasions, on horseback, to sit within the choir, and to put on his hat at the elevation of the host, though these privileges have often been obstinately contested by the clergy.

The present lineal representative of Hernando del Pulgar is the Marquis de Salar, whom I have met occasionally in society. He is a young man of agreeable appearance and manners, and his bright black eyes would give indication of his inheriting the fire of his ancestor. When the paintings were put up in the Vivarrambla, illustrating the scenes of the Conquest, an old gray-headed family servant of the Pulgars was so delighted with those which related to the family hero, that he absolutely shed tears, and hurrying home to the Marquis, urged him to hasten and behold the family trophies. The sudden zeal of the old man provoked the mirth of his young master; upon which, turning to the brother of the Marquis, with that freedom allowed to family servants in Spain, "Come, Señor," cried he; "you are more grave and considerate than your brother; come and see your ancestor in all his glory!"

Within two or three years after the above letter was written, the Marquis de Salar was married to the beautiful daughter of the Count ——, mentioned by the author in his anecdotes of the Alhambra. The match was very agreeable to all parties, and the nuptials were celebrated with great festivity.

THE CATSKILL MOUNTAINS.

HE Catskill, Katskill, or Cat River Mountains derived their name, in the time of the Dutch domination, from the catamounts by which they were infested; and which, with the bear, the wolf, and the deer, are still to be found in some of their most difficult recesses. The interior of these mountains is in the highest degree wild and romantic. Here are rocky precipices mantled with primeval forests; deep gorges walled in by beetling cliffs, with torrents tumbling as it were from the sky; and savage glens rarely trodden excepting by the hunter. With all this internal rudeness, the aspect of these mountains towards the Hudson at times is eminently bland and beautiful, sloping down into a country softened by cultivation, and bearing much of the rich character of Italian scenery about the skirts of the Apennines.

The Catskills form an advance post or lateral spur of the great Alleghanian or Appalachian system of mountains which sweeps through the interior of our continent, from southwest to northeast, from Alabama to the extremity of Maine, for nearly fourteen hundred miles, belting

570

the whole of our original confederacy, and rivalling our great system of lakes in extent and grandeur. Its vast ramifications comprise a number of parallel chains and lateral groups; such as the Cumberland Mountains, the Blue Ridge, the Alleghanies, the Delaware and Lehigh, the Highlands of the Hudson, the Green Mountains of Vermont, and the White Mountains of New Hampshire. In many of these vast ranges or sierras, Nature still reigns in indomitable wildness; their rocky ridges, their rugged clefts and defiles, teem with magnificent vegetation.

Here are locked up mighty forests that have never been invaded by the axe; deep umbrageous valleys where the virgin soil has never been outraged by the plough; bright streams flowing in untasked idleness, unburdened by commerce, unchecked by the mill-dam. This mountain zone is in fact the great poetical region of our country; resisting, like the tribes which once inhabited it, the taming hand of cultivation; and maintaining a hallowed ground for fancy and the Muses. It is a magnificent and all-pervading feature, that might have given our country a name, and a poetical one, had not the all-controlling powers of commonplace determined otherwise.

The Catskill Mountains, as I have observed, maintain all the internal wildness of the labyrinth of mountains with which they are connected. Their detached position, overlooking a wide lowland region, with the majestic Hudson rolling through it, has given them a distinct character, and rendered them at all times a rallying-point for romance and fable.   Much of the fanciful associations with which they have been clothed may be owing to their being peculiarly subject to those beautiful atmospherical effects which constitute one of the great charms of Hudson River scenery.   To me they have ever been the fairy region of the Hudson.   I speak, however, from early impressions, made in the happy days of boyhood, when all the world had a tinge of fairy-land.   I shall never forget my first view of these mountains.   It was in the course of a voyage up the Hudson, in the good old times before steamboats and railroads had driven all poetry and romance out of travel.   A voyage up the Hudson in those days was equal to a voyage to Europe at present, and cost almost as much time; but we enjoyed the river then; we relished it as we did our wine, sip by sip, not as at present, gulping all down at a draught, without tasting it.   My whole voyage up the Hudson was full of wonder and romance.   I was a lively boy, somewhat imaginative, of easy faith, and prone to relish everything that partook of the marvellous.   Among the passengers on board of the sloop was a veteran Indian trader, on his way to the lakes to traffic with the natives. He had discovered my propensity, and amused himself throughout the voyage by telling me Indian legends and grotesque stories about every noted place on the River,— such as Spuyten Devil Creek, the Tappan Sea, the Devil's Dans Kammer, and other hobgoblin places.   The

Catskill Mountains especially called forth a host of fanciful traditions. We were all day slowly tiding along in sight of them, so that he had full time to weave his whimsical narratives. In these mountains, he told me, according to Indian belief, was kept the great treasury of storm and sunshine for the region of the Hudson. An old squaw spirit had charge of it, who dwelt on the highest peak of the mountain. Here she kept Day and Night shut up in her wigwam, letting out only one of them at a time. She made new moons every month, and hung them up in the sky, cutting up the old ones into stars. The great Manitou, or master-spirit, employed her to manufacture clouds; sometimes she wove them out of cobwebs, gossamers, and morning dew, and sent them off flake after flake, to float in the air and give light summer showers. Sometimes she would brew up black thunder-storms, and send down drenching rains to swell the streams and sweep everything away. He had many stories, also, about mischievous spirits who infested the mountains in the shape of animals, and played all kinds of pranks upon Indian hunters, decoying them into quagmires and morasses, or to the brinks of torrents and precipices. All these were doled out to me as I lay on the deck throughout a long summer's day, gazing upon these mountains, the ever-changing shapes and hues of which appeared to realize the magical influences in question. Sometimes they seemed to approach; at others to recede; during the heat of the day they almost melted into a sultry haze; as the day declined they deepened in tone; their summits were brightened by the last rays of the sun, and later in the evening their whole outline was printed in deep purple against an amber sky. As I beheld them thus shifting continually before my eye, and listened to the marvellous legends of the trader, a host of fanciful notions concerning them was conjured into my brain, which have haunted it ever since.

As to the Indian superstitions concerning the treasury of storms and sunshine, and the cloud-weaving spirits, they may have been suggested by the atmospherical phenomena of these mountains, the clouds which gather round their summits, and the thousand aërial effects which indicate the changes of weather over a great extent of country. They are epitomes of our variable climate, and are stamped with all its vicissitudes. And here let me say a word in favor of those vicissitudes which are too often made the subject of exclusive repining. If they annoy us occasionally by changes from hot to cold, from wet to dry, they give us one of the most beautiful climates in the world. They give us the brilliant sunshine of the south of Europe, with the fresh verdure of the north. They float our summer sky with clouds of gorgeous tints or fleecy whiteness, and send down cooling showers to refresh the panting earth and keep it green. Our seasons are all poetical; the phenomena of our heavens are full of sublimity and beauty. Winter with us has none of its proverbial gloom. It may have its howling winds, and thrilling frosts, and whirling snow-storms; but it has also its long intervals of cloudless sunshine, when the snow-clad earth gives redoubled brightness to the day; when at night the stars beam with intensest lustre, or the moon floods the whole landscape with her most limpid radiance;—and then the joyous outbreak of our spring, bursting at once into leaf and blossom, redundant with vegetation and vociferous with life!—And the splendors of our summer,—its morning voluptuousness and evening glory; its airy palaces of sun-gilt clouds piled up in a deep azure sky, and its gusts of tempest of almost tropical grandeur, when the forked lightning and the bellowing thunder volley from the battlements of heaven and shake the sultry atmosphere,—and the sublime melancholy of our autumn, magnificent in its decay, withering down the pomp and pride of a woodland country, yet reflecting back from its yellow forests the golden serenity of the sky!—surely we may say that in our climate, "The heavens declare the glory of God, and the firmament showeth forth his handiwork: day unto day uttereth speech; and night unto night showeth knowledge."

A word more concerning the Catskills. It is not the Indians only to whom they have been a kind of wonderland. In the early times of the Dutch dynasty we find them themes of golden speculation among even the sages of New Amsterdam. During the administration of Wilhelmus Kieft there was a meeting between the Director

of the New Netherlands and the chiefs of the Mohawk
nation to conclude a treaty of peace. On this occasion
the Director was accompanied by Mynheer Adrian Van
der Donk, Doctor of Laws, and subsequently historian of
the colony. The Indian chiefs, as usual, painted and
decorated themselves on the ceremony. One of them in
so doing made use of a pigment, the weight and shining
appearance of which attracted the notice of Kieft and
his learned companion, who suspected it to be ore. They
procured a lump of it, and took it back with them to
New Amsterdam. Here it was submitted to the inspection of Johannes de la Montagne, an eminent Huguenot
doctor of medicine, one of the counsellors of the New
Netherlands. The supposed ore was forthwith put in a
crucible and assayed, and to the great exultation of the
junto yielded two pieces of gold, worth about three guild-
ers. This golden discovery was kept a profound secret.
As soon as the treaty of peace was adjusted with the
Mohawks, William Kieft sent a trusty officer and a party
of men, under guidance of an Indian, who undertook to
conduct them to the place whence the ore had been
found. We have no account of this gold-hunting expedition, nor of its whereabouts, excepting that it was
somewhere on the Catskill Mountains. The exploring
party brought back a bucketful of ore. Like the former
specimen, it was submitted to the crucible of De la Montagne, and was equally productive of gold. All this we
have on the authority of Doctor Van der Donk, who was

an eye-witness of the process and its result, and records the whole in his "Description of the New Netherlands."

William Kieft now despatched a confidential agent, one Arent Corsen, to convey a sackful of the precious ore to Holland. Corsen embarked at New Haven in a British vessel bound to England, whence he was to cross to Rotterdam. The ship set sail about Christmas, but never reached her port. All on board perished.

In 1647, when the redoubtable Petrus Stuyvesant took command of the New Netherlands, William Kieft embarked, on his return to Holland, provided with further specimens of the Catskill Mountain ore, from which he doubtless indulged golden anticipations. A similar fate attended him with that which had befallen his agent. The ship in which he had embarked was cast away, and he and his treasure were swallowed in the waves.

Here closes the golden legend of the Catskills; but another one of similar import succeeds. In 1649, about two years after the shipwreck of Wilhelmus Kieft, there was again a rumor of precious metals in these mountains. Mynheer Brant Arent Van Slechtenhorst, agent of the Patroon of Rensselaerswyck, had purchased in behalf of the Patroon a tract of the Catskill lands, and leased it out in farms. A Dutch lass in the household of one of the farmers found one day a glittering substance, which, on being examined, was pronounced silver ore. Brant Van Slechtenhorst forthwith sent his son from Rensselaerswyck to explore the mountains in quest of the supposed

37

mines. The young man put up in the farmer's house,
which had recently been erected on the margin of a
mountain stream. Scarcely was he housed when a furious storm burst forth on the mountains. The thunders
rolled, the lightnings flashed, the rain came down in cataracts; the stream was suddenly swollen to a furious tor-
rent thirty feet deep; the farm-house and all its contents
were swept away, and it was only by dint of excellent
swimming that young Slechtenhorst saved his own life
and the lives of his horses. Shortly after this a feud
broke out between Peter Stuyvesant and the Patroon of
Rensselaerswyck on account of the right and title to the
Catskill Mountains, in the course of which the elder
Slechtenhorst was taken captive by the Potentate of
the New Netherlands and thrown in prison at New Amsterdam.

We have met with no record of any further attempt to
get at the treasures of the Catskills. Adventurers may
have been discouraged by the ill-luck which appeared to
attend all who meddled with them, as if they were under
the guardian keep of the same spirits or goblins who
once haunted the mountains and ruled over the weather.
That gold and silver ore was actually procured from
these mountains in days of yore, we have historical evidence to prove, and the recorded word of Adrian Van
der Donk, a man of weight, who was an eye-witness. If
gold and silver were once to be found there, they must
be there at present. It remains to be seen, in these

gold-hunting days, whether the quest will be renewed, and some daring adventurer, fired with a true Californian spirit, will penetrate the mysteries of these mountains, and open a golden region on the borders of the Hudson.